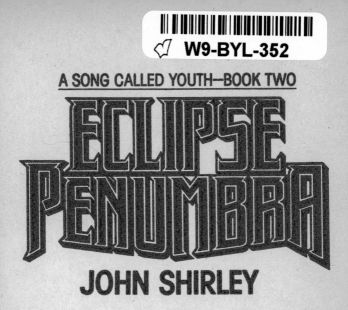

A SONG CALLED YOUTH—BOOK TWO

ECLIPSE PENUMBRA

JOHN SHIRLEY

POPULAR LIBRARY

An Imprint of Warner Books, Inc.

A Warner Communications Company

**The end of the world has come and gone.
And the situation is going from bad to worse.**

The Leader—He had gone to war, sacrificed friends, risked his life. But for Steinfeld, no sacrifice could be too great . . . for freedom.

·

The Warrior—In the beginning, he was just another survivor, struggling for his life. Then the NR had forged Hard Eyes into a dedicated freedom fighter, a killing machine struggling to preserve his humanity in a world turned to hate and despair.

·

The Mother—Trapped in the violence that shattered the peace of the space colony, Kitty would stand against anyone who threatened her radical technicki husband, or their unborn child.

·

The Spy—Once Karakos had been a major asset to the New Resistance, but that was before the SA caught him, broke him, stripped his mind, and sent him back—reprogrammed to betray his own.

Also by John Shirley

ECLIPSE

Published by
POPULAR LIBRARY

For Stephen P. Brown,
in gratitude for much help and much friendship

The author wishes to thank Corby Simpson, Rob Hardin, Bruce Sterling, Tyler Sperry, Martha Millard, Frederic Allinne, Norman Spinrad, William Gibson, and Jim Frenkel.

Special thanks and my love to Kathy Woods Shirley.

A man and a little girl were strolling down a white beach, in hazy sunshine. The year was 2021 A.D. The Caribbean surged lazily beside them, white on crystalline blue. The man was tall and dark and gaunt. A crow perched on his left shoulder, a blot of blackness on the beach, its head ducked against the sun. The girl, who walked between the man and the lapping lacework fringe of the surf, was about nine or ten. No one was quite sure of her precise age. She was dark brown, her wavy black hair caught up in the bright yellow scarf common to the women of the island of Merino. She had hold of the belt loop on the man's left hip, holding it as if she were holding his hand. It was too warm to hold hands.

The man and the little girl wore sandals made from tire rubber and hemp; he wore khaki shorts and a blue silk short-sleeved shirt; it was an expensive shirt but he'd lost three buttons from it and hadn't bothered to replace them. The girl was wearing a yellow cotton shift.

The man was Jack Brendan Smoke. The little girl was named Alouette. Smoke had adopted her a few weeks earlier. She was a child of this island. Her parents had died a year before, in a hurricane.

"Do you think I'm a clever girl?" she asked him. Her island accent was strong, but her English was good.

"Yes. You are the cleverest girl your teachers know. But you mustn't hold yourself above the other students."

"I won't. But if you think I'm clever, why don't you tell me things?"

"What things?"

"What your work is. Why you came here. What your people are doing. I know they're doing something special."

He hesitated. Then he decided. "All right. You know about the war?"

"Yes. The Soviets invaded Eastern Europe because they were afraid of the aggressiveness of the Yankees. The Yankees were very aggressive."

"The Soviets wanted to take the initiative."

"They considered a good offense to be the best defense. Do you know why there wasn't a nuclear war?"

"Because of the Conventional Aggression Treaty, and because of the warning systems. It wasn't practical."

"That's right." He wondered if she'd learned this by rote only, or if she'd understood it. "Do you know what happened because of the war, in Europe?"

"The armies destroyed lots of cities and everyone went into refugee camps and there was riots and people stealing everything and robbers."

"Exactly. The Soviets and the United States let their bulls loose in the world's china shops and everyone suffered. Because of that, NATO hired . . . you know what NATO is?"

"Yes." A little annoyed. "Of course!"

"Okay. NATO hired the biggest international private-police company. They provided security patrols and anti-terrorist squadrons and all kinds of mercenary business. They were called the Second Alliance. Did you know that?"

"No," she admitted.

"The Second Alliance International Security Corporation. We just call them the SA. NATO hired them to police Europe, to keep order behind the lines. They were a big army all by themselves. Bigger than anybody thought. And nobody knew they were waiting for a chance like this. There was a conspiracy. . . . Well, anyway, they occupied lots of Europe behind the lines of fighting. They took control of it. And it turned out that the people who ran the SA were Fascists."

"Fascists are Nazis. I saw them on movies. They torture people. They want to control everything."

"More or less correct. The SA is controlled by some very, very extremist Fundamentalist Christians who aren't really Christians at all. Christ would have despised them. They are believers in racial purity. Genetic purity. A man named Rick Crandall in America, and another man named Watson in Europe, those are their top people. Rick Crandall is a preacher of sorts. They have power in the United States now too. They have friends in the government. Maybe even the President."

"Mrs. Bester?"

"Yes. President Bester. And they control some very big American companies. They're using them to influence the American people, through the media. There's a depression in the United States. I think President Bester provoked the Soviets into aggression so she could have a war that would help the economy and big business. Anyway, the depression and the war make a lot of pressure on people, and that makes them think that Fascism might be all right . . . for a lot of reasons. And the Fascists control the Space Colony now. They took it over."

"The Space Colony! I want to go there!"

"You know all about it?"

She nodded eagerly. "It's a building in space bigger than Merino. Floating out there. Thousands of people live in it. It has trees and everything, way out in space. It's sealed so the air can't get out, and it recycles everything. But the Soviets have block-kaded it in space, so it's running out of food because it can't raise enough for all its people inside."

"Yes. When we take it back from the Fascists, we can go there for a visit."

"That's what your work is, then? To take it back?"

"Yes. And Europe. To give Europe back to its people. The SA used tricks and set up puppet leaders so that the people of Europe think they have their own leaders, but those new leaders really belong to the SA. And the SA is promoting Fascism in the people. They're hungry and angry and they want order, and Fascism promises food and order, so they think they want Fascism. But they don't know it means they won't have any freedom and they'll have to hate their neighbors."

"How are you fighting these people?"

"We have the New Resistance. The NR. We're fighting them with guns and with information."

"With guns?" She looked at him. "You might have to fight with guns?"

He put an arm around her shoulders. "No. Not me. I use words and ideas. I'm no good with guns. People like Steinfeld and Hard Eyes are using guns and strategy and tactics. . . ."

"Steen-field. Hard Eyes."

"They're leading our guerrillas—that's *guerrillas*, not—"

"I know the difference between guerrillas and gorillas." She pouted at him.

He smiled. "Sorry again. Let's head back now and get something to drink. I'm thirsty."

"Yes." They turned and moved away from the water toward the NR compound.

"Hard Eyes," she said when they were almost to the road, "is a stupid name."

Smoke laughed. "You're right. Hard Eyes is an American named Dan Torrence. The nickname sort of embarrasses him now. . . ."

"I can see why."

"But he's a good man. He doesn't think he's better than anyone else, and he has given himself completely to the Resistance. Because he saw what the Fascists did to some people, and he saw what the future could be like."

"Why do people decide to be Fascists?"

"Almost anyone could be Fascist under the right circumstances. If they get scared enough. That's why we have to fight it so hard. Because it never quite goes away."

_____ ONE

SOUTHEASTERN FRANCE. The Alps.

Three olive-drab trucks and an icy-blue dawn. The shadows still black in the craters on the two-lane mountain road angling up through the French Alps. The dark steel of the sky to the east going blue-white between the snowy peaks. The rough texture of the peaks' western faces was still etched by darkness; the dawn light created a kind of ecliptic corona around the silhouetted mountaintops.

In the lead truck, Hard Eyes was riding shotgun, literally holding a twenty-round CAWS fully automatic shotgun propped up between his legs. Steinfeld was driving. It was a stolen U.S. Army truck, an old diesel built by Ford thirty years before, in 1990. It creaked with age and overuse, its mileage indicator long since numerically exhausted. The rusty floor was cracked; engine heat pushed fumes up at them, along with the grunt and clash of the gears as Steinfeld downshifted for the steepening road grade. The headlights flickered when the truck hit a pothole, and swiveled out over the canyon drop-off to their left as Steinfeld swung the truck around to avoid a crater. On the western side of the road, a craggy cliff face rose two hundred feet above them before sloping back toward the top of the ridge; snow, loosed by the vibrations set up by the truck, skirled down from shelves in the rock to glitter in the headlight beams. There hadn't been a fresh snowfall for three days. Morning melt-off and the passage of other vehicles had cleared the road of most of it. Now and then the rumbling engine roared in frustration as they hit an icy patch and the wheels spun, Steinfeld cursing through his thick black beard as he wrenched the wheel in search of traction.

Hard Eyes was tired. Gritty tired and aching tired. Physically, mentally, emotionally tired. He cranked the side window open a little more, to let the cold air wash over his face, revive him a little. He wouldn't let himself sleep, because Steinfeld was there, and Steinfeld never seemed to sleep, never showed his weariness except in a sort of tangible moodiness, a tendency to lapse into scowling silences. . . . There were forty-four of them, in three trucks, moving southeast toward northern Italy, as they had been for almost four days. They were supposed to rendezvous with the rest of the French NR in twelve hours.

But most of the French New Resistance probably wouldn't make it. Most of them were probably dead, or swallowed up by the SA's "preventative detention camps." And two hundred of them had died when they'd broken through the blockade around Paris. They died to get Steinfeld safely through. Which, perhaps, was why Steinfeld never seemed to sleep.

Hard Eyes had lost his three closest friends in Paris, at the end. Rickenharp and Yukio and Jensen. Killed by the Fascists; crushed by the Jaegernauts like small animals under a jackboot's heel.

But he'd found Claire, in Paris.

Now she was curled up in the back of the truck, probably asleep beside Carmen and Willow and Bonham and the others. Claire was a short, frail-looking woman who'd killed seven of the enemy back in Paris, one of them with a knife.

Hard Eyes wanted to climb into the back of the truck and curl himself up around her, try to keep the warmth of her humanity from slipping away into the mountain shadows. Like the warmth in his hands, drawn off into the cold metal of the auto-shotgun.

But Hard Eyes remained sitting stiffly in the passenger seat, staring blearily out the mud-spattered windshield. Feeling his eyelids twitch from exhaustion, his back ache from the hours in the truck.

Steinfeld shifted his bearlike bulk in his seat, stretching as much as he could in the cab's confines, wincing. "Find cover soon," he muttered. "Satellites'll pinpoint us. Soviets will think we're NATO; NATO'll know us for Unauthorized in this area; they'll collate it with the Fascists." His voice was gristly with fatigue.

Hard Eyes nodded. "You know a place?"

Steinfeld shook his head. "Don't know this stretch. Just hope I'm where I think I am."

A single short honk from the truck behind them.

Hard Eyes felt a chill, then a hot surge of adrenaline wakefulness. They wouldn't be honking unless something was wrong.

He looked in the passenger-side mirror. "They're stopped —looks like they're stuck. . . ."

Steinfeld cursed in Hebrew and pulled over, close under the cliff side. He put the truck into park, left it idling as he got out, breath pluming in the chill air, and went back to see what was wrong. There wasn't enough room between the truck and the stone of the mountainside for Hard Eyes to get out on the right side, so he slid across the seat and climbed out the driver's side door, grateful for an excuse to stretch.

Levassier was the driver of the second truck. He was standing in the headlight beams, arguing in French with the big, bald Algerian.

Levassier had driven a little too close to the edge of the road, on the eastern side. The road's shoulder was badly eroded by winter weather and the shock of the air-to-ground missiles that, earlier in the year, had torn up the roadbed. The road had crumbled away under the left front tire. The truck tilted dangerously into the ravine. The Algerian—Hard Eyes hadn't found a chance to learn his name—was saying, so far as Hard Eyes could make out, that Levassier should simply back farther up onto the road. Levassier was making grand gestures that seemed to say, "What an imbecile!" as he maintained that there was ice under the rear wheels, so the truck wouldn't make progress backward, but might well slip about, slide into the ravine.

Steinfeld was crouching, looking at the rear wheels.

Hard Eyes lifted the edge of the canvas tarp and looked into the rear of the first truck. Claire was sitting up with her back to the cab, staring into the shadows. He looked for

Bonham, the other refugee from the Colony, saw him curled up on a sleeping bag, snoring through his beakish nose, wide mouth open. Reassured to see that Bonham wasn't sleeping beside Claire, Hard Eyes looked over at her again. She didn't look up at him. He could just make out her eyes, open in the darkness, staring at the truck bed. Blinking, staring.

Why wasn't she asleep? Why was she sitting there in the dark, staring at nothing?

Steinfeld shouted, "Hard Eyes!"

Hard Eyes walked back toward Steinfeld. Looking at the sky as he went, wondering if they were under surveillance. And wondering if a Second Alliance patrol plane might not happen by. Or the Soviets. Or NATO.

Everyone was their enemy.

Steinfeld had appointed Hard Eyes as captain. He had no bars, no insignia to show his rank. He wore blue jeans and a ski jacket and black hiking boots. But Willow and Carmen and the Spaniard, Danco, went instantly into position when he told them, "You three—grab the S.A.G. and the grenade launchers, stand watch for air attack."

Hard Eyes walked on, found Steinfeld and Burch unloading a heavy tow chain from the rear of the third truck. Burch was a stocky, glum black from the People's Republic of South Africa. He wore a parka and wire-rimmed glasses.

Without looking over, Steinfeld said, "Hard Eyes, detail a crew to hook this up."

Half an hour later they were still trying to move the teetering truck. It was packed with ordnance; there wasn't room for the stacks of rifles and ammo boxes in the other trucks, and Steinfeld didn't want to leave it behind, so they continued to struggle with several tons of metal poised on a cliff edge. Hard Eyes had cut his hands on the chain as they added manpower to the rear truck's pull. His hands ached with the cold; the knuckles were swollen. The shadows had shrunk, the growing light was blue-gray; it was a watered-down light, but they no longer needed the headlights. The sun was edging over a mountaintop that looked to Hard Eyes, in his weariness, like a Klan hood slightly cocked to one side. There was just a faint suggestion of sun warmth on the top of his head.

They couldn't back the towing truck very far, or it would

have gone over the edge behind it. So they couldn't use its full power to move the one it was pulling.

Steinfeld made up his mind. "Unload the rest of the gear, anything useful; we'll run the truck over the side, make do with two. Hope they'll get us up over the pass."

Hard Eyes gave the orders. All the time looking at the sky, or at the first truck, wondering about Claire. Looking up at the austere mountainsides; listening to their voices sounding tinny and lost in the mountain vastness. Thinking he'd be moved by this place, another time. The scenery, the heady purity of the morning air . . . but now it was just another pain in the ass, something to hump over, trudge through. . . .

He heard a distant thudding sound. Soft and repetitive but distinctly man-made in its ominous regularity.

He looked around, frowning, losing the sound in the noise the others made as they unloaded a crate of ammunition . . . there it was again, louder.

He felt his scalp tighten, the hair rising on the back of his neck. He looked around for Carmen, saw her perched on a boulder with a grenade-fitted rifle in her arms. She was looking at the sky, frowning. He started toward her.

Steinfeld shouted, "Where are you going, Torrence?" Steinfeld was using Hard Eyes's real name, something he did to warn him he was about to get chewed out.

Hard Eyes opened his mouth to reply—and the reply caught in his throat when he saw Carmen pointing, and then saw what she was pointing at.

Three aircraft. Side by side, close formation, coming at them from the east over a serrated shoulder of mountainside, a little more than a quarter of a mile off. And closing. A jet accompanied by two choppers. One of the new models of the Harrier jumpjet; not particularly fast, but lethal in its copterlike maneuverability. Shaped like a hunchbacked triangle. And flanking the jet, the autochoppers, American-made, equipped with sidewinders and 7.62-mm miniguns. They could spray a target area with six thousand rounds per minute.

Carmen was shouting; the others saw it now too. Levassier was looking through field glasses at them. Seeing the Second Alliance Christian crosses on the undersides of the jumpjet's wings, the black and silver of its trim. "SA!" he shouted.

They could hear the thudding of the chopper blades clearly now; the whine of the jet. Coming in slow for a jet.

Second Alliance. *Maybe,* Hard Eyes thought, *they'll see the Army trucks, take us for NATO.*

No. They'd see we're all out of uniform. They've been looking for us in this area. There are a half dozen other telltales. They'll know.

As he thought this, he was looking around. There was no time to drive the trucks out of the way. They'd have to find cover.

The cliff face to their right, on the western side of the road, rose about a hundred feet. But about forty feet ahead of the lead truck, there was a fissure running back into the cliff. It looked as if it might be wide enough to run into, but narrow enough to give them cover. He couldn't see anything else.

Steinfeld had come to the same conclusion. He was shouting orders. Everyone was running now; some of them with crates of ammo slung between them; some running to the lead truck, shouting at the others to get out, make for the fissure: Levassier arguing that they should get in the trucks and drive like the devil. But the trucks would make excellent targets on the road.

Hard Eyes shouted, "Get what you can carry and run for that opening in the cliff! Over *there*! Go, go, *go*!"

The jumpjet and the copters were almost on them; they occluded the sun, sending their shadows racing like hungry panthers over the ground ahead of them. The cannons mounted on the nose of the jumpjet were tilting downward. The jet and the autochoppers swung off to the north, and for a giddy moment Hard Eyes thought they'd decided not to engage—but then he saw they were coming around for a strafe run, angling to follow the north-south course of the road so they could come in low. The choppers followed the jet in precise flight-path replication: they were Bell *Heeldogs,* entirely automated, robot pilots responding to the orders of the human pilot in the jet.

Weariness was forgotten. Mouth dry with fear, Hard Eyes looked around for Claire, saw her climbing out of the back of the truck, carrying a light machine gun, her face white, her lips pressed to a thin line. She was the last out. Steinfeld and the others were mostly up ahead. Someone—Burch, maybe—had gotten into the lead truck, was starting it, and driving ahead to block the gunships from the main body of guerrillas. Drawing fire.

Hot knives clashed in Hard Eyes's lungs as he reached Claire, shouting, "Leave the fucking gun!" She shook her head angrily, continued to carry it, staggered under its weight. He slung the CAWS over his shoulder and wrenched the machine gun from her, tossed it aside, took her elbow, and dragged her along, knowing that if they survived, she'd lecture him about women carrying their own burdens. But he didn't care because now the autochoppers—commanded by the jumpjet pilot—had let go four sidewinders. He heard a quadruple *thud* and the scream of rending metal as the air-to-surface missiles struck the two rear trucks; Hard Eyes felt heat on his back, and the arrogant shove of shockwaves. He stumbled, but Claire steadied him and they ran on, the world dancing jerkily around them—

Something sizzled past them, drawing a line of white exhaust in the air, the line finishing in the back of the lead truck, which still trundled awkwardly up the road, and a second later the truck Hard Eyes had ridden in all night was consumed in an orange-red ball of fire.

Heat and the zing of shrapnel. Reflections of fire shimmering from the patches of snow; a long, thudding echo off the mountainsides.

Burch, one of the best of them, was dead.

Claire shouted, "Here they come!" and tugged Hard Eyes into the poor shelter of an outthrust of cliff rock as the Harrier and the autochoppers bore down on them. The rocks around them spat chips and sparks as the steel-jacketed rounds impacted. Something stung Hard Eyes's cheek; something more slashed at his neck. Slight wounds from rock fragments. He and Claire tried to press farther into the hollow; their backs were bruised by knobs of cold rock.

Hard Eyes thought, *If they pull up and turn toward us, we're fucked. They'll mince us.*

But the killing machines kept going, chasing the main group of the rebels, who'd just reached the fissure, twenty yards ahead; Bonham paused at the opening to look back, probably looking for Claire—then he ducked inside. Carmen was crouched in the opening with her rifle propped on a small boulder; she fired, and a grenade bounced off the underside of an autochopper, exploded; the chopper rocked in the air but showed no other effect as it whipped by, following the Harrier.

Hard Eyes pulled at Claire's arm, and they were running toward the fissure, wondering if they could get to it before the choppers and the jet circled back. Passing three bodies sprawled in red splashes. No time to see who they were. . . .

The jet slowed, stopped in midair, and the autochoppers obediently came to heel.

Take out the jet, Hard Eyes thought. Somebody take out the fucking jet.

The jet and its faithful dogs were coming at them, about fifty yards up, angling down, red sunlight gleaming on the cockpit and flashing off the steel curve of the autochoppers' blind front ends.

Running hard, Claire beside him, Hard Eyes saw an autochopper swiveling toward him and Claire, lining them up in its sights. He felt her hand in his, palm moist with sweat, fingers rigid with tension, and there were things he wanted to tell her—

And then she was pulling him into the shadows of the crevice as 7.62-mm minigun rounds screamed off the rock a few feet behind them. Someone returning fire with the ground-to-air missile launcher . . . a satisfying *ka-whump* as the missile struck an autochopper.

Hard Eyes threw himself down into a pebbly alcove between two low boulders, Claire hunching down beside him, both of them gasping, shaking with fear, but amazed to be alive, feeling a transitory buzz of triumph . . . until he saw that Potter and the Algerian were splashed over the rocks near the entrance to the crevice. They'd been caught coming into it.

Hard Eyes felt despair like a weight. But he forced himself up, to look for Steinfeld.

There were four volunteers near the entrance to the fissure, shooting at the aircraft in order to draw fire, to give the others a chance to move back into cover, away from the road. The fissure was about forty feet deep, V-shaped; it was about eighteen feet across at the top, narrowed to a snow- and pebble-packed floor, angling upward toward the mountainside; the crevice floor varied from a yard to two yards wide. There was a slight overhang on the south side that gave them a little aerial cover. The sun shone almost directly into the crevice; the bluish light was broken up here and there by sharp blades of shadow.

"How many . . . how many of us?" Claire asked, her knees drawn up, arms propped on her knees, face buried in her arms.

He said, "Looks like we're down to about thirty-two." She said something more, but he couldn't hear it because of the bark and chatter and scream of gunfire from the front of the fissure. Steinfeld and Levassier were just turning a corner farther down the crevice, moving up to deeper cover. Cursing at the patches of snow and uneven rock in their way, other guerrillas carried wounded, and a few crates of weapons, food, guns. They hadn't gotten away with much.

The wounded were screaming.

Some mocking inner voice told Hard Eyes: *You wanted to be where the conflict was real. This real enough for you?*

The remaining autochopper opened up with long, blanketing bursts of its miniguns at the four guerrillas drawing fire at the opening of the fissure.

Hard Eyes saw the rough *V* of the fissure's opening blur with dust and rock chips and smoke and spattered blood. He saw the bodies of the four volunteers jerking, slamming against the stone with the impact of the bullets. He saw the *Heeldog* hovering fifty feet up, wind from its rotors swirling dust and smoke and snow. Like an opaque-helmeted SA security guard, it had no face. It was computer-driven; it was a machine for killing and nothing more.

The jet was coming in from the opposite direction, looking for targets. Claire had gotten her breath. She stood and they followed the others back into the fissure, feeling like small animals running from an exterminator.

They turned the corner in the fissure just as the rock behind them erupted with a cannon shell from the jumpjet. The ground seemed to ripple; the shock thickened and distorted the air, and the ground seemed to leap out from under Hard

Eyes . . . till he found himself lying facedown, his ears ringing. Thinking, *Have I been hit?* Someone was pulling at his arm, shouting over the screaming roar of the jet, the thump of the autochopper blades, "Get up, damn you, Hard Eyes!" Claire's voice. "Come on, Torrence!"

Torrence? Hard Eyes? He remembered the names, remembered everything that had brought him here. It seemed nonsensical now—now as he forced himself up, got his rubbery legs moving, as he and Claire stumbled back into the crevice—it seemed absurd, a meaningless exchange of chaos. *They throw chaos at us, in flying bullets, shrapnel, explosions; we throw chaos back at them. Waves of chaos heaved back and forth, driving me up a mountain for two days, then on foot into a mountain fissure. Waves of chaos driving us like field mice before a thresher. Small animals under the jackboot again. The Jaegernaut in all its manifestations.* The ideological origin of the conflict was an excuse. The conflict, the killing, had a life of its own.

And he wanted out of it, just then. In that exhausted, meaning-drained instant he wanted to hide in a hole till the wave of chaos passed him by; till he could crawl back down the mountain, find his way to the sea, to a ship or a plane, back to the USA and the walled-in enclaves of safety his parents lived in . . .

But then he looked at Claire and saw no despair in her. He saw fear and anger, but no tears. He felt her hand in his, and the sensation was somehow the organizational locus for meaning. In that instant all meaning proceeded from her touch. Steinfeld, the New Resistance—all that was distant just now. Now they were running, struggling to survive, together; and that *together,* by itself, had to be meaning enough, paltry though it was. It was like using a small, leafless tree as your only shelter against a raging desert sandstorm.

There were three more volunteers up ahead, where the fissure widened for a short distance. They were setting up a missile launcher, which wasn't much more than a ten-foot tube of olive-drab metal on a tripod. A rifle fitted with a grenade leaned against the stone wall to one side. The jet and copter were converging overhead.

Hard Eyes had a choice, then. He could pick up the rifle,

join them in drawing fire away from Steinfeld, and be killed. Or he could tell himself: *I'm a captain, officers are necessary, important to the Resistance, I'd be squandering a resource. And Claire is with me. I brought her into the NR. I feel responsible for her.* Tell himself all of that . . . and use it as an excuse to scramble for safety.

Some irresistible clockwork mechanism of his personality made the choice for him. He pulled away from Claire as they came up to the volunteers, shouted, "Go on, join Steinfeld, I'll be there in a minute!"

"That's bullshit, Hard Eyes! Come *on!*"

But he'd grabbed the grenade rifle, was wedging it in the hollow of his shoulder (wondering if she was going to get killed because she wouldn't leave him here, killed because of his gesture, his gesture of selflessness ultimately selfish because it sacrificed her too), aiming at the autochopper . . . its blades blew grit in his eyes . . . he saw the jet loom up, its wings vibrating from its hover-retros; he felt it emanating heat, poised over them like a monstrously oversize sword of Damocles . . . he shifted aim and fired . . . the grenade arced toward the jet and—didn't explode. A bum charge. *Fuck!* He was going to die for nothing. . . .

The chopper's miniguns opened up, but it was a few yards too far south, and most of the rounds rang off the rock overhang; a ricochet caught one of the volunteers in the eye, a young black woman who clutched at her bloody socket, screamed and crumpled as the other two fired the missile. The launcher belched: white flash and a white rope of smoke behind the missile. It struck the sidewinder tubes on the right side of the autochopper. At the same moment the jet's cannon fired—its aim thrown off by the shockwaves from the exploding autochopper, its shell struck the rock wall over the two surviving volunteers.

Hard Eyes seemed to see an orchid of fire that blossomed gigantically to consume his field of vision, and he felt himself flying backward—

Hard Eyes was sitting with his back to the curved stone. A patch of snow making his rump wet, chilling his tailbone. His head seemed to reverberate. He heard a metallic singing. Red and blue smoke swirled. The red smoke wasn't real; it vanished. The blue smoke remained, so he decided it was real.

Claire?

He turned his head, winced. Saw her sitting beside him, laughing. Her upper left arm was laid open, thickened blood making the cloth of her coat indistinguishable from the torn flesh of her wound. Her hysterical laughter was almost lost to him through the roaring, metallic ringing in his ears. He looked up (wincing, biting his lips with head pain) and saw that the sky was clear over the fissure. Where was the jumpjet?

The natural stone wall across from him was painted uniformly red. The paint was still wet. He looked at it for a long time before he knew it was blood.

A man's raggedly severed arm lay nearby in an iridescent patch of snow; the fingers were curled as if the hand were playing the piano. The skin was blue-white.

All the time there was the hissing, roaring, in his ears, an aural motif for the scene.

And then Willow and Carmen were there, bending over him. Their faces seemed fish-eye distorted. Willow was a gaunt, straw-haired Brit, with bad teeth and a perpetual air of quiet suspicion; Carmen was a lanky punk in an Army surplus ski trooper's jacket, waterproofed green canvas with a hood; the hood was thrown back to show her ring-clustered ears, her black hair shaved on the sides and the back of her head, spiked like an anarchist crown atop.

"Anything broken, mate?" Willow asked. Each word accentuated by the white puffs of his breath in the cold air.

Hard Eyes thought, *Everything's broken everywhere.* Willow meant bones. He moved experimentally. The movements brought some aches and a whirligig of nausea. But none of the grating pain accompanying broken bones. "I think I'm all right. Just kinda . . . blurry."

"You'll be okay," Carmen said.

Claire had stopped laughing; she sat rocking with pain, silent. Carmen put a tourniquet on Claire's arm, and then she used a medikit to clean and close the wound. Claire made hissing sounds between clenched teeth. "It's a nasty-looking cut, but it's shallow," Carmen said. "Artery's intact. Nothing imbedded. Looks worse than it is."

Hard Eyes didn't want to move. He wanted to lie there. Stay there. Sleep, maybe.

He must've mumbled something aloud about it, because Willow said, "We got a camp, up the crack. Sleeping 'ere's not on for you, mate." Willow helped him up. Hard Eyes groaned.

"The jet . . ." Claire said huskily.

"Gone," Carmen said. "I think it was damaged when the second chopper blew. But it'll be back. *They'll* be back. Trucks are gone. We can't use the road. Steinfeld says we hide up in the mountain. . . ."

The island of Merino, the Caribbean.

Jack Smoke tapped the broad, wafer-thin computer screen and said, "They're somewhere in here . . . about ten miles northeast of the Italian border." The big, glossy-black crow perched on Smoke's shoulder fluttered a little when Smoke moved.

Witcher, standing beside Smoke, was frowning at the map on the screen. He nodded and tapped the terminal's keyboards for zoom magnification on one small segment of the map. That part swelled to fill the screen. "There's nothing much around there. No villages . . . just the pass . . ."

"And it's a high elevation, not much cover except rocks. They're exposed."

Smoke and Witcher were in the Comm Center, at the place called Home: the heavily fortified New Resistance world headquarters, on the island of Merino, somewhere between the Antilles and Cuba. It was not a comfortable room. It was hot and oppressive between the thick, white-painted concrete walls, the gray concrete floor splashed with paint around the edges where the painters had been sloppy; white plastic, aluminum, and black plastic equipment crowded the room, and in some places you had to turn sideways and press hard to get through between the monitoring gear. Two technicians sat at satellite link monitors at the other end, recording information about SA, NATO, and Soviet troop movements, and alert for information pertaining to Steinfeld. The technicians were a man and a woman; the man was black. Both were topless, wearing only shorts, because the room was stifling, turgidly hot. Smoke and Witcher each wore white shorts, sandals. Witcher wore a gold polo shirt, darkened by sweat to clay color under his arms. Smoke wore a flower-print Hawaiian shirt, mostly blue. And in a way he wore the crow.

Smoke was silently cursing Witcher's fear of air conditioners. Mention air conditioners and Witcher'd mutter darkly about "lethal mutations of the American Legionnaire's bacterium." But Smoke had come to accept Witcher's fits of hypochondria, his mercurial shifts from expansive openness to tight-lipped reserve. Witcher was the angel of the New Resistance, its billionaire backer, and if his eccentricity should shift him from supporting the NR, it might well collapse.

They were too dependent on him, Smoke thought. Perhaps Steinfeld should take steps to reduce their reliance on—

"Smoke," Witcher said suddenly, "what about the contingent at Malta? We could air-drop some assistance."

Smoke shook his head. "That'd be just another group of NR trapped in the area. We're too badly outnumbered to help Steinfeld that way. If we could get the men in, it'd have to be from a high-altitude drop. The airspace there is monitored by three armies. If we had some helicopters, something that could fly in under radar, but big enough to pick up forty men . . ." He shrugged.

Witcher grimaced. "We tried." He'd dispatched a ship disguised as a tanker, with six copters hidden in holds designed for oil. One of the NR's American operatives had been captured, interrogated with an extractor. He'd known about the tanker, because he'd supervised the construction of its false walls. The extractor* had told the SA about the tanker and its destination. The SA pulled strings, and NATO simply sank the ship, fifty-five miles west of the Strait of Gibraltar.

"Maybe we could stage a diversion, draw the SA away from him," Witcher said.

---

*Extractor—a device that uses advanced techniques in molecular biology to extract information from the brain.

"I considered that. But we've intercepted their field transmissions. They've ID'd Steinfeld. They're certain it's him. Getting first priority."

"So what do we do?"

"Hope Steinfeld finds a way out on his own."

"You saying there's nothing we can do for him?"

"It looks that way." His voice flat, emotionless. But he reached up and stroked the crow, as if comforting it.

Southeastern France.

If was late afternoon when Hard Eyes woke, but in the cave it was twilight. It was a shallow cave, only forty or fifty feet deep, with a high, cracked ceiling that effortlessly swallowed their campfire smoke. Hard Eyes sat up and looked around.

He was in the back of the cave, sitting on a sleeping bag. Claire lay on a bag beside him, asleep. He wanted to reach out, stroke her hair, but he didn't want to wake her. And they'd never made love; there was no real physical intimacy between them.

The fire popped and sizzled. It was a skewed pyramid of thin, twisted tree branches gradually collapsing into the wavery column of yellow flame. The wounded lay nearby, seven of them; one groaning, the others too quiet. Two of them looked like they'd died. On the far side of the flame the little, spike-bearded Spaniard, Danco, sat with an old AK-49 across his knees, staring into the fire.

Hard Eyes looked at his watch and saw that the crystal had splintered into a coarse star; the digits were frozen.

He stretched, biting his lip at the pain. It felt like he had some cracked ribs, sustained bruises, and a lot of little wounds.

He felt dull, creaky, and hungry. But the disorientation, the panic—all that was gone.

Scowling, muttering, Levassier came into the cave carrying a packet of freeze-dried soup mix and a bucket of snow for melting. Hard Eyes tried not to stare at the food. They might not have enough for anyone but the wounded.

But everyone ate. Bonham sitting near Danco on the other

side of the fire, eating greedily, staring at Claire and Hard Eyes. Claire woke when she smelled the food cooking. By degrees, as the guerrillas talked over the mess kits of soup and canned stew, Hard Eyes pieced the picture together. They'd found the cave a mile and a half up the mountain from the road. There were twenty-five of them intact enough to fight.

Two SA jets had gone over, probably looking for them. The sentries were fairly sure they hadn't been spotted. There was cloud cover, blocking satellite reconnaissance. Steinfeld had used a pack-radio to try to reach the other SA units, and the Mossad, transmitting coded messages. No reply so far.

The SA was probably triangulating troops in the area by now. They'd be along, soon enough.

So what do we do? Hard Eyes wondered. It would be tough to run farther, with the wounded, and with scarce supplies.

Steinfeld looked grim.

After the meal—it would be their only meal that day—Hard Eyes took a shift on guard duty, outside the cave. The clouds that had drifted in at mid-morning had thickened, began to unspool thin streamers of sleet. Hard Eyes trudged from one miserably uncomfortable spot to another in the shallow, open area of broken rock outside the narrow cave mouth, slipping on ice-glazed patches of gray snow. A faint wash of smoke drifted out of the cave entrance but was quickly sucked away by the drizzly wind. The wind burned his nose and ears, and the auto-shotgun was a dead weight on its shoulder strap.

He was dismally grateful when, an hour after sunset, just when it was getting *really* cold, Steinfeld sent out the dour, pallid Frenchman, Sortonne, to relieve him.

Hard Eyes found Claire sitting cross-legged on the sleeping bag, cleaning a rifle, forehead creased with concentration. Danco had taught her how to clean the rifle just the day before.

Now Danco watched, grinning, as Hard Eyes sat down beside her, his hands and fingers tingling in the sudden warmth from the campfire.

They didn't speak for a while. Then Claire said, "The sky clear out there?"

"No. You wondering about the Colony?"

She hesitated, then nodded, frowning over the assault rifle. She'd put it back together perfectly. "No news. When I left, it was on the verge of anarchy. And the Soviets were closing in. I'm not even sure if the damn place is still up there. Just to see it . . ."

He asked, "You can see it with the naked eye?"

"If you know how to look. It looks like a star."

"I guess you're not used to being down here yet. Joining the NR is a bad way to readjust to the planet."

She stared at her grime-blackened hands, her broken, dirt-encrusted nails. She shrugged and looked around. "Actually . . ." She smiled sadly. "The cave is sort of comforting—the Colony's corridors weren't so different, really. . . . God, I just wish I could know if—" She broke off, squeezing her eyes shut.

"Wish you could know if he's dead?" Hard Eyes asked.

After almost ten seconds she nodded, very slowly. "If Dad is dead."

They didn't speak again for nearly two hours. The fire burned low; darkness gathered itself around them. Steinfeld, Levassier, and Danco talked softly at another campfire nearer the front. Most of the others were asleep.

Hard Eyes and Claire sat side by side on the sleeping bag, knees drawn up, hugging themselves for warmth. Suddenly she said, in a whisper, "It's getting cold in here. But I . . . it's like I can hardly feel the cold, like the feeling is in someone else. I left the Colony to get away from the fighting, and to get away from the way the place was falling apart—the place I lived all those years—and, shit. Look at me."

"You could get to the States. Steinfeld could probably arrange it."

She shook her head. "The SA took the Colony. Enslaved everyone there. It was bad enough I ran away from them once. I couldn't live with twice. And for Dad's sake . . . this is my way to fight Praeger." It was difficult to make out her expression in the dimness. "Maybe I should've stayed in the Colony. Fought them there."

"What would have happened if you'd stayed?"

"I'd have been arrested. Interrogated. Probably killed. They'd have made it look like the rebels killed us, I guess."

"So how can you feel guilty about not staying? You couldn't have fought them, you were trapped, cornered."

"How often are guilt feelings really rational? I mean, how many times in a person's life do they feel guilty for something they can't really control?"

"Know what you mean."

"And today I got so . . . I just felt *fucked*. Those things that weren't even human were hunting us . . . machines—" Her voice broke. "I was more scared than I thought a person could be without their heart blowing up."

"Me too."

"Were you?" She sounded surprised.

"Scared shitless." He reached out, tentatively laid his hand on hers. Started to withdraw when he felt her move— but she turned her hand palm upward, squeezed his hand, leaned toward him, and pressed her head against his shoulder.

He had an overwhelming urge to embrace her—and he gave in to it. She returned the embrace. He felt her shaking as she sobbed softly.

He held her for a long time, being careful of the wound on her arm, till it was too cold to stay atop the sleeping bag. "Let's get under the covers," he whispered. "And sleep," he added, to let her know he wasn't going to make a move on her.

She nodded. They took off their boots and climbed into the double sleeping bag. Both of them smelled sour. But it had been a long time since that had mattered.

They held one another against the cold, and the fear.

He'd almost gone to sleep when he felt her moving against him, a kind of blind nuzzling of her hips. He felt his cock harden; she felt it, too, and pressed her crotch against it. Both of them ached, and her wound burned on her upper arm—but that made the caressing more piquant, a deeper relief. She unbuttoned her blouse and pressed his rough hands to her breasts.

There was some fumbling with zippers, and pants buttons, but in a few minutes they were joined, with Claire on top, straddling him, sighing softly, almost sobbing; she was very warm, and very wet, inside. And when she came, she pulled his face to her breasts and he was amazed—exquisitely amazed—to experience the sheer, silken luxury of them here, in this place, this animal's den on the cold shore of a battlefield.

At ten the next morning Steinfeld, Levassier, Danco, and Hard Eyes held a conference. They looked at maps on the glowing blue screen of a hand computer; they collated what data they had about SA, NATO, and Soviet troop movements and came to a bitter conclusion. To leave there was probably suicide. To stay there was to await execution.

They decided to go through the mountains. The wounded would have to be abandoned—or put to death. No one said this but everyone knew it. There was real sorrow in Steinfeld's eyes.

They'd never had to do it before. Hard Eyes wondered if they could bring themselves to go through with it.

The question was moot, because before the guerrillas could move out, the enemy came.

They heard the thudding of choppers, and an electronically amplified voice booming outside the cave entrance, its absurd verbosity echoing between the rocks: *"This is the Second Alliance Security Force acting on behalf of the North Atlantic Treaty Organization. Come out of your camp unarmed, with your hands on top of your heads. If you surrender, you will not be harmed. Repeat, if you surrender . . ."*

There was no question of surrender. They would put them under extractors. You can't keep anything back from an extractor. They'd know what Steinfeld knew, and that would mean arrests, hundreds of arrests. . . .

Steinfeld looked almost relieved. They wouldn't have to abandon the wounded.

They looked at Steinfeld. Steinfeld said, "Deploy for defense."

Hard Eyes had a sister. He assumed she was safe in the same fortresslike housing project their parents lived in, near New York City.

But Dan's sister, Kitty, had married while Hard Eyes was in Europe. She'd married a technicki (a *black* technicki, to the barely contained disgust of her parents). She'd emigrated to FirStep, the Space Colony, to be with her husband, Chester, who was a communications technician. That was just before the Soviets blockaded the Colony.

She'd married, but her best friend, a feminist, had persuaded Kitty to keep her last name. She was still Kitty Torrence.

FirStep, the Space Colony, recycling center.

Kitty's job was simple and ugly. She kept the sludge pipes from clogging.

The recycling center was an enormous barnlike room with aluminum-gray walls and six-foot-thick flat-black pipes; the joints of the pipes were dull silver. Harsh fluorescent light buzzed overhead; steam and rancid smells escaped from loose pipe joints; the atmosphere was faintly cloudy, like a glass of gin left out for a couple of days.

And it roared all day. Roared and groaned, as discarded garments and other refuse from the previous two days, heated by the same chemical process that liquefied it, bubbled and slopped through the pipes. No one knew why the pipes gave out those pathetically human groaning noises, but the superstitious technickis assumed the ghosts of Samson Molt and Professor Rimpler were trapped in the pipes, because probably Admin had simply fed them into the recyclers. The younger technickis—the younger ones were more superstitious—would hear the groans and mutter, "Cover me, Gridfriend. . . ."

The four biggest pipes emerged from the wall to the right, slanted down to the first separation vats; smaller pipes led away from the vats at a right angle to the big ones, heading for the room in which the separated wastes were reprocessed into the blocks of raw garment material and other things; a catwalk ran along the pipes and around the enormous vats, and Kitty walked along the catwalk, checking to see that the pipes weren't clogging. The colonists used disposable clothes most of the time because laundering would consume too much volume, too much water on the Colony, and because there were strict weight limits on what could be shipped up from Earth; the weight allowance for clothing was small. Each dorm or living unit had its own garment printer; blocks of the raw garment material, to be fed into the printer like reams into a photocopier, were delivered once a week. Some wore cloth clothing on the Colony; there were even boutiques. But most preferred the economy and flexibility of disposable clothing. Print it out in any style you programmed the printer for that day. Wear it twice and toss it into the chute. The chute took it to the sludgepipes, where it was soaked in Breakdown, which broke it down into sludge with the other recycled trash; its components were drawn by inertia and the Colony's centrifugal force, down to recycling, down to the big pipes where Kitty walked along the catwalk.

Kitty was five months' pregnant, but she didn't show a whole lot. She wore a shift to help conceal it. She was afraid they'd lay her off if they knew she was pregnant. Her supervisor had guessed. But the supervisor was technicki; she knew what conditions were like for technicki, she knew Kitty and her husband needed the work credit.

Kitty's legs hurt, and she was thirsty. Parched. Her lips were cracked. There was a steady, dull background heat in the room, and in it swam the smell of the human odors wrung from the disposable clothing. The heat, noise, and smell were always there, and after a while it felt strange to go out into the corridor where the air was cooler and cleaner.

Every five steps she had to stop and slide open the little window on the top of the pipe; usually a little sludge spat up at her when she did this and she'd snatch her hand away to keep from getting sludge and Breakdown on it. She'd hold on to the rail and peer into the pipe, and if she saw it was gumming up, she'd use the sludgefork clamped inside the window to clear away the blockage. Then she'd close the window and go on to the next joint. And when she got to the vat, she'd cross over to the other side, go back up the pipe. And when she got to the wall, she'd cross over, go back down the pipe again. On and on like that all day. She guessed it was better than working down in Sewage where Mary Beth worked. There weren't enough jobs to go around, because the traffic between Earth and the Colony was so reduced, and the Colony had been damaged in the vandalism, sabotage, the riots of the Technicki Rebellion. Kitty's husband, Chester, was a comm specialist. But now that the comm lines were damaged—and they were waiting, seemingly endlessly, for comm parts to be sent from Earth, the things they couldn't manufacture here—Chester had to make do with occasional video maintenance work. Part-time. The Colony wasn't going to let anyone starve, it was said; if you couldn't pony up the work-cred for food, they gave you rations. Bad food and not enough of it. These were difficult, transitory times, Admin said. Have to tighten the belts a few notches. But it would be over soon.

The rebellion was over, after all. The mirror-helmeted Second Alliance bulls were everywhere. Praeger and the Admin council had complete power. The union assemblies had been suspended. Martial law was still in effect.

But somehow the sabotage was still happening. At least, things were breaking down. The TV lines had been disrupted by some vandal—wild laughter, static, distorted images. The extra air-purification parts in storage had been damaged by runaway warehouse robots. The food in cold storage was damaged when the refrigeration had turned itself off, refused to go back on for twenty-four hours. And yet there seemed to be no whisper of an active technicki rebellion. . . .

What would happen, she wondered, if the Soviets won the war on Earth? Would they take over the Colony? Would they blow it out of the sky?

Kitty was a wide-framed woman, her hair brown and coarse, her features blunt, hands and feet a little too big. She'd once overheard someone calling her "horsey." Okay, she was not a pretty woman, and not unusually intelligent. But she was strong and determined, and her eyes were a nice shade of blue, almost violet, and Chester adored her.

A broad ripple of nausea ran through her; the rancidness from the pipe seemed to deepen, the heat seemed to increase. She had to stop and lean on the railing of the catwalk, turn away from the pipes, and retch for a few moments. God, how she had wanted to get pregnant, have Chester's baby. A beautiful little brown baby, caramel like its dad . . . but she regretted it now . . . now that she had to hide it. If they found out, they'd make her leave her job, go to Colony parenthood monitoring to see if they'd even permit her to have the baby. And since Chester was black, and the SA was running things, they probably wouldn't issue the permit. They'd find some excuse to disallow it. Unless she could wait long enough, so the baby was a fait accompli. But moments like this . . . feeling sick and too heavy and tired all the time . . .

She saw the supervisor, Mrs. Chiswold, standing by the vat, looking up at her with a worried expression. She was probably worried she'd have to let Kitty go.

Kitty smiled, and stretched as if she'd just been taking a little rest, then turned back to the pipes, forced herself to stare into the endless subterranean river of sludge. And let her mind wander till she found herself wondering what had become of her brother, in Europe. Danny. Poor Danny. He was probably dead.

SouTHEASTERN FRANCE.

Hard Eyes was thinking, *We'll probably be dead by sunset, the latest*.

He and Claire and Danco were hunkered down in a shallow, crater-shaped depression atop a house-size mound of rock, waiting for the SA choppers to make another pass. They squinted against the austere winter sunlight, shivered when the breeze knifed them. Hard Eyes's hands were stiff on the auto-shotgun. Claire, sitting beside the small missile launcher, blew in her hands to keep them warm.

"How they find us?" Danco wondered aloud, his dark eyes darting from side to side as he scanned the sky. He said something else, but it was lost in the rattle of gunfire as Willow's group met another onrush from SA ground troops, up ahead, with a wall of bullets. Danco had a brown, saturnine face; bristling, arching eyebrows; a small, pointed beard; and the devil's own red mouth. He wore fatigues, a watch cap, and a battered brown leather jacket.

"Probably found us with infrared scans," Hard Eyes said. "This is a good area for it. Not much else up here that's warm to confuse the tracking. Doesn't matter." He heard the resignation in his own voice and thought, *I sound dead already*.

"It matters how they did it," Claire said. "They could use the same technique on the other Resistance outfits. . . ."

Hard Eyes nodded. She was right. She was right a lot of the time.

He heard a rattle of pebbles behind him and looked over his shoulder. Bonham and Sahid—a Palestinian whose shattered right arm was limp in a rude splint—were dragging the wounded out of the cave on sleeping bags, and into the shelter of another cluster of rocks. Bonham looked as if he were thinking of surrendering to the other side. He probably was. Sahid was a pinched, yellowish man whose lips hung slack as, wincing with pain, he tugged the wounded guerrilla with his left arm.

Nature had anticipated their need for a good defensive setup. The tumble of rocks, some ancient glacial deposit, was arranged in a kind of half-moon shape an acre across around the cave opening, with the moon's curve facing outward from the cave; the maze of rocks was made up of granite and basalt, gray and dull black, knobbed and craggy, but most of them roughly squarish or beveled like housetops, ten to twenty feet tall; between them ran crooked corridors of stone; the floor of each "corridor" was a moraine of smaller rock, mortared together with snow.

The guerrillas were looking east; the sun was almost overhead, here and there glancing brightly off the assault rifles of the three other NR teams placed in the warren of stone; four more were dug in around the approach to the cave.

Claire and Danco were to operate the launcher. Hard Eyes was there because that's where Claire was. The three of them were sitting ducks up here for the choppers—but they had to be on high ground to get a good shot with the launcher.

The SA had unloaded troops from two transport choppers, the long kind with two sets of copter blades each; they'd let them out down the mountainside a ways. Maybe a hundred men. SA Regulars, without heavy armor or the visored helmets, but well armed, fanning out to approach the cave area. Steinfeld had set up Willow's command out front. Willow had waited till the SA regulars were almost on top of them before jumping up and opening fire. The SA, caught by surprise, lost eight men before getting under cover—they'd expected the Resistance to hole up in the cave. A man sat behind a damaged, unusable machine gun in the mouth of the cave. A Frenchman Hard Eyes didn't know. He was terminally wounded; he'd volunteered for decoy duty. Suicide.

"Here comes another chopper," Claire said.

Bonham was alone now, dragging the last of the wounded from the cave—as Hard Eyes watched, Bonham stopped, startled, dropping his end of the sleeping bag at the sound of an assault-rifle burst somewhere not far behind him. He turned and looked in that direction, seemed to waver on the point of running.

Hard Eyes muttered, "Breached our flanks," as he turned and started down off the rock, half sliding down a snow-and-ice-encrusted incline. Claire would be all right for a while.

He made the ground and ran through the chill shadows, between the high rocks, toward Bonham. Hissing, "Get 'im undercover, damn you, Bonham!"

Bonham cursed but bent and dragged the unconscious man off to the right—as behind him two men emerged from a crevice. SA. Their guns still smoking from the execution of the NR sentries they'd surprised.

They were SA regulars, Hispanic, maybe Guatemalan, in

gray-black uniforms, trousers tucked in at the boots, and SA-insigniaed ski jackets with imitation sheepskin collars. They carried Heckler & Koch assault rifles, grenades on their khaki belts buckled over the coats. They were fifty feet off.

And they were looking at the mouth of the cave where the Frenchman sat hunched over the machine gun, forty feet to their right. Their attention was focused on the cave. Hard Eyes approached in heavy shadow. They hadn't spotted him. One of them raised a rifle, pointed it at the quiet, hunched figure behind the heavy machine gun. Hard Eyes realized the guy had already died. The other SA tapped his friend's shoulder and shook his head. Reached for a grenade. The machine gunner seemed to be looking toward Hard Eyes, away from the approaching soldiers.

Hard Eyes heard the thwacking blades of approaching choppers. He ignored it, moved forward carefully, trying to make as little noise as possible, keeping close to the craggy rock wall on his right, thinking, *Any second they'll realize the machine gunner's dead, they'll look up, see me, open fire. Those assault weapons have better accuracy than the shotgun at this range.*

The soldiers were moving closer to the machine gun. One of them had a grenade out, put his other hand on the pin. The choppers thwacked nearer. Hard Eyes was thirty feet away from the two SA. Twenty-five . . .

His foot dislodged a stone. One of the SA swung toward him.

Hard Eyes ran at them screaming, hoping to unnerve them into paralysis as he leveled the shotgun, bracing it against his hip, squeezing the trigger.

It was like firing a small cannon. The 12-gauge rounds slapped into the chamber at a rate of three per second. The gun leapt in his hands, viciously wrenching his wrists, kicking bruises into his hip, thundering, thundering, so the rocks echoed big rolling booms and the shadows vanished in strobing muzzle flash and—

In four seconds he'd sent twelve 12-gauge rounds into the two men, the load spreading just right at this range but compact enough to rip deep, slamming the two soldiers off their feet, and before they struck the ground, additional rounds slashing into them again and again so that their bodies jerked around in the air . . . spinning, blood flying . . .

They fell like things that had never been alive, their rifles clattering. One of the men almost torn in half above the waist.

Hard Eyes saw the grenade, with its pin gone, rolling on the ground nearby.

He leapt for a boulder as it went off, felt a hardened slab of air smack him in the back, send him head over heels so he ended on his back with his head pointed back the way he'd come.

He lay there for a moment breathing hard, feeling that icy pinching in the back of his legs that said he'd been hit by grenade fragments. Hoping the flak hadn't severed tendons. Lay there, trying to sort out the sounds. A harsh rattle of a chopper's minigun (maybe cutting Claire to pieces: *Fuck, Torrence, don't think that*) and a dull thud, a whoosh, an explosion—that would be Claire and Danco's surface-to-air. WHAM.

A flash of light glimpsed from the corner of his eyes as he got up on one elbow; saw a ball of fire tipping down into the rocks, vanishing in some fissure, huffing up blue smoke after itself . . . heard a ragged cheer . . .

They'd gotten one of the choppers.

Buoyed by elation, he got to his feet. He was dizzy, and his legs were shaky, they hurt like a bitch, but it didn't feel bad. He'd taken small fragments mostly in the meat of his thigh. It hurt when he walked, but . . .

But he hurried toward the rock Claire was on, heard the brittle *snap-snap* of rifle fire, glimpsed Danco opening up on someone below, then ducking down from return fire. Judging from the down-slant of Danco's rifle a moment before, his target was close to the rock. Hard Eyes circled the rock, heard two voices that sounded Dutch, maybe Boer, Afrikaans. The rock up ahead was shaped like the prow of a ship; the mazelike way between the rocks angled sharp right and left around that prow. He took the left-hand path. It was narrow; he had to turn sideways to slip through. The rock's dull-knife edges against his tailbone, shoulder blades. And then he emerged into a wider corridor. The rocks were more

open, up above, it was brighter here; he blinked against the
sudden sunlight as he turned the corner and saw two, no
three, SA regulars just under thirty feet down the narrow
rock corridor from him, hunched down, one of them fitting a
grenade on a launching rifle, the other two slapping fresh
clips into their magazines. Shit! Hard Eyes realized he'd
forgotten to reload. The magazine on the auto-shotgun now
held only four or five rounds. It'd have to be enough, they'd
spotted him; one was raising a rifle, shouting, "Hold it right
there!" the others snapping their heads around to look, jerky
with fright. Hard Eyes and the one who'd spotted him
opened up at the same time. But in a place like this, Hard
Eyes had the advantage. The assault rifle ricocheted its
rounds off the rock just over Hard Eyes's head, rock chips
hissing away as Hard Eyes squeezed out the rest of his magazine, the shotgun painfully loud in the enclosure, hurting
his arm like a son of a bitch now.

He was too close—too close because he got a good look
at their faces. Blue-eyed Dutch faces, rosy-cheeked, all
three of them probably teenagers. Racists, yes; Fascists, yes;
maybe even brainwashed robots in a sense. But they had
faces that registered fear and hope and even a kind of wist-
fulness. And he had a split-second flash-card image of those
faces as boys, three boys playing where they weren't supposed to be . . . caught by the adults and punished. . . .

Dan Torrence closed his eyes against what his auto-shotgun did to those boyish, blue-eyed faces. Ripped them off
the skulls. One of them screamed. Kept screaming, one
long, screaming tone, like someone continuously pressing
down a car horn. Was still alive screaming as Hard Eyes
opened his eyes and stepped over to him . . . the young soldier's red-splashed body, bubbling out blood now, mingled
with the others in the narrow space . . . broken bodies
crammed in one atop the other between broken, blood-drip-
ping rock . . . the boy screaming because his face was gone
and part of his head and most of the fingers on his left hand
. . . slapping that fingerless hand against a flap of skin, his
goddamn rosy cheek torn from the bone of his jaw, exposing
the blue and mucous yellow of oozing under-tissue.

Hard Eyes retched. Then took a deep breath, got control
of his lurching stomach, and pulled the knife from his belt,

bent, slashed through the boy's windpipe and jugular. The knife was a little dull; took several seconds. Hard Eyes trying to ignore the spongy feeling transmitted through the knife: flesh resisting, parting raggedly, making him remember cutting through the neck of a chicken on his uncle's farm as a boy.

Stomach pirouetting, Hard Eyes turned away. Muttering, "Go home to your ancestors, kid." He wiped and sheathed the knife, and started to walk away from the dead . . . and stopped, looked at the auto-shotgun in his hand: *His damn rosy cheek torn from the bone of his jaw, exposing the blue and mucous yellow of oozing under-tissue . . .*

Hard Eyes tossed the shotgun aside.

He turned and went through the ordnance that had been dropped by the enemy dead. He selected an M-20 U.S. Army assault rifle, automatic, and a pouch of ammunition. Then he went in search of communication with the living.

Many miles overhead, a satellite turned its cold eye on the maze of boulders, the stony ridges of the mountain, the patchwork snow, and sere granite. Over the mountains to the west, other satellites watched the deserted shore and a picket of Soviet ships on the ruffled jade of the Atlantic Ocean. When the reach of sea seemed infinite, finitude came as a shore, like a slap in the face. American shores, studded at regular intervals with new batteries of antiaircraft weapons, new radar installations, preparations for a Soviet invasion. (Moot preparations: if the invasion came, the Americans would launch a preemptive nuclear strike. The Soviets knew; so far they hadn't tried it.)

American satellites watched over the new Air Force installations, over receiving stations for the microwave power beamed from orbit. Above the shopworn American landscape, the crenelated and wallpaper-patterned vastnesses of housing projects, each bordered by its own walls and concertina wire, nocked by checkpoints for Security Guards. Some of the satellites were controlled from the CIA installation at Langley. Around the installation, more fences, wire, cameras, checkpoints. A series of nondescript government buildings with polarized windows.

In one of those buildings was a man named Stoner, alone

but for the camera that watched him. He was hunched over a keyboard in a researcher's computer WorkCenter. He was both large and small; his upper half was large, with a thick chest, wide shoulders, and a well-padded middle; his legs were shorter than most, his hips seemed miniature. He had a pudding-bland face, except for his sharp blue eyes. His short brown hair was combed and brilliantined in strict imitation of an old photo he'd seen of Hank Williams. He wore jeans, a red plaid shirt—real cloth—and a cream Western-style jacket.

But his mind was focused through his sharp blue eyes on the word-processing screen, sifting data. Finding in it events and observations that were like pottery shards to an archaeologist; he could fit them together, come up with a whole more than the sum of the parts. He could see the man hidden in the file.

The agents observed, photographed, snipped out bits of information about a man, so as to make the man into a file, reduce him to a lot of data; it was Stoner's job to make the file and its data back into a man. To study the man and make recommendations concerning him. Stoner had to reconstitute the man in his own mind.

Just now he was studying the thin file on a man named Daniel Torrence. Called by his *companeros* Hard Eyes.

The file had been provided to the CIA Domestic Branch by the Second Alliance International Security Corporation; the file's approval-of-transfer had been initialed by Sackville-West himself. Evidently the SA held Torrence in high regard as an enemy.

Stoner sat back in his chair, felt a tingle of gratification as it readjusted its contours to his movement. He patted his shirt pocket for his cigarettes, and then remembered that his wife had taken them that morning, had kissed him and taken them from his pocket at the same time. "You're giving them up, remember?" she said.

He smiled and sipped tepid ersatz coffee, to give his hands and mouth something to do. The file said that Torrence had been a college student at the outset of the war. An American, born in Rye, New York, he had lived most of his life just north of San Francisco, in Marin County. Upstate middle-class family. He'd gone to London to study political science. Torrence had been only marginally interested in his studies. He seemed to be "doing it to have something to do," according to the dean at the New London School. Some kind of exchange-student thing. He leaned toward Democratic Socialism but with "no particular zeal." When the war began, Gatwick air traffic was tied up, so Torrence tried to get out through Amsterdam. Found himself stuck there instead. Became leader of a gang of scavengers ducking the worst of the war as it moved through the Netherlands, trying to survive day to day and "presumably waiting for transportation to the States." Recruited into the New Resistance by unknown persons, "probably in return for promises of food and eventually transportation home." Evidently Torrence became ideologically entangled. Became convinced that the NATO forces and the SA were in some kind of racist collusion, judging from the text of pamphlets the NR circulated (file appendix 12, sec. C & D).

Stoner shrugged.

So what was the big deal? The agency had given the NR a Focus One rating. That meant that all overseas experts and a significant number of Stateside personnel were to focus on the guerrillas. There were less than a thousand active guerrillas in France. Admittedly they'd significantly inconvenienced the SA several times. But essentially they had to be some sort of bandit outfit, just another gang of scavengers feeding off the leavings of those two monstrous predators, the Soviet and NATO armies.

Stoner could understand the SA's involvement. But why the CIA Domestic, to this extent? There were said to be less than fifty NR agents in the United States. They were not known to sell information to the Soviets. They had performed no bombings, no robberies. They *had* been linked to two assassinations—one attempted and one successful. Rick and Ellen Mae Crandall. But the New Resistance had a sort of feud with the SA—it wasn't really a matter of National Security. Keep tabs on them, yes—but Focus One?

There was a war on, after all. Common sense dictated, from Stoner's viewpoint, that all available agency personnel focus on counterintelligence—counter the Soviets. Sure, the SA was performing a useful service for NATO by keeping order behind its lines, discouraging saboteurs, helping stabilize logistics. But the CIA, it seemed to Stoner, was allotting too much manpower and too many man-hours to the concerns of the SA. The President herself had signed a Classified Executive Order adjuring them to "give all necessary aid to NATO's peacekeeping force."

And the file on Hard Eyes had been stamped *PrS*.—Priority Subject.

> Torrence quickly graduated from a complete outsider to become one of the top five in the European NR. Torrence has been directly involved in every major guerrilla action since his recruiting, and one eyewitness described him as "ruthless and a little crazy when he's leading an attack" (extractor ref. SA872) and "a leader but also the guy is a dog at Steinfeld's heels" (*ibid*). Subject believed to have engineered the capture of the Arc de Triomphe shortly before its Jaegernaut demolition in SA Operation Cold Bear and the subsequent evacuation of Steinfeld and NR core from Paris. This subject experienced a profound motivational shift, with subsequent radicalization, after Paris training. Computer personality analysis and projections foresee extensive militant political involvement and volatile potential for Movement Leadership. Long-term survival of subject Torrence is counter to the best interests of SAISC/CIA projects. Advise subject be terminated with extreme prejudice. . . .

"Can't kill what you can't reach," Stoner murmured. *Extractor reference*. The SA had access to extractors? That was news to him. And Operation Cold Bear—military nomenclature.

There was a military slant to the SA. And the guerrillas claimed the SA was actively racist. It made Stoner nervous, because it made him wonder about Kupperbind.

Emmanual Kupperbind. CIA liaison to the Mossad. Kupperbind had submitted—unsolicited—a report on the "extra-contract activities" of the Second Alliance International Security Corporation in the Netherlands, Belgium, Italy, and France. He'd claimed the SA itself was a security risk. He alleged "systematically racist activities" and "the implementation of a European apartheid" that would, among other things, inevitably alienate Israel, at a time when American intelligence was already in danger of losing access to Israeli intelligence—some of the best in the world.

Not only had Kupperbind not been taken seriously, he'd been recalled and put out to pasture. Retired four years early.

There was a rumor that Kupperbind's dismissal was a function of agency politics: Pendleton, the director, was said to have gotten his job partly through the influence of the SA's panel of international security "experts"; the panel advised the President, from time to time, on terrorism and saboteurs. Pendleton owed the SA favors, it was assumed.

Whatever, all copies of Kupperbind's report were gathered up and shredded.

All except one. Stoner had a copy. He hadn't read it in detail. He'd been busy, and the whole thing had smelled of eccentric alarmism.

But when the clerk had come around asking for the report, Stoner had made excuses. Told them it was locked up in one of his cabinets and it was a hassle to dig it out just now when he had so much work to do. He'd drop it off later that afternoon.

Only he never did drop it off. He wasn't sure why he'd never turned the report over. Ought to get rid of the damn thing.

But, after all, he was under assignment to study the so-called New Resistance. The NR existed—so it said—to oppose the Second Alliance. And any information on the Second Alliance could conceivably apply to his investigation of the NR. He could read Kupperbind's report. Skeptically. Perhaps pan a few small nuggets of useful information out of the silt of Kupperbind's paranoia.

He was startled by a buzzing from his console, almost jumped out of his chair.

Words flashed for his attention on the screen: INCOMING CALL. SWITCH TO FONE MODE FOR RECEIVE.

Stoner punched for Fone Mode. The file page on the screen compressed to a thin line; the line expanded to become something else entirely. A man's face. Unger.

The black-and-white TV image of Unger smiled. Squat,

almost jolly face, laugh lines around the eyes, always smiling when he first saw you, hail-fellow-well-met. Always wanted something. Stoner had never trusted Unger, but Unger was section chief, so Stoner smiled and said, "What can I do for you?"

"You could switch on visual so I can see if it's you or somebody doin' an impersonation!"

"Sorry." He punched for transmission tie-in with the lens beside the computer's disk drive.

"There you are, by God! How's it hangin', Kimosabe?"

Stoner winced inwardly. Kimosabe. Where'd he get that stuff?

"Fine. Great."

"Good—well, hey, Kimosabe, we're just trying to get some loose ends tied up here, and we find, going over the checklist for Recalls, that you never turned in that File-178-Report-43 we asked for. Says here you promised to bring it in yourself."

Stoner felt a chill at the synchronicity of it. File-178-Report-43 was the Kupperbind report. "Well, I'll look it up, see what I got. I don't know as I have it; they maybe forgot to check it off when I brought it in. I'll see."

Unger's black-and-white grin melted into something flat, appropriate for the colorless image. "Say there, Kimosabe— we got a Focus One on the NR. That file concerns the NR; we need it in here right away."

The file's more about the SA, Stoner thought. But he said, "If I've got it, you'll sure get it. Right away."

Unger nodded. Stoner hoped Unger was going to break the connection, but after a moment he said, "I wonder if we could take a quick meeting, say in the commissary in about an hour—we need to talk. Things are moving. Changes coming down. We need to know which side of the changes you stand on."

"Uh—"

"Seriously, Stoner. The commissary. One hour."

"Uh—okay."

Unger broke the connection. Stoner thought: *We need to talk?*

SOUTHEASTERN FRANCE.

Claire almost shot Hard Eyes when he turned the corner. He saw her shudder, the color draining from her face. She lowered her rifle.

Claire and Danco were crouched in the frozen rubble between two sheer rock walls, under the boulder they'd used for their surface-to-air launching. A curtain fringe of thin gray ice hung in little spears down the shadowed rock walls beside them. Both Claire and Danco were haggard; Claire was trembly with cold or fear. Hard Eyes wanted to go to her, put his arms around her, but he thought she might resent being comforted in front of Danco, so he held back.

"Your shotgun," Danco said. "Damaged? It works no more?"

"It works too well," Hard Eyes said. He looked up, hearing a fresh spate of gunfire. Unconsciously he'd turned so that his back was to the rock, Claire and Danco on the left, a view down the crooked corridor of chill stone to his right.

Movement down there. Hard to make out clearly in the shadow what it was. But in that direction . . .

"Here they come," he muttered.

Danco's walkie-talkie was nattering at him. He pressed it to his ear, frowning, then nodded. "Okay. *Si*." He put the walkie-talkie back on his belt and told them, "We regroup around the cave. The SA, they are pressing. They are coming in to finish us."

A cold, weary late afternoon. The sunlight streaking pale between the megalithic stones imparted no warmth. About twenty guerrillas were posted at the openings between the rocks, and in the approaches to the cave from the sides. Two more NR—Sahid and the fatalistic Sortonne—crouched in the crater atop the square boulder, a little bit in advance of the main group; Sortonne with a rocket launcher, Fahid beside him to help reload.

Quiet. The SA had moved into position. Probably deploying seeker missiles, maybe light artillery.

Steinfeld's command group squatted on its haunches, mouths and nostrils trailing steam as they talked, hands tucked in their armpits for warmth. Steinfeld saying, ". . . the extractor makes it that way. The only course we can take from here. We hit them with everything, we force their hand. I . . ."

Steinfeld hesitated, his mask of calm slipping. It hurt Hard Eyes to see it. He relied on Steinfeld's courage, his seeming indefatigability. But being cornered one too many times had worn Steinfeld down.

Steinfeld looked at the ground, and when he looked up at them again, his gaze was broken. He couldn't look directly at any of them. He said, "I must insist that you kill me. The moment the line breaks. Be sure to shoot me in the head, several times. A shot to the body won't necessarily. . ." He cleared his throat.

Levassier turned away, cursing in French.

Hard Eyes felt leaden. Like he'd never get warm again. They'd patched him up, but he was suffering from blood loss. Dizzy when he moved too quickly. It didn't matter, obviously. He looked up toward the line at the edge of the amphitheater area around the cave mouth—a woman there toppled over backward. They heard the distorted crack of the gunshot a half second later, echoing *shuh-shuh-shuh* through the twisted corridors of rock. The woman lay on her back, a bullet hole in her forehead. It was Angeline, someone he scarcely knew. Steinfeld was bellowing orders, and Hard Eyes automatically went into position with the others. Claire beside him, and the black woman, Lila, as they crouched behind a block of stone the size and shape of an overturned credit-transfer booth.

Ahead, the crooked corridors of rock were sunk in shadow; dark, hunched figures shifted there. Lila said, "We cannot see them. Their uniforms are colored like the rock. Dark there." She took a flare gun from a pack lying on the ground beside her, dropped a shell in it, fired it ahead, into the shadows; the shell arced up, down, and splashed the gray dimness with sparks and the blue-white dazzle of burning magnesium. Someone screamed, and even Claire smiled at that. *Burn, you bastard, because you're going to kill me.*

And then they saw something else in the light of the flare.

Hard Eyes remembered snorkeling once, off the coast of Florida, seeing a shark nosing slowly toward him among the coral formations. That's what this thing looked like, from here. The shark in the undersea maze had swum past him, ignored him. This one wouldn't do that.

It was a seeker missile, moving slowly—not much more than hovering in place, just drifting forward as it picked out a target—held up by jets on its underside, its tail rocket dormant, waiting for the missile's microcomputer to make a decision, wavering in and out of the flare light behind it. It was a sleek thing of chrome, a sensing grid on its nose looking for heat in human-body outline. Nosing this way, that. Why was it taking so long?

Maybe the flare heat behind the missile, reflected from the rocks, confused it. Soon it'd pick the heat from a group of people, though, and it'd find its way—

One moment the missile was drifting in and out of shadow, almost absently; a split second later, rattlesnake flash, it struck, impacting with the top forward edge of the cratered boulder where Sortonne and Sahid had been . . . had been.

The two men spinning from a fireball, torn outlines of men, dolls some sadistic kid had torn the hands and head from. Warm droplets spattered Hard Eyes's cheek. Chunks of rock flew from the blast, and one of them smacked meatily down onto Levassier's shoulder, who'd been kneeling by someone wounded, smashed down himself now, shoulder crushed, upper arm nearly mangled away, hanging by shreds. Steinfeld was running to him, removing his belt for a tourniquet. Hard Eyes felt blood—Sortonne's? Sahid's?—running down his cheek toward his mouth. He smeared it away with the back of his hand so he wouldn't have to taste the blood of other NR. Blood already cold to touch.

Shouts of outrage; someone sobbing; spastic volleys of gunfire; two more on the line fell back, one gut-shot, shit from his ruptured intestines adding its ugly sweetness to the iron taste of blood in the air, the scratchy tang of gunsmoke; the second wounded NR writhing as a rift through his neck pumped out his life. The other NR turned away from the man with his neck shot out; there was no helping him, they had to ignore his frantic hand signals—*Help me!*—try not to see him, look down the sights of your gun. . . .

"Don't shoot without a clear target!" Steinfeld yelled.

NR firing slowed and stopped. Echoes and then quiet. Hard Eyes looked for the enemy and saw no one. . . .

Motion. Gleaming metal motion. *Another* seeker. The sight freezing his bowels as it nosed into a band of wan sunlight, sniffing for group heat.

Hard Eyes squeezed off a three-shot burst at the seeker, hoping to detonate it while it was still a hundred yards away. Glimpsed sparks as the rounds ricocheted from stone. Anyway, it was well armored, you'd have to hit it precisely, squarely, in the nose, almost impossible at this range. Try again—no, wait!

Claire had taken something from Lila, was up and running ahead of them, toward the missile.

"Claire!" Hard Eyes heard himself shout.

She was bending beside Sortonne's body, lifting it up, her hands under its armpits, her face twisted with revulsion. What the fuck was she *doing*? Recovering bodies? *Now?*

The seeker missile was drifting closer, its tail rocket beginning to show flame as it picked out a target. Any second it would lance out, blow two or three or five of them to shreds.

Claire had set up Sortonne's body so it leaned on a boulder. She fired the flare gun into it and turned to run.

The body's chest erupted with flare heat.

The missile sensed the heat, saw the body outline; the heat more than enough for a group. It streaked to the decoy, exploding it along with bits of boulder. Still running, Claire stumbled, caught in the shockwave or by shrapnel, fell flat, skidding. Hard Eyes shouted something and vaulted over the boulder, ran to her, picked her up in his arms . . . she was heavier than she should have been; his legs were wobbly. He felt a stickiness on the back of his legs; he'd started bleeding again. But he staggered back to the low boulder with her, the others laying down suppressive fire to give him cover.

He laid her on her back behind the stone. Bullets ripped the air overhead. His ears ached from the gunfire noise of the guerrillas, just to his left. Claire's eyes were open, moving. Alive. But registering nothing.

A tympanic roll announced the tons of killing machine suddenly blocking out the sky overhead, a machine giant's voice booming shakily through the thudding copter blades, *"NR, if you surrender, you will not be killed. If you surrender—"* The words were shattered by light machine-gun fire as someone opened up at the copter; it returned fire with its miniguns, and someone screamed and sobbed at the top of their lungs. All the time Hard Eyes was looking at Claire's face. Was she hit? Internal bleeding? "Claire?"

Danco and Lila were shouting something at him. "More choppers!" someone yelled, and something more in French. He looked up and saw a group of large brown choppers moving in, guns alongside firing. Red stars on the doors. And a red CCCP. Soviet choppers. The Soviets were involved. Why? He didn't really care.

His eyes stung from dust in the rotor backwash. "Claire . . . ?"

A shell—he had no idea where it had come from—threw bushels of the stony ground into the air maybe twenty feet from him and slapped him down with the hot ripple of its blast, sending a single sharp ringing tone through his head as he fell sprawling across Claire. *Am I hit? Is she hit?*

"Claire?"

After a moment he realized he was lying facedown across her, his body making an *X* with hers. And he was holding his breath. He let it out, becoming aware of a whirlwind of noise and motion, of people running nearby, fire chattering in their hands. It seemed to him that it was all mixed up now; it wasn't the enemy over there, NR here—the enemy had overrun them, were all around; the NR was there, too, emerging and sinking in smoke. Hard Eyes saw two SA regulars running toward him. He found his rifle, fired from a belly-down sniper's position, gun propped in the hollow of his shoulder and in his hands, its butt kicking at him as one of the SA fell. The other one was still coming, pointing a submachine gun. Any second he'd feel the slugs. But that one fell, too, seeming to explode into flame as he fell, dropping his gun, clawing, making a swimming motion on the ground . . . somebody'd hit the guy with an incendiary grenade . . . after a moment the soldier lay still, facedown, quietly burning. But the Soviet choppers were looming like great golden dragons overhead as they descended, rotors whipping the smoke.

"Dan?" Claire's voice. "Let's get up, let's get under cover." Sounding weak. But she was all right.

But . . . *Fuck, the Soviets are going to take us,* Hard Eyes thought. *Fuck that. They'll torture Claire and then they'll execute us. That's what they do. Wring you for information and kill you for convenience. I got to kill her myself. Save her from torture.*

Rifle in hands, he got to his knees beside her. She was turned on her side, away from him, starting to get up.

He pointed his rifle's muzzle at her head. *So they don't torture her.*

He pulled the trigger.

Nothing. Magazine empty.

He tossed the rifle aside, looked around for another gun.

And then Steinfeld was kneeling beside him, pulling him up.

"Got to kill her before they. . ." Hard Eyes said. Or tried to say, he wasn't sure which. He felt like he was made of soggy cardboard. His lips didn't want to work; his tongue felt thick. He managed, "The Soviets—"

The choppers were settling down in an open space just ahead of him. The SA had taken cover, driven back by cannon blasts from the Soviets.

Steinfeld said, "They're not Soviets. That's cover. Kind of camouflage. That's the Mossad. They got the transmission. They've come to get us out."

Hard Eyes must have lost consciousness for a while. But not more than a few minutes. Because when the fuzziness around him resolved into shapes, he was inside a helicopter, hearing Steinfeld say, "They've gone into the cave. They sent in ten regulars, it looks like . . . I doubt they send in any more. Go ahead, Danco."

Hard Eyes heard Danco chuckle as he reached for the remote-control detonator.

Hard Eyes was distantly aware that there was a field IV plugged into his arm, a Mossad medic kneeling beside him holding up a plastic bottle of plasma, Claire sitting up across from him, her leg bandaged, staring into space, but she was alive, Lord she was . . .

Heard Danco laughing. "Hey, *pendejos, vaya con Dios!*" as he threw the switch on the detonator. And the cave blew, taking ten SA with it.

Hard Eyes smiled and went back to sleep.

THREE

LYONS, FRANCE.

Jean-Michel Karakos stood at the window looking at the prisoners in the detention pens below. On either side of him stood Dr. Cooper and Colonel Watson. Behind Karakos loomed an enormous Second Alliance guard—the man must have been close to seven feet. Karakos could *feel* him back there, hulking over him. Karakos's hands were cuffed together, and the cuffs were locked to his belt buckle.

Karakos, Watson, and Cooper were looking through the polarized window at a nightmare concocted with the simple-minded efficiency of a high-school science fair project. "It's an interesting experiment," Watson was telling him. "It was Cooper's brainchild." Watson was a tall, thick-bodied Englishman in his early fifties, with a round, weathered face, a brickish complexion, and poker-chip-blue eyes. He wore a black-and-silver SA officer's uniform but stood in a kind of boyish slouch, as if to defuse the uniform's punctilio. He was the SA's Chief of Tactics, a title that encompassed a great many public and private responsibilities. Some said he was the number-two man in the Second Alliance.

"Oh, well," Cooper said with a modesty that was clearly insincere, "the experiment is actually an old sociobiological concept—we're merely bringing it to life." Cooper was about forty, Karakos guessed, though it was hard to tell with an albino. He was stooped, potbellied; he had one pink eye and one blue eye, hair that looked like mold, and an unsettling waxiness to his skin. It looked as glossy as a balloon. He wore a blue lab smock over a tweed suit.

"You are a sociobiologist, then?" Karakos asked, as if he were a magazine interviewer and not a prisoner.

"A sociobiologist? No, we're beyond that here." They were standing at the second-story polarized window that looked out over detention pens ten, eleven, and twelve. Karakos didn't know where he was; he'd been brought here in the back of a big windowless truck, packed in with seventy others. The trip had taken only half an hour—he was sure only that he was still in France. The building was big, drafty, echoey, built of a dull white alloy that looked like plastic, but was in fact alumitech.

Watson, selecting Karakos from the other prisoners being transferred from the main detention facility in Lyons, had taken the air of a proud man of property giving a friend the tour, telling Karakos they'd put the place together from its component parts in two weeks, once the foundations were sunk. There were fifteen "pens," most of them not visible from here; pens ten and eleven were side by side under the window; pen twelve was as big as ten and eleven together and ran alongside them to the right. Each pen was separated from the others by two chain-link fences, and each fence's crown of thorns was concertina wire. Between the two fences was a five-foot concrete path patrolled by helmeted SA guards.

Karakos was deceptively brutish-looking. He was stocky, brown-eyed—his eyes were sunken now, from poor diet— had thick lips, a wide mouth full of widely spaced teeth from which the gums were beginning to recede; oily, stringy brown hair; and eyebrows that grew together. He wore a detainee's polyplas bright orange overalls—for maximum visibility in case of escape—and a yellowed T-shirt. He had ten days' growth of coarse brown beard, and in the months he had been in detention, he had been so long without a bath that he could no longer smell anything but himself. He was not an elegant figure. But as Watson had written in his Extraction Experiment 5F evaluation for Sackville-West, "Karakos was one of the NR's most effective propagandists. His scathing attacks on the SA [for the banned newspaper *Egalité*] were noteworthy for their eloquence and sheer panache, and it is said he worked closely with Steinfeld in planning the NR's first field campaigns."

"No," Cooper was saying, "I'm not a sociobiologist. We left that behind years ago." Tight, smug smile. "I'm a social geneticist."

Karakos noted Watson's reaction, an arch look that Cooper interpreted as humorous acknowledgment, but which probably signified Watson's barely contained contempt for the albino. Cooper was, after all, a genetic aberration himself. But he was useful to the SA.

Was there a way to drive a wedge between the two men? Karakos wondered.

You're grasping at straws, he told himself. *It's hopeless.*

But Karakos had the habit of hope. It was a survival skill, for the "detainees." A monstrously false term, *detainees*. As if it was only temporary. As if they'd ever go free.

"As you can see, Michael," Watson began, "the detainees in the three pens are divided, roughly, into three skin-color groups." Watson's manner, talking to Karakos, was amiable, respectful, with a touch of the paternal. Just as if he wasn't a prisoner wearing handcuffs and guarded by a professional thug in a mirrorglass helmet. Watson went on, "And, in fact, each of the three pens is on a different dietary regimen. The black-skinned group in number ten are fed rather well and given a number of privileges, such as cigarettes, the others don't receive. The brown-skinned group in eleven is on an average diet, with average privileges. The lighter-skinned 'coloreds'—half-breeds essentially—in pen twelve are being starved. Dr. Cooper's theory holds that interracial mistrust is instinctive, but that instinct is often dormant until survival-stress factors are significantly increased. You'll note the subjects are in most cases imprisoned, in this experiment, with their families, in order to tap into their protective instincts. Each penned group has been informed that fighting is to be severely punished—the equivalent of the civilizing social inhibitions that check violence in urban settings—but Dr. Cooper believes that given a sufficient increase in survival-stress factors, all such restraints will be overwhelmed and aggression will take place, if it has the opportunity. And we intend to provide opportunity."

"People who starve get angry, yes," Karakos said. "And they'll strike out against whoever's around. Race has nothing to do with it."

"We have another group, on the other side of Control, in pens thirteen, fourteen, and fifteen," Cooper said, in an oozily patronizing tone. "In those pens the races are mixed—light-skinned side by side with black and so forth—and we find that they do not respond to survival factors nearly so uniformly as those who are incarcerated with their own race."

"Even if it's true," Karakos said, shrugging, "it doesn't prove anything about the superiority or inferiority of races involved."

"We have other experiments—" Cooper began a little angrily.

But Watson cut him off with an incisive hand motion. "It's of no real relevance in the long run, which race, if any, is the superior. First you must understand that this experiment is laying the groundwork for experiments on a larger scale in the outside world. We can induce race war with the right social pressures applied—"

"*Colonel* . . ." Cooper said warningly.

A flicker of satisfaction showed on Watson's face. *He's using me to bait Cooper,* Karakos thought.

Watson went on blithely. "The question of race superiority is only of academic interest—to me, at any rate. What matters is that races are inherently programmed to be in conflict with one another—and the only true path to world peace is to see to it that the conflict is resolved by carrying it to its logical conclusion; its bitter but inevitable final solution."

Karakos was half Greek, half French. After age ten he'd been raised in London. Reading the trashier sort of English fiction, he'd come across the word *thunderstruck,* and it had always seemed excessive. Now he understood it. He felt as if he'd been struck by a thunderbolt between the eyes. He looked at Watson. He gaped. "I—uh . . ." He shook his head in disbelief. "I always assumed that you wanted to, ah . . ."

"To enslave?" Watson smiled. "Or perhaps merely to exploit the other races?" He chuckled. "It's no longer practical.

There's too much uncontrolled information polluting their cultural integrity, poisoning them with discontent and ambition. No, in the long run the only real solution is genocide. Many genocides. Oh, for now we need the lesser races for economic reasons. But we're already at work breeding a sub-race of workers who'll be quite incapable of challenging us. We call them 'subjugate breeds.' The subjugates won't be human at all, you see. No smarter than dogs or horses, but they'll be idiots savants when it comes to fulfilling whatever low technical work—technicki work—needs to be done."

Cooper was fuming. Even the silent SA guard behind Karakos was shifting restlessly. In a carefully flat tone Cooper said, "Colonel, you have a tendency to enjoy the sound of your own discourse to the detriment of security—"

Watson silenced Cooper with a look. It wasn't a hard look, particularly. Once more, it was incisive. "When I speak to Karakos, I'm speaking to a blackboard."

Karakos knew what he meant. He meant the extractor. He meant he would be *erased*.

They'd already put him under the extractor once, for interrogation purposes. But they hadn't gotten anything useful: The resistance had shifted its headquarters since he'd been imprisoned. All the partisans he'd known about had long since fled France. He had no idea where Steinfeld and the others were now.

But next time the SA would erase him, would take not only his personality, his convictions, but also everything he knew that might be useful to the Resistance. And now he knew something that could make all the difference. If the rest of the world knew...

Karakos felt ill, sick with responsibility. He had to get word out somehow. Because Watson was not insane. He was probably a sociopath, yes, but not truly insane. It seemed impractical: a plan to exterminate every race on Earth but the Caucasian—and the Caucasian's special "subjugate breeds." *Wildly* impractical.

But maybe not. The SA's New Life Lab was known to be involved in genetic engineering of microorganisms. And during the Middle Ages a single strain of microorganism, the bubonic plague, wiped out something from one third to one half of the population of the world. Indiscriminately, of course. But suppose someone engineered a discriminatory virus or bacterium. Some had claimed that the CIA, in the twentieth century, had come close to developing a germ that killed only Slavic races . . . like the Soviets. But the project had been canceled as impractical because too many Americans had Slavic blood.

But suppose the SA developed germs that were more selective. That killed only the black race, the Jewish race, the Chinese.

"But what would you do about the Soviets?" Karakos asked.

"The Soviets will lose the war," Watson said. "We'll absorb them. Racially they're close enough to us that—"

"Colonel Watson," Cooper interjected, strident now, "suppose something were to go wrong—an attack on this building, say—and this man were by chance to go free? He—"

"He'll be taken care of very soon, I assure you, Cooper," Watson said sharply. Losing patience. Dropping Cooper's *Doctor* honorific.

Karakos thought, They're off-balance with conflict now. Try it. "I understand your multiple genocide is even now being cooked up in the New Life Labs." Deadpan. Trying to sound as if he knew it to be true.

Watson and Cooper were staring at him. Watson had gone almost as white as Cooper. He began, "We extracted you, you had nothing about—" But then he snorted and shook his head ruefully. "You are playing a game with me." His blue-gray eyes had seemed watery; the water turned to ice now, as he stared at Karakos. He'd been wheedled into an admission. He'd been manipulated, and it was as if Karakos had spat a wad of phlegm onto Watson's ego. Watson went on. "You shouldn't, you know. Shouldn't try to play me that way. I have you, you see. I own you now. I can do as I like with you. And I really don't think you've quite considered the implications of that."

Karakos's stomach lurched.

"I brought you here," Watson said, "to prepare the ground for you in some way. Or to prepare the ground *in* you. The extractor will change you, yes. We will erase you, rebuild you from the ground up—but simply chemically installing a new mind-set in a man doesn't seem adequate to me. I felt you needed to be prepared. I felt that somewhere in you there's a seed of genetic purity that resonates with the beauty of what's happening here—a beauty that emerges from truth."

"You're preparing me . . . mystically?"

"Spiritually, perhaps." Some of the edge had left Watson. "I . . . always felt you were rather wasted on the other side. I suppose I wanted to try to convert you the ordinary way first." He shrugged. "Strange impulses arise in one from time to time." He looked down at the pens. "Ah. The fourth stage. Have a look, Karakos."

Karakos forced himself to look. Till now he'd tried not to look at the pens too closely. Afraid of his own anger. Now he saw the prisoners squatting in groups here and there, held nearly motionless by the weight of misery. Saw that the "privileged" pens' detainees had clothing; the others were humiliated by being kept naked and shivering with cold. Saw them huddled for warmth and rocking on their heels, mothers clasping listless infants. Some of the younger men seemed to have gone into the gray blankness of simple despair; others were looking around with a maddening repetitiveness: Look first this way, see the fence, the locked gate, the guards, the wire; look *that* way, see another fence, wire, guards; look another way, see the wall, the opaque window behind which they knew more of their captors watched them; turn, look behind, and see the fence, the guards, the walls. Start over again: See the fence, the locked gate, the guards, the wire. . . . No matter how many times you looked, it was still the same.

Even from here, Karakos could see the marks of malnutrition on the "unprivileged" prisoners. The distended bellies, the sores. The dullness in the faces. The ones who sat and rocked; and the ones who didn't move. But all of them, from time to time, staring sullenly at the other pens.

The gate opened, four SA guards strolled into the nonprivileged pens, picked out prisoners at random, and began to beat them. "And, of course," Karakos said, his voice just a croak now, "those in the privileged pens are not usually beaten."

The prisoners were cringing, running, clawing at one another to get out of the way as the guards swung cattle prods and Recoil Reversal sticks.

"You begin to see," Cooper remarked, "how very animalistic the prisoners are. They revert so easily."

"Animalistic?" Karakos could not believe it. He fought himself. Feeling the dull throb of hatred inflame and squirt searing bile in him.

But he didn't move. It was as if he stood balanced on the tip of a flagpole. He didn't dare to move. He simply stood at the window, trembling, sweat running into his eyes.

As Cooper spoke into a microphone, ordering the guards. As the guards opened the gates between the pens.

As pens eleven and twelve were opened onto number ten.

The guards withdrew from the area. None could be seen from the pens.

Slowly the larger group, made up of the prisoners in eleven and twelve, began to move toward the frightened, huddled blacks in ten.

It began gradually. But in ten minutes the fighting had begun, and in fifteen minutes four, perhaps five, of the blacks had been beaten to death.

Karakos was choking, gagging. Not with squeamishness —he was beyond that—but with undirected rage at the way these people had been shorn of their humanity, twisted into new shapes, all the hunched shapes of brutality.

"I think we have room forty-four set up for Michael, don't we?" Watson said, speaking into a fone he'd taken from his belt. "Good."

I have to make them kill me, Karakos thought. *Or they're going to use me and I'll be part of this.*

This. The men tearing other men to pieces below. And women. And children.

He could no longer contain himself. He slipped from the flagpole, turned toward the guard, and, forgetting his cuffs, tried to raise his fists against the man and screamed in frustration when the shackles restrained him—and something bit him on the arm. He looked, saw that Cooper had given him an injection. He had time to think, *They're going to use me*. And to feel the horror that followed on that thought, before all thinking was eclipsed and the darkness was complete.

Washington, D.C.

"So what did Unger say?" Howie asked.

Stoner shrugged. "Not much—just something ambiguous about how things are 'hopping' and 'we're all gonna have to watch our step, you read me Kimosabe?'"

Howie laughed.

The two CIA career men were in a bar in Washington, D.C., on Connecticut Avenue. It was not a fashionable bar. It had a jukebox in it, instead of a U-Select programmer at the bar stools; the music was the umpteenth reissue of Patsy Cline or George Jones or Hank Williams, people like that, twentieth-century country music instead of Minimono or chaotics or ska-thud or angst rock. The floor was wood instead of concrete or plastipress, and it sagged in places with age. The bar stools weren't confoam; they were torn, taped-up vinyl.

There was a mirror behind the bar instead of a vidflasher.

The jukebox was playing Ned Sublette's "North Dakota," and Ned was wailing about "mosquitas big as helicopter choppers and the wind's a permanent part of your hair," and Howie and Stoner were sitting in a scarred wooden booth drinking Lone Star beer, imported from Texas, and talking shop. They were almost the only people in the bar, except for a barfly on a stool at the far end of the bar, the bleached-blond barmaid, and a snoring fat man four booths away. It was eight P.M., and Stoner was tired from work—but at the same time he was wired on a nagging anxiety that never quite articulated itself.

Howie was a barrel-chested black man wearing half-glasses and four gold rings on his left hand. An enormous white cowboy hat was tilted back on his head—he'd worn it as a joke, because Stoner was a country-music fan. His right eye was electronic, an implant; it moved a little differently than the other, but it was fairly realistic. They'd even traced fake veins on the corner of the white. When you looked at the iris closely, you could see the overlapping sections of its shutter closing. Howie was fifty; but except for a sag around the cheeks of his broad face, he was one of those black men who seem ageless.

"He came into AD this morning," Howie said. Howie worked in the CIA Domestic's Accounting and Disbursements office now. Once he'd been a field agent. "Said he had a special project needed funding and the director was unavailable, could he talk to our supervisor? What the hell, he thinks Fench is going to give him money without top-off approval? Man's crazy." There was something more than office-gossipy derision in Howie's voice. Something personal, even sullen.

"All he wanted from me—in a material way—was the Kupperbind file," Stoner said, watching Howie's face.

"Was that all." Flat like that. No question mark.

"And he . . . mentioned you."

Howie had been staring at a moth-eaten elk's head over the bar. Now his eyes jerked back to focus on Stoner; the artificial one took a moment longer to line up with the other.

"How's that implanted eye treating you, Howie?"

"Uh—okay. I had some ghost-image problems with it. It picked up some TV station, I was seeing football players running through my office. And one of those AntiViolence executions, some guy getting his head blown open in front of a studio audience . . . I saw *that* in the fucking cafeteria. Blew away my appetite. Had to get my eye reinsulated. What'd he say about me, goddammit?"

"Unger? He said he heard you were a good buddy of mine. I said yeah. He said, 'Alignment is everything, Stoner.' I said, 'Huh?' and he said, 'You should be careful who you pick to be your friends, Kimosabe. Pick people who're on their way up.' " Stoner waited for Howie's reaction. Howie just sat there, looking leaden, motionless, staring at his beer bottle. "What is it with you and him, Howie? What the hell was he talking about?"

"He was talking about the new Hiring Assessment Program, Stoner. They make it sound nice with a name like that. Whitewash it." He smiled bitterly at some private joke.

"Go on."

Howie shook his head. "He's an asshole, but he gave you good advice. You don't want to know any more about it."

"Yeah, I do. Come on, man. We known each other for a while. Hell, I married your niece, Howie. Come on."

Howie sighed. "Okay. You asked for it. You're going to think it's paranoid bullshit, though. You ever wonder why I'm in AD now, after eighteen years in the field?"

"Sure, I wondered." With a little embarrassment, because he'd assumed Howie had fucked up in some major way.

"Let me tell you something, I wondered too. I got twelve Special Commendations, I figured that was enough. I applied for desk work, figured something supervisory in Langley. Wanted to settle back with my family. So they transferred me, all right—to the fucking accounting department. Man, I got seniority, experience, training, education, and know-how over every fucking one of my five immediate superiors. You know? I got my masters in psych, I got—" He broke off, swiped at an imaginary fly. "They don't care about any of it. They said the Assessment Program evaluated me as being best suited for accounting. So I looked into this Assessment Program. It's supposed to be based on a new 'personnel efficiency study.' Only there never was any such study. It just doesn't exist. The whole thing was cooked up by Unger and the director, and so far it's only been applied to blacks, Hispanics, Orientals, Jews, and anyone who's even politically moderate. Nobody else."

Stoner stared at him. Shook his head in disbelief. "You're saying they're using this Assessment Program for racial discrimination? To 'keep the niggers down'?"

"That's just for starters. When they can, they *fire* blacks. And remember Winston Post?"

"Tall guy, used to be a basketball player, worked in personnel?"

"Yeah. It was him first found out that this 'efficiency study' was bogus. He started complaining, talking lawsuits. Where is he now?"

"Come on, you don't really think—it was a car accident, man, brakes went out, that could happen to anyone."

"Sure happened at a convenient time. His wife tells me

she called an ambulance, but it didn't come for almost an hour and a half. She asked them how come they took so long and they said some plainclothes cops pulled them over and hassled them. And Winston bled to death in the wreck."

"Jesus. That sounds like . . ."

"Yeah. But don't say you heard it here. I'm retiring as soon as I can. I'm getting out, man."

"Maybe I ought to get out too."

"What for? If Unger bothered to warn you, means he wants you to change sides. They've decided you're valuable. You got that famous memory of yours, that talent for data search. And you're not exactly a liberal when it comes to Communists. They know you got a bug up your ass about Communism—"

"Christ, the Soviets are blockading the Atlantic ports, blockading the Space Colony, and invaded half of Europe, and you're telling me I got a *bug up my ass* about 'em?"

"Yeah, yeah. Anyway, you and Unger are in the same camp that way—he hates the Reds too. So they want you solidly with them when they purge the Agency. And when they purge the rest of the government, and maybe the whole fucking country. . . ."

"Hey—*now* you're getting paranoid."

"Right. Sure. But you know who's behind this Assesssment Program? Our friends in the Second Alliance. The SA. Post saw the memo—it was on their recommendation. Who you know that's more racist than the SA, man, huh? You read that Kupperbind file. And where's Kupperbind now? Let me tell you something, Stoner . . . these bastards have just begun. Before they're through, it's going to be a white, white world, my friend. . . ."

The Island of Malta.

"We can't really be alone," Steinfeld said. "But sometimes it feels as if we are."

Hard Eyes nodded.

They were in a villa, on the island of Malta, in the Mediterranean Sea. A little chill was creeping into the evening air, but compared to the Alps, it was almost balmy here. Deep winter in Malta was like early fall in New York.

The villa was a Mossad safe house. It was high and narrow, an anomaly in the landscape. Nothing but trees and scrub and boulders around it, for ten acres square. The villa's designers could have sprawled it out comfortably, like many Mediterranean country houses. But they'd chosen the gaunt effusion of an Italian town house. It was three narrow stories, with a balcony on each of the upper stories; the top balcony faced north, the lower faced east. There was a ten-foot brick wall around the property, topped with barbed wire. Cameras and infrared detection devices were snugged discreetly in the trees. It was perfect for the Mossad's purposes: It commanded a view of the fields and olive orchards beyond its grounds; it could be defended from the balconies in two directions, and the wall would help ensure privacy. To the east, beyond an olive orchard, was the sea. To the south, forty yards behind the house, was the barn, actually a hangar, just big enough for a chopper with its switchback blades secured.

Steinfeld, Hard Eyes, Claire, Danco, and an Englishman, Chiswell, were sitting around the old wooden table in the gray stone kitchen. Chiswell was a tall, basset-faced man with wispy brown hair and an air of melancholy intensity.

Hard Eyes shifted in his seat, wincing, feeling the bandages rasp on his wounds. He sat on pillows, because the Mossad medic had dug some fragments from his buttocks.

They were into their third cup of coffee after dinner. They were cleaned up, in clean clothes, and well fed, and in safe, warm surroundings—and they all felt like hell.

The light was fading, the room darkening visibly minute by minute. No one felt like getting up to turn on the light. Their faces were increasingly veiled by deepening shadow.

Steinfeld sat across from Hard Eyes, hunched over the table, an empty pewter coffee cup between his hands. He turned it back and forth in his palms like a potter with clay. "What we've got is this: about four hundred coming from France, Italy, Holland, Switzerland. Solely NR. And we're in touch with the alignments: the Communist party of France, the Italian Leninists, a cadre of anarchists . . . all of them have gone underground, so it's hard to say how many they number, and harder still to work steadily with them. But we're in touch. The Communists, especially, are doing some very good organizing." He sounded distant, almost mournful.

Claire sounded even more distant when she asked, her voice almost too faint to hear, "Isn't it...unwise to bring everyone here? We'll all be one target, then." Hard Eyes looked at her, wondering again if she'd been through too much. She was wearing a gray pilot's jumpsuit the Israelis had given her. As she spoke, she sat with her hands folded in her lap, looking out the window at the tangerine smear of sunset.

Steinfeld said, "Yes, it's a risk for us all to regroup in one place. But the Fascists have made it impractical for us to work the way we worked before, at least for now. They've got complete military control of France, Belgium, Holland, West Germany, Spain, Portugal, Austria, Italy, and Greece. They're consolidating control in six more countries, including England. Legally speaking, their control is supposed to be temporary, and it's supposed to be only in terms of law enforcement, but in most places they've succeeded in placing their native puppets in administrative positions. They've got a lot of grass-roots support from the white, native Europeans because wherever they appear, things *do* become orderly, and where there are still rails intact..."

"The trains run on time," Danco said, snorting.

Steinfeld nodded and went on. "And, of course, the white Christians see them isolating the Algerians and the other blacks and immigrants in assigned ghettos, arresting anyone black or Arab or Jewish who so much as sneezes. And the white Christians who are prejudiced respond favorably when they see that. And even the ones who were formerly liberal..." He shrugged. "Jack Smoke once said that war has a way of making conservatives. When there is privation, famine, constant danger, some low instinct seems to make people suspicious of strangers, or of anyone at all different. Open minds slam shut...." He paused to sigh. The darkness thickened in the room. "There are only a few courses open to us. We can run to the States and work there to try to awaken the public to what's going on over here. The SA's

American people are manipulating the news, censoring things without seeming to. Here, they don't permit journalists to accompany NATO troops in Europe. People in America don't know what's happening here. But Smoke and Witcher and their team are working on changing that already, and if we leave Europe, the continent's only nonfactionalized resistance core will be gone."

By insisting on keeping all political activity out of the NR—except, of course, for its primary mandate—Steinfeld had made the New Resistance a resource available to Communists, capitalists, anarchists, republicist conservatives, liberals; all flavors of those persuasions, as long as they were opposed to the Second Alliance. New NR recruits—sometimes joined on their own, sometimes assigned by other areas of the underground, such as the Communist Workers Party—were required to take a mortally serious vow that clearly stated they would put all political disagreements with other Resistance fighters aside, giving first priority to the struggle against the new Fascism. The NR supplied the sundry Communist and anarchist resistance cadres with money, weapons, and sometimes hiding places; in return, the Communists provided the NR with intelligence, safe houses for traveling NR actives, and sometimes military reinforcement. They coordinated their sabotage efforts, and together managed to keep the SA off-balance.

Occasionally there were polite ideological arguments in the NR ranks. Some of the republicists muttered about "collaborating with Communists," and the danger of giving Communists resources that would help them survive so they'd be around after it was all over.

But Steinfeld had said, "There will always be Communists. They are a fact of life. I'm against all dictatorships—even dictatorships of the proletariat. But we have to learn to live with Communists—and perhaps we can gently persuade them to keep their Communism nondictatorial, if they come into power."

At such times Levassier, who was a Trotskyite, would complain bitterly of Steinfeld's patronizing tone with respect to the People's Revolution, and he would insist that the dictatorial phase of Communism was only temporary in order to enforce revolutionary reforms, and he would go on to quote Marcuse's claim that the so-called free world was a dictatorship that, instead of gulags, used media and conformist conditioning—in modern terms, the Grid—to enforce its dominion.

NR political discussions were always mild and rhetorical, never became real infighting.

"If we escape to the USA, the other resistance groups will be severely weakened," Steinfeld said. "But SA surveillance on the continent is so tight, we're finding it tougher and tougher to get away with anything. And people are frightened." He made a gesture that almost seemed to convey despair. It was difficult to tell; his face was lost in shadow. "They're beginning to turn our people in."

"So what does that leave us?" Hard Eyes asked.

And the room grew darker yet.

Steinfeld took a deep, rheumy breath. "The Fascists have two European headquarters—Paris and Palermo. The Sicilian headquarters is also their center of communications, and one of their top air bases. According to our information, Colonel Watson and five other top Second Alliance officials will be in Palermo in early March to evaluate the European situation. They'll be in conference with Crandall by satellite. If they decide the situation is amenable, they'll move into the second phase of their campaign to take control of Europe. They'll announce something called the Self-Policing Organization of European States. SPOES will claim it's the core of a new economic and political unity that will protect it from the ravages of Soviet and American interference, and from the war itself. It will be—"

"A new Axis," Danco burst in. "Mussolini, Franco, Hitler, and Tojo, in the last century. Now we will have Le Pen, Sinsera, and the other SA puppets."

Steinfeld said simply, "Yes." After a moment he added, "In effect, they will be announcing the birth of a new Fascist state."

No one spoke for a full minute. Then Hard Eyes said, "You want to raid their Palermo HQ? That it?"

Steinfeld grunted in assent. His chair creaked mournfully as he shifted his weight, leaned back.

Hard Eyes looked out the window. The last shreds of saffron light were melting away. A single ray of orange-red flicked on as a cloud shifted at the horizon. And suddenly switched off, as the sun sank farther, as if someone had thrown a switch to turn off a searchlight beam.

Steinfeld said, "I have in mind a large, concerted raid, timed to hit the island when they're having their conference. Ideally we will kill Watson and the others, destroy their sat dishes, their transmitters, whatever aircraft are on the ground. It won't stop them, but it will slow them—and perhaps delay the announcement of SPOES. The longer they wait to put SPOES into effect, the more chance we will have to expose it for what it is."

Chiswell said, "Rather awfully breezy, the way you say it, Steinfeld—but that island will be defended like nowhere else in their territory. I don't think we have the manpower or the air power to make it work. Unless the Maltese help us—"

Steinfeld said, "No, they're Socialist, so they oppose the SA. But not actively—not even very vocally. They give us shelter, but no help with materiel or troops or transportation. The Mossad will provide some planes, some choppers, some amphibious vehicles. But it must operate secretively too. There's a severe limit to how much they can help us. Witcher is doing what he can, but he's finding it tough to get anything through the Atlantic Blockade."

"Then we do what we can with what we've got," Hard Eyes said, thinking, as the room grew darker still, *And we'll probably die doing it*.

A young black woman came into the room. Lila, an NR captain from Martinique. She spoke to Steinfeld in rapid-fire French. He nodded, replied in the same language. She left. Steinfeld said, "It seems Levassier is going to live. He will lose an arm, however." Cold silence in the room till he went on. "And one other piece of news: Michael Karakos has escaped from the detention camps. He's on his way to us. He's a good man. He'll be a great help."

And the darkness in the room was almost complete.

_____ FOUR

There was a can of people, floating in space. It was the Space Colony, FirStep, but to Russell Parker, just then, it was only a very big tin can.

Russ Parker—he thought of himself as Russ—was Chief of Colony Security. He sat at his desk in Central Admin, hating his job, hating his current home (if you could call it a home), hating his boss, and hating himself. And asking God's forgiveness for all that hatred.

It had just hit him as he sat there looking over his schedule of interviews for the day. _He hated_. It had boiled up in him from somewhere hidden—and it had come as a complete surprise.

Russ was six-foot-two, weighed in at two twenty-five. He wore an Admin sky-blue Security jumpsuit—the color of the original security force's uniforms, before the SA—and an old-fashioned wristwatch with a watch face and hands. He was middle-aged but boyish-looking, blue-eyed, tanned, seam-faced, and he usually managed a friendly expression. He sat in a compact office, twenty feet by thirty, with the claustrophobic seven and a half feet between floor and ceiling, typical of the Space Colony's offices; the walls were postered with old Arizona Highways photos of the American Southwest's deserts and mesas and sunsets. His desk was real walnut—he'd built it himself, having imported the wood over a six-month period a piece at a time—and centered on it was a white plastic computer console.

He wished to God you could smoke on the Colony. Even after all these years . . .

Russ took a deep breath and closed his eyes for a moment,

leaned back in his squeaking swivel chair—he refused to let them oil it, he liked it to squeak—and put his booted feet on the desktop.

He'd just come from his session with Dr. Tate, the Admin chief psychiatrist. Had gone to him about his ulcers, which his physician felt were stress-related. Tate had had partial rejuv, had his face and back rebuilt, so he looked thirty years younger than his sixty-five—and Russ himself was fifty— but Tate seemed paternal somehow, anyway. Patient but not patronizing. Had expertly gotten Russ to talk about himself. Airing the misgivings he'd been having about the job, and how the job conflicted with his religion. And Tate had asked some leading questions that made Russ examine his feelings. Specifically, made him examine his hatred.

Looking at it, he realized that only part of the hatred was real. The part about hating *himself*. The rest of his feelings about the job, the place, were colored and exaggerated by his self-hatred. And his self-hatred, as Tate had hinted, was rooted in the shame of religious hypocrisy.

That thought came to him while he was looking at the list of names on the computer screen.

Beside the name of each Security Risk he was to interview was a short summary of the interviewee. Ninety percent of them were either black, Jewish, or married to a black or Jewish person. The other ten percent were Marxists or known to be associated in some way with the people who'd fomented the Technicki Rebellion. Those he could understand. The rest just didn't make sense. There was no particular correlation between the technicki rebels and race. Only thirty percent of them had been members of a racial minority group. And those weren't the ringleaders. The issues giving rise to the Technicki Rebellion just weren't race-related.

The Colony's new chief administrator was a man named Praeger. The list had been made up by Praeger's special committee on post-rebellion security measures. And everyone on the committee was, like Praeger, an SA Initiate.

Russ took a deep breath, turned in his swivel chair, and tapped the button that would buzz Administration. He glanced at his watch. It was three P.M., Colony Time. Praeger should be back from lunch by now.

Praeger's TV image appeared on the upper left-hand

screen of the four monitors, two stacked over two, that stood to the left of Russ's work console. Praeger said, "Hello, Russ, what can I do for you?" Praeger, wearing his rimless Coke-bottle glasses, running a hand over his eraser-pink bald head, making an inquisitive cone of his prissy red lips.

Russ controlled his surge of revulsion and said, "Well, now, Bill, I was just looking over the list of Risks, and I just can't see why most of them are on there. I feel it's inappropriate to use race as a—"

"Everyone on the list is there for a good reason," Praeger said briskly. As if he were impatient with stating the obvious. "The reason doesn't necessarily show up on the stats attached to the list. Sometimes the reason isn't provided. Our agents just give us the names, and there are too many names for them to get specific about each one. We want you to interview them and see what you can find out."

Russ struggled to maintain his mask of serenity. Like nothing rattled him. Objecting mildly, "That doesn't make sense, either. They know I'm Security Chief. I reckon they're not likely to open up to me. No, sir. And, hell—I don't know what I'm supposed to be lookin' for—"

"Don't you?" A hint of real annoyance in Praeger's flat voice now. "Saboteurs, for a start. Who sabotaged the food storage refrigeration? Who's been interfering with Inter-Colony TV transmissions? Who's been freezing up Admin's elevators?"

"Probably just servicing breakdowns, Bill. We haven't got the parts—"

"Some of those systems were newly installed."

"There was no direct evidence that it was sabotage, Bill."

"Electronics informs me that they think it was done with a power surge, which was deliberately introduced into the systems."

"I've got that report. I see it as a lot of wild digging for excuses to cover up the fact that they can't find the real problem."

"They might as well say that the statement you just made is *your* way of covering up *your* inability to find the saboteurs."

There was a tense silence. Then Praeger chuckled, to let

Russ know that what he'd just said wasn't serious. But they both knew it hadn't been entirely a joke, either.

Behind that chuckle was the slightly veiled implication that Russ's job might be on the line.

Sure, Russ had come to despise the job. But he was trapped on the Colony till the blockade was lifted. If he resigned, he'd be an object of suspicion. He'd be on the list that was on his computer. He just might be arrested. On general principle.

"Maybe you don't know, Russ—there've been reports of unusual activity at Life Support Central," Praeger said.

"I've got that one. Wild changes in power output levels. You think it's connected to the power surges in the other parts of the Colony?"

"I don't know. But I want you to see what you can find out about a kind of technicki cult around Professor Rimpler."

"A what? A *cult*?"

Rimpler? Rimpler was dead. Bludgeoned by Samson Molt during the uprising. Rimpler, who'd founded the Colony, had turned against its Admin Committee, had become a rebel sympathizer.

Praeger shrugged. "For people who work every day with state-of-the-art hardware, the technickis are remarkably superstitious. Evidently some of them believe Rimpler's spirit is haunting the Colony. It could be that this cult around his 'spirit' has found out about his, ah, cerebral/cybernetic interface . . . which is now in place in Life Support Central."

"Run that 'un by me again there, boss, will ya?" Drawling it, making light of it. But Russ was stunned.

"When we found his body, it wasn't quite brain-dead. He was interested in cerebral/cyber interfacing, he had all the equipment here to experiment in it . . . and the life-support computer system was on its last legs. We didn't have time to get in a new life-support computer—we can't get in the equipment fast enough with the blockade. The air was getting bad. It's that simple. We risked a total breakdown in life-support systems without some kind of guidance computer. A brain interface was the quickest way—the only way we had. The principle of cerebral interfacing is—"

"I understand the principle." He understood it in a general

way. Human brains store much more information than a computer in a *much* smaller space, and they respond to some things more quickly; brains could be grown, or surgically removed, from people who've signed their bodies over. Once perfected, using an interfaced human brain as an extension of a computer costs less than an elaborate computer storage system. "But, Bill . . ." He shook his head again, laughed hollowly. "It's all experimental! And, anyway, it'll never be practical for the Colony's *life support*! We discussed this, and the committee voted against it! Brain tissue is too fragile; it deteriorates, ages, has a number of unpredictable qualities . . . and—for God's sake!—you used *Rimpler's* brain?"

"As for its deteriorating—the wetware link is only a temporary expedient till we get a hardware system. We're keeping the tissues alive with a nutritive fluid. It's fascinating, really, don't you think? Admittedly, it's an experiment that, ah, interests me . . ."

Russ suspected that Praeger took some kind of perverse pleasure in using his old adversary's brain tissue as a convenient spare part. It was like a medieval ruler making the skin of his enemy into a seat covering for his chair, or drinking ale from his skull. It was a celebration of his complete triumph over him.

Praeger, Russ thought, you're a sick man.

Praeger went on. "And as for its being *Rimpler's* brain—this isn't a Gothic by Mary Shelley, Parker. Do you suppose we sent Igor out for a good brain and he dropped it, came back with Rimpler's? There's no shred of Rimpler's personality left in it. We have a primitive extractor here . . . not adequate for interrogation, but it *will* erase. Rimpler's memories were erased. A great deal of the brain was cut away; we're only using the tissue that's interfaceable. Dr. Tate used electrochemical amino-acid breakdowns to translate the computer's impulses into neurohumoral transmission units which—"

"*Dr. Tate* did this?" Russ broke in, startled.

"Yes." Praeger's expression was as glassy and flat as the TV screen. "Why?"

"Uh—nothing." So Praeger was working closely with

Tate. How much had Tate told him about Russ's problems? Did he stick to professional confidentiality? Was Tate SA?

"It could be some of our Security Risks know about Rimpler's brain," Praeger said. "There could be a connection."

"Seems pretty farfetched to me. To be honest, I don't think excessive security is *good* security. It makes people angry at authority, makes them hard to deal with—we could end up *making* rebels. I just don't see the necessity at this—"

"You don't see the necessity." Praeger's voice was terribly calm. He reached for something offscreen, punched some buttons. An image appeared on the lower right-hand TV monitor.

It was a telescopic TV image of a spacecraft; something like a standard space shuttle but knobbier, with heavily bolted plates, and generally cruder: a Soviet vessel. Their spacecraft always looked directly descended from the *Monitor* and the *Merrimac*.

"You see that?" Praeger asked.

"I see it."

"They're out there. The Soviets. Less than a hundred kilometers from our outer hull. Directly in the way of the approaches to our hangars. They're armed. They have—you see the dishes?—a great variety of communications gear. They could be communicating with someone on the Colony, for all we know. They could even have had accomplices at the air locks."

Russ listened with amazement to the rising tone of hysteria in Praeger's voice. Praeger looked cool, but . . . he'd begun talking rapidly, and his pitch had risen half an octave.

"I see," Russ said slowly. Soothingly. (Thinking, *This man is making life-and-death decisions about people . . . about me . . . he's capable of having me killed. . . .*) "Well, uh, I surely see your point and, ah, that puts a different light on things." Adding humbly, "I'll get right on it, Bill."

"You do that, Russ."

Praeger cut the connection.

Russ stared at the blank screen, thinking that he just hadn't had the courage to bring up his real objection to the brain interfacing. It seemed immoral. Blasphemous some-how.

But Praeger would've laughed at that. Praeger was an atheist.

And now he was expected to take part in systematic racial discrimination. And he just couldn't see any way out of it.

Russ turned slowly to his console, to the list of names. Thinking, *God forgive me.*

The first five people on the list were all waiting in the outer office.

He noted the first name on the list and called his secretary on the intercom. "Sandy, send in Kitty Torrence, please."

The Island of Malta.

She saw men who were also wild dogs. Wolves, jackals, wild dogs. They went on their hands and feet, running in a crouch; unnaturally long arms, unnaturally short legs. Each lean muscle clearly etched in the moonlight; skin mottled pink and mange-gray. Hairless but for a strip of fur down the back. Wagging, semitumesced sexual organs. Their hands and feet black with grime, their faces—

Their faces were the worst part. She saw lust for murder and rape in those faces. But—and this was the horror that kept her from looking twice—they were human expressions. Expressions that, till now, she'd glimpsed in men's faces for only a microsecond before the veil of civilizing conditioning was drawn again.

There were two packs. One had made a sort of camp around the mouth of a burrow, a small cave in a bank of dirt, under the dark cypresses dripping with Spanish moss. Smaller dogwomen licked and suckled dogman-infants. Others stalked the edges of the feces-littered camp, snuffling the hot swamp breeze, tick-studded ears listening, sorting through the croc grunts and cricket calls. Listening for . . .

A splashing. Pricked-up ears caught a rustle, a panting. A prescient silence.

And then the second pack lunged from the shadows, attacking the camp.

She saw two of them rending one of the dogwomen; the

dogwoman bitch tried to run but was caught with one set of jaws on her rump, the other on her neck, pulling her two different ways, pulling her apart so blood spurted, hotter than the steamy night air. While three more leapt on her husband, rending with tooth and filthy talons.

She saw one of them raping a mother whose breasts swung heavy with milk under her as she tried to claw away from him, as he sodomized her while biting into the back of her neck . . . biting deep. She saw them maim their victims so they could no longer move and then thrust their human faces into the wounds of the still living—

Claire sat bolt upright in bed, choking, trying not to vomit, but a sound between a gurgle and a scrape was all that escaped her throat.

The room yawed, and a dark, tooth-bared man-face thrust itself into her line of sight.

She screamed and clawed away from it. It was barking at her.

"Claire! Hey, Claire!"

The last membrane of the dream dissolved.

It was Hard Eyes. Danny. It was Danny. She looked around, found she had backpedaled off the bed, had fallen, was sitting on the cold floor, her back against the cool wallpaper. Sweating. Her tailbone bruised.

"I'm sorry," she said. Her voice sounded funny in her own ears. "I—shit, what a nightmare."

"Sounded like. You okay?" As he bent over her, nude, he helped her to stand. His touch on her arm making her skin crawl (a flash of the filthy talons ripping pink into red).

She pulled away from him. Wearing only panties, she went out the bedroom door and down the dark hallway. It was three in the morning. The house creaked with her footsteps. It felt fragile and porous around her, after the Colony; you could feel all its boards straining in the night wind to burst free of their nails. (Nails! God, the house had been *nailed* together! One step from mud huts . . .)

She found the bathroom and gratefully turned on the light, looked around at the old ceramic surfaces of the sink, the bathtub—she looked quickly away from the tub. It had brass legs shaped like an animal's, complete with claws. . . .

She washed her face and went back to the bedroom.

· She stood for a moment in the door of the bedroom, looking at Hard Eyes in the indirect light from the floor lamp. She felt all right now, about getting back into bed with him. He looked normal, relaxed, friendly. He was lying on his back, hands behind his head, nude under a sheet; she could see the outline of his penis angling to one side like a clock's hand at three o'clock.

She felt a sexual stirring, which played tag with the half-suppressed sense of loathing left over from the dream. . . .

Hard Eyes felt the old brass bed tilt and creak as Claire lay down. She stretched out close beside him, under the sheet and woolen blanket, but not quite touching. He could feel her body heat; that warmth was itself an intimacy.

Hard Eyes had stayed up talking to Danco, Carmen, and Willow. Had heard Bonham complaining to Steinfeld, and Steinfeld calmly planning to sacrifice all of them—including himself—in what amounted to a suicide raid.

When he'd come to bed, Claire was already asleep. He was unable to sleep: too horny, lonely, worried.

He was grateful the bad dream had awakened her, then disgusted with himself for being glad she'd had a nightmare.

"Want to tell me about the nightmare?" he asked.

"No."

"You sure? Maybe it'd help."

"*No*. Men are arrogant. Think they can analyze everything, cure everything."

He felt the stab of resentment. He'd been trying to help her.

"Did Steinfeld decide for sure?" she asked.

"About the raid? Yes."

"What, um, are they going to do with Bonham?"

He glanced at her, wondering how she felt about Bonham. She'd promised herself to Bonham, and in return he had agreed to get her safely down to Earth. He'd done his part; she'd reneged on hers. She said she loathed him—but maybe she felt she owed him.

He said, "I don't know. Bonham seems to think we have some kind of obligation to him. He wants money, a passport, transportation to the States. He claims he can give us some useful information about the Colony—he did say one thing that grabbed Steinfeld's interest. That Crandall's planning to use the Colony as his headquarters once the Soviet space blockade is lifted. But I don't think Steinfeld trusts Bonham enough to let him go."

"When he's frustrated, he's dangerous."

"We'll watch him." He couldn't restrain himself any longer. He turned on one elbow, looked at her for a moment, bent and kissed her. She responded, but weakly.

Then she turned her head away.

He saw her face contort as she fought tears. (And as he fought frustration.) "What's wrong, Claire?" With as little pressure as possible in the question.

She bubbled it out all at once, her voice pitching on the edge of a whine. "I'm all—shit. It's weird, I was wondering when this'd . . . see, I was killing people. I never thought I could really kill anyone. It seems so—this is a smug term but—so *unevolved.* And then I got caught up with you guys . . . and I killed those men. And I didn't feel anything about it! It was so amazing. I didn't feel disgust or remorse or . . . or anything. But I guess I *did,* because it's all coming out now. Here, where the pressure's less. It comes out in the nightmares and—God, when I saw you kill people with that shotgun . . . I mean, you're all *my friends,* and my friends are tearing bodies apart with these tools *made* for tearing bodies apart, and . . . how could I just *accept* it?"

"Like you said, you *didn't* accept it. But you coped with it. You think there was anything else we could've done?"

"Yes. We could have let them kill us. Maybe that would be better than having to tear people apart."

He didn't say anything for a few minutes. Finally she looked at him and asked, "You mad at me?"

He shook his head. "No. But, Claire—they're *planning another Holocaust.* All the signs point to that. If we don't stop them, more people will be murdered."

"We have to murder a few to keep them from murdering a lot?"

"That's it."

After a moment she said, in a small voice, "I guess. I guess it makes sense. But . . ."

"I know how you feel. It's like nothing makes sense when you see it happening. I felt the same way more than once."

"But, Danny . . . you *like* killing people."

A knot pulled itself tight in his stomach. "No. Or . . . the truth is, I do and I don't." He was desperate then, to change the subject. He turned over, sat on the edge of the bed. "I like this old house. I wonder who it belongs to, really. You know, the others are all crammed together in six rooms. Steinfeld was almost sentimental, giving us this room to ourselves. Something about morale—theirs as much as ours. Hey!"

He'd noticed light glinting off something half hidden behind a rack of thirty-year-old yellowed English paperbacks on a wall shelf. The glint of a bottle. He got up, crossed to it, pulled it out. Accidentally tipping a collection of Clive Barker stories onto the floor.

"Scotch!" A stubby, triangular bottle, half full of amber liquid. Pinch, it was called.

He brought it back to the bed, unscrewed the cap, and sloshed some into the empty water glass on the bedside table. Drank off half. "Damn!"

"Well, don't *hog* it."

Twenty minutes later they both felt considerably more relaxed. In fact, he felt a little too relaxed.

She was in his arms, undulating against him in that way she had. . . .

They kissed for a long time and then . . .

"No, wait," she said.

Oh, no, he thought. His hard-on was so rigid, it hurt.

"I want to, but . . . we can't actually fuck, okay? It's too much like something in my dream. It's too much like stabbing tonight. But maybe we could . . ."

He relaxed as she ran her fingers—still Colony soft—over the pulsing silk of his rigid cock, as she cupped the head in the palm of her hand and drew sensations from him, began to squeeze and pump on it.

He was lying sideways, his head tilted over hers so he could kiss her, feel her darting tongue, trace her lips with his own tongue, her right breast nuzzling his chest as he gently parted her labia with the index and middle finger of his right hand, dipped into the wet core of her, gathering a little lubricant onto the tip of his finger, running it up onto her clitoris. She groaned and pressed against him, jacking his cock faster as he stroked her clitoris. She reached across with her left hand to move his fingertip up a little higher, to a place that was not too sensitive. He could feel the tumesced stalk of her clitoris through the satiny clitoral hood. He stroked his musk-lubricated fingertip up and down the short length of it, a little to one side, slowly at first and then faster, to match the rhythm of her hand on his cock, until both of them abandoned themselves completely to sensation, sensation focused *almost* as much in the intimacy of their locked mouths as in their genitals . . . till some minutes later she gasped, bucked her hips, and he let go the orgasm he'd been holding back . . . holding it back with an exquisite desperation . . . and he came, thick and sticky, across her heaving belly.

Later still, he sat up to pour them both a drink.

They heard a truck approaching, saw lights glowing upward from the drive outside.

He got up, looked out the window onto the front of the house.

Two men he remembered from the Mossad were getting out of a van. Now there was a third man walking ahead of them into the house. Not their prisoner. *One of our people,* he thought, straining to see who it was.

The man seemed to feel Hard Eyes watching. Just before stepping onto the porch, he looked up at the window. Hard Eyes saw his face clearly then.

"Who is it?" Claire asked.

"It's Michael Karakos," Hard Eyes said.

_____**Five**

Watson was summoned to the Comm Center, in the Lyons SA installation, at three in the morning.

His bedside console had chimed, its screen lit up with three sets of identical numbers: 33–33–33. The code for the SA's final authority. Watson dressed hastily, woke his personal bodyguard, Klaus, who always slept in his clothes, and together the two of them trudged across the frozen mud of the compound, past the guards at the checkpoints, who stepped reluctantly from their electric-heated stations to approve passage. Into the cube-shaped building with its rooftop orchard of antennas and sat-dishes.

Watson was mildly surprised to see that the big, console-crowded viewing room was dark—except for a single green-glowing screen at the far side.

He stood in the doorway for a moment, staring at the screen, pinching the bridge of his nose. He was getting one of those blasted sinus aches from the cold.

Klaus stood behind him, a foot taller than he was, and sixty pounds heavier. Tonight Klaus made him nervous. Not because he was big. Not even because he was wearing that damned opaque helmet. But because Watson had recently realized that Klaus was not at all stupid. And therefore his loyalty could be an act.

Across the room, that green light glowed, like some kind of graveyard phosphorescence. A gravestone of green light pulsing alone in the darkness. For him, for Colonel Watson, for no one else.

Get a grip on yourself, man. "Klaus, turn on the blasted heat, eh?" Watson said, fumbling for the light panel. His fingers brushed the panel, and the lights came on, in sequence across the room—flick, flick, flick, flick. He crossed to the screen, footsteps echoing in the room's chill metallic spaces, eyes blinking in the harsh blue light, as Klaus lumbered away to find the thermostat.

Watson activated the console, and the holotank above and behind the screen lit up. He'd grumbled about the expense of having a holotank installed here. TV would have done as well, he'd thought. But now he saw why Crandall had insisted on it.

His gut twisted as Crandall appeared in front of him, life-size in the holotank, his three-dee image glimmering as if from some numinous inner fire.

Crandall was sitting in a plain wooden armchair, his head tilted forward a little, his eyes shadowy, that same shadow playing around the faint smile. His craggy face looked gaunter than ever. His short hair, combed back from the angular forehead, had thinned. And there was something curiously inert about the set of his legs.

It occurred to Watson that he hadn't seen Crandall standing for a while, not since the night of the ritual in the Cloudy Peak chapel. The night Johnny Stisky killed himself and Crandall's sister, Ellen Mae.

Crandall had been secretive about the extent of his wounding after the assassination attempt...after the NR had tried to kill him...

Maybe he was crippled and didn't want them to know because it would reduce his power over them. He was supposed to be a man protected by God himself. He was almost the Messiah—he allowed some to suggest that he *was* the Messiah. Would God allow his Christ to be a cripple? (What was that old American expression, "Christ on a crutch"?)

"Well, Colonel," the figure in the holotank said in his soft accent, "I've heard some mighty disturbin' reports. I knew that you would be unable to sleep well till you cleared up the matter with me. How about you do a little quick explainin'."

Watson shook his head. "Rick, I—"

"Now, I see that I'm-sorry-Rick-I-don't-know-what-you're-talking-about look on your face, so I'll pretend you're not joshin' me, and I'll tell you here'n now: You've been telling our enemies all about our most classified project."

Watson did indeed know just what Crandall was talking about. And knowing made him feel like he was coming down with the flu. Weak, feverish, and green around the brisket.

"I deny telling an enemy about anything classified," he said, gazing serenely up at Crandall, hoping his face was as proud and unafraid as he was trying to make it look. The holocameras in a semicircle just above the holotank showed his image to Crandall, transmitted by satellite across the ocean. To Cloudy Peak Farm, where Crandall had remained, with tripled security, since the Stisky affair. Watson had heard Crandall was living behind bulletproof glass now, with only his doctor having physical access to him. And Crandall wasn't even sure he trusted his doctor.

Crandall asked, with soft incredulity, "You deny it? Do you think you're in some headmaster's office, Colonel? Are you a boy denying having stolen the sweet biscuits?"

"I deny that Karakos is an enemy, Rick. At the time he was, technically, but—"

"I'm familiar with your plans for him." The Southern drawl had left his voice, bit by bit, replaced by the bitter cold of crystallized steel. "Suppose something had gone wrong. Suppose he'd escaped. Suppose he'd won his way to the NR. They have media contacts in the States. How long before the headlines read, SECOND ALLIANCE PLANS WORLD GENOCIDE. What is it you're about to say, Colonel? That no one would believe we'd attempt something so impractical? Ah, but everyone is familiar with the 'wonders of modern science,' Colonel Watson. Don't you think American journalists are capable of putting two and two together?"

The inside of Watson's mouth had turned to cardboard. "Ah, well, Rick—"

"You have lost the privilege of using my first name, Colonel."

Watson felt a deep, deep chill run through him.

"The truth is," Crandall went on, "you're a windbag. You've always been a windbag. You're also a talented man, but that's not enough. We need reliability. And you simply like to talk. To boast, to pontificate. It's in your character. It's a weakness, Colonel."

Crandall was talking quickly. Was himself strangely loquacious today. With that and the gauntness, Watson began to believe the rumors he'd heard were true: Crandall was taking some kind of amphetamines.

Crandall leaned back in his chair, and the chair creaked. Equipment at Cloudy Peak Farm picked up its creaking, transmitted the creak of the wood to a satellite somewhere over the Atlantic, which sent the creak down to the receiver on the roof of the Comm Center. The sound of wood creaking. "We're taking under consideration the possibility that you might be better off if part of your, well, now, your background on all this were extracted—"

"No!" Watson burst out. If they extracted his knowledge of Project Total Eclipse, his whole relationship with the SA would be surgically altered. He might be used as a soldier, a strategist, but he'd no longer be an insider. His power would be irreparably undercut.

"You might not like the alternatives, Colonel," Crandall said softly.

Watson swallowed; his tongue sandpapered the roof of his mouth. "See here, Ri—Reverend Crandall—I admit I've been a trifle, ah, insubordinate. Truth is, I find it hard to continue working with the albino. He's obviously a genetic inferior. His hubris is insufferable. I suppose what happened was a product of my distaste for him. I realize that's no excuse. I can assure you that from here on in, I'll keep a tight rein, ah, on my tendency to, ah—"

"Very well. But you are aware, I'm sure, that your restraint will be closely monitored."

"I . . . I would have it no other way, Reverend Crandall."

"All righty, let's get on up the hill a ways. What've you got to tell me, Colonel?" Crandall's false Southern affability had returned. He leaned his chin on his fist and yawned.

"Very good, sir," Watson said. "We're triangulating in on the People's United Front—"

"I don't want to hear about every diddly-squat little Commie outfit. The New Resistance is our priority, Colonel."

"The NR. Yes. We, ah, believe Steinfeld and his planning council to be somewhere in the Mediterranean, possibly on the coast of North Africa. We have, of course, our man in the field, who has every likelihood of linking up with them, and we expect a message from him shortly. In the meantime—"

"You had them, Colonel. Your people had them trapped. And now you don't even know where they are."

"Reverend Crandall..." Watson paused to corral his anger. He took a deep breath. "Reverend Crandall, I was not in charge of that operation; they didn't have time to consult me. I was here, shoring up security around the project installation. I—"

"You want to pass the buck? Fine. But from here on in, Colonel, I want you to leave *basic* security to Sackville-West. You are to go to our installation in Sicily, immediately, and you are to work from there to find Steinfeld and his people. I want them found, and I want them completely *gone* from our hair. They're small, but they're more dangerous than they look. Steinfeld has a knack for uniting factions. I know the knack when I see it: I have it myself. Take him seriously, Colonel."

"Reverend—"

But Crandall had cut the transmission. His smiling face rippled as the image faded, the ripple distorting the smile, warping it—or perhaps revealing it for what it was.

And then the holotank was dark.

Watson turned away, stifling a curse. Crandall could still be listening.

A giant's silhouette hulked in the doorway, across the room. Klaus.

Watson frowned in irritation. The man had a way of startling you.

Watson shrugged. He crossed the room, muttering, "Let's go."

A minute later, as their feet crunched the pockets of ice in the compound's frozen earth, Klaus said, "Colonel...?"

Watson glanced at him. "Yes?"

Klaus stopped in the middle of the compound and looked up at the stars. The stars were reflected, cold and brightly impassive, in the arc of Klaus's visor.

"Well, what is it, Klaus? It's cold out here."

Klaus looked toward him again. At least, his helmet was

tilted down. "I could not help but overhear your exchange with the Reverend Crandall. He's right about security matters, of course—"

"Just who do you think you—"

"But on the whole I question his competence to continue as our leader."

Watson stared at him, astounded that Klaus would speak treason so bluntly.

Klaus reached up and twisted a series of studs at his neck. The helmet's visor slid upward. Watson could see his craggy Eastern European face, with its hawkish black eyes and short-clipped black beard, the broad, red-lipped mouth. And he saw conspiracy in that face.

"He's going to be looking for mistakes, Colonel. And everyone makes mistakes sometime. You make fewer than most, of course. But eventually . . . and when you slip up, he's going to overreact, as they say in America. Perhaps the time has come to look for a way to . . . well, to remove him from real power. He is a necessary figurehead. But there is no reason he should have to be a *living* one. . . ."

Watson glanced around. There was a guard at the fence, but he was well out of earshot. "You're suggesting we . . . but the man's so heavily guarded." *This is insane. Am I actually considering this proposal?*

"Opportunity, Colonel. The opportunity will come. My brother, Rolf, is one of his private guards. The time is not yet here. But it will come."

"And what do you expect to gain?" Watson's teeth were chattering from the cold now, but he stood fascinated, staring up into Klaus's monumental confidence.

"A promotion. Sackville-West's job. At twice his salary."

Watson said, "This is a loyalty test of some kind. You're working for Crandall."

"You control a staff who can operate an extractor. I will submit myself to it, if you wish. Look into my mind. See the truth."

After a moment Watson nodded. "Very well. But we will not move against him until I decide the time is right."

"Of course, sir." Klaus reached up and snapped his visor shut.

They started back to the officer's quarters. Watson thinking, *Have I made the wrong decision? Have I let my anger with Crandall push me into making a fatal mistake?*

Overhead, the constellations turned, swinging slowly, slowly, through the night . . . and one star crossed the path of another.

Washington, D.C.

Janet had gained weight in the three and a half years since Cindy's birth; there were lines at the corners of her eyes, and she was less energetic than she'd been when she and Stoner had married, eight years before. Stoner was still in love with her.

It was Saturday afternoon. The rain had stopped. Everything was soaked in a pearly gray light. Stoner and his wife were on the back terrace of their Georgetown condo, sitting under the rain-scarred plastic bubble. Janet was sitting in the wicker rocking chair, looking pensively out through the plastic pane. She was peering through the slot between two other condos, onto the next street. A boy wearing a transparent antiacid rain slicker bicycled by, his tires slicing puddles.

Through the open sliding glass doors Stoner could see Cindy—her skin not the dark black of her Mama's but cocoa—sitting rapt in front of the TV watching some cartoon show in which blond, blue-eyed Danny Angel and his sidekick, Bucky Blast, foiled another plot of the evil Soviet scientist, Dr. Darkinsky. Reflected cartoon colors crawled over Cindy's face.

"You go over everything?" Janet asked dryly. "You check the Bible in my desk drawer? Might be a bug in there." She was sitting with her feet tucked under her for warmth. It was a little chilly on the porch. She was wearing a white sweater and cream pants. She ticked orange-painted, manicured nails against the wicker chair's armrest.

She was looking at the black satchel sitting beside Stoner's easy chair. It contained detection equipment. Stoner had been at it all morning and into the afternoon. He was fairly sure they weren't being bugged, at least out here. But he knew it couldn't last.

"We're clean so far," he said.

"If you want to talk to me without worrying about surveillance, why don't we go out somewhere?"

"I wanted to know about the house. I just wanted to know."

She said, "You're taking this pretty seriously."

She gave him a look that made him say, "You're afraid I'm going paranoid."

She shrugged. She smiled. "I go with you, honey. Anywhere, even paranoid."

He glanced at Cindy. Danny Angel had gone off; some noon news show had come on. She'd lost interest, was spelling things out on her I Teach Myself computer, sitting cross-legged and holding the little robin's-egg-blue console in her lap. Smart kid.

Stoner took a deep breath and told Janet about the Hiring Assessment Program weeding the non-Caucasians and moderates out of the CIA's power structure; told her about Howie; told her about the Kupperbind file. Told her, last, as unsensationally as possible, about Winston Post.

She was a strong woman. Just a little catch in her voice when she said, "You really think they"—she glanced at Cindy, lowered her voice—"you think they murdered him?"

He nodded.

"And you think they're watching you?"

He nodded again. "It's only a matter of time before they start home surveillance. And they're already reassigning my workload. I was keeping tabs on NR data. The Resistance people in Europe, they've taken me off that."

"How, uh—how far do you think they'll go?"

"I don't know . . . but right now I think Unger figures to use you against me for leverage, keep me in line behind him, so I support him in everything."

"What do you mean, *use me against you*?" She was outraged now. Violated.

"Their rationale is, blacks and other 'coloreds' are prone to sympathy with radical groups, because the radical groups are antiracist. So blacks are Security Risks. So is anyone closely associated with blacks." He shrugged. "They haven't used the Assessment Program to reassign me, because I've got a lot of seniority. Which means clout. I think they'd be more likely to arrange another 'accident'."

She stared at him. "Jesus."

"You think I'm paranoid?"

She shook her head slowly. "You never talked much shop with me, all these years. You were real tight-lipped. It was part of your job to be, I guess. If you're telling me things now, you got to be scared for real, for serious reasons."

He nodded, smiling ruefully. She was too smart to simply assume that he was right. She'd had to reason it out. "I can't play along with them, Janet. I can't handle it. It's . . . I'd be a traitor to my country to play along with them. Because *they're* traitors. This bullshit is un-American."

"Now I got something to tell you that you maybe didn't know."

He waited. She'd genuinely startled him.

"About my brother. I told you he was working overseas for Mobil. That was a lie. There's another reason you never met him. Stu's in New York. He's in the Black Freedom Brotherhood. But so far as we know, he hasn't got warrants out on him. I don't condone the Brotherhood, they're terrorists. That's what I told him too. But . . . he's my brother."

"Okay. You think the Company knows about him?"

"We don't know. There's nobody looking for him as far as I'm aware. You people know about all of 'em?"

"Of course not. Especially not the deep-cover terrorists, like the majority of BFB tend to be." He shook his head. "Christ, what if they find out?"

"I know. Eventually . . . so, I was thinking . . . well, first: What're you going to do about all this?"

"Do? See how bad it looks. If it looks bad, I take you and Cindy and we run."

"Uh-huh. Where? That's worth living in?"

"What else you want me to do?"

She hesitated.

"Go on," he said.

"Okay, um—well, look, honey . . . if we got to run, it's better if we have something to run to. An umbrella. Some people have already got shelters set up. Now, I don't condone the Brotherhood—and I wouldn't want to join them. But they could help us, put us in touch with these other people . . ."

"What other people?"

"The New Resistance."

His eyes widened. "You want to join the NR?"

She shook her head. "But they could *help* us. Maybe they'd expect something in return. Information, something. Why not?"

"But they're guerrillas. Criminals."

She nodded. "And so is my brother. But if you think the Company is going to kill you . . . what else have we got?"

He tried to think of a reply. He couldn't. He heard the TV talking with newscaster semi-seriousness in the next room. Saying something about another acid-rain alert. Secretary of the Interior warning that acid rain falling in the Midwest could cause wheat and corn shortages, but "*famine* is too strong a word." At this time. The President was asking Congress to give her emergency powers of absolute authority—on a temporary basis—to keep order as the danger of a Soviet first strike increased; citing the Soviet destruction of two U.S. orbital antimissile battle stations; citing also increased domestic terrorism from "race extremists on the left"—meaning black and Jewish activists. *Insisting* that the grant of absolute authority was only temporary. . . .

They were making it sound as if the threat of all-out nuclear war was nearing the flashpoint. Hearing that, he should have been scared. But all he could think about was: *Criminals. We'll become criminals if we run to those people.*

But when Janet asked again, "What else can we do?" he still had nothing to say.

THE ISLAND OF MERINO, THE CARIBBEAN.

"The strange truth is," Smoke was saying as his crow, Richard Pryor, fluttered restlessly on his shoulder, "most people don't see the Grid. That is, they don't know it for what it is when they see it. They aren't able to step back from it. Let's step back from it now and look at it squarely. . . ." He turned and switched on the big videoscreen that stretched across the wall like a blackboard behind him. It hummed, flickered with light. . . .

It was hot in the briefing room, though it was seven in the evening. The windows were open. Mosquitoes whined and ticked at the screens. Glancing out the window, Charlie saw the searchlight on the guard tower swinging over the sandy ground outside the NR's Coordination Center.

He looked back at Smoke and shifted on the metal chair, wincing at the pain in his buttocks. Metal chairs just weren't made for skinny people. His fingers hovered over the keyboard of his lap console.

Charlie Chesterton was one of the people they didn't make metal chairs for. He was also tall, bony, a little round-shouldered, a touch weak-chinned. He was twenty-three, and he wore his hair in a young man's fashion: the triple mohawk; three fins, each a different color and each color significant, the middle one signifying he was a Technicki Radical Unionist; the one on his right was blue for his profession, videotech; the one on the left was green for the neighborhood he'd grown up in, the floating boro New Brooklyn. He was wearing a sleeveless videopic T-shirt, this one looping through a Jerome-X video.

There were six other NR trainees in the hot room, in the New Resistance CC, on the tiny island of Merino.

Behind Smoke, the videoscreen, its volume muted, flashed through its parade of media baubles, a weirdly inappropriate backdrop for him.

Smoke, in his sleeveless black jumpsuit, was gaunt, hawk-nosed, tired-eyed, dark; his movements were swift, almost abrupt. But sometimes he'd slide seamlessly into a deep calm that seemed so smooth, so untouchable, you felt you were looking into the face of a man who'd spent his life in a monastery.

He had a look on his face like that now as he paused, faintly smiling, looking sedately at them from the front of the briefing room. And then he came out of it with a sudden slash of his hand, making them rock back in their seats, his crow flapping irritably to a perch on the windowsill, as he said, "It's going to shape you, your family, your friends, unless you—unless we—shape the Grid first! Learning to shape it starts with redefining it. The Grid is a three-leveled system. The first level is Worldtalk-type packaging of products, people, ideas, styles of behavior, socially useful prejudices, and, of course, some 'news,' all mixed into a solution of entertainment or simple distraction. That level is then fed into the second level, which is all the transmissions: all forms of TV and holo transmission; standard radio and bone-implant receiver radio; vidcassettes in homes, in schools; tabloids that print out through the home computer; daily papers you buy at the printout kiosk on the street; electronic billboards, video billboards; modem and every other kind of long-range communications between computers. Visorclips, earmites, records, tapes: all filtered through the Grid in some way. Even Charlie's T-shirt there. . . ."

Charlie shifted uncomfortably in his seat. Smoke's crow tilted its head to peer at him suspiciously with its glittering eyes.

Charlie wanted badly for Smoke to like him. He'd read all of Smoke's essays, books of them written before Smoke had been caught up in the chaos surrounding the war in Europe. Smoke had been abducted by the SA, tortured, escaped through one of the war's multitude of wild variables; wandered lost in the deepest circles of hell. And had come back, resurrected from what his public had thought was his death and what had been, at least, the death of his sanity. Had emerged not unscathed but unbroken. Smoke was a legend in the underground.

Smoke went on, "The third level of the Grid are the receivers, the public. More specifically, the public's brains, and its prosthetic sensory organs. The electronically enhanced collective unconscious. The important thing to remember is that while the Grid is made up of three levels, it's *all one system*. And the third level dovetails back to feed into the first. . . ."

On the screen, a sex-com sniggered by, then a commercial for a new camera-linked computer that monitors the entry of strangers into your neighborhood—deliverymen, workmen of all kinds, would-be renters, shoppers. The system looks for type-anomalies, such as racial variations, economic class variations, clothing style variations; a scaling up of type-anomalies could mean the neighborhood's in danger. The neighborhood security team that uses a TADS, Type Anomalies Discrimination System, is one that protects its neighborhood. The slogan: *"TADS weeds out weirdos!* A Second Alliance International Security Corporation product" . . . then a newsblip showing clips from the successful retaking of

Vienna, and the President saying, "We're making great strides! With your support we'll win the war—without recourse to nuclear weapons!" . . . then a ten-minute Science Special suggesting "new studies by experts would seem to indicate that interracial marriages create offspring who seem to be unusually vulnerable to disease or birth defect." And then a five-minute religious program . . . and then a sitcom in which a white couple, Dan and Joanie Clifton, are annoyed by Mr. and Mrs. Wog, the Pakistani couple who've moved in next door, whose overwhelming curry cooking smells and practice of defecating in the hallway give rise to a number of sardonic remarks on the part of Mr. Clifton . . . and then a public-service commercial informing the public that Soviet spies are rife in the tech centers, best not to speak to anyone you haven't known for years . . .

Smoke went on. "The thing saturates the public—worldwide—with information in wave after wave, each wave hitting all the local receiving centers, the cities, more or less simultaneously. There's more of the Grid's information—superficial as each unit of information is—coming faster than ever before. Doesn't matter if it's a lie or not, it's all information.

"People receive the information simultaneously, and they soak it up passively. If the government claims there's a new strain of AIDS that you get only from talking to Communists, then eighty percent of the people hooked into the Grid will believe the Communist AIDS story implicitly, instantly. Everyone they run into has heard the same thing. They all got it at once. So it seems to confirm itself by its very instantaneous prevalence. Since little real substance exists in this hypothetical broadcast, there's nothing much to stimulate questioning. There's simply the basic bullshit story line, and 'testimony' from a few 'experts' the government keeps on tap for when it needs their tailor-made quotes to give the appearance of credibility. Maybe a flash of a chart to give us an impression that some serious study's been done. And bang! everyone believes it. And it becomes 'true' for the public, as a kind of Consensus Reality develops from the instantaneousness and ubiquity of the story. That sort of thing makes the Grid a powerful tool for shaping society.

"And none of this was lost on Crandall and the other

planners for the SA. The SA had the foresight to buy the world's biggest PR outfit, Worldtalk.

"They're still reasonably subtle in their use of the Grid, but they're getting bolder. They're blaming the depression on immigrants, non-Christians, the so-called 'Zionist conspiracy'; and they can blame the war on Communists, of course.

"The public's being programmed to be knee-jerk supportive of the government and, by extension, the SA, which, as a 'private-sector' security and peacekeeping force, is now operating under a government contract. All classes of the Caucasian public is being programmed to blame its ills on outsiders, immigrants, non-Caucasians. It's being set up to give its backing to a race war."

On the screen was a "public-service ad" warning that "visitors from other countries" have "inadvertently introduced" a series of new flu viruses recently, particularly one strain that may be fatal to children. Until the crisis is past, it might be best if your children played only with native-born Americans. U.S. Weather Service acid-rain alert, keep windows closed, don't go out without goggles tonight. Fallout shelter drills for all public schools announced tomorrow. Public service announcement: "Remember, harboring draft resisters or deserters is giving aid to the Soviets." The announcement concludes with a slogan from the U.S. Department of Public Information: "The only way to win the war is to win together! Warning: Illegal TV or radio transmissions *will* be traced! Perpetrators *will* be prosecuted! The Undergrid is the Underworld—don't let criminals whisper in your ears!" Premiere of a new nighttime drama, *Ghetto Cop*. Slogan: *"He does what he has to."*

Smoke continued. "And there's only one way to sensibly fight it. We break into the Grid, we reprogram it, where we can, we use Jim Kessler's antipropaganda software to force the Grid to reveal itself for what it is. We step up our input into the underGrid. We try to reach the concerned journalists—sure, there are some—in the overGrid. The Grid is really too vast for the SA or the government to control effectively. It's more porous than they know. We *can* get into it. Jim Kessler's going to be here"—he glanced at the wall clock—"in just a few minutes, to train you in doing just that."

A weary hour later, after Charlie's fingers had begun to ache from tapping notes into his console, training was over for the night. Charlie rose to follow the others out of the room.

Smoke was standing near the door, the crow perched on his right hand. He held it near his cheek and murmured to it.

Charlie was feeling logy, thinking of bed. He stretched, rubbed at his numb buttocks once, and started to walk out past Smoke.

"Hold it, young Chesterton," Smoke said, looking at the crow but smiling for Charlie's benefit.

Charlie stopped, waited, wondering if Smoke was going to reproach him for something.

"You'll continue antipropaganda training, Charlie," Smoke said, "but we won't be placing you in a network mole position."

Charlie stared at him. "I can do it. I was a little sleepy tonight, but I followed the whole—"

Smoke shook his head. The crow cawed raspily, almost like laughter. "No problem with your alertness. We need you elsewhere. You know about video-evidence tampering? The AntiViolence Law programming?"

"Just the first briefing. Not much."

"We've got a special project for you. You'll be part of a team that's going to be working with a U.S. senator."

Charlie stared. "What?"

"Oh, yes. If you volunteer."

Charlie shrugged. "You're Smoke. You're Jack Brendan Smoke. Without you, man, I'd still be asleep. You need it, you got it."

The Space Colony. Married Workers' Dormitories.

Chester was home, just stepping into their unit. Kitty Torrence heaved herself off the bunk and couldn't keep from groaning. She ached in a dozen places; when she stood, the dull aches became sharp ones, making her suck air through her teeth. The baby squirmed in her swollen belly.

"*Duhgedda*," Chester said.

"Chester, we said we weren't going to talk technicki because the baby should learn standard, right? We got to get in the habit before—"

"All right, okay. Don't get up, I said."

"Got to. Time to fix dinner."

"Kind of thing it is, I can do it just as well. Your belly like that, isn't room for two of us to walk around in here, anyway."

She laughed and lay down; the dozen aching places that had begun to scream quieted to whining.

She watched him fix dinner. On the Space Colony, while they were on rations, "dinner" meant he took two airline-food dinners from the storage unit and put them in the microwave. "Be good when we can afford some real food around here," Chester muttered. He was a small, wiry man; it was as if he'd been bred for the twenty-five-by-thirty-foot studio unit they shared. There was a queen-size bunk in its own nook, a wafer-thin sofa that folded down from the wall, a "kitchen" area with a "dining bar" about the size of an outdoor café table. There was thin foam rubber over the floor; the walls were coated in light blue syntex, which was mottled around the edges with mildew. Once a week she hung fresh drapes of garment material over the bed alcove and above the little sofa. The light was from a soft white ceiling fixture. A small videoscreen was flush with the wall to the right of the door—the door covered it when it was open. Just now it was dialed to a soothe-scene. There was a selection of six soothe scenes. It also served as a TV for the techniwave channel and the twice weekly movies Admin was supposed to provide. Only there'd been more equipment failures, and they hadn't had a movie for a month. Chester frowned over the videoscreen, trying to change channels. "It's on the fritz."

"What you trying to get?"

"The mountaintop scene. Where you can see the wind blowin' the snow off the mountain." Chester's favorite. "There it is . . . see if I can get it in better—"

"I guess you'd rather play with that thing than give me a kiss. I don't blame you, the way I look now."

He chuckled and came to her, bent to kiss her. "You are

the prettiest thing in creation. Of course, I need an eye implant pretty bad."

She laughed and pretended to punch him in the shoulder. He acted as if she'd broken his arm, making the arm swing loosely, hamming it up. She smiled up at him. He may be small but he's a handsome man. And he's smart.

The microwave went *ding!* and he got their meal. He put pillows behind her so she could sit up, leaning against the wall, holding the tray on her pregnant belly. He sat beside her, scowling as he ate. He resented the airline food. It was an issue with him.

The nausea caught up with her halfway through the meal, and she put the tray aside. "Chester. You were later than I thought you'd be. Does that mean, um—"

"That they gave me work? Wish it did. Another bullshit day wasted in a waiting room. No fucking work. Another week of subsistence creds. I'm late 'cause I stopped off at Bitchie's to talk to Carl." He hesitated. "And the others. They asked me to talk . . ." He sounded almost puzzled.

The others. He'd gone to a meeting, then. Colony New Resistance. The only argument she'd had with Chester in a month happened after they'd gone to an NR meeting together. The New Resistance rep, Carl Zantello, had said some things about Admin and the SA she thought were crazy. He'd claimed they were part of some enormous racist conspiracy. Crackpot stuff. She'd agreed that Admin was mishandling the Colony, was treating people badly. But saying they were part of a new international Nazi party or something . . . Zantello was watching too many movies, she'd told Chester. And Chester had yelled at her that she'd believe it if she were black, because if she were black, she'd feel the SA people looking at her. The way they look at blacks, at the other races, the way they treated them. A black man could *feel* it all coming down. Maybe some kind of survival skill evolved in American blacks, Chester said. A keen awareness of prejudice in others; a talent for sensing the plans that followed the prejudice.

Two weeks after the meeting she'd been called to the Security office, to see Russ Parker. Not a bad man, she thought. But he'd talked to Chester, too, and Chester had come home angry. *"They've been watching me,"* he'd said.

"So—they asked you to make a speech?" she asked now.

"Kind of." He grinned. "I guess it was, yeah. I talked about the prejudicial work-assignment practices. I swear to God—I never expected to see this on the Colony—they're hiring Caucasians, and a few ass-kissing Spanish and Japanese. And nobody else is getting work assignments. So nobody else is getting anything but subsistence creds. Most of the technickis—even the white ones—are bitching about it. In private. But everybody's afraid to bitch in public because of the 'preventative detention' bullshit." He ticked off the names of the technicki political prisoners on his fingers. "Judy Wessler, Jose Arguello, Abu Nasser, Denny Bix—all of 'em arrested, no one gets to talk to them. Shit, we don't even know if they're still alive." He took a deep breath and then, staring fixedly at the snowy mountaintop scene, said, "So me and Carl decided the time's come for another general strike."

"Chester, shit!" She wanted to shout at him. But she knew how he'd react. She needed to change her tactics. She carefully modulated her voice, said, "Chester, you're right. We should all go on strike again. It's called for. But—we got to think about *timing*. While the Soviet blockade's on, the SA can do what they want with us. I mean, you said they were some kind of Nazis, right? And they know you're a Marxist. Black is bad enough—but Marxist! If they're Nazis, they don't have any conscience about hurting people—maybe even killing people—that stand up to them. Especially black Marxists, Chester. They'll—"

"That's exactly the reason we ought to stand up to them," he said. "Because it's immoral to give in to people like that. And giving in's even more dangerous, maybe, in the long run, than fighting. They're consolidating their power. We've got to take some of that power from them while we can. We got to face the risks."

She repressed the outburst of exasperation she felt at his bravado. It wasn't easy. Being pregnant made you cranky. She wanted to yell, to grab him and shake him. But you tried not to argue when you were in the units. The claustrophobic compactness of a unit acted like an electrical transformer on the current of anger, pulsing it up to absurd extremes.

"Okay, we ought to stand up to them. But . . . but don't you think it'd be more, um, more powerful . . . that it'd give us, you know, a better chance, if you wait till the blockade's over? So they don't just use it as an excuse to come down on you? They've got to lift the martial law alert eventually."

He frowned. He shook his head. But he said, "Maybe. Maybe so."

The videoscreen gave off an uncharacteristic crackle. In the image, electronic snow fell over the videotaped mountain snow. They stared at it, both wondering the same thing: Are they bugging us? Listening in on this? Is it that far along?

And then a voice spoke from the intercom grid over the door. It was a computer simulation of a woman's soothing but firm voice. Little Mom, some of the Colonists called her. Or else they called her Libish. Technicki for "lying bitch."

"Please take note. Please take note," the voice said sweetly. "The Boulevard of Lights"—that was Corridor C—"has been sealed off due to flooding. Do not attempt to enter the corridor until entry is reauthorized. The corridor flooding is believed to be caused by sabotaged pipes. If you have any information about the vandals, your security report will be treated confidentially. Should your report lead to the apprehension of the vandals, you will be rewarded, also in confidence. Remember, helping Security maintain order is helping *you*! Thank you for helping yourself!" She repeated the message in technicki.

So someone had sabotaged the pipes at Corridor C.

Kitty looked at Chester questioningly. He shook his head. "It wasn't us."

The videoscreen gave out another raucous buzzing—and then the image cleared. Kitty and Chester stared at it. They looked at one another; then back at the screen.

It was different. The scene was an endless tape loop, and it should always be the same sequence, wind blowing soft banners of powdery snow from a Himalayan mountaintop; feathery whiteness blown from the stark, dignified peak, trailing into crystal-blue sky. But now there was a man in the image. He was sitting on the mountaintop, kicking the snow up with his feet like a little kid, laughing. He was *nude,* for

God's sake, on a mountaintop. And he was an old man. Skinny, potbellied, white-haired. And evidently crazy.

"*Fugg'nshid!*" Chester swore in technicki. "*Hoofugzit?*"

"I don't know," Kitty murmured. The image of the man was small. It was hard to see his face. "But he looks familiar. . . ."

In another part of the Colony, at exactly that moment, someone else found the image familiar.

"Shoot me for a wetback, but by God I think that's Professor Rimpler!" Russ burst out.

"It is indeed," Praeger said. He was on a separate screen in Russ's office, monitoring the transmission anomaly from his quarters. "This reinforces my opinion: There is a Rimpler cult. And they've broken into our system somehow."

"Maybe you're right. I don't know what else it could be. But if the guy's a hero to them, why they making him look . . . like that? Seems to me—shit!" The mountaintop image had vanished, replaced by a close-up of Rimpler's leering face. The face tried to speak, but the words came out garbled.

The image on the screen flickered, vanished. The snowy mountaintop returned, sans Rimpler.

"What are our chances of tracing the source of the superimposed images?" Praeger asked.

"I don't know. I'll have to ask the techs. But until we know when it's going to happen ahead of time, it's hard to be prepared to trace—"

"Then have the computer continually monitor all channels for anomaly. At the first anomaly it should trace automatically."

"That'll take time to set up—in fact, with the damage that's been done in Central, I'm not sure if—" Russ was interrupted by the red flash from the Security Priority screen. He thumbed the acknowledge button and tapped to tie it in to Praeger's line.

One of Russ's technical investigators came onto the priority screen. It was Faid, a tech-intelligence officer who'd come to the Colony from the People's Republic of Palestine; he'd been one of Russ's own men before Praeger brought the

SA in. He was one of the few left from the original security roster. "Right, we have source of water leakings in Corridor C, Chief. Martinson is having it for you, what?" That was just the way Faid talked. "He is made determination."

"Put him on."

Martinson's lean black face came on the screen. "The valves are auto-operated by the Tertiary Life Support System. The computer opened two of the unconnected valves. It simply opened them and increased water pressure in them. Whoever programmed Tertiary most recently..." He shrugged.

"Must've been. Thanks. The water shut off?"

"Shut off and permacapped. They're draining for recycling now. And that's all we've got for you."

Russ nodded and cut the transmission.

"Why are those men still in the field?" Praeger asked.

Russ was caught by surprise. "Uh—Faid? Martinson? Why?"

"According to the new personnel guidelines, they should have been replaced. Especially this Faid person. He's culturally contraindicated for Security."

"Because he's an Arab? Sir, he may be a wog, but he's a damn efficient one. You saw how fast he got on top of—"

"Replace him. And when you find out who programmed Tertiary, let me know."

Praeger cut off, and Russ stared at the blank screen where his image had been. There was an ugly taste in his mouth. Damn Praeger, that arrogant, bigoted son of a bitch!

But after a moment he muttered, "Nothing I can do about it." Faid would have to go, maybe Martinson too. It was stupid, but it was unavoidable.

He ran the check himself on the programmer for Tertiary Life Support. It was Kevin Brock. Kevin *Brock*? Brock was SA! Hell, he was one of Praeger's toadies.

Russ shook his head in wonder. Had someone turned Brock? Converted him to a radical saboteur? Fat, middle-aged, overpaid, bigoted *Brock* had become a revolutionary?

Bullshit.

Someone unauthorized had gotten into the computer somehow. Life Support computers were triple-protected against unauthorized access and tampering. How had it been done?

The valve control tampering, the image of Rimpler—none of it should have been possible. It was as if the computer itself had it in for them. Which wasn't possible, either.

Somewhere on the Island of Malta.

Steinfeld had ordered them out for assault exercises.

The Maltese Army was holding exercises on other parts of the island's coast. NATO, and hence the SA, knew about the Maltese exercises. If spy satellites used infrareds or other sensors to penetrate the cloud cover, they'd be camouflaged amongst the Maltese activities.

Today, one hundred and eighty NR were out in boats. Six boats, thirty guerrillas apiece. They were green U.S. Army amphibious landing vehicles, creaky old buckets with the insignia painted out. Witcher had bought ten of them from war surplus, had them partially refitted, smuggled them here in one of his false-bottomed oil tankers.

And it was getting dark. It was nearly time to begin. . . .

Claire and Hard Eyes stood on the top deck with the coxswain, looking through the gloom at the rocky coastline. A soft wind coming up the coastline from the south carried the sweet rot of brine and the diesel reek of the other amphibious boats. The sky was beaten brass above the sunset; the sea was a heaving infinity of copper and verdigris. The engines rumbled; the wake hissed behind them as the boat carried them south, a quarter of a mile out from the coast. Claire could just make out the hulk of Steinfeld in the lead boat, hunched over a chart.

"I wonder if Steinfeld is lost," she said, for something to say.

Hard Eyes took the remark seriously. "There are hardly any beaches on this island. He'll know it when he sees it. Everything else is rocks and cliffs."

She nodded and shifted her assault rifle to her other shoulder. It was getting heavy. Hard Eyes looked at her as if he might offer to carry it. She could see him think better of it.

"What are you smiling like that for?" he asked suddenly.

"Nothing. Why shouldn't I?"

He shrugged and went down the gangway; Claire watched him go, wondering what she'd done to annoy him. She'd seen him put up with grueling conditions of all kinds; with cold, hunger, wounds, and firefights to make a seasoned veteran piss his pants in fear—and he'd shrugged it all off. But say the wrong thing, hurt his feelings, and he sulked like a little kid. He had become a professional fighting man—and at the same time he was absurdly immature.

His immaturity was exasperating, but . . . it had a certain appeal.

And when he made love, he was as patient as he was passionate.

Still . . .

Did she want to commit herself to him?

And then, silently, she laughed at herself. Worrying about emotional commitment as if she were some cow-eyed debutante in Long Island. The chances were excellent that they were going to be dead in a month or less. Even without the likelihood of death in the assault on Sicily, there were half a dozen other deaths waiting for them, incubating in the teeming corridors of possibility. The Soviets could move in on Malta, take it over, imprison them all, enslave or kill them. The SA could find them, bomb them in their hideouts, or send in commandos to slaughter them in their beds. Or she could find her way to the States—and Praeger's hirelings could locate her. Kill her. Or the Third World War could escalate into nuclear holocaust. A fire-storm death, or a slower demise from wind-carried fallout . . . or death by cold and starvation in a nuclear winter. . . .

And with all that heaped on my plate, I'm thinking, Should I commit myself to Hard Eyes? She shook her head and told herself: Bury those feelings. Feelings about anything long-term. The desire to make a home somewhere. Bury it deep, but don't kill it. Not yet.

"You look very thoughtful," Karakos said, coming onto the deck. He had a pleasant accent and a mild, unassuming expression. He'd been cleaned up, and in the week he'd been there, his face had filled out a little. His face was not a handsome one, but it was attractively masculine, mature, deeply etched with character, and sometimes his eyes showed just a hint of the suffering he'd been through.

He hadn't talked about what he'd been through, what he'd seen, except to say that most of the time he'd been in solitary confinement. He seemed unable to talk about his imprisonment at the hands of the SA, and that was understandable.

He stood at the rail beside her, gazing into the gloom. "Stars are coming out," he said. "We get caught up in trying to stay alive, we forget to look at things like that." He glanced at her, smiled. Boyish, that smile. She liked it. "But I guess, Claire, you've had enough of seeing the stars, eh? Up there."

The Colony. The screw pinning her stomach to her spine bit another thread deeper. It showed on her face.

"I have said something that hurts?" he said.

He put his hand on her arm and smiled sadly, as if to say, "I'm sorry. There is enough pain."

His touch felt good. It felt—she wasn't sure.

But she found herself looking up at the sky, wondering—as the screw tightened another turn in her belly—if in fact her father was dead.

"You look lost," Karakos said. "I, myself, am feeling lost. I'm wondering if I belong here. . . ."

She glanced at him. "You're tired of fighting," she suggested. "I don't blame you."

"It isn't that. It's . . . I feel as if Steinfeld doesn't want me here."

"Are you serious? You have a great reputation in the NR. Steinfeld has nothing but respect for you."

"And yet—he has told me nothing about what our plans are. I'm participating in an exercise to prepare for a mission I know nothing about. I'm not used to that."

She hesitated. She was one of half a dozen people who knew about Steinfeld's plan for an attack on the Sicilian SA base. The others knew an action of some sort was planned, but they didn't know where and when. It was best that few as possible know. "Steinfeld's told almost no one. It's not that he doesn't trust the people he's not telling—it's his fear that they might be caught by SA agents before the assault."

Karakos snorted. "And he thinks I would talk? *I?*"

"No, probably he's worried about an extractor. All the willpower in creation won't help you against an extractor."

"Extractors! It is a myth that the SA has them in Europe! They are extremely rare, expensive devices!"

"How the hell do you know it's a 'myth'?" Hard Eyes asked as he stepped onto the deck from the gangway.

He was staring at Karakos's hand, which was still on Claire's arm.

"One of their people confided in me," Karakos said briskly, removing his hand from Claire's arm. "I made friends with him." He shrugged. "He says they spread the rumor they have extractors so that prisoners will talk freely, will assume it's hopeless to hold back."

Hard Eyes spat over the rail into the hissing sea. "Bullshit!"

Karakos shrugged again and moved stiffly away, down the ladder.

Hard Eyes looked at her expressionlessly. "What did he want to know?"

"What makes you think he wanted to—"

"*What did he want to know?*"

She stared at him. "He was understandably concerned about Steinfeld's assault target."

"Was he. I don't trust that son of a bitch. Not with our plans, and not with you."

"Dan, you're being childish—" She broke off as Lila came up the ladder. She was captain of their assault unit, a tall woman with night-dark skin, wearing black. They saw only her starlit silhouette and the glitter of her eyes. Claire had often wondered about her. Lila could speak English, French, and Martinique pidgin fluently—but speaking was something she rarely did. She was one of those people who communicated more with the subtle posture of her body, her eye contact, her timing. She made Claire think of Yukio.

Lila was neat, compact in all her movements, graceful even when loading and firing a gun. She never seemed at a loss for something really useful to do. Never distracted or spaced-out. When there was a lecture on strategy, she listened raptly, not taking her eyes off the speaker. When there was work to do, she did it vigorously and gave it her full attention. When she was done and there was really nothing more to do, she slept, just like that. She'd lie down, and she'd be asleep in seconds. She didn't even snore.

Claire had a vague urge to make friends with Lila. But in the two weeks she'd known her, she'd never seen her make small talk. Or talk about herself. Or smile.

Lila gave them each a headset. "We hit the beach in about twenty minutes. Hard Eyes will be in charge of Platoon *A* for this unit, I'll be in charge of *B*; Hard Eyes will also be under my command."

Hard Eyes and Claire nodded. Steinfeld had already told them the chain of command.

"The objective is a ruined building. It used to be where they pressed olives. We are to blow it up with MPGs, then to secure what remains. *A* will be approaching first; *B* on radio command. Do not fire weapons without positions confirmation. The new code applies."

She went on for a few minutes more. Without stumbling on a single word, without a need for clarification, holding their eyes with the intensity of her gaze.

When she was done, Hard Eyes nodded and went down into the troop transport deck area, to where the others sat on the benches, talking softly.

Lila turned to go—and then stopped, seemed to hesitate.

Claire watched her in fascination, relieved to see her showing some human uncertainty.

Lila turned to Claire and looked her in the eyes. She smiled.

She reached out, tentatively, and touched Claire on the cheek. She turned and went down the ladder. Claire stared after her, amazed.

She saw Lila talking to Karakos, below. Hard Eyes on the other side of the boat, fairly glaring at them. What was with Hard Eyes? "I don't trust that son of a bitch," he'd said.

Claire shook her head and shrugged her rifle off her shoulder. She held it in her hands and prepared to rehearse a massacre.

The Caribbean. The Island of Merino.

"No," Alouette said. "It didn't hurt."

"How about now?" Smoke asked her.

"No. But it is making a little itch," she said, reaching up to touch the spot on the back of her head. But she drew her hand back, remembering she wasn't to touch the incision.

"The itch means it's healing up," Smoke said. He wasn't sure if that was really true but he wanted to reassure her. "But if it starts to swell or anything you must tell the doctor."

They were sitting together on the examination table in the clinic. The miniblinds were halfway closed; the subtropical light slanted brilliantly to the cement floor, next to the white bulk of the x-ray holography machine. Across from them, in a locked glass cabinet, other silicon chips—actually, each was a matrix of many nanochips—were laid out on the black foam-rubber tray like a display of individual fish-scales. The room was warm. Alouette wore white shorts. She had no top on, because the doctor had been examining her. She was far from budding breasts. Smoke was wearing an islander's white cotton shorts, and buttonless overshirt. They sat on the table, swinging their legs, waiting for the doctor to come back, each being brave for the other.

"Before they put it in, I understood this thing, this chip," she said. "But now I wake up and I don't understand it."

"You're having what we call cold feet, I think," Smoke said. "That's normal."

"Cold feet. Like . . . de peur de un hoyo?"

Smoke smiled. She'd mixed French and Spanish. The island had been colonized by the Spanish first, then the French, then the Spanish fought to take it back, then the French once more . . . wrested back and forth like a child between divorced parents. The result was a mix of French and Spanish, in the names and dialect of the islanders. De peur de un hoyo. The fear of a hole. An island expression; being afraid to walk about at night, for fear of falling in a hole. "Yes," he told her, "de peur de un hoyo. It's the same idea. Afraid to go forward because you're not sure what's there."

"I understand what's there. But . . ."

"But at the same time you don't? I know the feeling. It's to protect you, Alouette. The chip will use your bioelectric field to communicate with us. When you get a little older you can use it to help you think when you have problems. It could save you. Neural-interface chips have been tested for twenty years. I'm convinced that this one is safe. . . . Well, I didn't decide to give this chip to you overnight. It connects with your brain and—I was afraid it might be dangerous. But we are . . ." He hesitated. He didn't want to frighten her. But there was a war going on. There was a war within a war. And because she had been adopted by the NR, she was part of the war. Probably, she would see some of it. He had to prepare her. "We are all of us in danger. This will protect you against that danger, a little. Its risks are outweighed by—" He looked for a way to explain it in words she'd understand.

"We're in danger because of the Fascists?"

"Yes. And lately . . . I'm afraid the CIA is looking for us. We think they've been spying on the island with a satellite. They're very dangerous. They're working with the Second Alliance."

"CIA?" She frowned. "James Bond's friends?"

He blinked at her. "Who's James Bond?"

"They showed him on movie night in the auditorium. He's a spy hero. He's from England. He has a friend named Felix who's from the CIA who helps him sometimes." She drew her feet up onto the padded table, crossed them, and scowled over a blister on her heel. She prodded it, squeezed it.

"Leave that alone," Smoke said. "You'll get it infected or something."

She turned and poked the foot at his stomach, laughing. He caught her ankle and held it, tickled her foot. She squealed and pulled it away—and almost fell off the table. Smoke grabbed her, his heart pounding. God. What if he lost her like that. Something stupid. Fall and hit her head.

She regained her balance, and lowered herself to the floor. She looked up at him gravely. "The CIA are trying to hurt us?"

"They're . . . not James Bond's friends in real life. They're a sort of secret government within the government of the USA. Every so often the rest of the government catches them at something they shouldn't have been doing and they, um, rein them in a little. Like a dog on a leash. But the dog gets away again eventually. And it has."

"What did they do that they shouldn't have been doing?"

"Oh God. Maybe we'd better wait till you're older. It's complicated."

She gave him her chilliest glare. There was something very adult in it that made him laugh. "I'm not stupid," she said.

"I know. Okay. Well—I'll give you some examples. After World War Two the CIA recruited Nazis—like Klaus Barbi, a man who tortured and murdered a lot of people in France. They recruited them to be spies. Later on they helped them escape to Central America. These were the worst kind of Nazis, too . . . Something else the CIA does is, it overthrows democratically elected governments."

A certain distance in her eyes told him he'd lost her on that one.

Smoke went on, "You know what democracy is. You know what elections are."

"Oh yes." That glare again.

"I know, I know you know." He smiled. He put a hand to his right shoulder. Empty. The crow wasn't there. The surgeon wouldn't let him bring him in. He was in a cage, poor fellow. "Anyway, um, America pretends to approve when a country elects its own government democratically. But the American CIA used covert operations—secret spy operations of a very ugly sort—to overthrow and assassinate some very decent democratically elected leaders. Like the president of Iran. This was in the twentieth century. He wanted to nationalize the oil industry, which wasn't convenient for American companies. So they pushed him out—they said he was a Communist, but he wasn't—and they installed the Shah instead and that led to a generation of torture and killing and repression, things the Shah did to people who disagreed with him, all with the help of the CIA, and *that*, the repression, that led to a revolution run by people who hated us. The Ayatollah. It was a big mess. And the CIA overthrew the democratically elected president of Guatemala—I think this was in the 1950s—ah, they overthrew him because he wanted land reform to help the peasants and that was not convenient for an American company called the United Fruit Company. They said he was a Communist and they got rid of him. He wasn't a Communist but they said he was. Then they set up a military dictatorship that tortured and murdered people for generations. They did this in Chile and a lot of places. There was always a big mess afterwards. They always made things worse for everyone. It was a question of protecting the interests of big Amerian companies who had a stake in the . . ."

He let his voice trail off, seeing her distress. She was standing there with one foot on the other, chewing her lip, frowning at the floor. She hadn't been able to follow it all, and didn't want to admit it. He was relieved. He didn't want to have to tell her these things. She was just a little girl. He was afraid she would ask him about the torture. The murders the CIA had sponsored. He didn't want to have to tell her.

And it was a relief to see the limits of her comprehension, the limits of her precosity, because he wanted her to be a little girl. His child, his daughter. His retreat into innocence.

"You get the idea," he said gently. "The CIA pretend to be the friends of freedom but they're the opposite. They're the friends of rich people. They'll kill innocent people for those rich people. So we have to protect you from them. And the chips are going to change the world, and we have to get a sort of jump on that change, to use it for our protection."

She looked up at him, bobbing her head. "I know that."

"Good. I'm tired of waiting for the doctor. Let's go find him."

"Okay. I have to pee."

_____Six

"The Soviet Union is losing the war," the man on the giant screen said. "They've been driven back to the old Warsaw Pact lines in Central Europe. They hold only a small corner of Afghanistan, and only unimportant territories in Iran. The orbital battlefield has been static for some time, with the U.S. and NATO holding the important orbits; the Soviet Orbital Army's only advantage is its blockade of the Colony. . . ."

Charlie Chesterton was standing against the wall in Grand Central Station, just below and to one side of the enormous clock over the electronic lettering strip. He glanced at his watch. Three-fifty. His contact was due at four.

The crowd in the vast, hangarlike spaces of the old train station wasn't big at this hour; but it was feverish. People walked by with single-minded haste, their paths crisscrossing, a perpetual, chaotic intermeshing.

Opposite the clock, the big videoscreen, slightly washed out in the daylight, flashed through a series of gigantic images illustrating the remarks of the commentator. The screen was silent unless, like Charlie, you wore a headset tuned to the screen's sponsor station, on which you'd now hear the commentator continue, "While it is true the Soviets control the key shipping lanes in the Atlantic, their 'superior' sea power is already beginning to show its weaknesses; ships in greater numbers simply do not make up for inferior technology. The great risk now is this: If they feel they are losing, they may assume we will take the initiative and invade Russia itself. Rather than abandon their way of life and their independence, they may attempt a nuclear first strike."

"Jesus," Charlie said.

"No, it's Angelo," Angelo said, walking up to him. "Hi, Charlie, 'sap, my man."

"Angelo! You're the . . .?"

"Yeah. Fuck the passwords. I forgot 'em, anyway. But it's me. They didn't tell you?"

"Shit, no, I thought it'd be some Pakistani in shades or something. Damn!" They clasped hands.

Charlie had known Angelo for twelve years, since they were kids. It was Angelo, four years before, who'd recruited Charlie into the NR.

Angelo was small, thin, as pale as his curly hair and eyes were dark. He had a wide mouth that split into a big, luminous grin at almost any stimulus at all. He wore an old black leather jacket and beat-up jeans, black tire-rubber boots. His eyes flashed around as if he were walking into a party and expecting to see someone he recognized. He was like that no matter where he was.

"That guy," Charlie said, nodding toward the screen, "claims the Soviets have lost the war. You think so, or is that propaganda bullshit?"

Angelo looked at the screen. "Naw, that guy's a liberal. Not one of the Administration's flunkies. If he says they losing, they probably are."

"He says they might panic and first-strike us."

"Shit . . . fuck it. Out of our hands. You got a tan, Charlie. You look stupid with a tan. Come on, we gotta go right to class."

"*More* classes. About what?"

"Video animation. You know anything about it?"

"Programming basics."

"This goes way, way beyond. This stuff is classified. Public doesn't even know it exists. . . ."

"What's this stuff about a senator?"

"Don't talk about that in public, man. Don't even think about it. . . ."

"Shit! Look at that!"

Charlie pointed at the videoscreen. The program had changed. Now it showed the Arc de Triomphe, the image rocking as if it had been shot from something moving erratically toward the arch. It swelled in the screen as the camera got closer and closer.

Charlie turned up his headset and heard, ". . . footage obtained from an assault vehicle of some kind, possibly a Jaegernaut, shortly before the destruction of the arch last month. This footage would seem to refute NATO claims that the arch was destroyed in aerial bombing carried out by the Soviet Union—"

"So what about it?" Angelo asked.

"Smoke told me about this—this is some stuff arranged to get on the air, he got it to Judy Kotz at Cable Enterprises, and damn if she didn't run it! Shit, I'll bet it gets confiscated. See that, those guys on top? You can see the muzzle flashes. That's *our guys!*"

"Fuck, Charlie, keep your voice down."

But the station was raucous with train announcements, music blaring from passing beat-boxes, the perpetual rising and falling drone of people talking and walking.

As the camera got closer to the arch, a contiguous mike picked up noise generated from the arch's top. The structured squeal of an electric guitar and the chilled-out rhythm of programmed percussion.

"Man!" Angelo said. "That's *Rickenharp!*"

Charlie nodded. Both of them stared up at the screen, awed. The tape of Rickenharp's final minutes. As the commentator said, "These two resistance martyrs—one of them has been tentatively identified as former rock star Rick Rickenharp—drew the SA's attention to the arch in order to provide a decoy so that other important Resistance operatives could escape . . . using a porta-amp and guitar, a mini-PA system, and sheer defiance, they drew not only the fire of the SA troops but the devastating attentions of the Jaegernauts. . . ."

They heard Rickenharp shouting over the music, "Hey, you, with the machine gun! Come on, give me your best shot!"

. . . and Rickenharp, a tiny figure up there, almost unseeable. But hearable. His voice and his guitar, kicked through those mean little Marshals, were audible even over the gunfire. Some original tune now . . . you couldn't make out the

lyrics but you knew what it was about . . . you'd heard a thousand permutations of it. It was an anthem, and it was about being young. Maybe it should have been called Youth.

And then the Jaegernauts rolled in from the east and west, two of them converging on the arch. They came like the neo-Fascist war machine itself. They came on like mortality. Looking from below like five-story spoked wheels, the spokes digging into whatever was in the way. There were clouds of dust, showers of bricks. The neo-Fashes scattered, cheering. Yukio kept sniping at them and more than one fell. . . .

The echoes of his gunshots rolled like bass lines for Rickenharp's electric wailing. Rickenharp had cranked the amps all the way up; he could be heard over the squealing of the oncoming Jaegernauts. . . .

The two Jaegernauts converged on the arch from opposite sides, began to grind away at it, spinning in place at first, then crunching down as the microwave beams took the fight out of the stone. Yukio's bullets whining off the blue-metal scythes . . . metal bit down on stone with a screaming that was another kind of heavy-metal jamming with Rickenharp's final chords: fat blue sparks shot out from the machine's grinding spikes; cracks spread like negative lightning through the huge monument . . . the arch's great crown bent, buckled inward. . . .

"Holy shit," Angelo breathed as they watched the Arc de Triomphe implode into a cloud of dust, boulders bouncing, gravel raining.

A final furious and defiant guitar chord and a burst of gunfire from the arch's top, and then the arch fell into itself —and was replaced, for a moment, by a great pillar of dust and a monolithic silence. . . .

"The sacrifice of these two men was more than a means of decoying the enemy from their friends. It was a symbolic act," the commentator said. "It was their way of saying no to the SA's unquenchable brutality. . . ."

"You hear that?" Charlie breathed. "That's fucking *great*."

"No way the government's going to let 'em show that stuff again," Angelo said.

"I don't know. Maybe if enough people saw it, they wouldn't dare repress it . . . I mean, check it out, some of 'em were paying attention. . . ."

Here and there, around the station, a few of the people wearing headsets were staring up at the screen, looking into the dust cloud surrounding the wreckage of one of the wonders of the world. They'd heard. They'd heard Rickenharp's final chords. How many more had heard?

Charlie and Angelo looked at each other. Till now, they'd always felt, privately, that the NR's struggle was a hopeless one. Was more of a gesture than anything else. But now, that look, that silent exchange . . .

FirStep: tHe Space Colony. Security CentRal.

"I've got to be wrong," Russ muttered, rereading the personnel lists. "Praeger wouldn't go that far."

It was 8:10 A.M. Originally the Colony had gone by military time—0800, 0900—but Professor Rimpler had seen the need for "Earth homey" touches. So it was nine in the morning. And the light in the street-wide main corridors had a gray-blue tinge, like early-morning light, from six till eight. By now it was yellow. The few "cafés" still open along the Strip would be exuding the smell of eggs and bacon—though both were artificially made, artificially scented—and the vents would be pushing a brisk morning breeze along the corridors and through the shrubbery of the Open.

Russ wished he were there, in the Open, where you could see real, though reflected, sunlight; where you could see the grass wave in the air-conditioned wind. . . .

But he was sitting in his tomb of an office, drinking ersatz coffee that tasted like sawdust mixed with thrice-used coffee grounds, and frowning at his work-screen's list of personnel for the day's outer-hull repairs.

It was routine, since the sabotage had begun, for Russ to approve all personnel lists for in-space repair. And he recognized twelve—count 'em, twelve!—names on the morning's list for Repair Module 17. They were all names from the Security Risk list. And they all belonged to blacks or Jews. And Praeger had already approved the list.

It didn't add up. Praeger had made it clear to hiring agents that blacks, Jews, Arabs, and Pakistani/Indians were to be hired minimally if at all. He claimed they were Security Risks who couldn't be trusted on the outside. And now he'd approved a whole shipload of them. The only Caucasian personnel were people like Carl Zantello, an Italian . . . and a notorious radical.

Must be some mistake. Praeger's assistant must have approved the list for him, without really looking at it. Something.

Unless . . . maybe Praeger had magically gotten himself some political savvy. Realized that he was only making trouble for himself by refusing work assignments to minority groups and radic technickis.

Forget it. No way. Praeger was too pigheaded to see that racism was impractical.

What was he up to?

Less than a quarter of a mile from Russ Parker's office, Kitty Torrence was wondering more or less the same thing. She was thinking, What are they trying to do?

She and Chester were in the Open. They each had about forty minutes before they were to report for work, and they'd decided to use up one of their last passes to get into the park. It was much less crowded at this hour, and in the "mornings" the breeze, carried on the badly filtered ventilator systems, was only faintly tinged with putrefaction.

They stood on a low hill, looking up into the circumscribed sky, talking. Chester was frowning—which surprised her; she'd expected him to be happy he'd gotten a work assignment that day.

But she understood when he told her about Billy Glass.

"Billy didn't know what it was," Chester said. "They told him they were forming a new technicki union, and that if he went, he stood a better chance of getting some work. But they hassled him about how he felt about things, about the dark brothers and the radics. He wanted the work, so he played along. He felt bad about it. Anyway, he went to their meeting, and there was nobody there but white technickis— except there were guys he figures are undercover for Security. The Security spies talked technicki. Said it was the radics who were screwing up for the rest of us. Said they were in league with the Soviets, and the Soviet blockade is what's put us on half rations. Said the blacks and the Jews were working together to vandalize things. They pointed out that three of the prisoners in Detention for LSE* are black. They asked Billy and the others to take a vow: If armed conflict comes up, they got to take up arms against the rest of us. Billy got freaked out. Went out the back way, came looking to warn us. . . ."

Chester and Kitty stood in silence for a while after he finished his explanation. Chester sullenly watched a helmeted guard walking by on the path below the hill. Kitty looking up at the hurricane's-eye swirl of clouds at one end of the immense green-furred tube that was the Open, wondering if Admin was really doing what it seemed. "Well, anyway," she said, glancing at her watch, "in ten minutes you'll have some real work."

"Yeah. I got RM17. Lot of my friends going out on this one. Guess this is the token nigger mission."

"Mmm . . . what they got you doing?"

He shrugged. "RM17's going out to repair meteor damage. Pinhole stuff. They got me maintaining video comm with Repair Central. Which is kind of weird, because Judy Forsythe is going, too, and she's the same rating. I don't know why they need two comm techs. I'm surprised they need one. Maybe there's a solar storm, so all the communications are screwed up, need us for constant adjustment." He reached over and patted her stomach. "They won't let you work much longer. Maybe if my job works out, you can quit right away."

"Chester, I—" *No, don't tell him.* But it came out on its own, all in a rush: "I'm scared to keep going to work. I'm afraid one of the supervisors'll notice I'm pregnant and check to see if I'm on Parenthood Monitoring. They'll make me go to PM, and PM'll tell me the baby's a risk from the radiation here or something and they have to abort it—"

She broke off and looked at Chester a little sheepishly.

He was looking at her like he couldn't believe it. "They

*LSE—Life Support Endangerment. Can be applied to anyone who makes trouble for Colony's administration. Any disorder is regarded as a threat to Life Support Systems and therefore to all life on the Colony.

wouldn't do that—not with a baby that far along! Would they?"

"They did it to Betty Carmitzian. Her husband's an Arab. They said the baby was deformed, but . . ."

"But maybe they murdered it because its daddy was a wog?" Chester looked so grim, it scared her.

She touched his arm—and quickly withdrew her hand. He was trembling with repressed fury. "If they touch our kid . . ." he said softly, his eyes glassy with rage. "If they touch *you* . . . I'll abort their fucking Praeger right out the fucking air locks."

She threw her arms around him. "Don't get all worked up, Chester," she whispered. "You'll get in a fight or something. They'll throw you in Detention."

She felt some of the tension draining out of him as he put his arms around her. "We're gonna get out of this shit can, baby. I promise you. Safe and sound . . ."

She nodded into his shoulder.

"Hey," he said softly. "I got to go to work. You too. Don't push it, huh? Take it easy when you can."

"Sure."

They took one last look around at the trees, the grass, the half-finished condo housing in Rimpler Meadows, the mist of sky, and, beyond it, the curve of more of the inside-out land overhead.

Kitty stretched. It felt good here, up on the hill. The gravity was less here, and it was easier on her pregnancy-burdened back. She sighed and took Chester's hand. Together they walked back to the passageway that led to Hollywood Boulevard: Corridor A.

Russ had been trying for thirty minutes, off and on, to get Praeger on the line so he could verify the RM17 worker list, and he just couldn't get through. Have to step up to his office and see him in person, maybe. Damn screen was fuzzing over. All the interference on the comm lines lately. Maybe it was the saboteur again. . . .

On an impulse Russ turned to his Security console and punched for Suspect Check, asked for the transcripts of the surveillance tapes.

He scrolled through the transcripts for a while, scanning

the highlighted stuff Praeger's men felt indicated "incriminating conversation." It was mostly ordinary grousing. Like, "Fuckin' Admin's playin' games with us again; they're moving us around. Kate and I got moved to a fucking lower deck unit, thing smells like the sewage recycler. . . ."

And another, *"Libish triguttusa sinker ginny—"*

Russ punched *TFT* for translation from technicki. The computer translated, "The Lying Bitch will try to get you to sink [i.e., betray] your own grandmother."

Big deal. Russ shrugged and scrolled onward, stopped at the transcript of a conversation between Kitty Torrence and her husband Chester.

"Okay, we ought to stand up to them, but . . . but don't you think it'd be more, um, powerful . . . that it'd give us, you know, a better chance, if you waited till the blockade was over? So they don't just use it as an excuse to come down on you? They've got to lift the martial-law alert eventually. . . ."

"Maybe . . . maybe so."

Russ frowned. He scrolled up, scanned through the parts he'd missed.

He stopped at a remark the marginal notation attributed to the woman. "If they're Nazis, they don't have any conscience about hurting people—maybe even killing people—"

Russ's gut contracted.

Well. There it was. A woman, a pregnant woman, soon to be a mother. Warning her husband about the storm troopers.

And he, Russell Parker, was one of the men she was talking about.

He'd taken an interest in Kitty Torrence. Maybe because when he'd questioned her, she made him think of his wife, who'd died eight years back. A plain woman, like Kitty Torrence, but as sweet and pure as creek water.

Russ had intervened. He'd checked up on her, found they were going to send the Parenthood Monitoring officers around to bring her in for a mandatory abortion. He'd scotched that and managed to slip it past Praeger. For now. The baby wasn't really safe till it was born. . . .

Was it safe even then? Not if they were the kind of people she said they were.

Her Chester was a troublemaker, all right. Smart, leadership qualities, and a Communist. Bad combination.

But if he could help Chester and Kitty, he would.

And Chester was scheduled to go out on RM17.

Thinking about RM17 made him shift uneasily in his seat. It'd been chewing at the back of his mind for almost an hour now.

He stabbed a finger at General Communications and this time got through.

"Bucher here," said the face on the screen. "Rear Launch Deck. Can I help?"

"This is Russ Parker, Security. I want you to hold that RM17 launch for . . . ten minutes."

"You got it, Chief."

Russ changed frequencies and punched for Praeger's office.

Praeger's image, scowling, appeared on the screen. "Yes?"

"Hey, how yuh doin' there—"

"Cut the corn pone and get on with it, Russ. I'm in conference."

Russ cleared his throat. *Keep your cool.* "I've been checking the passenger list for RM17. Must be some kind of mistake—you check this list personally?"

"Yes, what of it?"

"It's almost all Suspects and High Risks. Blacks, radics, you name it. I thought you wanted—"

"You wanted me to give them more work, did you not? 'Defuse their anger,' I think you said. Well, I've done it."

But Russ didn't buy it. There was something more. Even in the two-dimensionality of the videoscreen he could see it in Praeger's face. "Just exactly why—"

He broke off, cursing as the screen fuzzed over with snow.

And then, gaping, he stared at another face forming in the visual white noise . . . a face forming out of the boiling field of white flecks. *Rimpler.* Old man Rimpler.

Russ had the uncanny feeling Rimpler was looking out at him. At him, personally. Was seeing him, was that instant staring back. . . .

"Russ . . ." A small, raspy voice from the comm speaker.

Startled, Russ leapt back, overturning his chair. He fell on his ass.

The screen laughed. "Russ!"

Russ got to his feet. "What the hell!"

"*Russ!*" Rimpler's voice. But Rimpler was dead.

Russ stabbed the reset button on the console. The screen flickered. The snow returned. So did the face, a face of white on white, with empty eyes.

Russ went to the door, thinking, *Get help*. Part of him wondering, *Help against what? What are you scared of? A glitch on a TV monitor?*

But he slapped the open panel on the door.

It didn't open.

He swore and pulled open the access box in the wall to one side of the door, reached in, threw the emergency open switch. The door slid aside.

He started to step through—

The door slammed shut on him, pinning his chest, wedging him in, crushing. A vertical bar of hot pain in his chest. He yelled and tried to push the door back. The door's servos whined. . . .

One of the guards came into the hall outside his office, stared for a second, then ran up to help him. Together they pressed the door open. Suddenly it switched off. It was as if it had stopped trying. It slid meekly into the wall.

"What happened, sir?"

"I don't know. My whole damn office went haywire. Get tech security up here."

"Yes, sir." The guard loped away.

Russ turned to look back into his office. He saw that one of his wall cameras had moved. It was a camera used by his comm system to pick up his image for transmission—and it had shifted toward the door. The camera moved only when it was electronically commanded to. He had given it no such command. So why had it moved?

To follow him, when he'd gotten up to go through the door. . .

To follow him so that someone—whoever it was—would know when to slam the door on him.

He rubbed his chest. It was bruised. It stung. Was the

attack a practical joke? Or had someone really tried to kill him?

On the Colony's rear launch level, A-Deck, the deck foreman looked at his watch. Russ had said ten minutes. It was now fifteen.

His screen pulsed, and Praeger's image appeared there.

"Bucher!"

"Yes, sir?"

"What's the delay?"

"Chief Parker said—"

"He's out of line. Launch it now!"

"Yes, sir."

Bucher turned and looked out the foot-thick tinted glass window into the Launch Deck area. The seventy-foot gray-metal bulk of Repair Module 17, roughly beetle-shaped, was sitting in its deck collars, its pilot windows lit up, its launch lights glowing red.

Bucher hit a button, and the launch lights went green. He hit another button and spoke into a mike extending from the wall. "Clearance, 17."

"Roger," crackled from the speaker.

The enormous air-lock doors slid aside. There was no whoosh of air: the launch area was already pumped airless. The collars unlatched from the beetle's legs, and it drifted up. Small jets on its aft sent it sliding neatly into space.

It became a black insect-shape snipped out of the field of stars, and then slipped like a shadow to Bucher's left, out of sight, as it followed the curve of the hull back to where the temporarily sealed punctures were.

As the doors were closing behind it, Bucher saw something odd.

There was a two-man EVA module, just a bucket shape with clawlike arms extended in front of it, drifting by the doorway, from Bucher's right. It looked as if it were following the RM17. That was odd, because it didn't appear on his duty charts.

He switched on his extra Launch Deck cameras and saw a flattened image of the RM17 drift by. And then, thirty seconds later, the EVA module, coming close on the RM17's heels.

* * *

Russ stormed into Praeger's office, pushed past the secretary—and stopped short when he saw Praeger looking up at him. He felt his nerve draining away, leaking through the holes Praeger's glare made in him.

"You have a reason to come barging in, Russ, you'd better give it to me *fast*."

Russ's mouth was dry. Sitting next to Praeger was Van Kips. Her normally immaculate flaxen hair looked a little mussed. Something odd about the way Praeger was sitting behind that desk too. And the room was dialed to dim illumination. It was almost dark in there. Could they have been . . . ?

No, ridiculous. Not in here, not now.

"Well," Russ began. "My comm was down and I wanted to talk about that personnel list of the—" He stopped, his attention caught by the screen across from Praeger's desk. It showed a TV image of the outer hull of the Colony, curving away like a metal plain. Four things crawling over it. No, two things, and their shadows. Repair Module 17—he could see the big numbers painted on the side—closely followed by a two-man EVA bucket.

"It's already been launched?" Russ asked, his voice sounding hollow in his ears.

"Yes." Smugness in Praeger's voice. "Yes, why shouldn't it? I was just monitoring it because"—Parker could feel Praeger pause to make up a lie—"ah, as you had expressed some concern about it. It seems to be just fine."

"Isn't it unusual for an EVA bucket to work so closely around a—"

"Yes," Van Kips said hastily. "We just put in a call to it. We—couldn't get through. That crazy interference again."

"Well, we'd better try again—"

"Oh, leave it alone, Russ. Go back to your station," Praeger said.

Russ started to tell him about the "glitch" that had trapped him in the doorway . . . but nothing came out of his mouth. He was staring at the image on the screen. The EVA module was moving in closer. Moving in on the cylindrical fuel tanks on the underside of the RM17.

The arms on the EVA bucket extended—and punched

through the metal of the fuel tanks. A crackle of electricity along the arms, a billow of gas from somewhere on the front of the bucket . . .

The RM17 exploded.

It was eleven o'clock and Kitty's supervisor had sent her home early. She was riding in a sort of train, in one of twelve small, rubber-wheeled cars pulled by something resembling an oversize golf cart. It made her remember being a little girl riding in a "train" not so different than this one at the Bronx Zoo, past a lot of tired, dull-eyed patchy-furred animals.

She sat across from a boy who held a hand-size TV set on his lap. He was watching rock cartoons.

The people in the street-wide corridor—Hollywood Boulevard—were of all kinds. Unsmiling and dull-eyed, most of them—but there were people laughing here too. There was a group of boys wearing real-cloth jackets—covered with technicki patches of all kinds—using markers to leave their gang tags on the walls. She couldn't read the stylized graffiti writing. The train swept past them, rocking as it turned a corner, and she winced as the inertia chased a snake of nausea up through her. She'd almost collapsed at work today. The supervisor had said, "You're past the time you can do this kind of work."

It seemed her super could no longer pretend she didn't know Kitty was pregnant. Kitty wondered if she'd reported it. They were supposed to report it in case the parents didn't.

She sighed. She closed her eyes. She hoped Chester was behaving himself.

Her eyes snapped open when the TV on the boy's lap broke from its mindless minimono yammering to announce: "Special news report from Colony Central. A repair module working outside the Colony has exploded, with all hands lost. However, no major damage to the Colony's hull was done. Although not yet Admin-confirmed, RM17 was reportedly destroyed by an accidental collision with a drone EVA module. A list of casualties will be—"

"Jeez," the kid said.

Kitty screamed.

* * *

Russ sat on his bunk, in the darkness, listening to a tape called "Night Noises in the Desert." Smelling the fragrance disk he'd put in the scent player: sage, wood smoke, mesquite. He was sitting on his hands. When he didn't sit on them, he tended to pound them against his temples, and that hurt, so he had to sit on them.

This is stupid, he told himself. So he took his sweaty hands from under his haunches and tucked them into his armpits for a while.

Goddammit. Goddammit son of a *bitch*.

They did it, all right. They had all the answers too soon. Too pat. "Guidance mechanism on the drone EVA bucket poorly insulated, misdirected by RM17's computer navigation signals." They had it twenty minutes after the thing exploded.

He squeezed his eyes shut but still saw, against the darkness of his unlit chamber, the white flash, the fireball quickly snuffed out in the vacuum, the expanding ring of debris—

—Yeah, twenty minutes after the RM17 exploded, Praeger was printing out a statement for release at 1800. Poorly insulated guidance mechanism; the EVA bucket sent out to assist the RM17 was simply the wrong one, was the one that should have been in repair dock. Some equipment dispatcher would get the blame. Maybe someone the SA wanted to get rid of.

Just to put the cherry on the sundae. Get rid of one more, after killing all those men and women on RM17. All those troublemakers.

No, Russ told himself. No one's going to take the fall for Praeger. Not that he could accuse Praeger. Yet. Too risky. Praeger would have him removed from his job, before the accusation could become public. Praeger's people—under Judith Van Kips's supervision—censored all the Colony's media now. Nothing went on the air or into printout without Van Kips's approval.

Removed from his job? Praeger wouldn't stop there. If Russ fought him, Praeger would simply have him killed.

And most of the SA guards were loyal to Praeger.

There had to be a way.

* * *

Someone tried to talk to her. She was walking down the narrow corridor, in the dorms section where most of the technicki lived, seeing only what she had to, hearing nothing.

Kitty was trying not to think, to perceive as little as possible, to feel nothing. Because if she let herself feel the pain, it would fall on her like gasoline on a man smoking a cigarette; she'd be a human torch with it, she'd run howling with it . . . where? Where would she go? To her parents? How many thousands of miles of interstellar space was she from her parents?

What else was there? Some peaceful spot on Earth where she could let herself feel, let her surroundings heal her. The state park her parents had taken her to, one of the only parks not ruined by the acid rains. How many thousands of miles of radiation-charged vacuum between her and that park? How many air locks and bulkheads and men with guns?

But still she felt the pain moving in on her, unreasoningly implacable.

The baby. Oh, Jesus. Living here *alone* with the baby. Oh, shit; she wished she were religious. The baby. Without Chester.

(Faces drifting by, like shapes in smoke. Voices speaking to her in a meaningless string of syllables.)

If she killed herself, she'd be killing the baby. Maybe that'd be better. It was only going to get worse and worse here, under the Nazis. They might kill her baby, anyway, because it was Chester's.

And, of course, she knew they'd murdered Chester.

(Her hands moving automatically to tap the coded sequence on the lock unit, opening the door.)

It might be a blessing to the baby if she killed herself. At least then it wouldn't be the Nazis (stepping into the apartment) who'd killed the baby, it would be—

He was sitting on their bed. "Hi, babe," Chester said sadly, sitting up, yawning. "Damn, can you believe I missed out on that job? I got back from the Open too late, couldn't get through the crowd around the assignment center, foreman said they'd overhired, weight limit wouldn't let them put anyone else—hey . . . what's the matter, Kitty? You okay?"

She moved across the room in a dream. *Touch him*.

She touched his lean, muscular arm. He was real.

She melted onto him. He threw his arms around her. "Why you cryin'—oh, the job, yeah, well, I'm sorry, babe, I just—"

"Chester, you—you didn't hear about the RM17?"

"No—what the hell happened?"

"Chester, I heard there's a way to get off the Colony. The Soviets let one ship through every two weeks. It's almost impossible to get on it. But there must be a way. Chester, let's get off this thing, please. I don't care if we don't have any money left. Let's go back. Please. Please."

"What happened to the—"

"You won't run out and start something if I tell you?"

"No." But his face went hard. "Tell me."

Russ lay on his back, smelling sagebrush, listening to the maracas of desert insects, the fluting of the desert owl.

And seeing two things in his mind's eye, alternately. First, the explosion on the screen. Ball of white fire, expanding ring of char. Second: Van Kips leaning over Praeger, the light from the screen image of the explosion lighting up their faces in that dim room . . . exposing, somehow, a febrile delight in Praeger's face . . . and Van Kips's hand moving under the table. He couldn't see what she was doing, but . . .

Van Kips had her hand on Praeger's cock. Was fondling him while the two of them watched the explosion.

They were that . . . what was the word? *Perverse? Demented? Inhuman?*

Efficient?

Yes. (Russ laughed bitterly.) Efficient. Extract the maximum from everything. Pleasure too.

And, Jesus forgive him, he was one of them. He was on their side.

And he had to be. Sure he did.

Or, anyway, he had to sit back and let it all happen. Try to get involved as little as possible.

But he remembered something his mother had said: "If you don't choose a side, the side will choose you."

The Island of Malta.

The ship is my best opportunity, Karakos thought.

The ship would have a stat-link to SA headquarters. In all the confusion, he could slip away from the other hijackers, get to the radio room.

Ten P.M., and they were in one of the top-floor bedrooms of the old manor house. An old, mildewy room, with peeling rose-patterned wallpaper, an empty wooden wardrobe standing open beside the wall's single decoration: a framed, yellowing photo of a droopy-mustached man standing in front of the Maltese capitol building in Valetta.

Eight guerrillas were seated in a semicircle around Steinfeld, shifting to ease the discomfort of the wooden seats as Steinfeld tapped the map, talked of currents, sea lanes, Soviet surveillance routes, the probability—or improbability— of interference from Soviet or NATO submarines, the temperature of the Mediterranean this time of year, and the projected route of the target ship.

"The ship will be coming from Malaga, on the coast of Spain, then east along the North African coast and through the Strait of Sicily, rounding Sicily on the eastern coast," Steinfeld had said. "It will be unescorted and without cannon, so as not to draw the attention of the Soviets, but it'll be accompanied by at least twenty-five SA infantrymen. They'll be heavily armed."

It wouldn't be easy for the NR to hijack the ship, Karakos thought. During the skirmishing there might be time to radio the location of the NR stronghold to Watson.

Doing it aboard the ship was risky. But he wasn't authorized to use the NR's radio, and there was always someone on radio watch. He'd decided against trying to get access to another shortwave elsewhere on Malta. Not practical. It didn't seem possible without drawing attention to himself. If he was caught wandering around the island alone, trying to locate a radio, they'd become suspicious. And there wasn't a phone he could use: the international telephone links had been destroyed by the Soviets, just before they pulled out of the area.

Karakos felt odd when he looked around the circle of faces. He felt . . . constricted. As if something were tugging in his brain and tightening in his throat.

But it was not as if he'd lost his resolve. Not at all. He knew that the only way to truly liberate Greece was to unite his homeland under a one-party nationalistic rule. Nothing else would render Greece strong enough to survive its endemic factionalism, the incursion of Communists, the predations of the Soviets and the Turks, the sedition of the Jews. And the only means to ensure a strong nationalist state in Greece was the Second Alliance. Watson had shown him by direct brain transferral—poured truth into his brain electronically and electrochemically—and it had been as if someone had turned on a light, blazing away the fog of ethical and political gray areas, leaving only the stark clarity of a single steely principle: "Strength is Security. And the SA gives strength."

But still . . .

Sitting here with the others—including Danco, who'd fought beside him in the first campaign against the SA (incredible now to suppose he'd actually fought his homeland's greatest benefactors!); the woman Lila, surely the finest woman soldier he'd ever met (impossible not to notice the way Lila was looking at this Claire Rimpler); Willow; and the others—the ghost of the old camaraderie made him tingle, made him shiver, just a little. It was as if his new conviction was an upright monolith of stainless steel in the expanse of his mind. But it was a haunted monolith. . . .

Steinfeld was talking about techniques for ducking the ship's radar, avoiding its infrared scans. But this man Hard Eyes was not listening, or was paying attention with only half his mind, for he was staring at Karakos.

The Yank suspects me, Karakos thought.

Karakos gazed back at Hard Eyes with wide-open, clear, guileless eyes, smiling like a big brother.

He could see Hard Eyes's jaw muscles clenching.

"The ship is the *Hermes' Grandson,*" Steinfeld was saying.

And Karakos thought, *It's a sign. The messenger of the gods will be my messenger to the SA.* . . .

And he must do something about the hijacking, of course. The *Hermes' Grandson* was carrying supplies of all kinds to the SA.

But it was a formidable weapon. It might be the wave of the future. He could not permit it to fall to the Resistance.

"Ship-assault training commences at 1600 tomorrow night," Steinfeld was saying, rolling up his charts.

The others were going out. Except Hard Eyes and Claire; Hard Eyes waited to talk to Steinfeld. "How about we assign Claire shore-correspondence duty for the assault on the ship," Hard Eyes was saying. Claire turned a glare at him. He ignored her. "I don't think she's ready to go back into combat just now. She's had too much too soon—"

"Who the hell do you think you are, Torrence?" Claire demanded.

"The question of Hard Eyes's personal sense of identity is moot," Steinfeld said dryly. "I had already decided that you are to do shore correspondence that night, Claire. Hard Eyes's suggestion was unnecessary. You've got good comm training, you'll be most useful there."

He tucked his satchel of charts under his arm and beat a hasty retreat, hurrying out into the hall.

Karakos pretended to follow. But he lingered in the hallway. He could hear very well from there; the door was not quite closed.

"Be realistic," Hard Eyes was saying. "You're sick of killing, Claire; you're not even sure the killing is the right thing to do. Those nightmares . . . when you're shaky like that, you risk the other people—"

"Torrence"—her voice wavered between outrage and tears—"I don't need you to tell me that I'm not ready for a mission right now. I know when I'm ready and when I'm not. And this stuff about risking other people is bullshit. *You're doing it to protect me.*"

"Come off it—"

"I know you, Hard Eyes." Saying his nickname with that sneering undertone that meant the name carried some sort of objectionable freight of machismo. "I know your condescending, paternalistic bullshit."

"That what you call caring about someone?"

That slowed her up for a moment. Two moments. But not three. "I'd be lying if I said I didn't want you to care about me. But I don't want you to make my decisions for me. You could at least have discussed it with me before going to Steinfeld."

"You're being childish. There's a chain of command here."

"Fuck that, it has nothing to do with you being a captain, you took it over my head because you like being in charge of me—"

"Fuck you, then," Hard Eyes said coldly, evenly. "Take care of yourself. You aren't going to like it."

He started through the door.

But Karakos had sensed that the argument was peaking. He was on his way down the stairs, thinking, *Maybe the girl Claire is the way.*

_____**SEVEN**

The New York City subways hadn't changed much. In 2021, they were still rackety, grimy, graffiti-ugly, plagued by aging equipment and vandalism. They were still under-maintained, due to the notorious laxity and greed of the Transit Workers Union; they were still dangerous.

Stoner was riding the subway that night for all those reasons.

The noise would cover their conversation; the danger and discomfort kept most potential eavesdroppers away.

But Stoner was worried. He was worried about the two guys he was meeting here. He could see them through the window in the door to the next car down, two men lurching

with the swaying of the rocketing train. The husky black guy
in the real-cloth gray suit was Stu Brummel, his wife's
brother (his terrorist brother-in-law, for God's sake!) He
could understand the suit; it went with Brummel's cover. He
was a lawyer. But did he have to wear something so expensive? Was that politically correct? The little Spanish guy in
the blue printout was the Nicaraguan, whom Stu referred to
only as Lopez. Stoner had found him in CIA Domestic files,
though: Carlos Lopez. He was a lieutenant in the SA. Lopez
was the son of the puppet government's Minister of Culture,
personally recruited by Crandall on the fourteenth anniver-
sary of the U.S. occupation of Nicaragua; six years later
Lopez had submitted a grievance to his SA superiors. He'd
complained that he'd been a lieutenant for six years, and he
felt his promotion to captain was being deliberately delayed
by someone. The filing agent had passed Lopez's grievance
off as the sour-grapes whine of an underachiever. Brummel
had told Stoner the rest: The NR had its SA moles. One of
them had come on Lopez's grievance. He let Lopez know
that he had been passed over simply because he was Hispanic. Despite all the SA's promises, none of the Hispanics
would become influential in the organization. There were a
few who seemed to have been promoted to higher offices.
But they were impotent figureheads.

The NR's mole cultivated Lopez's resentment and fanned
it into outright rebellion by letting Lopez in on the SA's
long-term plans for South America: complete subjugation.

Lopez was turned, had changed sides, but was kept in
place in the organization. Eventually he was transferred to
New York, where, ostensibly, he worked as an adviser on
SA Security Activity in the Latin ghetto. But his actual
function was to be an intelligence funnel for the New Resistance.

Brummel wasn't NR. He was a Maoist, and he considered
the NR politically tainted, suspect, to be contacted and used
only when necessary. Which is why he'd contemptuously
told Stoner too much about Lopez.

But, hell, Brummel could be up to anything. Maybe he
was going to deliver Stoner into the hands of men who'd
take Stoner hostage, demand money from the government
for his release. Maybe he was a cold motherfucker who'd

decided that his sister—who didn't approve of him, after all—had to be sacrificed for the revolution.

Maybe he was on the level. Maybe . . .

As the train roared around a turn in the tunnel, racing to meet the line of lights in the ceiling, Brummel and Lopez came into Stoner's car, looking around.

It was after midnight; they were alone.

They stood close together in the center of the cold, trash-strewn car, holding on to the grimy chrome stanchions, forced by the car's motion into an absurd, jerky dance, lurching to the percussion of the wheels, shouting to be heard; shouting what would get them arrested in other places.

Stoner looked at the two men and felt a long, slow, sickening wave of disorientation go through him. Something in him shrieked silently, *What am I doing?*

And he told himself, *I'm doing it for Janet. For Cindy. And because I have to survive.*

But still he felt like he was two men inside, and one of them hated the other one.

"You sweep your house again?" Brummel asked. His expression was always the same: sullen amusement.

Stoner nodded. "Found one in each room. And I've picked up a tail. Pretty sure I lost him today."

Lopez, a fox-faced man with shiny, short-clipped hair, small eyes, and a way of snapping his head around to look eagle-intensely at each man who was talking, said, "But—you are not completely sure?"

"Sure as anyone can be. Which means, not completely."

"You bring it?" Brummel asked.

Stoner snorted and shook his head. "I'm not going to hand files over to you guys till I know what I'm getting in return."

"How we know we trust you?" Lopez asked, smiling through it, raising both shoulders in an exaggerated shrug. "Could be you want to penetrate us. You could be a plant for CIA Domestic."

Brummel nodded. "Possibility exists."

Stoner gave Brummel a look of exasperated appeal, said, "Come on, I'm your sister's husband. She'd never set you up."

"But you might *use* her to set us up, man. Without her

knowing. Or you could be using extractors on her, twisting her mind around. CIA scumbags capable of anything."

Stoner hesitated. It seemed he had to give them something. . . .

Maybe he ought to blow this whole thing off. Grab Janet and Cindy, head out on his own somewhere.

Only, chances were, the Company would find him. He needed an underground route that someone had already set up.

The decision hovered on the edge of his will, just out of reach. And the lights on the train went out.

The three men ignored the blackout. The lights went out on the subways all the time. Light from outside strobed the windows as the train shot past the tunnel lamps, light flickering Brummel's face in and out of darkness. On, off; on, off; light, dark; trust and no trust; trust and no trust; on, off. . . .

Then the train's interior lights came back on.

And Stoner made up his mind. "I'll give you something that no plant would give you," Stoner said. "They've taken me off the SA/NR stuff, but I can still access the files on library console; I've still got top clearance. I'll get you something. . . ." But not his ace in the hole. He'd keep that back till he really needed it: the fact that there was an SA agent planted in the European NR. Someone close to Steinfeld himself. He'd hold on to that as a final bargaining chip. Maybe never have to tell them about it at all. It went against his grain, his years of training, to give them even an iota of classified stuff. And he was going to have to give them a hell of a lot more than an iota.

It made him feel sick inside all the time.

"You bring us something we can really use," Lopez said, "we get you out of the country, set you up good."

Stoner nodded. The train screeched into a station.

"We'll be in touch," Brummel said, turning toward the opening door.

But both doors leading out onto the platform were occupied. There were eight men standing in them, four in each. And there were knives in their hands.

Men? Almost men, mostly boys. Eight black teenage boys in fragments of military uniforms, bits and pieces stolen from servicemen on leave. Air Force flight jackets with NASA patches, Orbital Army patches, Naval Moonbase patches; fatigues, khakis, dress trousers incongruous with combat boots; goggles, diver's masks, Army-issue medinject units; Marine Corp ties worn as sashes. Helmets from five services; cunt caps and sailor's caps. One green beret. The tougher the service, the more prestige in taking the trophy off a serviceman. Stoner wondered what had happened to the men they'd taken the stuff from. Were they dead, crippled? Or did they take it off them while they slept off a drunk in a subway car?

As if choreographed—maybe they rehearsed it to scare you—the eight gang punks stepped left foot first, into the car. *Stomp*: Their boots came down together. The subway car hooted, and the doors closed behind them. The train began to move.

Stoner thought, *I'm stupid*.

He'd followed instructions, which meant he'd come unarmed, and it was going to end stupid. Caught up in a scheme to ditch CIA Domestic and you don't watch where you're going, you fall into bullshit like this. Like a man running cross-country from bloodhounds, looks over his shoulder, doesn't see he's blundering into a barbed-wire fence. Tangled, slashed, bled to death. *Stupid*.

The one in the green beret was brandishing his Navy Seabee knife. Blued seven-inch blade, leather-banded grip, iron end-knob. Bluing worn off the blade's razor edge, catching light where it had been recently honed; small nick four inches up the blade.

The details of the knife were forever imprinted in Stoner's mind.

Run? He glanced over his shoulder at the door into the next car.

"Forget it," Green Beret said. The knife in his hand waved in the air with a sawing motion imparted by the swaying of the car. The train hissed and grumbled and clacked.

Stoner said, "What we got, you can have. This is your turf and we respect that."

"Then why you bring this suck-ass nigger in the suit

whichoo?" Green Beret asked. His head was tilted a little to one side.

The other gang punks moved into an orderly semicircle around the three men.

"I don't like no suck-ass suit-nigger."

Stoner glanced at Brummel. Brummel was impassive. He wasn't going to bring up the Brotherhood. Rub them even more the wrong way with that. *Ohhhh, he's political, huh? Thinks he's more righteous than us, zat right, huh?*

"Take money," Lopez said, digging into his wallet.

"Money isn't enough," Green Beret said. His pupils were expanding, shrinking, expanding, shrinking, in waves. . . .

Which drug was it? Stoner wondered.

"Money onna outside, money onna inside," said a boy in goggles, holding up a polished surgical scalpel.

"Organs pay better," said a guy in a Marine Corps helmet, grinning. He held up a satchel clinking with jars.

The satchel was open, and Stoner could see the blue-tinged organs glistening in their preserving syrup.

Stoner felt cold and hollow, like he was a fire-gutted tree cooled to fragile ash. Kick it and it falls over, crumbles. Janet. Cindy.

And then a number of things happened too quickly.

The door to the next car banged open behind Stoner; someone back there pushed him aside and ran at the gang; someone else behind the first someone, following close, and Stoner saw them both as he fell back against the vibrating metal wall: two Second Alliance cops, hired by the Transit Authority to patrol the cars, both in armored suits of gray-black cloth—flat black, striated armor reminding Stoner of fencing vests—and mirrored helmets, RR sticks upraised, the one in the lead with his machine pistol out, amplified voice booming from his helmet: "YOUR CHOICE IS STOP WHERE YOU ARE OR DIE. I REPEAT, STOP OR WE SHOOT YOU SICK LITTLE ASSHOLES!"

The gang scattered, turned to run, one of them pulling a pistol, firing over his shoulder, the sound of the gunshot lost in the screech of the brakes as the train pulled into another station; the round catching the cop square in the chest but even at close range ricocheting from the armor, smacking through an ad in a ceiling panel that read, THE ONLY SECUR-

ITY IS FULL SECURITY: SAISC! The cop returning fire with a machine pistol spitting three-shot bursts, gang punk spinning and falling; another kid running, dropping the organ satchel, jars rolling, smashing, a kidney, a bladder, a heart, all nice and fresh, skidding nasty wet across the floor to slide into a heap of grimy paper and plastic cans, the organs becoming just more trash; the SA cop swinging the RR club down on the boy's head. Recoil Reversal stick splitting the kid's head open like a burst organ jar, his brains splashing the wall; Stoner gagging, kid crumpling, cop catching the others, firing at their backs, running after them into the next car as the train pulled up ... second cop cornering two other boys, smashing their faces into their cranial cavities ... bodies slumping, cop straightening over them ...

It was quiet for a moment as the train paused in the station ... and as the cop turned with bloodied club toward Stoner and Brummel and Lopez.

A faceless cop, his head hidden in the helmet; a distorted reflection of the interior of the subway car in its visor ...

Stoner got to his feet, turned to follow Lopez and Brummel toward the door. Lopez made it through, but Brummel had to stop when the cop pointed a machine pistol at him and boomed, *"Hold it, nigger, or you're dead!"*

Brummel said mildly, "I look like I'm a teenage kid wearing gang colors, officer?"

"YOU LOOK LIKE A NIGGER AND MAYBE YOU WAS HERE TO SELL 'EM DRUGS OR SOME SHIT. NOW TURN AROUND, PUT YOUR HANDS ON THE FUCKING WALL, OR YOU'RE DEAD!"

Stoner muttered, "So it's gone that far now. . . ."

"Yeah," Brummel said. "A long time ago."

"SHUT UP, NIGGER, AND FACE THE WALL, HANDS BEHIND YOU." With a practiced motion the cop used his free hand to replace his stick on his belt and unhook handcuffs from the belt, almost in the same motion, opening them for Brummel.

Stoner's heart was banging, his mouth papery, but he managed, "He's—he had nothing to do with them. He's a lawyer—"

The cop's enigma-chilled visor turned toward Stoner, the muzzle of his gun coming Stoner's way too. Stoner thought,

Oh, no, don't do it, Brummel! when he saw Brummel reach into his coat, draw the little gun. . . . It looked so small, like a cap gun, it couldn't possibly penetrate that armor, he was a fool. . . .

But then Brummel's gun hissed and a tiny hole appeared in the belly of the cop's black-armored outfit and Stoner thought, *Explosive bullet with armor-piercing Teflon coat.*

As the cop screamed, the gun in his hand spitting fire but the shots going wild, smashing out windows, the cop clutched at himself. And then his armored uniform ballooned outward, swelling in a split second to an almost spherical shape, grown five times bigger with his blood and the force of the explosion that was going off in his gut . . . blood spurting in a thin stream from the hole in the suit . . .

Stoner running behind Brummel, out of the car and up the stairs, thinking, again, *So it's gone that far.* . . .

A Suburb of Chicago, Illinois.

"First of all," the walleyed prizewinner said, "it's a feeling of power like you never had. I figure that's especially the case here, see, because it ain't like you're doing it in self-defense, or in a war where it's in a hurry—you got time to, you know, think about it first. . . ."

Spector was watching the walleyed guy on TV. The guy was tubby, was wearing a stenciled-on brown suit, one of the cheap JC Penney's printouts where the tie blurs into the shirt collar. And green rubber boots. Spector puzzled over the green rubber boots till he realized they were intended to look military.

A ghost image of another man's face, ragged-edged, began to slide over the AntiViolence Law winner's; the new face was bodiless, just a face zigzagging across the image with kitelike jerkiness. A punky face, a rocker; leering, laughing. His tag rippled by after his face like the tail after a comet: JEROME-X.

It was television graffiti, probably transmitted from a shoplifted minitranser. The year 2021's answer to spray paint.

Annoyed, Senator Spector hit the switch on his armchair,

turning off the TV. The broad, inch-thick screen slotted back into the ceiling. In a way, the program was his responsibility. He'd felt bound to take stock of it. But watching it, the gnawing feeling had begun in his stomach again.

Spector stood up and went to the full-length videomirror in his bedroom. It was time to get ready for the interview. He gazed critically at his fox face, his brittle blue eyes. His black crew cut was widow's-peaked to hint at minimono styles—to let the youngsters know he was hip, even at forty-five.

He wore a zebra-striped printout jumpsuit. It'll have to go, he decided. Too frivolous. He tapped the keyboard inset beside the mirror and changed his image. The videomirror used computer-generated imagery. He decided he needed a friendlier look. Add a little flesh to the cheeks; the hair a shade lighter. Earring? No. The jumpsuit, he told the mirror, would have to be changed to a leisure suit, but make its jacket stenciled for more identification with the average American. He'd never wear a stenciled suit out to dinner, but just now he needed to project a man-of-the-people image. Especially as the interviewer was from the under-Grid. Both Spector's Security adviser and his press secretary had advised him against giving an interview to an underground media rep. But the underGrid was growing, in size and influence, and it was wise to learn to manipulate it—use it, before it used you.

He tapped out the code for the suit, watching it appear in the mirror, superimposed over his jumpsuit. A cream-colored leisure suit. He pursed his lips, decided a two-tone combination would be friendlier. He taped the notched turtleneck to a soft umber.

Satisfied with the adjusted image, Spector hit the print button. He shed the jumpsuit and waited, wondering if Wendy had contacted his attorney, Heimlitz. He hoped she'd hold off on the divorce till after the election. The console hummed, and a slot opened beside the glass. The suit rolled out first: flat, folded, still pleasantly warm, smelling of chemicals from its fabrication. He pulled it on; it was high-quality fabricant, only slightly papery against his skin. He used Press Flesh for his cheeks, tamping and shaping till his face conformed with the image of a friendlier Senator Spector, the 'Flesh appearing to blend seamlessly with his skin. Cosmetics lightened his hair, widened his eyes a fraction. Then he went to look over the living room. Shook his head. The room was done in matte black and chrome. Too somber —he had to take great pains to avoid anything remotely morbid or sinister, because of the AntiViolence Laws issue. He dialed the curtains to light blue, the rug to match.

The console chimed. Spector sent to it and flicked for visual. The screen lit up with the expressionless face of the housing area's checkpoint guard. "What is it?" Spector asked.

"People here to see you in a van fulla video stuff. Two of them, name of Lerman and Baxter, from a cable channel called UNO. Citident numbers—"

"Never mind. I'm expecting them. Send 'em up."

"You don't want a visual check?"

"No! That would offend. And for God's sake, be friendly to them, if you know how. . . ."

He cut the screen, wondering if he was being cavalier about security. Maybe—but he kept a .44 in the cabinet beside the console, as a security backup. And there was always Kojo.

Spector rang for Kojo. The Japanese looked small, neat, harmless as Spector issued his instructions. Kojo's official title was secretary. He was actually a bodyguard.

Flawlessly gracious, Kojo ushered the two underGrid reps into the living room, then went to sit on a straight-backed chair to the left of the sofa. Kojo wore a blue printout typical of clerks. Sat with his hands folded in his lap; no tension, no warning in his posture, no hint of danger. Kojo had worked for Spector only two weeks, but Spector had seen the Security Agency's dossier on him. And Spector knew that Kojo could move from the bland aspect of a seated secretary to lethal attack posture in under a quarter of a second.

The "alternative programming" reporter wore "rags"—actual cloth clothing, jeans, T-shirt, scuffed black boots. Silly affectations, Spector thought. The interviewer introduced herself as Sonia Lerman. The big black guy, Baxter, was her techi. A silver earring dangling in his left ear; his head was shaved. Spector smiled and shook their hands, making eye contact. Feeling a chill when he met the girl's eyes. She was almost gaunt; her dark eyes were sunken, red-rimmed. Not a happy woman. Thin brown hair cut painfully short. But she and Baxter seemed neutral; not hostile, not friendly.

Spector glanced at Kojo. The bodyguard was relaxed but alert.

Take it easy, Spector told himself, sitting on the sofa beside Sonia Lerman. His body language, carefully arranged, read friendly but earnest; he smiled, just enough. Baxter set up cameras, mikes, fed them into the house comm system for transmission to the station.

The girl looked at Spector. Just looked at him.

It felt wrong. TV interviewers, even if they intended to feed your image to the piranhas during the interview itself, invariably maintained a front of friendliness before and after.

The silence pressed on him. Silence, the politician's enemy. Silence gave people time to think.

"Ready at your signal," Baxter said. He looked *big,* hulking over hand-sized cameras on delicate aluminum tripods.

"Now, what shall we talk about?" Spector asked before the cameras were rolling. "I thought perhaps—"

"Let's just launch into it," she broke in.

He blinked. "No prep?"

She smiled thinly. Baxter pointed at her. She looked at the camera. Serious. "I'm Sonia Lerman, for the People's Satellite, interviewing Senator Henry Spector, one of the key architects of the AntiViolence Laws and an advocate of the AVL television programming. . . ."

For a while the interview was standard. She asked him how he justified the AntiViolence Laws. Looking at her solemnly, speaking in an exaggeration of his Midwestern accent (the public found it reassuring), he gave his usual spiel: Violent crime began its alarming statistical growth trend in the 1960s, continued to mount in the 1970s, leveled out in the 1980s for a few years, and then feverishly resurged in the 1990s and . . . so on.

"The AntiViolence Laws are a heck of a deterrent," Spector said. "Violent crime is down sixty percent from five years ago. It continues to drop. In a few years the Security checkpoints and the other precautions that make modern life tedious—these may vanish entirely. Oh, yes, because of our sped-up judicial pace, a few people a year are perhaps unjustly convicted. But the majority of the people are better off, and it's the majority we must administrate for."

"Even accepting that people are better off," Sonia Lerman said, "which I don't, how does that justify the executioner's lottery, the AVL TV?"

"First, it's more deterrent. The humiliation and the awfulness of being executed on TV—well, if criminals see it every day, it scares them. Also, the program gets the public involved with the criminal justice system so that they identify with society and no longer feel at odds with policemen. And it acts as a healthy catharsis for the average person's hostility, which otherwise—"

"Which otherwise might be directed at the State in a revolution?" she cut in, her neutrality gone.

"No." He cleared his throat, controlling his irritation. "No, that's not—"

He was even more annoyed by her interruption, and her tone, when she broke in. "The phrase 'healthy catharsis' puzzles me. Lottery winners are winning the right to beat or execute a convict on public television. Ever watch the program *What It's Like,* Senator?"

"Well, yes, I watched it today to see if in fact—"

"Then you saw the way people behave. They giggle when they're getting ready to hang the convict. Or shoot them. They'll give out with a happy whoop. A man or a woman, gagged in stocks; the winner blows their brains out . . . and they cackle over it. And the more demented they are, the more the studio audience cheers them on. Now you call that *healthy*?"

Stung, he said, "It's temporary! The release of tension—"

"Two of the lottery winners were arrested, tried, and executed for *illegal* murders, *after* their participation in 'Anti-Violence' programming. It seems fairly obvious that they develop a permanent taste for killing, reinforced by public approval when they—"

"Those were flukes! I hardly think—"

"You hardly think about anything except what's convenient," she snapped, "because if you did, you'd have to see that you, Senator, are no better than a murderer yourself."

Her veneer of objectivity had cracked, fallen away. Her

voice shook with emotion. Her hands clenched her knees, knuckles white. He began to be afraid of her.

"I really think you've lost all, um . . . I don't think you're thinking about this calmly. You're hysterical." He said it as coolly as he could manage. But he felt fear turning to anger.

(Feeling, in fact, he was near losing his own veneer, his cool self-righteousness, feeling he was near snapping. And wondering why. Why had all the skills he'd developed in years of facing hostile interviewers suddenly evaporated? It was this fucking AVL issue. It haunted him. Nagged him. At night it ate away at his sleep like an acid . . . and the damned woman went on and on!)

"Everyone who has been killed, Senator—the innocent ones, at least—their blood is on your hands. You—"

Some inner membrane of restraint in Spector's consciousness flew into tatters, and anger uncoiled in him like a snapped mainspring, anger wound up by guilt. (Fuck the camera!) He stood, arms straight at his sides, trembling. Shouting. "Get out! Get *out*!"

He turned to Kojo, to tell him to "escort" them to the door . . . and saw Baxter stretching his right arm toward Kojo; in Baxter's hand was a small gray box like a garage-door opener. And Kojo had frozen, was staring into space in a kind of fugue state.

Spector thought, *Assassins*.

Kojo stood and turned toward Spector. Spector looked desperately around for a weapon.

Kojo came at him—

—and ran past him, at the woman. A wrist flick and he was holding a knife. She looked at him calmly, resignedly, and then she screamed as—his movements a blur—he closed with her, drove the slim silver blade through her left eye. And into her brain.

All the time Baxter continued filming, showing no surprise, no physical reaction. Spector gagged, seeing the spurt of blood from her eye socket as she crumpled. And Kojo stabbing her methodically, again and again. Spector stumbled back, fell onto the sofa.

"Kill Spector after me, Kojo!" Baxter yelled. Baxter turned a knob on the little gray remote-control box, dropped it—and the box melted into a lump of plastic slag. Spector stared, confused.

Baxter stepped into the TV cameras' viewing area, closed his eyes, was waiting, shaking, muttering a prayer that might have been Islamic—then Kojo rushed him, the small Japanese leaping at the big black man like a cat attacking a Doberman guard dog. Baxter just stood there and let Kojo slash out his throat with one impossibly swift and inhumanly precise movement.

Kill Spector after me, Kojo.

But Spector was moving, ran to the cabinet, flung it open, snatched up his .44, turned, and, borne on a wave of panic, shot Kojo in the back.

Kojo would have turned on Spector next, surely.

But in the pulsing silence that followed the gunshot, as Spector looked down at the three bodies, as he stared at the big, red oozing hole his bullet had torn in Kojo's back . . . seeing Kojo's own Press Flesh had come off, exposing the puckered white scar on the back of his head, a scar from recent brain surgery. . . .

Looking at that, Spector thought, *I've been set up.*

And the Security guards were pounding on the door.

"Today on *What It's Like* we're talking to Bill Mitchell, from Vendorville, Pennsylvania, the first man to participate in an actual *legal duel* with an AntiViolence Laws convict. Bill, you wanted to execute the man 'in a fair fight,' is that right?"

"That's right, Frank, I'm a former U.S. Marine, and I just didn't want to shoot the man down in cold blood, I wanted to give him a gun, and of course I'd have a gun, and we'd, you know, *go at it.*"

"Sort of an old-fashioned Wild West gunfight, eh? You're a brave man! I understand you had to sign a special waiver—"

"Oh, sure, I signed a waiver saying if I got hurt, the government couldn't be held responsible—"

"Bill, we're running out of time. Can you just tell us quickly what it was like for you, Bill Mitchell, to kill a man."

"Uh, sure, Frank—killing a man with a gun has its *me-*

chanical aspect, like, you got to punch a hole through the guy, and that causes damage to internal organs, so they're no longer workin', and of course loss of life-givin' blood. Now, what it *feels* like to do that—oh, boy. Well, you almost feel like the bullet is, you know, a part of you, like you can feel what it would feel, and like, you imagine the bullet nosing through the skin, pushing through muscles and smashin' through organs, bustin' bone, flyin' out the other side of 'im with all that red liquid . . . just blowing the bastard away. And it feels good knowing that he's a criminal, a killer, that *he deserved it*. And you feel a kinda funny *relief*—"

"Bill, that's all we've got time for now. Thanks for letting us know . . . *What It's Like!*"

The Chicago City Jail.

The cell they'd moved Spector to that morning was significantly smaller than the first one. And dirtier. And there was someone else in it, wearing a bloodstained prison shirt. The guy was asleep, his back turned, on the top bunk. The cell had two metal shelves that passed for bunks, extending from the smudged, white concrete wall, and a lidless, seatless toilet. They wouldn't tell him why he'd been moved, and now, looking around at his cell, Spector was beginning to suspect the reason, and with the suspicion came the stink of fear.

Don't panic, he told himself. *You're a United States senator. You've got friends, influence, and the strings sometimes take a while to let you know they've been pulled. The defense contractors and the Pentagon need you for that military appropriation bill. They'll see you through this.*

But the cell seemed to mock all reassurance. He looked around at the cracked walls; the water stain on the white concrete near the ceiling looking like a sweat stain on a T-shirt; the bars in place of a fourth wall, dun paint flaking off them. The graffiti burned into the ceiling with cigarette coals: "Julio-Z, 2017!!" and "Who-ever UR, yer ass is *Fucked*!!" and *"At lease* [sic] *you a TV star!! once!?!"*

Spector's stomach growled. Breakfast that morning had been a single egg on a piece of stale white bread.

His legs were going to sleep from sitting on the edge of the hard bunk. He got up, paced the width of the cell, five paces the long way, four the short.

He heard a metallic rasp and a clang: echoey footsteps in the stark spaces of the hallway. Trembling, he went to the bars. A middle-aged, seam-faced man wearing a stenciled three-piece suit, carrying a tan vinyl briefcase, was walking up behind the guard. He walked as if he were bone-tired.

The bored, portly black guard said, "Got to look in your satchel there, buddy." The stranger opened his briefcase, and the guard poked through it. "No machine guns or cannon in there," he said. A humorless joke. He unlocked the door, let the stranger in the cell. Locked it behind him and went away.

"Senator Spector," the man said, extending his hand. "I'm Gary Bergen." Bergen's hand was cold and moist in Spector's.

"You from Heimlitz's office? It's about time he—"

"I'm not from Heimlitz," Bergen said. "I'm a public defender." Spector stared at him. Bergen looked back with dull gray eyes. "Heimlitz is no longer representing you. They formally withdrew from the case."

Spector's mouth was dry. He sank onto the bunk. "Why?"

"Because your case is hopeless and your wife is in the process of seizing your assets, garnishing your bank account, and she refuses to pay an attorney."

Spector suspected that Bergen was taking some kind of quiet satisfaction in all this. He sensed that Bergen didn't like him.

Spector just sat there. Feeling like he was sitting on the edge of the Grand Canyon, and if he moved, even an inch, he'd slip and go over the edge and fall, and fall . . .

He conjured some motivation up from somewhere inside him and said, "Senator Burridge's committee will provide the money to—"

"The Committee to Defend Senator Henry Spector? It's been disbanded. Public opinion was overwhelmingly against them—and they had to think of their careers. Frankly, Senator, the public is howling for your blood. For the very reason that you are who you are. The public doesn't want to see any favorites played. And they're sure you're guilty."

"But how can anybody be sure of that? I haven't gone to trial, there's only been a hearing—and by now they should have screened the TV footage. That should've vindicated me."

"Oh, they've screened it, for the judge, and on television for the public. Everyone's seen it. They saw you holding that gray box, pointing it at your bodyguard, making him attack those people. A close-up on your face as you shouted, 'Kill them!' The autopsy on Kojo turned up the brain implant that made him respond to the prompter against his will . . . and we saw you pulling that gun, shooting your bodyguard in the back—to make it look as if he'd gone mad and you'd killed him to protect yourself." Bergen was enjoying this. "Too bad you didn't have time to get rid of the videotapes."

Spector was unable to speak. Finally he managed, "It's insane. Moronic. Why would I go to that much trouble to kill Sonia Lerman, a woman I didn't know—"

"Your wife says you were obsessed with her. That you watched Sonia's editorials and they incensed you. You babbled that Sonia deserved to die—and so forth." He shrugged.

"That's perjury! I never saw the Lerman woman, on TV or off, before that interview! My 'wife'. . ." He snorted. "God, I had no idea she hated me so much. Wendy's lying, so she'll get everything. The tapes. The tapes—they *can't* have shown me saying 'Kill them.' I didn't say it!"

Bergen nodded slowly. "It may surprise you to know that I believe you. But the tapes contradict you. Of course, they were at the UNO station for twenty-four hours before the police picked them up. The whole thing was transmitted from your place through your comm system to the UNO station and recorded there."

"They tampered with them!"

"Possibly. But try to get the judge to believe that . . ." And he smiled maliciously. "You'll have two minutes for that at the trial."

"The brain implant—whoever set me up had to have arranged that! We could trace Kojo's recent past, find out who his surgeon was when he—"

"Before your defense committee disbanded, they tried that

tack. Kojo had cerebral surgery just after you picked him out from the bodyguard portfolio at Witcher Security. He was to have an implant inserted to improve his speed and reflexes. The technicki who provides implants for the surgeons was contacted by someone over TV-fone. The man he saw on the screen offered to transfer fifty-thousand Newbux into the technickis' account if he'd consent to some unauthorized 'adjustments' to the implant. He consented, and the implant's 'adjustment' turned out to've been one of the army's attack-and-kill mind-control instruments. Remote-control. Experimental. But apparently it works."

The guard came back, waited impatiently. Desperately Spector said, "The man on the screen must've been—"

"It was *you*, Senator . . . the technicki recorded the transmission . . . it's pretty damning evidence. But I'll tell you what—" His voice creaked with mockery. "I'll see if I can get you off with a 'mercy execution.' You know, death by injection, sedative overdose. I think you'll prefer it to being clubbed to death on television. Well, good afternoon, Senator."

The guard opened the door, let Bergen out, locked up behind him, and Spector was alone.

Except for the guy climbing off the top bunk. The guy looking at Spector and chuckling. "Hey, Spector, man, that guy's really got a hard-on for you, you know? Public defender! Shit! Unless you get a Special Pardon—and I can't remember the last time anybody got one—you're fucked but good, man. Screwed royal. They ain't gonna give you special treatment just because you're a senator. That's the PR cornerstone of the AntiViolence Laws, man: *Everybody* gets screwed—equally."

He was a wiry little dude with a yellowed, gap-toothed smile, flinty black eyes, and the spiky color-shifting hair of a Chaosist. It was hard to get a real handle on what he looked like, though, because of the bruises, the swollen tissue, and crusted cuts on his face from the public beating. Still, he looked familiar.

"Jerome-X," Spector muttered, recognizing him. "Great."

Jerome-X gave that slightly brain-damaged chuckle again. He was pleased. "'at's me, my man. Yeah. Yeah. I got the hot trans 'n they know it up'n'down the freak-en-seize. I do some music too. I got a band now—shit, why not? I got the style. I got the name. I got—"

"You got *caught*—" Spector observed.

"Hey, pal—thas better'n bein' *set up*. You were right, man—sure as shit, they tampered with those tapes. Not editing, pal—image reconstitution. You're talking to the VideoMan Hisself. I *know*. Computer analyzes a TV image of a man, right? Gets him moving, talking. Then codes its analysis digitally. Samples it. An' generates an image of the guy you *can't tell* from the real thing. Uses, like, fractal geometry for realistic surface texture. And they can animate you to do whatever they want. Sample your voice, synthesize it to make you seem to've said whatever they want—"

"But that isn't—"

"Isn't *just*?" Jerome-X shook his head. "You're too much. I didn't think justice was high on your list of priorities, man. I seen you on TV, Spector—I know about you . . . hey, how many people who 'committed robbery' or 'murder' were people who were annoying to the local status quo or the feds—or the SA? Especially the SA. So they're video-framed. Convicted on the evidence of some security camera that just happened to be there . . . *ri-ight*. How many people died like that, pal, huh? Hundreds? Maybe thousands. About half the people convicted go down for videotaped evidence these days. That's a lot of lucky cameras. Sure, maybe if there were more time, you could prove the tampering—but *you*, big shot, you've seen to it you got *no time* and no chance for appeal. . . ."

"Videoframing . . . I don't believe it."

"Hey, you *better* believe it. But most people don't know about it, so it's no use tryin' to tell the courts. The up-to-dates on computer-generated images is kept under lock 'n' key. They want the public to think it's really crude, see . . . and all the people involved, the government, the networks, no one wants to believe anything like that about it because, hey—this thing is a *moneymaker*! People got all jaded about violence from the last few generations of TV and movies, right? So they need it in big doses now—and the ratings are great on these shows so the advertising revenues are orbital, just sky-high, so the government makes big bucks off heavy-taxing that revenue and the networks—you get what I mean. No one wants to rock the boat . . . fuck it . . . me, I'm gettin' out in the morning, already got my beatings for pirate transmissions, videograffiti . . . but you—they're gonna splash you all over the studio, pal. 'Cause you're the Case now. And you're Big Ratings. . . ."

New York City.

"What you say, Charlie boy?" Angelo tapped the table with his credit card, meaning he'd pay.

"No, it fucks me up. The next day I always feel like shit." They talked loud, and in Standard, to hear each other over the music.

"Come on, you're not gonna get hung up on it, you're not where you can get at it most of the time. Come on, I don't like to do Room alone. And this is the best fucking Room in New York, absolutely bar none, no shit."

"You're a big help, Angelo. You know that?"

Charlie Chesterton and Angelo were in a dark place that was splintered with light. The club was a Funkz place called Worldbeat, all its music neo-Worldbeat. On the stage, four nearly naked blacks and two Puerto Rican girls, all of them direct-wired to the muscle synthesizers, shimmied out a black sound that was something like sexy bagpipes and electric alto sax over salsa percussion; and the light came from behind the band, lasers and colored spots backlighting them, ricocheting from their sweat-shiny skin to dazzle the black ceiling, but lost in the deep dourness of the smoky club. Black walls, black floor. Sitting at a black table beside the black wall, under a painting done in shades of black; one side of Angelo's face in darkness, laser splashes psychedelicizing the other side.

Charlie and Angelo were playing a game that was like sexual coyness. It was drug coyness. Charlie wanted to score some Room, but he was scared to get started doing that again, knew it wasn't responsible to the NR. So he needed to be able to tell himself that Angelo had talked him into it. And Angelo sensed that. Angelo knew that the best way to get Charlie to do Room was to play to his guilt, cultivate his depression, hold something over him he'd need to get out from under. Saying, "Hey, it wasn't like it was your fault. It was Spector's. No one responsible but him. . . ." But just mentioning it was telling him the opposite. Because Charlie felt funny about his part in setting up Spector. You watch a guy for days, you get a little sympathy for him, whether he deserves it or not. And he'd done more than watch Spector, he'd filmed him from behind the two-way in the panel truck when he moved around in public. They'd checked out the stock footage of Spector talking to the public—but that wasn't much use, he was too much on his guard then, the computers were confused by Spector's projection of a public image. The stuff Charlie got when Spector was walking around, was arguing with his wife in that café—that one, especially—now all that, that was something Charlie and the others could work with. Build up a computer data template of realistic movement style, speech style, grist for the animation. . . .

"What you let it bother you for, Charlie? The guy's an asshole. A hypocrite, a Fascist. Not SA himself, but he plays ball with 'em all the time. The AntiViolence Laws were an SA project, man."

"Yeah, I know. I just hate the TV execution stuff so fucking much, it gets me so upset—and now we're slotting somebody into it. I know all the reasons to do it. But it still . . ." He shrugged. "And then Sonia. And Baxter. Kojo. Killed real nasty."

"Shit—Kojo was SA. Sonia and Baxter volunteered for that, no one talked 'em into it. Sonia tried to kill herself twice because Coochie got busted and snuffed on TV. You know Coochie? She was fucking out of her mind, anyway. And Baxter, he was, like, into fanatic martyrdom stuff."

"Yeah, but maybe we shouldn't've played along with their sick problems for this—"

"Otherwise they woulda been destroyed for nothin', without us. Look, you gotta get your mind off it. We do some Room, that'll take you right out of your head. And into the Hollow Head, right?" He grinned. "I mean, fuck it, right?"

Charlie played hard to get for a while longer. But finally he said, "Okay. I got to make a report to Smoke, and then . . . I'll meet you there."

The Chicago City Jail.

Sometimes it's possible to bribe a man with *promises* of money. And Spector used all his politician's skill to persuade the guard. *Get a message out, friend, and you'll be rewarded in a big way. I'm still a senator, right? In with the in crowd, right?* Wrong, but the guard didn't know it had gone that far.

Gave the guard a letter telling Burridge about the computer-generated evidence; and telling him to work on it *seriously*—or Spector'd press-release what he had on Burridge: the death of a girl named Judy Sorenson and just where she'd got the goodies she'd OD'd on.

Three days later, nine A.M., the guard came to Spector's clammy cell, passed him an ear-cap, winked, and left. Spector put the capsule in his ear, squeezed it, heard Burridge's voice: "Henry, there's a method of videotape analysis that'll tell us if what's on videotape was genuine or computer-generated. First we'll have to subpoena the tapes. Of course, as you've already been convicted, that'll be hard. But we're pulling some strings . . . we'll see if we can get your conviction overturned in the next day or so. A Special Pardon. In the meantime don't get panicky and mention that mutual friend of ours to anyone."

But a week later Spector was being prepped for his execution. He sat on a bench, chained to five other convicts, listening to the prison's TV program director, Sparks.

The videotechs called Sparks "the animal handler." He was stocky, red-faced, with a taut smile and blank gray eyes. He wore a rumpled blue real-cloth suit. The guards stood at either end of the narrow room, tubular stun-guns in hand.

"Today we got a man won an execution-by-combat," Sparks was saying. "An EBC is more dignified than the execution in stocks, so you fellas should be glad of that much, anyway. You'll be given a gun, but of course it's loaded with blanks."

And then the chain connecting Spector's handcuffs to the man on his right jerked Spector half out of his seat as the small black guy on the other end of the bench lost it, just lost it completely, ran at Sparks screaming something in a heavy West Indian accent, something Spector couldn't make out. But the raw substance of it, the subverbal message in the guy's voice—that alone spoke for him. It said, *Injustice! Innocence!* and it said, *I've got a family!* And then it could say nothing more because the stun-guns had turned off his brain for a while and he lay splayed like a dark rag doll on the concrete floor. The guards propped him up on the bench, and Sparks went on as if nothing had happened. "Now we got to talk about your cues, it'll be a lot worse for you if your forget your cues. . . ."

Spector wasn't listening. A terrible feeling had him in its grip, and it was a far worse feeling than fear for his life.

At home—the condo his wife had sold by now—he'd opened his front door with a sonic key. It sang out three shrill tones, three precise notes at precise intervals, and the door heard and analyzed the tonal code and the interval code, and opened. And the voice of the man who'd tried to fight, the small, dark man . . . his voice, his three shrieks, had opened a door in Spector's mind. Let something out. Something he'd fought for weeks to lock away. Something he'd argued with, silently shouted at, again and again.

He'd pushed for the AntiViolence Laws for the same reason that Joe McCarthy, in the last century, had railed at Communism. It was a ticket. A ticket to a vehicle he could ride through the polls and into office. Inflame their fear of crime. Cultivate their lust for vengeance. Titillate their own repressed desire to do violence. And they vote for you.

And he hadn't given a rat's-ass goddamn about the crime problem. The issue was a path to power, and nothing more.

He'd known, somewhere inside himself, that a lot of the condemned were probably being railroaded. But he'd looked away, again and again. Now somebody had made it impossible for him to look away. Now the guilt that had festered in him erupted into full-blown infection, and he burned with the fever of self-hatred.

That's when Bergen came in. Bergen spoke to the guards, showed them a paper; the guards came and whispered to Sparks. And Sparks, annoyed at the disruption in his scheduling, unlocked Spector's cuffs. Glumly Bergen said,

"Come with me, Mr. Spector." He was no longer Senator Spector.

They went to stand in the hallway; a guard came along, yawning, leaning against the wall, watching a soap on his pocket TV. Voice icy, Bergen said, "I have an order to take you back to your cell, pending a reopening of your case. You're going to get off. A Special Pardon. Rare as hen's teeth. Burridge has proof the tapes were tampered with. It hasn't been made public yet, and in fact, the judge who presided at your trial is out of town, so Burridge arranged a temporary restraining—"

"Why is it you sound disappointed, Bergen?" Spector interrupted, watching Bergen's face closely. When Bergen didn't answer, Spector said, "You did everything you could to sabotage my defense. You were with them, whoever it was. Whoever set me up. I can feel it. Who was it?" Bergen stared sullenly at him. "Come on—who *was* it? And why?"

Bergen glanced at the guard. The guard was absorbed by the soap opera; tiny television figures in his palm flickered through a miniature choreography of petty conflicts. Bergen took a deep breath and looked Spector in the eyes. "Okay. I don't care anymore... I *want* you to know. Sonia, Baxter and I—we're part of the same... organization. Sonia did it because her lover, a girl she'd lived with for eight years, was videoframed. She was very dependent on her. Baxter did it because he was part of another organization too: the Black Freedom Brotherhood—they lost their top four officers to an SA videoframe-up. Me, I did it—I planned the whole damn thing because I saw one too many innocent people die. We thought if you, a senator, were videoframed, condemned, publicly *killed*, afterward we'd release the truth, we'd clear you, and that'd focus public attention on the issue. Force an investigation. And something else—vengeance. Simple revenge. We held you responsible. For all those victims."

Spector nodded like something mechanical. Said softly, "Oh, yes. I am responsible... and now I'm going to get off. I'll go free. And it'll be blamed on your people, your organization. They'll say it was an isolated incident, the only incident of videoframe-up. They'll pressure me to shut up about it. And once I was on the outside, where things are comfortable, I probably would."

And the realization came at him like an onrushing wall of darkness; it fell on him like a tidal wave: *How many innocent people died for my ambition? A thousand? Two thousand?*

"Yes," Bergen muttered. "Congratulations, Spector, you son of a bitch. Sonia and Baxter sacrificed themselves for *nothing*—" His voice broke. He went on, visibly straining for control. "You're going free...."

But the gnawing thing in Spector wouldn't let him go free. And he knew it would never let him go. Never. (Though some part of him said, *Don't do it! Survive!* But that part of him was broken, could speak only in a raspy whimper, as the other part said, aloud,) "Bergen—wait. Go to Burridge. Tell him you know all about the Sorenson incident. Repeat it back to me."

"The Sorenson incident. What—"

"Wait. And tell him you'll release what you know about her, about Sorenson, if he tells anyone about those tapes before tomorrow. Tell him this came from me. He'll stay quiet."

"But the restraining order—"

"Tear it up. And come with me—you've got to explain to Sparks that your paperwork was wrong. That you were mistaken about something . . ."

Spector walked out onto the stage. Glanced at the cameras and the studio audience beyond the bulletproof glass. Pointed the pistol loaded with blanks at the grinning man in the cowboy hat at the other end of the stage and walked toward him, toward the big gun in the man's hand. Walking up to a gun that was loaded with real bullets. Spector smiling softly, thinking, *This is the only way I'll ever go free....*

New York City.

Charlie'd say, "I'm into it once or twice—but you, you got a jones for it, man." And Angelo'd snicker and say, "Gives my life purpose, man. Gives my life direction."

You could smell the place, the Hollow Head, from two blocks away. Anyway, you could if you were strung out on it. The other people on the street probably couldn't make out the smell from the background of monoxides, the broken-battery smell of acid rain, the itch of syntharette smoke, the oily rot of the river. But a user could pick out that tease of amyl tryptaline, thinking, *Find it like a needle in a haystack.* And he'd snort, and then go reverent-serious, thinking about the needle in question . . . the needle in the nipple . . .

It was on East 121st Street, a half block from the East River. If you stagger out of the place at night, you'd better find your way to the lighted end of the street fast, because the leeches crawled out of the river after dark, slug-creeping up the walls and onto the cornices of the old buildings; they sensed your body heat, and an eight-inch ugly brute lamprey thing could fall from the roof, hit your neck with a wet *slap;* inject you with paralyzing toxins, you fall over, and its leech cronies come, drain you dry.

When Charlie turned onto the street, it was just sunset; the leeches weren't out of the river yet, but Charlie scanned the rooftops, anyway. Clustered along the rooftops were the shanties.

New York's housing shortage was worse then ever. After the Dissolve Depression, most of the Wall Street firms moved to Tokyo or the floating city, Freezone. The boom in Manhattan deflated; the city couldn't afford to maintain itself. It began to rot. But still the immigrants came, swarming to the mecca of disenchantment till New York became another Mexico City, ringed and overgrown with shanties, shacks of clapboard, tin, cardboard protected with flattened cans and plastic wrappers; every tenement rooftop in Manhattan mazed with squalid shanties, sometimes shanties on shanties till the weight collapsed the roofs and the old buildings caved in, the crushed squatters simply left dying in the rubble—firemen and emergency teams rarely set foot outside the sentried, walled-in havens of the midtown class.

Charlie was almost there. It was a mean motherfucker of a neighborhood, which is why he had the knife in his boot sheath. But what scared him was the Place. Doing some Room at the Place. The Hollow Head. His heart was pumping and he was shaky, but he wasn't sure if it was from fear or anticipation or if, with the Hollow Head, you could tell those two apart. But to keep his nerve up, he had to look away from the Place as he got near it; tried to focus on the rest of the street. Some dumbfuck pollyanna had planted saplings in the sidewalk, in the squares of exposed dirt where the original trees had stood. But the acid rain had chewed the leaves and twigs away; what was left was as stark as TV antennas. Torchglow from the roofs; and a mélange of noises that seemed to ooze down like something greasy from an overflowing pot. Smells of tarry wood burning; dog-food smells of cheap, canned-food cooking. And then he was standing in front of the Hollow Head. A soot-blackened town house, its Victorian facade of cherubim recarved by acid rain into dainty gargoyles. The windows bricked over, the stone between them streaked gray on black from acid erosion.

The building to the right was hunchbacked with shacks; the roof to the left glowed from oil-barrel fires. But the roof of the Hollow Head was dark and flat, somehow regal in its sinister austerity. No one shacked on the Hollow Head.

He took a deep breath and told himself, "Don't hurry through it, savor it this time," and went in. Hoping that Angelo had waited for him.

Up to the door, wait while the camera scanned you. The camera taking in Charlie Chesterton's triple mohawk, each fin a different color; Charlie's gaunt face, spiked transplas jacket, and customized mirrorshades. He heard the tone telling him the door had unlocked. He opened it, smelled the amyl tryptaline, felt his bowels contract with suppressed excitement. Down a red-lit hallway, thick black paint on the walls, the turpentine smell of AT getting stronger. Angelo wasn't there; he'd gone upstairs already. Charlie hoped Ange could handle it alone. The girl in the banker's window at the end of the hall—the girl wearing the ski mask, the girl with the sarcastic receptionist's lilt in her voice—took his card, gave him the Bone Music receptor, credded him in. Another tone, admission to Door Seven, the first level. He walked down to seven, turned the knob, stepped through, and felt it immediately; the tingle, the rush of alertness, the chemically induced sense of belonging, four pleasurable sensations rolling through him and coalescing. It was just an empty room with the stairs at the farther end; soft pink lighting, the usual cryptic palimpsest of graffiti on the walls.

He inhaled deeply, felt the amyl tryptaline go to work almost immediately; the pink glow intensified; the edges of the room softened, he heard his own heartbeat like a distant beat-box. A barbed wisp of anxiety twined his spine (wondering, *Where's Angelo, he's usually hanging in the first room, scared to go to the second alone, well, shit, good riddance*), and he experienced a paralytic seizure of sheer sensation. The Bone Music receptor was digging into his palm; he wiped the sweat from it and attached it to the sound wire extruding from the bone back of his left ear—and the music shivered into him. It was music you *felt* more than heard; his acoustic nerve picked up the thudding beat, the bass, a distorted veneer of the synthesizer. But most of the music was routed through the bone of his skull, conducted down through the spinal column, the other bones. It was a music of shivery sensations, like a funny-bone sensation, sickness sensations, chills and hot flashes like influenza, but it was a sickness that caressed, viruses licking at your privates, and you wanted to cum and throw up at the same time. He'd seen deaf people dancing at rock concerts; they could feel the vibrations from the loud music; could feel the music they couldn't hear. It was like that but with a deep, deep humping brutality, like having sex with an obviously syphilitic whore and enjoying it more because you knew she was diseased. The music shivered him from his paralysis, nudged him forward. He climbed the stairs.

Bone Music reception improved as he climbed, so he could make out the lyrics, Jerome-X's gristly voice singing from inside Charlie's skull:

Six kinds of darkness
Spilling down over me
Six kinds of darkness
Sticky with energy.

Charlie got to the next landing, stepped into the second room.

Second room used electric field stimulation of nerve ends; the metal grids on the wall transmitting signals that stimulated the neurons, initiating pleasurable nerve impulses; other signals were sent directly to the dorsal area in the hypothalamus, resonating in the brain's pleasure center.

Charlie cried out and fell to his knees in the infantile purity of his gratitude. The room glowed with benevolence; the barren, dirty room with its semen-stained walls, cracked ceilings, naked red bulb on a fraying wire. As always, he had to fight himself to keep from licking the walls, the floors. He was a fetishist for this room, for its splintering wooden floors, the mathematical absolutism of the grid patterns in the gray-metal transmitters set into the wall. Turn off those transmitters and the room was shabby, even ugly, and pervaded with stench; with the transmitters on, it seemed subtly intricate, starkly sexy, bondage gear in the form of interior decoration, and the smell was a ribald delight.

(For the Hollow Head was drug paraphernalia you could walk into. The building itself was the syringe, or the hookah, or the sniff-tube.)

And then the room's second phase cut in: the transmitters stimulated the motor cortex, the reticular formation in the brainstem, the nerve pathways of the extrapyramidal system, in precise patterns computer-formulated to mesh with the ongoing Bone Music. Making him dance. Dance across the room, feeling he was caught in a choreographed whirlwind (flashing: genitals interlocking, pumping, male and female, male and male, female and female, tongues and cocks and fingers pushing into pink bifurcations, contorting purposefully to guide between fleshy globes, the thrusting a heavy downhill flow like an emission of igneous mud, but firm pink mud, the bodies rounded off, headless, Magritte torsos going end to end together, organs blindly nosing into the wet receptacles of otherness), semen trickling down his legs inside his pants, dancing, helplessly dancing, thinking it was a delicious epilepsy, as he was marionetted up the stairs, to the next floor, the final room. . . .

At the landing just before the third room, the transmitters cut off, and Charlie sagged, gasping, clutching for the banister, the black-painted walls reeling around him. He gulped air and prayed for the strength to turn away from the third room, because he knew it would leave him fried; yeah, badly crashed and deeply burned out. He turned off the receptor for a respite of quiet. In that moment of weariness and self-doubt he found himself wondering where Angelo was. Had Angelo really gone on to the third room alone? Ange was prone to identity crises under the Nipple Needle. If he'd gone alone—little Angelo Demario with his rockabilly hair and spurious pugnacity—Angelo would sink and lose it completely . . . and what would they do with people who were overdosed on an identity hit? Dump the body in the river, he supposed.

He heard a yell mingling ecstasy and horror coming from an adjacent room, as another Head customer took a nipple. That made up his mind: like seeing someone eat making you realize you're hungry. He gathered together the tatters of his energy, switched on his receptor, and went through the door.

The Bone Music shuddered through him, strong now that he was undercut, weakened by the first rooms. Nausea wallowed through him.

The darkness of the Arctic, two months into the night Darkness of the Eclipse, forgetting of all light.

Angelo wasn't in the room, and Charlie was selfishly glad as he took off his jacket, rolled up his left sleeve, approached the black rubber nipple protruding from the metal breast at waist height on the wall. As he stepped up to it, pressed the hollow of his elbow against the nipple, felt the computer-guided needle probe for his mainline and fire the ID drug into him.

The genetic and neurochemical essence of a woman. They claimed it was synthesized. He didn't give an angel's winged asshole where it came from, right then; it was rushing through him in majestic waves of titanic intimacy. You could taste her, smell her, feel what it felt like to be her (they said it was an imaginary her, modeled on someone real, not really from a person).

Felt the shape of her personality superimposed on you, so for the first time you weren't burdened with your own identity, you could find oblivion in someone else, like identifying with a fictional protagonist but infinitely more real. . . .

But oh, shit. It wasn't a *her*. It was a *him*. And Charlie knew instantly that it was Angelo. They had shot him up with Angelo's distilled neurochemistry—his personality, memory, despairs, and burning urges. He saw himself in flashes as Angelo had seen him . . . and he knew, too, that this was no synthesis, that he'd found out what they did with those who died here, who blundered and OD'd: they dropped them in some vat, broke them down, distilled them, and molecularly linked them with the synthcoke and shot them into other customers . . . into Charlie . . .

He couldn't hear himself scream over the Bone Music (*Darkness of an iron cask, lid down and bolted tight*). He didn't remember running for the exit stairs. (*And three more kinds of darkness, three I cannot tell*), down the hall (*Making six kinds of darkness, Lord, please make me well*), out into the street, running, hearing the laughter from the shantyrats on the roofs watching him go.

He and Angelo running down the street, in one body. As Charlie told himself, *I'm kicking this thing. It's over. I shot up my best friend. I'm through with it.*

Hoping to God it was true. *Lord, please make me well.*

Bottles swished down from the rooftops and smashed to either side of him. And he kept running.

He felt strange. He felt strange as all hell.

He could feel his body. Not like usual. He could feel it like it was a weight on him, like an attachment. Not the weight of fatigue—he felt too damn eerie to feel tired—but a weight of sheer alienness. He was too big. It was all awkward, and its metabolism was pitched too low, sluggish, and it was . . .

It was the way his body felt for Angelo.

Angelo wasn't there, in him. But then again he was. And Charlie felt Angelo as a nastily foreign, squeaky, distortion membrane between him and the world around him.

He passed someone on the street, saw them distorted through the membrane, their faces funhouse-mirror twisted as they looked at him—and they looked startled.

The strange feelings must show on his face. And in his frantic running.

Maybe they could see Angelo. Maybe Angelo was oozing out of him, out of his face. He could feel it. Yeah. He could feel Angelo bleeding from his pores, dripping from his nose, creeping from his ass.

A sonic splash of: *Gidgy, you wanna do a video hook-up with me?* Gidgy replying, *No, that shit's grotty, Ange, last time we did that I was sick for two days I don't like pictures pushed into my brain couldn't we just have, you know, sex?* (She touches his arm.)

God, I'm gonna lose myself in Angelo, Charlie thought. Gotta run, sweat him out of me.

Splash of: *Angelo, if you keep going around with those people, the police or those SA people are going to break your stupid head.* Angelo's voice: *Ma, get off it, you don't understand what's going on, the country's getting scared, they think there's gonna be nuclear war, everyone's lining up to kiss the Presidential Ass cause they think she's all that stands between us and the fucking Russians—* His mother's voice: *Angelo, don't use that language in front of your sister, not everyone talks like they do on TV—*

Too heavy, body's too heavy, his run is funny, can't run anymore, but I gotta sweat him out—

Flash pictures to go with the splash voices now: *Motion-rollicking shot of sidewalk seen from a car window as they drive through a private-cop zone, SA bulls in mirror helmets walking along in twos in this high-rent neighborhood, turning their glassy-blank assumption of your guilt toward the car, the world revolves as the car turns a corner, they come to a checkpoint, the new Federal ID cards are demanded, shown, they get through, feeling of relief, there isn't a call out on them yet . . . blur of images, then focus on a face walking up to the car. Charlie Chesterton. Long, skinny, goofy-looking guy, self-serious expression. . . .*

Jesus, Charlie thought, is *that* what Angelo thinks I look like? Shit! (Angelo is dead, man, Angelo is . . . is oozing out of him . . .)

Feeling sick now, stopping to gag, look around confusedly. Oh, fuck: Two cops were coming toward him. Regular cops, no helmets, wearing blue slickers, plastic covers on their cop-caps, their big ugly cop-faces hanging out so he wished they wore the helmets, supercilious faces, young but ugly, their heads shaking in disgust, one of them said: "What drug you on, man?"

He tried to talk, but a tumble of words came out, some his

and some Angelo's, it was like his mouth was brimming over with small, restless, furry animals: Angelo's words.

The cops knew what it was. They knew it when they heard it.

One cop said to the other (as he took out the handcuffs, and Charlie had become a retching machine, unable to run or fight or argue because all he could do was retch), "Jeez, it makes me sick when I think about it. People shooting up some of somebody else's brains. Don't it make you sick?"

"Yeah. Looks like it makes him sick too. Let's take him to the chute, send him down for the blood test."

He felt the snakebite of cuffs, felt them do a perfunctory body search, missing the knife in the boot. Felt himself shoved along to the police kiosk on the corner, the new prisoner-transferral chutes. They put you in something like a coffin (they pushed him into a greasy, sweat-stinking, inadequately padded personnel capsule, closed the lid on him, he wondered what happened—as they closed the lid on him—if he got stuck in the chutes, were there air holes, would he suffocate?), and they push it down into the chute inside the kiosk and it gets sucked along this big underground tube (he had a sensation of falling, then felt the tug of inertia, the horror of being trapped in here with Angelo, not enough room for the two of them, seeing a flash mental image of Angelo's rotting corpse in here with him, Angelo was dead, Angelo was dead) to the police station. The cops' street report clipped to the capsule. The other cops read the report, take you out (a creak, the lid opened, blessed fresh air even if it was the police station), take everything from you, check your DNA print against their files, make you sign some things, lock you up just like that . . . that's what he was in for right away. And then maybe a public AntiViolence Law beating. Ironic.

Charlie looked up at a bored cop-face, an older, fat one this time. The cop looked away, fussing with the report, not bothering to take Charlie out of the capsule. There was more room to maneuver now, and Charlie felt like he was going to rip apart from Angelo's being in there with him if he didn't get out of the cuffs, out of the capsule. So he brought his knees up to his chest, worked the cuffs around his feet, it hurt . . . but he did it, got his hands in front of him.

Flash of Angelo's memory: *A big cop leaning over him, shouting at him, picking him up by the neck, shaking him. Fingers on his throat . . .*

When Angelo was a kid, some cop had caught him running out of a store with something he'd ripped off. So the cop roughed him up, scared the shit out of Angelo, literally: Angelo shit his pants. The cop reacted in disgust (the look of disgust on the two cops' faces: "Makes me sick," one of them had said).

So Angelo hated cops, and now Angelo was out of his right mind—ha ha, he was in Charlie's—and so it was Angelo who reached down and found the boot knife that the two cops had missed, pulled it out, got to his knees in the capsule as the cop turned around (Charlie fighting for control—dammit, Ange, put down the knife, we could get out of this with—) and Charlie—no, it was Angelo—gripped the knife in both hands and stabbed the guy in his fat neck, split that sickening fat neck open, cop's blood is as red as anyone's, looks like . . .

Oh, shit. Oh, no.

Here come the other cops.

The Island of Malta.

Same night, another time zone, another variety of darkness.

Hard Eyes walked through a vast, wind-scoured darkness, unable to see his feet or his hands in front of his face, guided only by the distant swatch of light ahead of him.

It was near dawn in Malta. Hard Eyes had just gone off watch on the approach road to the safe house. Danco, yawning and cursing, had replaced him, was making himself ersatz espresso in the little shack by the dirt road.

A cold wind blew the rich scent of the sea from the coast, a quarter of a mile south. Sounds seemed eerily detached and lucid out here. He could make out the smack and rumble of breakers over the soughing wind; his rifle clanked softly on its shoulder strap; his booted feet made grumpy, trudging sounds.

He felt as if none of it had anything to do with him. At

any moment the wind might blow his soul right out of his body.

He was glad when he reached the barn. He walked blinking into the barn's interior light. Two choppers sat there, looking glassy and bulbous and out of place, as foreign to the dusty wooden walls as flying saucers, their blades folded back on hinges overhead. Hard Eyes nodded at the guard lounging in the cockpit of the compact chopper by the stairs. The Italian, Forsino, an old-fashioned long-hair, a hipz in Stateside terms, looking put upon and bored.

Hard Eyes took the open stairs up to the dusty attic, hearing the old wooden barn creak in the wind, wondering if tonight was the night it would fall over.

Lila was on the radio in the attic, monitoring the military bands and anything else she found of intelligence interest, keeping a frequency open for communications from Witcher and the NR's affiliate groups. Wires ran to the next room— an old olive storage bin—where sat-link antennas, looking like miniature radar scoops, angled out an open window, listening to the babbling emptiness. . . .

An old electric light bulb burned naked in a white porcelain socket overhead; moths ticked at it, and it dimmed now and then when the wind blew particularly hard. Wearing a headset, Lila was seated at a table piled with a lot of arcane metal boxes that looked as out of place as the choppers in the rustic backdrop.

Lila was clear-eyed and alert, evidently ready for anything, even at this hour. She was so efficient it was maddening, Hard Eyes thought. She took off the headset and looked at Hard Eyes questioningly.

"I thought Claire was on tonight," Hard Eyes said.

Was there a flash of displeasure in her face? "I have relieved her. An hour ago."

"Nice of you to relieve her early."

Lila said nothing. She seemed to be studying the dust-heavy cobwebs shaking from wind vibrations.

"Hear anything interesting?" Hard Eyes asked, nodding toward the radio.

She shook her head.

He turned away, hesitated, then turned back to her. "Was she here alone, when she was on duty?"

Lila didn't reply for a full three beats. She looked at him blankly and said, "Karakos. He was here talking to her when I came."

Hard Eyes felt a chill. He went to the table, flipped open the comm log, looked down the list of dispatches, messages received and sent for the week . . . nothing at all for that day. "Karakos didn't transmit?"

"No."

"You sure?"

"Any transmission has to have written clearance from Steinfeld. Claire would not have let anyone use the radio without clearance. There are only four people cleared to do comm duty, and Karakos is not one of them. Claire knows that." A touch defensive on Claire's behalf.

"What did Karakos want here?"

"Probably couldn't sleep, wanted someone to talk to. How am I to know?"

"Okay." He turned away. She seemed hostile to him, in a subdued way. Why?

He went down the creaking stairs, dust rising with his every step, thinking hard, wondering if his feeling about Karakos was simply jealousy. *Or is it what I think?*

In forty-eight hours they'd hijack the *Hermes' Grandson*. Karakos was to go along.

He stepped into the windy night, crossed to the house, called out the password at the back door. Someone shined a flashlight in his face. He blinked irritably till they were sure of him, and went into the house. It was quiet; most of the others were asleep. But there was a steady creaking noise from upstairs.

Moving on sheer impulse, not thinking, borne along by some inner charge of urgency, he climbed the stairs, went to Claire's room—since their argument, she'd taken her own room. He knocked once, and before she'd finished calling out, "Who is it?" he opened the door and went in.

She and Karakos, in bed, a candle fluttering romantically in a draft from the door. The two of them naked in the soft golden light.

Somehow it was the candle that hurt most.

"It won't be tonight, Karakos," he heard himself say, "but

next time she's on the radio, that's when you'll talk her into letting you take it over for a while, right? That it?"

"I'm surprised it's the radio that's on your mind," Karakos said with a small laugh. "But what about it?"

"Torrence, get out of here." Claire's voice was flat, dead.

He looked at her. A dozen bitter remarks rose up in him, vying for his voice, but all he said was, "Okay. Sure."

He left, seared inside, thinking, Just jealousy? Just jealousy? Just jealousy? Just jealousy?

As soon as it was light, he carried his rifle to the beach for target practice.

Eight

The Space Colony. Bitchie's After.

Kitty Torrence was squatting with her back against the wall, in Bitchie's After. The room was dimly lit at her end, brighter at the other where the meeting was going on. The walls were metal, patchy with posters, faded pornography, and stitched with graffiti. Bitchie's was an illegal after-hours club, in a double-unit that also functioned as a brothel on certain days. The back room was thirty feet by twenty, the floor space taken up by foam-rubber mattresses. She would have liked to lie down. Not here, though. The mattresses stank; she was careful not to touch them with anything but the bottom of her shoes. She wished they'd pick another place to meet—but Bitchie's was one of the few places Chester's loose organization of radics felt safe. Admin tolerated Bitchie's as a brothel; they didn't suspect it as a meeting place for reformists.

Chester and the new NR Rep and Hasid Shood and Ben

Vreeland were sitting cross-legged in a circle, talking. Kitty could have taken part, but she felt like hanging back, staying out of it. She got upset when she took part in the meetings. Chu, the NR rep, was a serious, brittle-mannered Chinese woman in a dull blue Pilot's Aide jumpsuit. Short, glossy black hair, no makeup, a single silver hoop earring. She carried a blue canvas pouch on a shoulder strap, zipped half shut, and she kept her right hand always on it. Somehow the pouch made Kitty nervous.

"If we call for an investigation, as a group," Chu said dolefully, "we'll tip our hand; they'll know about us a group. If we demand an investigation as individuals, they'll know about us as individuals."

"They already know about us—as individuals," Chester said. "Russ Parker called me in. They been watching me."

"They know about you, and maybe about Shood, but probably they don't know about Vreeland yet, or about me. I have been very, very careful." Her voice was almost a monotone. But there was an underlying intensity that kept Kitty's attention riveted when the woman talked.

"I dunno," Vreeland said. "I don't think they got me ID'd. Unless maybe because Sonny was my brother... I dint get involved in nothing before now." He was a great chunk of a man, short-legged but thick, wide-shouldered. He wore a ship tech's white jumpsuit, grease-stained with insulation fluid, and a flattop crew cut divided into three technicki signification colors for his earth-home, profession, and seniority. He spoke Standard badly and laboriously. His brother had died on RM17.

"It takes not long," Shood said. "They will identify us eventually. Me they maybe know, for Silla was very much loud in the Union...." He swallowed hard after mentioning Silla. Shood was a compact, dark Pakistani with mournful black eyes, wearing a paper cash-suit of tacky red and yellow stripes, faded from two days' wear. He was a computer programmer, a Marxist, and "sharp as a razor," Chester said. He'd lost his wife to the explosion on RM17.

And I came so close to losing Chester, Kitty thought. And why? Because Chester went to meetings like this one....

"The longer we stay unidentified as activists, the better," Chu said.

Chester shook his head. "That's why they got away with murdering everyone on that repair module. Because most of them weren't publicly declared. So not enough people smell a rat. Well, a lot of people suspect, but most of 'em aren't sure it was murder—because they aren't sure the people on the ship were anti-Admin. If the people who were killed had declared their stand publicly, the SA wouldn't want to kill them; they'd be afraid it'd cause more riots...."

"Perhaps. But for what we have to do," Chu said, shrugging, "secrecy is the only way. It is hopeless to 'demand an investigation.' Nothing will come of it. I think you have an American expression about asking foxes to guard chicken nests. And the SA will take note of who is doing the demanding. No. There is only one way: to take power. The NR knows the SA's plans for the Colony. The SA plans to man the Colony with their own people only. The rest of us will be deported or...who knows? If the Soviets surrender to NATO—and it seems possible that soon they will either launch a first strike or surrender—the SA will transform the Colony into their headquarters. Rick Crandall himself will come here. It will be his...his ivory tower. He will tolerate nothing less than complete dictatorship here. We must prevent that or we lose it all. We begin like this: to stock arms —with great secrecy, with caution—and to make plans to use them. And then to use them, when they are not expecting it. We must take control of Admin Central. There is nothing else to do."

Shood looked at Chu and then, to Kitty's surprise, he nodded. "We must take by force."

Chester looked uncomfortable. He glanced over his shoulder at Kitty. Then looked at Vreeland. "What you think?"

Vreeland said, "It's suicide. But standing up to 'em *any* kinda way is suicide too. So fuck it. They gonna pay."

"Yes," Chu said. "Standing up to them in any way is equally dangerous. Suicide? I think not, not if we plan very carefully. It would take very few people placed in the right nerve centers to take over the Colony. Getting there is the hard part. But once we're there, once we have control of Computer Central and Life Support, the people will rally behind us."

"What if they don't?" Kitty said, standing. Her legs were going to sleep. Her back ached. She did a few knee bends, grimacing. "What if . . . what if everyone's too scared. They won't know who you . . ." Who *you* are? Or who *we* are? Diplomatically she chose the latter. ". . . who we are. If they think we're terrorists, they won't trust us at the Colony's control system."

"We will not be operating the Colony's system ourselves," Chu said. "We will be handing it over to competent people we can trust."

"They still might be too scared of the SA bulls to back us."

"It's a risk we must take. One of many. I take a risk coming here at all, meeting with Chester and Shood. I risk my cover. But I *must* risk it now."

Chester said, slowly, as if thinking aloud, "I think they'd back us."

And as he went on, Kitty thought, *God damn you, Chester, we have to get out of this thing, not get locked up in it deeper! We have to get out for the baby!* But aloud she said nothing.

"People are pissed off," Chester was saying. "A lot of them suspect the explosion was rigged . . . and the others blame the explosion on Admin's not caring much about worker safety. And we haven't got the housing reforms they promised. They keep putting housing negotiations back farther and farther . . . And the air's getting bad in the technicki section; it's still fairly clean in the Admin section. The food's been shitty, and there hasn't been enough of it. The curfews—people are going stir-crazy. Claustrophobic. Soviet blockade's preventing Earth visits, and the curfew's keeping them in their units during off-time. We almost got busted coming over here—"

Chu looked sharply at him. "Almost? How?"

"A guard stopped us. We had a permit to go to medicenter for Kitty, so he let us go. But he did it like he didn't want to."

"Did he run an ID check?"

"Yeah, I think he did. But he let us go—"

Chu stood. "You are a known agitator. Your permit is for your wife; they would not have let you go, too, at this hour, unless—" She looked at the door, spoke with brisk authority. "We must go. Everyone go, quickly. I will be in touch."

They stood, everyone suddenly uncomfortable, as she got up and walked hastily across the mattresses to the door, stooped, and stepped through. They heard the outer door creak and clang shut behind her. She was gone. Just like that.

"She spooks easily," Chester said.

"Maybe we better go too," Vreeland said uneasily.

Kitty's stomach churned with tension. Nausea welled up in her. "Chester, I think I'm gonna be sick. Is there a toilet here?"

"They took it out. You got to use the public down the hall. Go ahead, babe, I'll be there in just a minute."

She moved across the mattresses to the door, staggering a little on the soft and uneven walking surface, went through the door. Bitchie was there in the corner, alone, his makeup smeared, his paper dress in dingy tatters. His face was drawn, hollow-eyed, pasty with pancake. His hair was a stack of dirty yellow coils. He was loading the little medinject unit attached to his leg with his black market Demerol-and-amphetamine mix; she could see his genitals, like a droopy white snail, under his printout skirt. He'd been a pilot, once; he had the double unit by contract for two years, and his two years were almost up. He hadn't worked at anything but collecting rents from whores for a year. He couldn't stay off the drugs, and when he was on them, he couldn't stay out of drag. Drag queens are not generally considered the Right Stuff.

She looked away from him—the sight of him made her stomach writhe even more—and went out the half-open door into the back hall. Chu hadn't even closed the door. Kitty's stomach contracted again, and she nearly threw up on the floor of the narrow metal hallway.

She was running by the time she got to the bathroom. She went in and, with not a second to spare, threw up in the vacu-flush.

She felt better almost immediately. And embarrassed. God, she must be unattractive this way, all puffy, throwing up half the time. No wonder Chester was ready to—

Oh, don't be silly, that's not why he's doing it.

But she went to the sink, looked in the mirror, grimaced, tried to pretty herself up a little.

Five minutes later she gave up. She rinsed out her mouth and went out into the hall.

And saw two SA bulls dragging Chester away, down the hall . . . up ahead of Chester, three other bulls were shoving Vreeland along; he was resisting, and they jabbed him with shock-prods, making him tense up and stagger. Where was Shood?

But . . . Chester. They had Chester.

His hands were trapped behind him in permaplastic handcuffs, and he was bleeding from the back of his head, and she thought, *Chu was right*.

She started after them, but the bulls stepped into an elevator. The doors closed on them, and on Chester. And that was it, that was all: he was gone.

New York City Jail.

Charlie was alive and Angelo was dead.

Angelo was gone. Charlie had sweated him out, pissed him out. Burned him out.

But Charlie was here because Angelo, using Charlie, had stabbed a cop. Dead, Angelo had put him here.

It was an autonomic cell, robot-guarded, one of the newer cells; Charlie didn't rate a human guard. He was in the cell with another guy, a short, taciturn, spike-haired Chinese in a bloodied JAS who'd come in that morning from an AntiViolence Law beating. His face all patchy with red welts, bruises; the puffiness around his eyes narrowing them to slits so that they were even more epicanthic than normal.

Charlie had been in the cell alone, awake all night, till just after the pathetic breakfast, when they brought in the Chinese. Charlie tried not to stare at the Chinese when the trash can escorted him in. But he couldn't help looking at his battered face, wondering what they'd leave of Charlie Chesterton's face if that cop died. Or even if he didn't . . . Stabbing a cop. Great.

You're screwed to the max, Charlie.

The place was cold and echoey and unyielding. It was a great, slow-moving mower machine you were caught in.

Charlie paced around the little plasticrete cell. There was just enough room for pacing to *be* pacing. Moving around hurt, because when the cops saw he'd stabbed one of their buddies, they got him down and kicked him, maybe ten times; Charlie had just managed to cover his head with his arms. Before they did anything more than bruise the hell out of him and crack a few ribs, the sergeant came in and stopped them, told them, "He'll get all that's coming to him." So, right, it hurt to move, but he was too restless and scared to sit still, and anyway, it was cold in there.

The Chinese guy was sitting sullenly on a bunk and following him with his glare as Charlie paced. Past the two thin bunks, ripped-up platforms coming out of the wall; past the seatless toilet. Naked white walls on three sides marred only by dinge and a word someone had smeared in feces, *Shit-Pigs*, in ocher.

On the fourth side, bars floor to ceiling. Square-edged bars, not even comfortable to put your hands around. Some drugged jackass about two cells down was braying with maddening regularity, about every ten minutes, "*Yermasuxen sh'piz' n' hurb' d!*" Technicki, over and over. Your Mama sucks everyone, shit-pigs, and I hurt bad, your mama sucks everyone, shit-pigs, and I hurt bad, your mama...

"*Fuck off!*" Charlie screamed back after an hour of it. Adding in technicki, "*Yotta basherbruh awl cuzzabrufugznay!*" You ought to bash out your brains on the wall, 'cause your brains are fucked, anyway. The jackass paused his braying to laugh cretinously, then went back to "*Yermasuxen sh'piz . . .*"

"Shit pigs," Charlie muttered as the brain-damaged jackass bellowed for the three-hundredth time. "Now we know who was in this cell before us." Nodding at the smear on the wall. "You take the wrong designer drugs, mix 'em with video-direct, and you end up like the shit-pigger over there."

That's when the Chinese guy said the only thing he said the whole time he was in with Charlie. "More likely," the Chinese said hoarsely, "he got brain damage from the beatings."

Charlie winced and closed his eyes.

How long before they came for him? According to the AntiViolence laws, he had to be in front of a judge and sentenced within seventy-two hours because he was charged with assault with intent to kill. A couple days left till the deadline. But he'd stabbed a cop. Hurt him bad, maybe killed him. In a case like that they'd give him priority. And because he'd attacked a cop, they'd probably sentence him to death, even if the guy lived.

Sure, maybe since the senator had gotten himself snuffed, and since the NR was going to make sure the public knew the senator had been railroaded, Congress would have to reexamine the AntiViolence Laws. A few months down the line, they might even suspend it.

But it'd be too late for Charlie.

They'd given him his phone call. He'd tried to call his NR contact, but the fucking phone had rung thirty times before someone had answered, and before he even had a chance to tell them where he was, the operator cut in with "Please deposit fifty newpence," and his time was up and the cops were dragging him away from the phone and . . .

The NR didn't even know where he was. Didn't know what had happened to him.

He heard the squeak of the trash can's wheels at the bars.

Charlie looked over, thinking that maybe the Resistance had sent a lawyer in for him, or maybe they were going to bribe his way out, or . . .

But the trash can said, "Charles Chesterton, you are required for arraignment, judgment, and sentencing. Come with me." Its polite, characterless male voice a little warped from wear.

It was about the size and shape of a standard street-side trash can, except it was on wheels, and it had the camera eye and the speech grid and the two nozzles. One nozzle for tear gas, the other for some kind of of knockout shot. The robot guards were heavy little fuckers, and even if you managed to knock one over before it put you under, the gates to the hall outside the cell block were always locked, and there were flesh-and-blood guards out there with guns and RR sticks and prods. And if anyone fucked with the trash cans, they instantly transmitted to Control, and alarms went off, and your ass was on its way to being shredded.

So when the robot transmitted to the lockbox on the cell and the barred door swung open, Charlie did as he was told.

"Come out of the cell, proceed to your left at a brisk walking pace," the trash can said.

Charlie went out of the cell, his stomach twisting as he thought about sentencing. The trash can backed away, whirring, till Charlie turned left and walked on. It followed, out of arm's reach, behind him. The cell door rang shut.

A camera on the wall, near the ceiling, swiveled to follow his progress as he walked to the gate. A guard let him through, and Charlie screwed up his courage and asked, "Uh—did he die?"

"Not yet. But it don't make no never mind to you, asshole. Come on, turn around, bracelets time."

Not yet. Charlie didn't even know the name of the cop he'd stabbed.

Twenty minutes later he was in the bedroom-size courtroom and they were showing the videotape of his attack on the cop. Whose name turned out to be Arthur Anthony Gespeccio. The camera in the ceiling over the arrival chute for the prisoner capsule had been whirring away, and they hadn't had to enhance the tape. But at first Charlie couldn't believe it was him on the videotape, sitting up in the capsule like a vampire in a coffin. Stabbing in that convulsive movement. Looked like, well, like somebody else. Moved like Angelo.

Physically it was Charlie Chesterton, and the judge knew it. A dyspeptic, matronly judge whose wrist was probably sore from banging the gavel, *the court so orders,* she sighed and shrugged when he tried to explain he'd been out of his mind; she murmured barely loud enough to hear—as if he weren't worth the breath—that the law no longer recognized insanity pleas no matter what the insanity was "by reason of." And she gave him the standard sentence for assault with intent to kill, compounded by a drug felony. Adding that he was also culpable for complicity with Angelo's death. Something he'd never thought of. The gavel said *bang*.

Death, to be preceded by public beating.

He was led out of there dazed, his throat too tight even to yell at them. . . .

And then it sank in: He was to be beaten before being

executed. That meant they'd give you a short rest in a hospital so you looked good, or anyway, so you didn't look persecuted when it was time for your public execution the following week.

The hospital stay. Prison hospital. But maybe in transferring, he'd see a chance for escape. Grab that hope. Hold on to that. Flimsy, almost nonexistent, but grab it and hold it.

Hold on to that, he told himself, as they took him into the videotaping room with its blank walls and its sear of lights; as they attached his cuffs behind his back to the metal ring in the wall. "Whatever you do," one of the cops told him, "don't puke. Makes him *real mad* if the guy pukes." Then they left him there. He hated them, but he didn't want them

to go, to leave him there alone. They went out, closed the left-hand door behind them.

There was another door, directly across from Charlie. Charlie stared at it.

The door opened. The big man in the mirror helmet came in, hefting the rubber club. Charlie thinking, *Mirror helmet. I'll have to see my own face as the guy wrecks it.*

"You fucking sick voyeurs!" Charlie screamed at the hidden cameras. Knowing they'd cut out anything he said that wasn't penitent.

"Try to relax," the guy in the helmet suggested. That's all he said. And then he began.

Langley, Virginia.

Stoner tried not to look around as he went into Records, Classified, with his access chit. Got to look like it's all part of a day's work, an ordinary day's work . . .

Records was almost a vault, *was* a vault when the doors were shut and sealed, and despite the harsh lighting and cool waft of air-conditioning, the windowless place always felt claustrophobic to Stoner. There were two clerks behind the counter, Etta and Frank, and two lines. Shit. He wanted to put his request in through Etta. The line for Franklin was noticeably shorter. If he got in Etta's line, it would look wrong. The people who watched through the ceiling camera noticed anything odd that went down. It was their job to look for things that seemed out of place. Little anomalies. Maybe Unger was looking over their shoulder right now. . . .

But it had to be Etta.

Stoner got in Etta's line, behind fat-assed Springsdale in one of his imitation tweed suits. Franklin glanced over at Stoner. Franklin was one of those prissy young men who look old and wizened before their time; he wore a newly printed flatsuit and a gawdy gold watch. He'd noticed. Maybe he took it personally. People who took little affronts personally made trouble for you, Stoner thought. Snooty little bastard.

Stoner looked up the line to Etta. She was bent over her console, muttering to herself as she punched codes with arthritic fingers. She was eighty-four, had worked here since the twentieth century. Stick-thin, pallid, silly excess of makeup; thick glasses; globe of blue hair. Quick, birdlike movements. Round-shouldered, almost hunchbacked from osteoporosis.

She was long overdue for retirement, but she was a tradition at Langley, the CIA's concession to its roots. And she was still good at her job.

She was also one of those people who did favors for friends. She wasn't afraid of the Company. She might do it for him.

He had to get into the Blue Classification files on the SA. Lopez and Brummel wouldn't take anything less. Class Blues couldn't be accessed through the outside computer lines; they were issued in noncopyable disks that were to be entered by top-clearance personnel only. He'd lost his top clearance, thanks to Unger, four days before.

"Hey, Kimosabe," Unger had said, "you get my memo?"

"Sure. But, uh—" Stoner had feigned obtusity. "I'm still not sure what it is you want me to look for. I mean, all you said was, 'Keeping in mind our talk, look for evidence of Security Risks in these personnel' and then there was that interminable list . . ."

"You don't know whereof I speak, Kimosabe?" His oily gloss of humor rubbing thin now, the cold metal threat showing through. "I think you know what I'm talking about.

I'm talking about team players. Telling them from the others. And there's an easy way to tell them apart."

Stoner had lost touch with his common sense and replied without thinking. "Well, it looked like you wanted me to pick through the files and find excuses to downgrade and even prosecute everyone in government who was black, wog, Jewish, or liberal, but I know I couldn't have read you right, that couldn't be right, that isn't our standard criterion—"

"Stoner, the criterion for risk changed when we opened our eyes to what was happening in this country."

The change in Unger's tone made Stoner regret not playing along. Hell, he could've played the game, pretended to, long enough . . . until he got safely out. Too late, he tried to snow Unger into thinking he hadn't meant it the way he had. "I'm talking about repercussions, man! For God's sake, some of these people are congressmen. They'll scream 'Joe McCarthy!' at us, and when it's time for a budget review—"

"Those people are on their way out. They won't be alone." And then he'd walked out of Stoner's office.

The next day, Stoner found his clearance reduced. They made excuses about why it'd happened. Claimed it was because he wasn't working on Blue-relevant cases now, hence they'd decided to limit access for the sake of efficiency. Just efficiency, Stoner, that's all. *Crap.*

And now he was waiting patiently in Etta's line, Franklin glancing at him with pursed lips.

Etta finished with Springsdale, Springsdale turned, saw Stoner, winked at him, and walked past.

Hey. What had the wink meant?

Forget it. You're getting the shakes. Springsdale gives that bogus wink to everyone.

"Hi, Etta." Stoner said, stepping up to the counter. Fingering his chit. Hoping the cold sweat on his palms didn't smear it.

"How you doing, Cowboy?" Etta didn't smile, but there was a lightness in her manner that said she found Stoner a relief after Springsdale. "You still listen to that twangy stuff?"

"Sure. You listen to that Hank Williams album I gave you?"

"Once or twice. Wimpy stuff." She cracked her arthritic knuckles. "You know me: give me rock 'n' roll anytime. It's maybe archaic, but not as archaic as that stuff you listen to. When I was at the end of my twenties, I discovered Bruce Springsteen, and I'll never forget . . ."

He let her ramble through her memories for a while. He glanced at Franklin, just twenty, maybe twenty-five, feet away. The Priss was frowning over someone's access code on his monitor, had forgotten about Stoner. But he was close enough to hear, if he were paying attention . . .

There was nothing else for it. Lopez had insisted.

"What can I do you for?" Etta asked, smiling at her own ancient joke.

"Oh, uh—got it right here." He passed her the chit. Leaned over the counter just a little, enough for the merest shade of confidentiality. "I'm not exactly on for that." He didn't whisper it. Franklin would notice a whisper. "But it's a lot of red-tape hassle, and I was hoping to seduce you into letting me slide so I can get what I need before they get around to changing my classification back to where it oughta be." That was it. It was up to her. He hadn't pushed for a favor from her before. If he was right about her . . .

He was. "Why, shore, cowboy. I'm headin' out to pasture in a month, what I care."

"You retiring, really?"

"Going to the elephant's graveyard in Florida. I'm kinda skinny for an elephant. More like an ostrich." All the time punching through his request using her own access code. "Is there an ostrich's graveyard?"

"Stop thinking so morbidly. People are living to a hundred twenty now all the time."

"People who can pay for the hormone treatments. Don't think I want to, anyway. Here you are." She went to the chute, which discharged the packet of disks, and she brought it to him.

"Thanks. I owe you."

"Careful where you ride your horse, cowboy," she said, looking him in the eye.

She was on to him. She knew he wasn't supposed to have this file, and not only for reasons of technicality. She was warning him.

His mouth dry, he said, "I will. Don't take up surfing in Florida without lessons, okay?"

He walked numbly back to his office, feeling Franklin watching him go.

In his office he opened his desk, found the bottle, poured himself a shot of peat-cured Glenfiddich.

Then he got up and locked the door.

It took only about five minutes to attach the recording filter to the screen of his word processor. It was a transparent square that fitted neatly over the screen. It might've passed for an antiglare filter if not for the telltale wire trailing from a lower corner to the little gray metal box. The SA files were supposed to be noncopyable, but the recording filter read anything that was on the screen the way his eyes did and "drank" the light pattern.

He took out the first of the disks, accessed, began to read.

Same old stuff so far. The Second Alliance: World's biggest international private-cop outfit, its own sizable army, antiterrorist action, CIA-affiliated interrogations, et cetera, scroll ahead, more et cetera, go on to the next disks. And the next. Fresh reports from SA's European theater of action, cross-referencing with CIA on Socialist or partisan activists who'd oppose the SA's policing authority. Three of these people liquidated in France, two in Belgium. Harassment from the NR, retaliation against the NR, et cetera again, ho-hum stuff. Next disk. CIA endorsement of the Self-Policing Organization of European States.

What? What the hell was *that* all about?

The next section was in deep code. Only three people had that code, and Stoner was one of them. Which meant Unger was a step behind him.

Stoner punched in the decoding sequence and waited.

The section decoded, and he felt like someone had punched him in the gut.

SPOES was "the multination framework for a single centrally authorized European State." It was to be a dictatorship operated by the SA, using nationalist leaders as puppets. Europe's several social democratic governments would be dissolved, not allowed to rebuild after the war.

Stoner was a hidebound capitalist, not enthusiastic about Socialism even in the watered-down form of social democracy. But SPOES would eliminate all choice in the matter. And it would systematically eliminate anyone who militated for a choice.

And: "A realistic assessment of Western Europe's racial situation leads us to conclude that minority races represent a threat to political and economic stability. . . ." It went on to endorse the SA's policy of rounding up blacks, Arabs, Indians, leftist Jews—it stopped short of endorsing the proscription of all Jews—and other "chronic problem races" for expulsion or something called "labor realignment." Which Stoner read as *slavery*.

Identified security risks were to be liquidated. The SA estimates that forty percent of each "subracial community" were Security Risks.

Forty percent? They're going to liquidate forty percent of the non-Caucasians in Europe?

And why quit there?

He scrolled ahead, his hand shaking on the keyboard. He found what he was looking for. Progress reports. How well they'd done so far in carrying this out.

Eighty percent success in stage one, all secured areas.

Stage one was the business of rounding up and isolating "risk groups" and the liquidation of priority troublemakers. Anyone they had confined whom they'd identified as a rebel had been killed.

Stage one was bad. Stage two was worse. But it was stage three that left him scared.

Somewhere in Sicily.

Watson had made a resolution to get caught up on his reports that night. He was beginning to regret the resolution. But when he thought of shelving it, he remembered the look on Crandall's face . . . the look that said: "You're expendable now, Watson."

Watson was sitting in the Comm Center of the SA's Sicilian HQ, monitoring reports from around Western Europe, yawning, swilling coffee that didn't seem to help, fighting the fatigue that had dropped onto him at ten P.M. like a guillotine. The telexes hummed, and now and then one of them would chatter insanely to itself for a moment. The lights overhead buzzed. It was almost midnight, he was alone—except for his bodyguard, of course—and his eyes were aching from staring into video monitors. The facts were beginning to lose their meaning; he had to repeat them to himself mentally. Forty thousand fresh SA troops from the training camps deployed in four European capitals. Another four hundred Partisans arrested in Rome, three hundred more in Athens. All of them tagged for execution. Jews and Moslems in Dresden and Rouen impregnated with radio-traceable IDs and remanded to isolated sections of town. Reports from the NATO front, Soviets moving back across the Warsaw Pact borders, one last shot, pushing especially in Germany, piercing through Belgium and into northern France. Significant deployment of tactical nukes but none in use yet. Speculation from observers that this was the Soviet war offensive's last-ditch effort. If this failed, they'd surrender. Or turn to nuclear weapons.

But the NATO lines were frayed from sheer attrition. Maybe the Soviets wouldn't fail.

Watson's mind wandered. He found himself thinking about Crandall, wondering, How long before Crandall becomes confident of his safety? Supposing it happened, supposing there was a way to get an assassin through to Crandall—what about Crandall's extractor team? They routinely searched the brains of anyone who was to come physically near Crandall. But there was a new technique—the bloody damn albino had just developed it—a technique that would make it possible to lay down a smoke screen in a man's brain. The extractor team would search the three layers of the man's mind. But what if you added a fourth layer? A false bottom to the wetware; a neurological subconscious. In which a man could be programmed, without his own knowledge, to kill Crandall when the moment came. A moment he wouldn't know about till it arrived.

Watson would need an American, martially trained. Someone he could have access to here, where his own extractor team was. Better if it weren't someone established as SA. The camouflaging layer would change him, and his old cronies in the SA would know something was wrong. It would have to be someone else.

An American soldier, Watson thought. One who would be thought MIA if he disappeared. And a lot of them were MIA in northern France now.

Very well. He'd go to Rouen. He was overdue for inspecting SA facilities there, anyway. Oh, there was a great deal he could do there. Of course, Crandall had ordered him to remain in Sicily.

It would be risky. But he was committed to taking risks now. One had to risk all to win all.

Somewhere in the Mediterranean Sea.

Waiting in the Bullshit Belly.

Hard Eyes was sitting on a metal bench in the half-darkness, smelling rusting metal and raw petroleum. Watching Karakos.

There were forty of them in the hold of the tanker *Daniella,* in a gymnasium-big compartment with a thin metal ceiling beneath a camouflaging layer of oil. Against the back wall of the compartment, roped down, was a two-man minicopter, on wheels.

The ship's engine droned in the background. Danco and Willow sat near Hard Eyes, their faces picked out eerily in the yellow of electric lanterns near their feet; Carmen was sitting close to Willow. She wore only fatigues, boots, and, over her bare tits, a flak vest; she was nervously reassembling her Enfield. It was a "light support weapon," the combination of a rifle and a light machine gun she'd found on a British corpse in an overturned armored car, outside Paris. Standard NATO 5.56 ammo, lightweight, semi- and fully automatic firing modes, less recoil than most LMGs. Hard Eyes envied it. He was carrying an ancient FN-FAL assault rifle, and an old Smith & Wesson .45 pistol. Danco and Willow were talking softly, their voices echoing tinnily in the great blank spaces of the hold. "This Bullshit Belly," Danco said, "it's like that story *en la Biblia.* Jonah in the big fish." He said Jonah *Ho-nah.* He set his old, slender Sterling

9-mm submachine gun on the floor; the *clack* echoed like the snap of a whale's jaws.

"Jonah's roit, Oim bloody digesting in 'ere," Willow said. "Wot's it been? Seven hours, then?"

"More like five," Hard Eyes muttered. "We'll be there in about half an hour." Across from him sat Lila and, lined up along the wall, a couple dozen more guerrillas. He found himself watching a pale blond guy, Farks, no more than nineteen, who was talking uneasily with Helmut Kelheim, an experienced West German mercenary who had personal reasons for hating the SA. Kelheim was big, dark, and confident; Farks was slim, pale, and clearly scared. Scared of not measuring up, scared of getting killed, scared he'd made the wrong decision in joining the NR. A decision made out of idealistic impulse, without the gristle of real anger, which was an important component of dedication.

Too late now, kid, Hard Eyes thought. *Your pride won't let you turn back, and we need fighters too badly to just up and send you home.*

Hard Eyes wondered what Claire was doing now. He hoped she was scared for him. As soon as he hoped it, he felt like a jerk for hoping it. But he kept on hoping.

He glanced left, at the hydraulic pistons on the steel door that would open out onto the sea when the time came.

The eight black-rubber rafts were stacked, inflated, beside the door, each with its small de-noised engine, no bigger than a lawn mower's. Coiled up beside the rafts was the magnetic climbing gear, the grapples and fiberlon rope ladders.

All neat and prepared over there, Hard Eyes thought. And it worked on the training hulk. But the training hulk had been undefended. . . .

And there was Karakos. Sitting over there with his face in the darkness thinking anything, God knows, anything at all.

"I think he's a risk," Hard Eyes had told Steinfeld and Levassier. *"I can't prove anything, but we shouldn't risk it if there's even a—"*

"I've known Karakos for more years than you've had hair on your balls," Levassier had told him, in French, the stump of his missing arm lifting as if he wanted to shake the vanished fist at Hard Eyes in anger.

"*If we get too paranoid, follow every little feeling up,*" Steinfeld had said, "*we'll get lost, we'll splinter with the pressure. He's had experience assaulting ships. We need him on the* Hermes' Grandson."

"*We're making a mistake taking him along,*" Hard Eyes had said.

"*You're crazy from jealousy.*" Levassier had snorted, saying what everyone thought.

And now Karakos was sitting over there with his face in the darkness.

Willow caught Hard Eyes staring at Karakos. "Chisin' ghosts agin, 'ard Eyes? Maykes you superstitious when a ghost sleeps witcher lidy."

"I think I'm getting another fucking bladder infection," Carmen said, pressing her knees together. "No fucking place to pee in here."

"Pee in Willow's ears, there's room in his head where his brains oughta be," Hard Eyes told her.

Nobody laughed.

The ship's engines coughed, sputtered, fell silent. The ship was coasting along in a current, angling to intercept the *Hermes' Grandson*.

Fuck it, Hard Eyes thought.

He slapped a clip into his assault rifle.

A Trojan Horse, the *Daniella* drifted, wallowing slowly, in a current that would carry it west, toward the *Hermes' Grandson*. The SA ship, coming from their base in the Spanish Mediterranean port of Malaga, was steaming steadily east. At 0110, an hour and ten minutes after midnight, the *Hermes' Grandson*'s radar took note of the approaching bulk of the *Daniella*. Radar automatically informed the duty officer, who radioed the *Daniella* and asked for its ID number. The *Daniella* gave an ID number, which checked out, on the SA ship, with a registered oil tanker. According to the computer's registration search the tanker was American-made but now owned by a Spanish company that imported oil from the Persian Gulf.

The *Daniella*'s first mate explained by radio that the ship had been on its way to the Persian Gulf when it experienced engine trouble arising from a short in the ship's electrical system. The short not only froze the engine but also the electrical controls for the ship's gigantic anchor. It could neither move aside nor drop anchor. And it was squarely in the *Hermes' Grandson*'s way. However, it expected to get its electrical system working again in short order.

The duty officer on the *Hermes' Grandson* was under orders not to alter course except in emergency, since there were believed to be mines in the waters off-course. The captain would not consider this an emergency. So the *Hermes' Grandson* would have to pass close to the *Daniella*.

The ship churned closer to the *Daniella*. And now, turned sideways relative to the SA ship, it was directly in the way. It wouldn't be necessary to change course drastically to avoid the *Daniella*. They'd be a bit close together for a while. That was all. The SA duty officer swung starboard twenty degrees. The two ships slipped past each other in the dark. The *Daniella* was a squat black bulk against the starlight-tinged cobalt of the sea.

The duty officer of the *Hermes' Grandson*, who was young and overconfident, almost forgot about the *Daniella*.

Hard Eyes chewed his lip as the raft rode another swell. He wondered if the SA ship would slip out of reach after all. The ship was in no hurry—but the little engines on the rafts were even slower. They'd pushed off from the *Daniella* while the two ships were still parallel, the guerrillas' faces and weapons blacked, swallowed in the inky night. They saw the great light-edged bulk of the SA ship ahead, looming like an ancient fortress . . . blinked salt water spray out of their eyes, heard the grind of the target ships' engines, and felt its wash slapping the rafts as they plowed toward it with painful slowness. Hard Eyes could just make out Steinfeld in another raft, saw him looking over his shoulder at the *Daniella*. The sharpshooters, with their infrared sights, should be in place by now . . . and the minicopter should be taking off.

Aboard the *Hermes' Grandson*, the duty officer was reaching for a cup of coffee when the call came. The deck sentry, his voice crackly in the intercom speaker, was yelling something about men in rafts. Did he *want* men in rafts, or was there someone adrift out there, in a raft?

"No, dammit, sir, there are men in rafts with—" The sentry broke off in the middle.

"What? What did you say?" the duty officer demanded. No reply.

But he got another call, from radar, about a small helicopter. "Well, where is it?"

"Directly overhead, sir."

The duty officer punched the alarm button.

The sharpshooters had taken out three sentries, and the copter's crew had landed on the deck, fixed four ladders to the rail, lowered them—the upper sections of the ladders adhered to the hull magnetically, but the loose bottom rungs were whipping along behind the thrust of the ship, jumping at the waterline in the trough of the wake. Danco, at the raft's little motor, opened the throttle, urging the raft within six feet of the ladder. It was dimly visible through darkness and spray. Hard Eyes, rifle strapped to his back, said it for the second time that night: "Fuck it." And jumped for the polymesh ladder.

He fell short, cold sea water closed around him, and he wished he hadn't been too damn *cool* to wear a life jacket. He had a monstrously lucid image of himself lost at sea, treading water and spectacularly alone in the cold vastness with only minutes more to live before exposure and exhaustion dragged him under.

But his fingers closed over the synthetic smoothness of the rope ladder's lower rung, and he pulled hard, fighting the drag of the ship's wake and the momentum of the ship itself, feeling as if he could feel the whole dark breadth of the sea sucking at his legs as he struggled up onto the ladder, nearly wrenching his arms from their sockets.

Then he was somehow several rungs up, clinging, gasping. He heard Steinfeld yell. He got his footing on the ladder, turned, caught the rope Willow threw him. Tied the rope to the ladder. The other end was tied to a raft. He swung over to the next ladder, caught another rope, tied another raft on . . . gunshots and sirens from above. Bullets whipped up the waves between the rafts; pocked the rafts in places, emptying raft compartments but not yet sinking the little crafts. Answering gunfire rattled from the *Daniella* as the guerrillas scrambled up the ladders. Hard Eyes saw Karakos going up one of the ladders, all eager-beaver, damn him. He forced himself not to think about Karakos. *Just keep it out of your head, you've got a job to do*.

We've lost surprise, Hard Eyes thought. But then a lot of them are probably still pulling their boots on. And he and Danco and some of the others were almost up the railing.

There was a good chance he'd get to the top—and somebody'd blow his brains out the instant he stuck his head up.

He moved past the scuppers, saw the gray-painted gunwale up ahead, getting closer. Wished he could climb and get at his rifle too. Maybe the seawater hadn't damaged his .45.

He paused just long enough to tug the pistol from his jacket, clench it in his teeth. He continued upward, expecting that any second someone above would pick him off the rope with an SMG burst. His wet clothes were raspy and heavy on him.

But he reached the rail, put one hand on it, took the gun from his mouth with the other hand, and dragged himself up.

Below the sharp electric lighting of the superstructure was an expanse of gray deck, and four sprawled bodies, and a man pulling himself along in a welter of blood. The minicopter was there, too, with bullet holes in its windshield; one of its crew was slumped over, nodding his head monotonously from pain.

Hard Eyes climbed over; hit the deck the same moment as Willow, who was coming off one of the other ladders; and ducked when he saw a muzzle flash from the corner of the cane-shaped top of a ventilation shaft. He dodged left, toward the bow, wet clothing making him move sluggishly, firing wildly with the pistol toward the muzzle flash just to keep the guy down.

Unslinging his assault rifle, Hard Eyes reached the corner of the steel superstructure, out of the vent gunman's line of fire. He tucked the pistol in his coat, checked his rifle, and stepped out, around the corner.

Twenty-five feet away, a man in an SA regular's uniform,

but without his shoes, stepped out of a steel hatch, looked around, saw Hard Eyes coming at him.

At the same time Willow and Danco were working together, Willow circling the guy at the vent, Danco pinning him down with rifle fire . . . Willow coming up behind the guy and shooting away the back of his head . . . as other guerrillas poured over the gunwale, hit the deck, ran for position. Lila shouting orders at her team; somewhere else Steinfeld yelling commands . . . the crack of gunshots and the whine of ricochets from metal.

The SA guy without his shoes looked scared as he fiddled with the submachine gun in his hand, trying to get the clip into it properly—and then he saw Hard Eyes, and the scared look became terror. The guy's crotch went dark as he wet it. Hard Eyes hesitated—he could imagine himself in this guy's place all too easily, the clip going in wrong, an enemy coming at him with a gun and no way to defend yourself and knowing at this range that your enemy couldn't miss.

Don't stop to think, idiot! And he made himself level the assault rifle at the guy—

"Wait!" the guy squeaked.

—and squeeze the trigger, the burst catching the soldier square over his heart, slamming him back against the bulkhead; he slid down the steel wall, leaving a long, vertical smear of blood like a gravemarker above him.

Hard Eyes turned away and went on; felt a revolting combination of elation and horror as he shot two more men.

They'd lost the advantage of real surprise, but they still had the edge, had the initiative, and they had Steinfeld's leadership.

Hard Eyes paused at a gangway leading up the superstructure to the bridge and drew his headset from its watertight pouch, put it on. He heard Steinfeld's voice, strident in the little earphones: "Teams two and three, regroup at the main deck aft gangway. Teams one and four, secure the forecastle and fantail."

An explosion and a ringing ran through the deck as one of the other teams tossed a seismic grenade through a hatch. Most of the SA were still below, and Steinfeld was trying to contain them till the ship's controls and its captain were taken.

Hard Eyes waited in the shadow under a large metal fixture he couldn't identify, across from the hatch. His team started showing up; Carmen and Farks and Kelheim and Willow running up, a little bent over as they ran, Farks looking white from fear, his chest heaving. Asshole kid's going to hyperventilate. And then Hard Eyes caught a motion out of the corner of his eye from somewhere above. Looked up and saw a big guy in an armored SA uniform, complete with helmet, leveling an M-30 at Kelheim and the other guerrillas. Hard Eyes yelled, "Up there!" and squeezed out his last six rounds at the SA bull. They knocked the bull back but failed to penetrate his armor—and at the same moment the bull opened up with his M-30, directing it sloppily as he staggered.

Farks screamed and Kelheim cursed. Hard Eyes looked, saw Farks lying on his side, bending double and straightening and bending, opening and closing like a mealworm on a hot rock, gut-shot. Mewling. Kelheim on his knees clutching at his own inner thigh and looking panicky. Hard Eyes was surprised to see Kelheim react so strongly to a thigh wound till he realized the German was afraid for his genitals.

Hard Eyes took a clip from his belt pouch, slapped it into his rifle as Carmen and Willow, running up, opened fire at the guard on the upper deck. Carmen hissed, "Keep him pinned, I got the only piercer." She ran around the corner of the superstructure, fired at someone Hard Eyes couldn't see, on her way to the gangway. She had to get closer to the bull for the armor-piercing round to work—and Hard Eyes wondered if she'd gotten herself shot. The bull saw him, was crouched behind the rail, his armor's helmet a glinting arc in the light from the bulkhead, taking potshots at the guerrillas. A round scored paint from the cowl Hard Eyes crouched under, making him jump a little. He returned fire, saw sparks jump as his short burst sang off the bulkhead over the bull—and then Carmen was there, padding up from the left, raising one of the little guns that fired armor-penetrating explosive bullets. The bull saw her, turned toward her, aiming the carbine. She fired; he fired. He missed; she didn't. His armor ballooned and he screamed, fell back.

Farks was lying still now, and Hard Eyes couldn't keep himself from thinking the inevitable: What a waste.

Kelheim sprayed sealant on his leg and then stood up, turned to shout a question at someone, trying to adjust his headset. His head exploded, between his hands. Just like that. One moment he was standing there shouting, his confidence back, once more part of the fight—the next his skull had flown apart under the impact of a round from an assault rifle fired from the lower corner of the superstructure. An SA regular, a stocky Hispanic carrying an M-18, was there, looking around. He saw Hard Eyes at almost the same moment Hard Eyes saw him.

Hard Eyes was stepping out to get a clear shot at him. Avenge Kelheim. The Hispanic SA—holding his rifle braced under his arm—was leveling the gun at Hard Eyes.

One of those moments. The worst sort. When you can see the man you want to kill and the man you want to kill can see you, and you aren't under cover, and you aren't far from each other, and the outcome, your life or death, was contingent on a lot of factors, some of them out of your control. Not just a question of who shot better and faster. Could have just as much to do with whose gun jammed; who happened to have light shining in his eyes; who happened to be lined up best for a shot.

Who was simply more lucky.

They fired at the same moment. Bullets slashed by, Hard Eyes expecting with each millisecond to feel the sickening crunch of impact. But the other guy was spinning, going down.

Hard Eyes stood there for a moment, his bowels clenching, his heart hammering, hands shaking. Get it together.

But a wave of relief went through him as the call came over his headset, Steinfeld's voice through the fuzz of static, "All teams: The bridge is secured. We estimate half the enemy personnel dead. Hold your positions, and if you have enough people, send someone to the bridge to report. I believe we've got her."

Hard Eyes took a deep breath and felt some of his calm return.

Until the thought hit him. Where was Karakos?

A battlefield in France.

His name was Rory Hayes—he was a sergeant in the United States Army, infantry—and on March 28, 2021, he was finally past being scared.

They said it was a war, and they said it was in Europe, but this is what it was: The sky was a big, wet gray nothing, the ground was a big, muddy brown nothing, and Sergeant Hayes was clapped between, a nothing on two legs. And sometimes chaos came and chewed people up.

But you had to keep yourself *doing,* because if you acknowledged the nothing and gave in, all the piranha dreams from the medinjects wriggled out and ate your thinking alive.

So he took care of Parakeet. It was important to take care of Parakeet.

Parakeet: PFC Perry Katz, a wannabe comic, twenty-three, always chirping his stand-up act at the other enlisted men in E Company. Parakeet was handing out the new shipment of rations, taking it from a big green polymesh sack. All the rations were alike: dried fruit, freeze-dried soup, canned pseudomeat; but Parakeet was going on with, "Delvecchio, here's your rat sandwich like you ordered with the tail stuffed in his cute little mouth." Delvecchio played tough guy a lot. "Pflug, here's your Soviet testicles on rye with mayo." Pflug was gung-ho, a medinject spigot sucker. "Becher, here's your Easter basket." Becher was religious, and it was almost Easter. "Carmody, here's Breck's undies, toasted, on a stick." Carmody had a thing for their CO, Captain Patricia Breck. "Hayes, here's your mud pie with a side of sand." Because once, just once, Hayes bitched he was sick of mud, why couldn't they get transferred to the North African front, get shot at in the desert where at least it's dry and you don't get trench foot.

Northern France wasn't so bad that clammy late afternoon; it hadn't rained in almost an hour. Mist hung in swatches of blur over the low hills to the north; it glistened on concertina wire, thickened over the gently rolling land to the east, cloaking the Soviet lines; but here and there, in the unnaturally sedate no-man's-land, the slumped hulks of blasted autotanks blacked through.

The trench was lined in rock-hard insta. Hayes and Pflug had sprayed the insta down carefully when they'd dug in, but the mud tended to ooze over the camouflaged-colored lip of the rockhole, anyway, or the men would track it in, so now it was up to their ankles. The mud was cold and slimy and persistent. It worked its way between your boot and your foot a hundred ways; you got it down your pants, and in your weapons so you had to field-strip and clean them all the time. Hayes crouched lower in the trench, under the squat tripod of the tank killer, and winced at the tug from the medinject sunk into the meat of his left inner thigh. Come sunset, Breck'd send Shit Head around with the new med-ups for the push north. The thought made his stomach contract with nausea. *Make yourself eat.* He opened two cans of pseudomeat. Parakeet called it sewermeat. Parakeet hunkered down next to Hayes. Parakeet—Katz—was a short, stocky guy with wiry yellow hair teased up from being constantly pushed out of his eyes so it was like a bird's crest on his head. He had a narrow, bumpy, beaklike nose; small, glittery blue eyes; and slender hands. Now and then he'd make a quick shrugging motion, maybe because of a nervous tic, maybe because his back hurt. Like most of them he wore a slicker over a flak jacket, plastic-mesh mud-caked boots, fatigues patched gray from dried muck.

General sexual frustration punctuated E Company's bantering with homophobic jibes; men who buddied up were ragged on, even when there was nothing gay happening, so naturally tall, lean Hayes with his precise movements and quietness was "made in Gen Spec"* for stocky Parakeet with his nervousness and noise.

They ate their sewermeat gunk and chewed the rubbery fruit for dessert and gazed out over the green-brown, black-splashed terrain of spent farmland between their lines and the Soviets'.

Through mouthfuls of gummy food Parakeet sang a patri-pop tune. Only he'd changed the words. They were supposed to go like this:

My Uncle Sam went for a walk down by his property line
Saw a big red bear bustin' down the No Trespassin' sign
He said, "Say Russian Bear, you better back away!
And if you cross that line, you better learn to pray!"

Parakeet's version, with even worse meter, went,

My Uncle Sam ditched his wife and went to git some wine
Saw a hot-bod Commie bitch hanging out her Sex for Hire
*   sign*
He said, "Listen, baby, I got no money, but I'll deal just the
*   same*
If you give me some nookie, I'll trade you American grain!"

Carmody laughed. He was a government rat-killer with a saggy face, and his mouth always droopy. He laughed compulsively at anything to do with sex. "Hey, whatsa second verse, huh?"

But Hayes said, "Breck's sending med-ups over tonight, Parakeet. What you gonna do?" Katz had been refusing his meds.

Carmody said, "Hey, let him sing—"

"Shut up, Carmody. What you gonna do, Katz? Take the meds or not?"

Parakeet said, "To BR** or not to BR, that's the question. Answer: no."

---

*Gen Spec: Genetic Specialties, a black-market lab—possibly mythical—that purportedly cloned lovers to specification for high-paying buyers willing to wait fifteen years for the clone's maturity.
**BR: Behavioral Robot. An expression describing someone conditioned by drug therapy or other means to complete subordination.

Delvecchio came over to listen. Not to talk, just to listen. He was a sallow, ferret-faced guy who, lately, just sat around watching, listening, twitching at little sounds, ignoring big ones; his eyes were deep-sunk in the sockets, his hands shaky. He was on the med-ups a lot, more than ordered, and sometimes he didn't sleep for days; or else he'd binge on sleep-meds and doze out for twenty hours. Now he just sat there listening. Not saying a word, though sometimes his lips moved soundlessly.

"We got orders, Parakeet, and we're stuck with 'em," Hayes said. "You going to do the meds?"

Parakeet was humming the patri-pop tune, gazing blissfully west toward the brown humps of the CO's bivouac. After a moment he said, "No way."

Hayes could feel the place he kept quiet inside him twisting frantically, the piranha trying to break out. He needed Parakeet. He never laughed at Parakeet's jokes, but he needed to hear them. When he kept his mind on watching out for Parakeet, the dream piranha stayed away. Talking to Katz and keeping him squared away . . . maybe the relationship was *a place* he needed. Like a cupboard he could keep some hope in. It was the only one he had. And maybe he cared about Katz. Why it helped to care about people, he didn't know. "She'll put you on every patrol for a month, Parakeet. Edit you out, man."

"I'm not gonna suck a spigot for her."

"You signed for it," Carmody said.

Parakeet shrugged. "They lied to us about what it really was till it was too goddamn late." He said something else, but Hayes couldn't hear it because a squad of NATO Veetolls went booming over; the VTOLs—Vertical Takeoff and Landing fighter jets—rippling their furious noise over them all, a roar of anger that spoke for Parakeet, so it didn't matter that Hayes couldn't hear him.

Hayes sat in his Mylar tent, in his skivvies, taking the transparent tubes from the medinject pack he held in the palm of his hand. He inserted the tubes into his spigot.

The little plastic tubes snicked neatly into the medinject unit, flesh-melded to Hayes's thigh. Sent over with Shit Head from Captain Breck. Filled with a solution containing a molecule called CRF. CRF released ACTH, adrenocortico-trophic hormone, which stimulated the fight-or-flight response; but the CRF was cut with amphetamine and testosterone to make sure the response was *fight* and not *flight*. Turn the little release knob and you felt the stuff flow into your veins almost instantly. Your heart pumped faster, blood vessels supplying the skin contracted, and the skin goes white. Carbohydrates stored in the liver are released as glucose for exertion energy. To supply the glucose with plenty of burning oxygen, the chest expands; bronchial tubes widen; breathing deepens, speeds up. Muscles tense, pupils dilate, mouth goes dry, body sweats to cool itself for the action. Your hair stands on end.

But not yet. He didn't touch the little knob. There was a fourth tube for the fourth slot in the cardpack-sized medinject "spigot." The P-tube, with Bromocriptine to stimulate the dorsal area in the hypothalamus: the pleasure center. And he had other tubes saved up in his sleeve pocket; Vasopressin compounded with select neurotransmitters for alertness. Vitamins, amino acids. Additional amphetamine set up to dose out slowly, accumulating to a steady seventy milligrams—at a low dose, amphetamine makes you quick and euphoric, borishly friendly; at a high dose it invariably makes you aggressive. *Mean.* You synched the P-tube to the A-tube, the aggression tube, just before battle; the P-tube didn't work without the ACTH and other secretions that came with combat. You fought, it gave you a jolt of pleasure. You fought a little more, it jolted you nicey-nice some more. You killed the enemy. But you lost touch with self-preservation. You tended to get killed, if you didn't get lucky. Hayes dressed, went to find Parakeet. He was in the trench, with a lantern and a white paint-pen, painting graffiti onto the insta: *The Easter Bunny sucks eggs. It could be worse.* "My sentimental Easter message for Becher."

"I'll hold on to your tubes for you, Katz," Hayes said, skidding down into the trench. "In case you want 'em."

"Hold 'em, use 'em for suppositories, I don't care, man."

It was getting dark, and colder. The dark pooled in the trench like an oily liquid. The clouds turned to charcoal. Yellow at the horizon shifted toward orange; orange flirted with red. Distant *pock-pock* of rifle fire. Thud of a mortar.

Pflug kicked irritably at the mud, splashed it on the insta, started talking low to himself.

Irritability, insularity, talking to yourself. Some of the spigot's side effects. Hallucinations was another.

"They're saying it's cowardice," Hayes said. "That you're scared you'll get yourself killed."

"That what you think, Hayes?"

Hayes couldn't see Katz's face very well now. But he could feel Parakeet smiling. "No, Parakeet, dammit. You pulled Wiekowski out from under the Grinder, you blew up an Otto, you did more than enough—without spigots. You're not scared. But they'll lie, say you lost your nerve."

"Wiekowski. Jesus. Like draggin' an epileptic in a seizure back to camp. From spigots. You saw 'em, too, Hayes. They were names and faces. Wiekowski, Potts, Depardieu, Tuttle, Shockley. Turned to BRs that laughed out loud or just grinned and ran into it and... it chewed 'em up. We could've taken this sector without them havin' to die, man. It's a sick game an' I ain't gonna play." He looked past Hayes to the west where, beyond the second trench, were the insta-hardened bunkers of Command. Breck's safe little hidey-hole.

Hayes said, "I'll be back," as he climbed out of the trench.

"You coming back? No *kidding*, huh? Shit, I thought you was, like, going on a Club Pacific vacation."

Captain Breck was in the comm tent, sitting on a folding aluminum chair, frowning over a set of orders she'd just gotten in. She put them on the radio table and covered them with other papers when Hayes came in blinking with the lamplight. She was standard female-officer stuff. Crew cut; hair cut so short, you couldn't be sure of the color; warningly cold gray eyes; her breasts neutralized by the baggy khaki jacket she never took off; a clip of medinject tubes—which she never really used—displayed in her sleeve pocket. Pistol always on her hip. Her expression inquisitive but otherwise dispassionate; nothing feminine but nothing too aggressive, either, wouldn't want to come across as an overcomper. "Sergeant Hayes. Been half expecting you. No orders for you yet re the offensive, and in fact, it looks like I won't be—"

"I'm here about Katz. Write him a waiver."

"Just like that. Little boy doesn't want to take his medicine. He signed a contract. As part of the Army's pharmilitary experiment he gets double pay, he gets double furlow, he gets out sooner than—"

"He gets shot. He gets addicted to the sleep agents they give us to get us down from the aggression plateaus."

"Addiction? What makes you an expert on addiction, Hayes? I've got your file on disk." Sarcastically she ticked off facts on her fingers. "Says you were a foster child and you didn't like your foster parents; says you were a bounty hunter till you went into business cracking armored cars with a guy you were supposed to've brung in. Says you were an ex-con who got drafted from prison because the Army was short on men. Doesn't say a damn thing about you being a doctor. Or even a pharmacist. What the hell you know about addiction? The meds aren't addictive."

"Bullshit. Half the men in E Company are junkies to the stuff. They take the amphets out of boredom, cool out on the sleepers, do more amphets, and maybe once every four days they remember to eat. It isn't that way in my platoon. I keep it minimum. But the others . . . And when we get into an offensive, I lose control of my own guys."

"Experiment's got bugs to be worked out. In the meantime you have your orders. No waiver." She turned to the field computer on the light metal table beside the radio, snicked a cassette into the playback for its TV monitor. New subject. "Going to be a show here in the supplies tent at 0900. Going to show the boys some of this." On the screen was a TV image of a battlefield, shot from overhead. American troops overrunning Soviet positions. The Soviets in full rout, panicked, mowed down. Hayes felt an involuntary thrill. "For morale," Breck said. "Pentagon thinks they'll juice the men up with these, like with a football team—"

Feeling the thrill made Hayes burn with humiliation. And anger. "You pushed my buttons with that," he said, his voice breaking. "And they're probably not even real. Probably vid-animations. Using them like the drugs. Making BRs. Conditioning us. Leaves no room for fighting for our country, for a cause, Captain. We're fighting because we're programmed. Don't it make you sick even a little?"

She looked at him blandly. "You don't usually talk much, but tonight you're babbling like the Grid. You really got a feather in your ass about it. Well, listen: Get used to it. That's an order. You been out here four months, it's gonna be another eight at least, if they don't start usin' nukes. If the antinuke treaty holds. And tomorrow we got a new med-up." She reached into a box, plucked out a pack of medinject tubes, and tossed them to him. Displaying her mastery of that difficult female officer's affectation, the paternal smile. As she said, "Free sample. Dismissed."

Hayes sat cross-legged in his tent, looking at the new medinject pack with a flashlight. The label read: LIMBIC TX4. SECOND SEQUENCE.

Second sequence: It was to be released when the first surge of combat energy wore off. It was a second wind of aggression. He'd heard about it. It was said to be the biochemical distillation of pure rage. And it was said that a man using it in another company had killed his entire platoon. His own people. His buddies.

There was shouting from the front trench, the scared kind. Hayes tucked the medinject pack into his first-aid kit, grabbed his rifle, and ran. He jumped into the trench feet-first, splashing mud. "What we got?"

"Got us an Otto!" Becher yelled. Otto: autonomous assault vehicle, made in East Germany.

Hayes saw it hunching through the dimness, a black silhouette against the gray-brown field, its camera eyes and gun snouts reflecting orange from the setting sun. An unmanned thing, piloted by a computer, programmed to distinguish—if it didn't glitch—between Soviet troops, Soviet vehicles, and NATO. It was two hundred yards off and coming on strong.

The Otto might be just a probe, a stick to stir up the hornet's nest and see how well defended it was. Or it might be the point for a Soviet offensive.

He thought: *Do I? Use the spigot?*

Not now. Not unless he had to. And not with the P-tube. Never with the P-tube. Because that was how they made you

BR. With candy. A bite-size goody for the dog that jumps through the flaming hoop.

Don't think about it. He checked the load on the tank killer and took up his position at the firing post, looked through the infrared sight unit, its eyepiece cold against his skin. The Otto was a hunched shape of dull red. He adjusted the cross hairs. Parakeet looked at it through binoculars. "She's gettin' ready to open up on us, she's raising muzzle. Let's make a baby with her."

Hayes nodded and fired. The launch tube coughed its small missile; the infrared sensor in the tank-killer's sight detected the flare in the tail of the missile, computer-calculated its flight path relative to the axis of the sight, and issued flight-correction commands via microwave transmission. The missile detonated. And a fat red flame was born. "She's havin' our baby!" Carmody cackled.

Hayes shook his head, seeing the tank advance through the smoke. "Uh-uh. Intercepted." The Otto had intercepted the missile with a laser, detonated it before it struck. Parakeet had already reloaded the tank-killer. Hayes sighted in, fired. Nothing happened.

"Mud, oh, Gridfriend, it's the mud," Carmody whined. Mud jamming the weapon.

"LAC, Becher," Hayes shouted, while the Otto's brutish front was made hideously visible by muzzle flash as it opened fire. A long whine, the platoon ducked and—*thud*—the ground shook, spitting some of itself into the air. Gravel pattered down over them. The shell had come up short. Getting the range.

Becher was chattering into the radio for Light Artillery Cover, sneezing between coded sentences—he always seemed to have a cold—and the response came back almost immediately from Breck: "No can do, you're too close to the target."

You bitch, Hayes thought. Tank's a good fifty yards off. She's trying to force Parakeet to use his spigot.

The autonomous tank plowed through an old stone wall, pulverizing lumps of stone as big as a man's head; it snapped lengths of concertina wire, it splintered wooden posts, it came implacably on.

Pflug came sloshing up with the lantern. His grimy features—undershot jaw, eyes too close together, pug nose—lit up on one side as he said, "Come on, Katz, you and me."

Parakeet said, "Not procedure. We wait, we use a seismic grenade—"

"Cowards make excuses, Parakeet," Pflug said, the words coming in a rush, his lip curling. Hair bristling, his face vampirish. He'd turned on his spigot.

Hayes started toward Pflug, yelling, "Back off, that's an order!"

Parakeet put a hand on Hayes's shoulder, restrained him. "Pflug had a talk with the missus, s'afternoon. She throws a stick, Pflug fetches." He looked at Pflug. "Come on, Pflug, let's bury your bone, if it's big enough to find. Show her something. Pflug with his med-ups, me without. See who kicks more butt."

"Katz, don't—" Hayes began.

But Parakeet was already out of the trench, running toward the Otto.

Hayes got up to go after him, climbing onto the insta lip. The Otto's cannon flashed, a shockwave hand slapped him contemptuously backward into a pit where blurry forms of gray moved all slippery past one another...

Not unconscious but stunned. Defenseless as the piranhas came from the underplace in his head; he saw himself under water, saw the gem-bright, wriggling mass of them swarming his face, chewing it away, swimming aside for a moment just to sadistically give him a good look at the bloody skull mask where his face had been...only it wasn't what he expected: it was Katz's face, revealed bloody, smiling sadly, under the shreds of Hayes's own features...

His eyes focused, he saw he was in the trench. No sound but the ringing in his ears. Through a drizzling rain he saw a hemisphere of murky yellow lantern light around the stretcher, where Becher and the medic, Tetscheim, bent over Katz...Parakeet crying—soundlessly but crying like a baby as they sprayed dressing over the gouting stump of his leg. He saw Hayes and stopped crying. He gasped for air. Something went out of his face, and it became an empty thing. And there was no sound but the ringing.

Tetscheim covered Parakeet's empty face with his rain slicker. Delvecchio sat on his helmet, staring at Parakeet's covered body, snickering. Almost gone himself, another way. Tetscheim came to Hayes. "How you doing, Rory?" His voice sounded far away. Hayes was lying on his back in mud. Tetscheim wiped muck from his glasses to see Hayes better. "You don't seem to be bleeding. It hurt when you move?"

Mechanically Hayes moved a little, shook his head. His ears were ringing. But he was all right.

Pflug appeared at the lip of the trench, grinning. "Blew the sucker in half!" Blood running from his mouth. Eyes wild, chest heaving.

Hayes was up, pulling Pflug down, smashing his face into the mud, kicking him. Men pulled him off, held Pflug back. (Delvecchio just watched. Sniggering.)

"It's Breck," Hayes said to himself. "Not this spigsuck. Breck pushed Parakeet into it." He turned to look at the CO's bunkers. He closed his eyes. The piranha were swarming up out of the hole losing Katz had made in him. He had to do something for Katz—for Parakeet.

Tetscheim said, "Breck's gone. She went South to Rouen an hour ago. Transferred out. New CO's due in tonight."

Hayes decided. He opened his eyes, went limp so the others would let him go. They backed off, watching him warily. He said, "Pflug's crazy from med-ups. Anyway, Katz was right: Pflug does what Breck tells him. For P-tubes. So I won't kill him. But I'm going to kill Breck."

Hayes slogged down the trench to ordnance, and the others let him go. Delvecchio sniggering. All of them thinking he'd give up when he thought about it: that she was sixty miles south, at least. That there was no way to get to her. There were sentries on the trucks; they'd never let him take one without authorization. He'd cool off, they thought. Let them think that.

He stepped into the insta-bunker and looked around. In the sulfurous light from the lamp, the ordnance looked like it was coated with yellow dust, ancient like something found in an Egyptian archaeological dig. Racks of rifles; crates of grenades like scarabs in their Styrofoam sockets. And the suits. Scicon suits, hanging in their racks like the skins of some strange semihuman creature. Hayes stared at the suits and wondered if he should use one.

Britain's Scicon Cybernetics had designed the infantry-man's field suit for protection against weather, neurotoxins, germ weapons, napalm and shrapnel. Two layers of organo-metallic* nylon with integral electrical heating, powered and controlled from the backpack, which also contained the microcomputer. The fabric of the suit was supposed to block toxins, and to keep itself aerated through its filter-nozzles; its ergonomically integrated body armor was supposed to protect against light ammunition and shrapnel; the rigid armored soles and armored uppers of the cammie boots were supposed to protect against mines. The helmet was the real bitch. With its gyrostabilized laser designator, image intensifier and thermal imaging camera built into the crown; below that there was a visor screen with a head-up display from a video system, superimposed alphanumeric input from the computer for things like range, aiming marks, graphics for maps, tactical sketches, grid references, infrared imaging. Tempting.

The computer pumped a hundred Megabytes of memory with multiprocessing and symbolic processing. Voice activated. Tell the computer "Major caliber, one hundred fifty meters, four rounds," and the aiming mark corrected for range appears on the visor while the weapon—on line to the computer—selects the correct barrel, takes off the safety and prepares the rounds. You move the weapon till the slaved aiming mark is on the target and you pull the trigger and . . .

The weapon. The real seductress. Double barreled, upper firing a high explosive shell or flare or smoke charge; the lower firing a caseless cartridge rifle caliber; semi or full auto. Monster clip of lightweight ammo. And the backpack contained vertical-launch light mortar, programmable and slaved to the microcomputer.

Seductive.

But he knew better. He'd used the suits three times.

Breck wouldn't let them use the suits for day to day defense, unless there was a neurotoxin alert. They were still experimental, and expensive as a motherfucker, and they

---

*Chemical compounds consisting of a metal atom bonded with an organic atom or atoms. OMs have a variety of applications.

tended to develop glitches during extended use. They were for patrols, special ops, emergencies.

But if Parakeet had worn one he might be alive. Another mark against Breck.

Still, Hayes didn't like them. They weren't as light and easy to wear as they were supposed to be. The torso armor was chancy. It might stop a round, it might break or it might punch inward with the round so you had a few inches of suit in your gut along with the bullet. The helmet's sound amplifiers tended to blare things at you, confuse you. The computer screens reacted to electric fields generated by other suits and your picture'd snow out or go infrared when you didn't want it. Parakeet had claimed his visor kept picking up some British game show, but who knew if Parakeet were making it up. The thermostats were quirky. Step into a microwave signal and they freaked, you'd find yourself roasting or freezing.

And you felt isolated, in a Scicon suit. Never mind that you talked to the others on radio. That your hearing was enhanced. You felt like you were in a tiny plasteel room . . .

Interfered with your instincts. Frustrated the Indian fighter in you.

The only trouble was, the Sovies were supposed to be deploying particle beam cannons on the battlefield. Big, awkward fusion-powered things that cut through the air waist-high over flat terrain with a highly energetic stream of hydrogen atoms; literally cut a man in half. Hayes had seen the NATO prototypes testing in Belgium. They didn't look like cannons; they looked like giant, complicated fire hydrants, tricked out with wires and a muzzle like a radar antenna. When they were fired there was a violet glow around the muzzle, but the beam itself was just a waver in the air, a translucent shimmer. The violet glow was the same as the city-shine off the smog in an American city at night. Glum violet shine. Made him weirdly homesick.

The beams tended to disperse with geological magnetic fields, to diffuse when they hit fog; they were energy-hogs and the fusion reactors were expensive. Neither the Soviets nor NATO used them widely. Yet.

But if he should stumble into one, the suit would be the only defense.

Hayes snorted. Bullshit. They used those things on orbital battle stations to knock down ICBMs. If they could penetrate a missile they could penetrate a Scicon suit. Anyway, chances were small he'd run into them.

Fuck it. He'd go bare-assed.

He went through the conventional weapons. Strapped an autonomous missile launcher to his back. Picked a grenade launcher, a satchel of clips preloaded with SS-109 5.56-mm rifle cartridges and a NATO-issue Enfield equipped with a Laserscope. The Laserscope looked like an oversize telescopic sight atop the gun; the laser wasn't used as a weapon, directly—the problem of adequate power supply in hand-held killing lasers had never been solved. But the Laserscope aiming aid was lethal in its own electronically Taoist way. He heard two men pass the bunker, talking, one of them claiming the Soviets were on the move again.

The hell with the Soviets. He wanted Breck.

Maybe she'd known. Maybe it was cowardice, Hayes thought. She'd known the Soviets were going to push back, were trying to retake France down to the Rhône. She'd known they'd cut off E Company and the others from the rest of the division. Driving southwest between E's position and Rouen. Maybe she'd fled, getting through just ahead of the Reds. So it amounted to this: The Soviets were encamped between Hayes and Breck. Forty miles of them.

And he was AWOL, so there was NATO to deal with too. Once he thought he saw the silvery flutter of a drone surveillance bird overhead. Maybe they were tracking him. Might be either side. Them—or them . . .

Hayes encountered the Soviet *them* an hour before midnight. The fulsome sky was drizzling, gusting. Hayes was slogging through a field, mud sucking at his boots, shades of gray and black delineating erosion-dulled furrows and the barbed-wire fence he followed south; the frozen wave of darkness that was the hills at the horizon. He was chewing a particularly tough slab of dried fruit and beginning to feel the aches in his shoulders, which suffered under the weight of the missile launcher strapped to his back; the gnawing aches were little piranhas burrowing into his flesh. The assault rifle in his arms had grown heavier; his throat was constricted with fatigue. But it wasn't time for the spigot yet. He had to hold off—

He bellied down in the mud. The hulk of a shack ahead, where the fence ended. A man-shape beside it, outlined in a bluish light bleeding from the shack. Voices in Russian, or maybe Czech.

Hayes wormed through icy mud, getting it in his mouth, down his shirt, shivering with it. But getting closer. Hearing them laugh. Maybe they'd smuggled some vodka out to the guard post. The man-shape loomed up. The sentry spotted Hayes; left half of Slavic face showing a scared blue eye. *Don't look them in the eyes.*

Hayes wedged the butt of the stubby Enfield in the mud, deciding he was too close to need the laser-aiming device, letting his instincts aim for him, firing a burst of 5.56-mm rounds, splashing the frightened face apart. Then Hayes was up, firing into the shack, raking it, hearing men inside scream. He stepped up to the door, finished the one who was crawling. After that, sticky with mud, he continued south.

Forty yards over a low hill—a spread of lights. Men shouting. They'd heard the shooting. Over there: tarps over what was probably a fuel dump.

He caught the silvery fluttering, high up, out of the corner of his eye. No time to look. He was already unstrapping the autonomous missile launcher, setting it up, looking through the sights, forcing his cold-stiffened fingers to program it to fire its first two rounds into the fuel dump, the rest in its eight-round drum at anything that moved, within a certain scope—anything with a bulk-spread of two meters or more. Which might be a group of men and might be an armored vehicle. Or a stray cow. He wedged the autolauncher's tripod in place on the hilltop—and ducked as rifle fire unzipped the air by his head. They were coming up the hill, firing from the south side. He rolled down the north side and began to circle around. Behind him he heard the *shoompf! click, shoompf!* as the autolauncher let go two minimissiles at the fuel dump, then the *whirrrr* as it tracked the men coming up the hill at it.

Explosions painted the sky red and rearranged the other side of the hill. Hayes kept going, thinking: *Maybe I ought to switch on the spigot, go into overdrive. No. No, not un-*

less I have to. The enemy thought he was on the hilltop. They kept charging it, in bunches; the launcher kept flawlessly blowing them away. And Hayes kept circling the hill, coming around the flank, looking for a way through. Men loomed up in the darkness, limned with the background flames of the burning dump, forty yards off, looking like target silhouettes; he pressed the bladelike pressure switch attached to the forearm grip of the assault rifle. He held the gun at pectoral level; the laser lanced out, invisible now that it had stopped raining—invisible till it hit the chest of the first man running at him, making a red dot on his chest: a red dot harmless in itself, but telling Hayes he was sighted in. He squeezed the trigger, making the man's chest erupt blood. A second man came at him, firing one of the new Soviet Dragunovas, its burst making little geysers in the mud near Hayes's feet—the guy screaming when Hayes pressed the trigger, sighting in effortlessly. He slapped in another clip, laid the red mark on them as they came, cut them down again and again. Once between clips, he came on a man up close, had to gut him with a knife that he'd never used before except to open tin cans. Running. Exhaustion a weight on him . . . more men up ahead.

He reached down and moved the cover off the medinject, turned the knob. The nighted landscape of the interior Hayes lit up with a flash of biochemical light, and his heart started playing a drumroll, and he laughed and found himself running and firing through a group of men, lining up the red dot, firing, lining up the red dot, the Laserscope aiming for him, firing . . . chewing the dried fruit like a kid happily chewing gum as he cuts a lawn . . . seeing clearly now the surveillance bird watching him overhead, not caring . . . caught up in the roaring delight of what he hated most.

Two A.M., and Hayes was hunched under his slicker, in a cave of twisted, blackened metal: the overturned cab of a shattered truck. Hayes feeling like a mollusk in a sunken ship.

He sat shivering, dozing. He'd given himself an hour's rest. A film of rainwater curtained him from the roadside. Now and then he heard a *crump,* and a corner of the mercurial curtain lit up with a lightninglike flash from the shellings to the east. The rain sizzled and burbled on the metal overhead.

Another sound, growing. Rumble, metal gnashings, dronings. Vehicles coming, moving north to south. Going his way...

He fitted a grenade launcher onto his Enfield, stood up, and stepped out into the rain. Felt chills and nausea and weakness sweep through him. Wanted to turn back, hide in his shelter. Felt an overwhelming self-disgust as he thought of the men he'd killed when he was hyped on the spigot; killing them in a biochemically induced frenzy was... sickening. Repugnant. But he thought about Parakeet. And Breck. He reached down, turned the knob on his medinject. Felt the spigot shooting him up. Flash... go.

Two trucks, headlights rain-scratchy funnels of glare along the muddy road. He ran at the two trucks, seeing the red star on the side. Firing the grenade at the ground in front of the lead truck, his amphetamine-accelerated brain calculating the grenade's trajectory and the speed of the truck perfectly—so that the grenade went off directly under the truck's gas tank. He threw himself down: a ball of fire ate seven tons of metal and twenty shrieking men. Seeing the explosion, he felt a neon-edged rush.

As if frightened by the explosion, the rain stopped.

The second truck pulled up short, and Hayes charged at it, the spigot juice white-hot in him but giving him wicked razor-backed chills made of metal-flake colors and whiplash shapes. There were muzzle flashes in the truck cab's window, and submachine-gun rounds gnashed away part of his right thigh, two fingers on his left hand, a chunk of his left cheek. He felt the woundings as streaks of burn, and it inflamed him more, made him zigzag, come around from outside their shooting angle, jump on the running board, shove the muzzle of the Enfield into the cab of the truck. Shoot the men in the cab neatly in their foreheads... There were two others under a tarp between the rocket launchers in the back of the truck. He shot them with inhuman precision. They moved so slowly, it wasn't difficult, really, to kill them all.

Machines and dying men both steaming in the darkness.

Hayes sprayed sealant on his wounds. Then, too jacked up to feel pain, he prowled around the truck, dragging the limp bodies clear, checking out the intact truck in the shuddery light from the one that was burning. It was an enormous, eight-wheel, twenty-two-ton ZIL-300 tokomak truck, camouflage-painted, broad and low to the ground, each of its wheels five feet high—and on its flatbed were two big BM-31 salvo rocket launchers, each with four rows of ten missile-launching rails. Capable of firing forty 122-mm rockets from each launcher. At once. Murderously concentrated firepower.

Hayes looked at the control equipment. Analogous to the NATO variety. He smiled.

It was a checkpoint. They looked up, bored, when they saw the truck coming, blued in dawn light, with its tired-eyed driver.

Hayes, wearing a Soviet overcoat, nodded to them and started to drive through. One of them raised a hand to tell him to stop and, yawning, said something to him in Russian, probably asking for travel orders. When the sentry saw Hayes wasn't going to stop, he raised his rifle—Hayes pointed a Soviet pistol through the window and shot him. And his friend. He drove on.

Downshifting to go up a muddy hill, and before he got to the top, he saw a platoon of Soviets outlined against the sky. One of the guys at the checkpoint hadn't been quite dead, must've accessed a radio. Because bullets were making crooked stars on the windshield, glass fragments stinging his cheek. He was already adjusting the salvo coordinates. The first rocket launcher behind the cab swiveled, tilted. He punched the fire button, and the truck shuddered. A noise like a razor strop magnified ten thousand times and then in multiple thunder the top of the hill—and the men on it—vanished into a fireball that heaved bloodied dirt and stone into the air.

Hayes swung to the right, off the road; circled the smoking, flame-flickered crown of the hill; and saw the camp laid out in front of him. More men coming at him.

Hayes lowered the first salvo launcher, raised the second, reset it for four ten-rocket salvos at four ranges. Fired.

Like instantaneously planting rows of autumn trees, trees with trunks of fire and roiling-smoke foliage. Kind of pretty.

The BM-31 could be reloaded once automatically—and then the reloaders would have to be restocked with rockets. He pulled the levers for reloading, waited nervously while machinery rattled and creaked to itself, and the fires diminished and the smoke tattered. Men picking themselves up, some of them literally, and coming at him again. Bullets whining from the grille of the ZIL-300.

The machinery stopped creaking; a green light went on in front of him. He fired one salvo in four sets. Another grove of hell-trees, the ground shaking, the sky echoing with artificial thunder.

He glimpsed a recon bird. There—and gone in the pall of smoke.

He drove on, through slow waves of fume and smolder. An armor-penetrating round struck the ZIL's engine casing. The engine spouted steam from the bullet hole, coughed. But kept turning over.

Hayes found a mostly intact highway, and on it a sign read ROUEN 20 KM. Exactly parallel to the sign, the engine died. Just as well, he was coming to NATO lines. He took off the overcoat and got out of the truck.

By the time he got to the first NATO checkpoint, his nerves were frayed through, and his wounds were beginning to hurt. It was like the piranhas were in them, burrowing. There were winter-stripped trees by the roadside, stark against the gray sky, and to Hayes they looked like his nerve endings, exposed and creaking in the icy wind. His senses were sharpened till they cut him. He could feel his clothes rasping his skin, feel the sickening meatiness of his limbs, the clicking interaction of his joints, the soreness of his feet, feel it all too clearly, and the sensations razzed him, nagged at him. He hated the feel of his own body. Hated the stink of it. Everything he looked at annoyed him. He knew it was drug fatigue, but he couldn't help it; he hated the sight of the road, the grass by it, that damn recon bird, the clouds, the abandoned farmhouses. Everything. And he was gagging from exhaustion.

A checkpoint. French soldiers on walkie-talkies. They said something to him in French and he shrugged. He was prepared to kill them. To kill anyone who stood between him and Breck.

The guy with the walkie-talkie got an order about Hayes. He spoke to the other man, who gestured for Hayes to come with him. Hayes decided to play along for a while. They might just take him to Breck.

They did. First they took him to an infirmary, got his wounds patched up. Then, over the objections of the Army doctors, they took him to an old hotel that had been appropriated by NATO, converted for military use. Turned him over to an MP who surprised Hayes by not trying to take his weapons away. The MP escorted Hayes upstairs and into a suite that contained a number of mismatched desks, collected piecemeal from around town. Breck was there alone, sitting at a dented metal desk, drinking coffee and looking at a TV monitor on the desktop. He came to stand by the desk, a yard from her, the Enfield held casually in one hand. "Coffee, Hayes?" she asked, dismissing the MP with a wave.

"No." Kill her now? Just like that? It seemed anticlimactic. He'd know when the moment came.

"Why'd you go AWOL, Hayes?"

He just looked at her.

"You might have been shot for desertion. Except for this." She turned the monitor around so it faced him.

He saw himself, filmed from above, running at the Soviet troops, cutting down three men. Another shot showed the burning fuel dump. Another shot of Hayes, shooting the men in the truck . . .

"It was just luck, of course," she said. "The drugs and the hormones helped, I'm sure. But with all those odds against you, you should've been killed half a dozen times. You had a streak of luck."

He nodded. She was right.

Breck leaned back in her chair, making it creak. "Still, Hayes—you're a hero. We need footage like this. We won't have to alter it much at all. And you can give some testimony, maybe some inspirational talks to the troops." Her voice dripped with cynicism. "It'll be cushy duty . . . you okay, Hayes? You look like you're about to fall over."

He shrugged.

She nodded toward a door on her left. "General Moreland is in there, with Major Kessel. They're talking about the spigots, the pharmilitary experiment, the whole drug project —and about you. They were on the point of recommending that the project be canceled, but it seems your little performance here has convinced them the thing works, after all." She smiled thinly, adding, her voice crackling dry, "Congratulations."

He felt like someone had kicked him in the belly.

She chuckled and lit a cigarette.

Bitch. "Maybe," he said, speaking with difficulty through a parched mouth, "I can change their minds."

He leaned over, pushed the muzzle of the Enfield against her cheek. "How many others are in there?"

"Hayes, what are you—"

"Shut up. No, don't shut up, answer my question."

"Half a dozen. And an MP."

"Good."

"What?"

He took the Limbic TX4 from his first-aid kit. "Show me your spigot."

"I haven't got one." Saying it between clenched teeth. But there was more fear than anger in her eyes.

He set the TX4 on the desk, took a syringe from his first-aid kit. Using one hand, keeping the gun on her with the other, he sucked the TX4 up into the syringe.

"Hayes, that's a full dose. If you put that into me, it'll kill me."

"Probably not. But you won't know what you're doing once the full dose hits you. The *over*dose. Anyone in your sights . . ." He jabbed it expertly into her arm, probed till he found the vein, saw her bite her lip with pain.

"Hayes!"

He emptied the syringe in her, then hit her on the jaw with the rifle butt. She went over backward. Bang and clatter as the chair fell—but no one came in. She lay there, dazed, disoriented. He took her by the collar, dragged her to her feet, took her to the door that led into the room where General Moreland and Major Kessel and the others were. He put the Enfield into her hands and held her firmly, till he saw the rage come into her face, saw the TX4 going to work. Her face contorting, eyes dilating, foam showing at the corners of her mouth . . .

He opened the door and shoved her into the room, told the startled faces, "Whoever survives, test her blood afterward to see what she was on." Then he left the room, fast.

The shooting started almost immediately.

Down in the street, five blocks away, Hayes found an old French grocer who spoke English. The old man was willing to sell him some civilian clothes. Hayes changed into them and then he went to look for a way out of town.

He'd need to move fast, he might have to kill some NATO sentries and a few MPs, and he was exhausted. So he had to use the spigot this last time, had to. He turned the knob on his medinject. Feeling as if fuses were burning out in his brain when the stuff hit him. Searing him, banging his heart like the hammer on a fire-alarm bell.

He saw men materializing from shadowy doorways on either side of the narrow street. Soviet soldiers, some of them missing portions of their skulls, their limbs, some of them with neat, round holes in their chests, smiling at him with a sort of melancholy camaraderie. They surrounded him. But he didn't feel threatened. Didn't feel he had to fight. One of them had an arm hanging by a shred of skin; the arm fell off, and another bent, smilingly picked up the arm, tucked it under the man's intact armpit. Then he turned to Hayes, said with a Russian accent, "We have to get a move on, Rory. MPs'll come soon."

Hayes said, "I'm hallucinating you."

The Soviet nodded happily.

"I'm sorry, man. I'm sorry," Hayes said.

"It's okay." And the dead soldiers patted Hayes on the back to show him it was okay.

Then they all hurried down the street together. The dead Soviets and Hayes, a crowd of friends.

FirStep, the Space Colony, L-5 orbit.

Kitty stepped off the lift at level 3, corridor C13, and saw the SA bull waiting on the other side of the glass wall.

Was it glass or some kind of plastic or what? She wasn't sure.

She hesitated outside the elevator, looking at the big man in the padded gray-black suit, his face completely hidden behind the mirrored visor. She couldn't tell if he was looking at her or not, and that bothered her. He stood there with his legs braced apart, his hands locked behind him, motionless. He might be asleep in that helmet, or leering at her, or his face might be angry or . . . anything.

She wanted badly to see Chester. But she was scared of the guards. *Go on*, she told herself, *Security gave you a visitor's pass, what are they going to do?*

She walked over to the glass wall. She yelled, so he could hear through the glass, "I'm Kitty Torrence."

The guard pointed to an intercom grid in the wall. She heard his amplified voice. "May I help you?"

Surprised by his politeness, she stammered a moment till she managed, "I'm here to see . . ." Then she remembered the pass, which would explain everything. She took it out of her pocket, pressed it to the glass.

The guard touched something on the wall to his left, and the glass lifted into the ceiling. "Go ahead on back. You'll see a door on the right says D5, the guard there'll escort you."

"Thank you."

Kitty walked by him with a little ripple of anxiety, half expecting him to turn and grab her from behind. Don't be stupid, she told herself. But she jumped a little at the noise of the glass wall coming down behind her. Hum, click.

She walked down to the hall, looking at door numbers. Her belly had grown a lot lately, making her back hurt, and making her feel awkward when she walked. She found D5, touched the door panel, and it slid aside. She went into a small gray metal room and spoke to a young, bored guard, plump and blond, sitting at a metal desk—this guard was, thank God, without a helmet. He looked at her pass. She saw him glance at her pregnant belly. He shrugged, took her handprint, then said something into an intercom. He listened, then nodded to himself and said, "Come with me, please."

They went down a long, narrow hall to a door stenciled

D5, VISITORS. The guard used a code-key to open the door. They went in, the guard second. It was a small room, harshly overlit, featureless except for a number of metal chairs along the walls and a vent. Sitting in one corner, a tearful Asian woman was talking earnestly, in Chinese or Korean or something, to an Asian man in a detainee's numbered blue printout. Paper pajamas, they called them. The opposite door opened, and Chester came in, trying to look proud in his own blue paper pajamas, a guard behind him. "You folks sit anywhere, you've got a half hour," Kitty's escort said.

Chester looked around sullenly till he saw her. He smiled and strode to her; she met him halfway and hugged him. She heard him suck his breath in quickly, and she asked, "I hurt you, huh? They bruise you pretty bad?"

"No—ribs are cracked, is all. They taped 'em up." He put his arm around her, and they went to sit in the corner opposite the other couple. The guards stood together at the visitors' door, talking in low voices about a glider race in the Open.

Kitty and Chester sat with their knees together, holding hands. They kissed. For a few minutes they looked at each other and Chester told her not to cry. But it was Chester whose eyes were filling.

When they spoke, it was in technicki.

"They beat you up since you been here?" she asked in a whisper.

"No. Just before they brought us in, if we even twitched a little. Here they mostly treat us like they're dogcatchers and we're the dogs. Dogcatcher doesn't beat the dogs, but he ain't nice to 'em, either."

"She was right." Meaning Chu. She didn't want to say her name here. "They haven't got her yet. They . . . interrogate you?"

"Twice. Real politely the first time. Second time I think they were gonna use electricity, maybe drugs, but then Russ Parker came in, told them to send me back, he'd oversee an interrogation at 'a later date.' They didn't like that. It's like" —he glanced at the guards, lowered his voice further—"it's like there's some kind of feud between the SA security and the old security. Which is, you know, kind of interesting. Maybe we could—"

"Chester..." She made a sound of exasperation. "I can't believe I'm doing this—I mean, I'm getting into this thing where the woman tells the man, 'Please don't do it, darling!' I don't like getting stuck in those clichés, Chester. Don't make me have to plead like that, okay?"

She was angry, and she wasn't sure if it was at Chester or the SA or both. She was buzzing with it, and it was too much to handle; it made her want to cry.

"Well, babe, what you want me to do?" he asked, patting her baby-big belly.

"I want you to play their game. Play Uncle Tom if you have to. We've got to get off this thing. Out of the Colony. Chester, what about RM17?"

She glanced at the guards and saw with a chill that both of them were looking at her. One of them, the black-haired one with the long sideburns, looked at her with uncut contempt. *You let that nigger knock you up,* his look said. She wanted to spit in his face. But she turned back to Chester. "They piss me off, too, Chester. But they have the guns and we don't. They know about you. And Shood and—the others."

He took a deep breath and closed his eyes. One of the tears that had been waiting there was freed to streak past his nose. He laughed softly at himself and wiped it away. "Crying. I'm a wimp, huh?"

She shook her head, feeling close to tears now herself.

"Thing is," he said, his voice breaking, looking at the floor, "there's no way they're going to let me out of the Colony, even if the blockade drops—maybe not even here. They don't want people on Earth talking them down. They got politics to worry about. I mean, you know where I am, here? I'm in a jail within a jail inside *another* jail. I'm in the lockup, and I'm jailed by being black here, and I'm jailed by being in the Colony at all, nothing but vacuum around us." He shook his head. "No way out. May as well fight it out. Nothing to lose."

"What about this?" She took his hand, put it on her belly. They both felt the baby move. He smiled.

"How is he?"

"He? It's going to be a girl!"

"You had a gender test for it?"

"No, but I just know—"

"Bullshit, it's going to be a boy."

"A girl."

"A boy."

They laughed a little, and that felt good. Then she started to cry for real.

He took her in his arms and said, "I don't know. Must be a way. This guy, Russ Parker . . . maybe you could talk to him. I can't see him, they won't let me. I already asked."

She drew back from him to ask, "What about an attorney?"

"They're all appointed for you, and they all belong to SA. And even if they're sympathetic, they can't do shit because of the emergency-martial-law thing."

She shrugged. "I don't think they'd let me see Parker."

They embraced again, but then the guard who'd given her that look came over and tapped her on the shoulder. "Come on, time's up." He had halitosis.

"It hasn't been a half hour," Chester said, and she could see him working hard to control his temper.

"I don't care. I can't stand looking at this unnatural relations here no more—"

Chester stood up, drew his arm back, shouted, "You fucking—"

And the guy hit him with the RR stick he had ready in his hand. It happened too fast to see where he'd hit him; she didn't see any blood, but Chester went to his knees, stunned, and Kitty—sobbing, "Stop it!"—pushed between them, bent to put her arms around him.

The other guard came over. "That's enough, lady. Come on, he'll be all right." He took her by the elbow, dragged her firmly out the visitor's door. She yelled something and he ignored it and . . .

A few minutes later Kitty was in the elevator, going back to the dorms alone, shaking and holding her heavy middle, trying to control the sobbing.

But as she passed Admin's level, she punched for stop and reset the elevator. She went back up to Admin. To see Russ Parker.

ROUEN, FRANCE.

It was another wet day in Rouen, and Watson was tired of the place. The old quarter of town had a certain charm, with its narrow, cobbled streets, its rococo eighteenth-century buildings. But he'd come now to the abandoned supermarket they were using as a detention center; it was in the "new" quarter, which was already dilapidated, the high rises dreadfully ill-kept, and the streets chocked with trash and war debris.

It was nine A.M. He'd had a meager breakfast of stale croissants, souring orange juice, and excessively sweet coffee, and he was still hungry. The rain had been sputtering on and off all morning; it returned as he stepped from the SA staff car to the cleared path that led between heaps of soggy trash and wet rubble, to the barren supermarket. The building looked markedly truncated between two high rises. They'd left ten-foot heaps of rubble around it as a defensive bulwark against NR attacks.

Watson wore his most elaborate uniform, just to cut back on red tape, and a shiny billed cap he himself had designed. Rain dripped off the bill as he stepped up to the metal doors and showed the helmeted guard his ID. He was ushered quickly inside.

It was more like a cattle barn than a supermarket now. The shelving had been removed, replaced by rows of pens to one side, wire fences between them, guards on the walks between fences. The pens were crowded and it was sickeningly obvious that some of the chemical toilets were overflowing. He must see that they had the prisoners clean them out, as they presented a health hazard for the guards.

High on the wall to the right was a glass mirror panel that housed the offices and once had provided a vantage for spying on shoplifters.

He went to the steps leading to the offices. He was looking for Chilroy.

He found him in Interrogation 9, at work. He was a trim, muscular young man, into health foods and working out; brisk, friendly, eager to please, generally considered on his way up. Watson disliked him for his cheerful willingness to impress everyone by overworking, never letting you forget he was overworking; and for his insincere geniality. He knew that some of his dislike was fear of Chilroy's ambition.

"Colonel Watson!" Chilroy said brightly, making sure his face lit up as he registered recognition of his superior. "This is an honor, sir!"

"Hullo, Chilroy. Bang at it as usual, I see."

"I've cut back, sir. Never more than fourteen hours a day."

It was a small room, perhaps once used for detaining shoplifters. The walls were institutional green. There was a doctor's examination table in the middle of the room. On it, strapped down under a dangling light, was a nude, pasty-skinned, Hasidic Jew, bearded, with the curls behind his ears, the classic hook nose right out of one of the old German propaganda posters. Watson made a face. This was the most demonstratively Jewish of the Jews. The man was shaking his head from side to side, muttering in what sounded like a mixture of French and Hebrew, bloody foam trailing from the corners of his mouth. The leather restraints creaked with his convulsive movements as Chilroy applied a smoking, white-hot electric instrument to the Jew's twitching skin, talking as he did it like a video metal-shop teacher demonstrating a soldering iron. "Some of them just seem to have the wrong brain chemistry for the extractor, and the darn thing is so expensive to use, we've fallen back on old-fashioned techniques for most of—"

"What is it you're trying to find out here?"

"Ah . . ." Chilroy looked nonplussed for a moment.

Watson enjoyed that. He'd forgotten why he was torturing the man!

"Oh, ah," Chilroy said, "we're trying to ascertain the whereabouts of his Rabbi. The Rabbi's an activist, a partisan."

"His Rabbi? Do I have the file on this man?"

"Yes, sir, we sent it to you by telex. I just hope it gets through with the other material we've sent along. The Soviets have been cutting lines and scrambling again."

"Mmm. Not important for the moment. Don't spend too much time on him. He isn't worth it."

Not that Chilroy knew fuck-all about interrogation, any-way. He was too young for the job. He had no subtlety. He was a sociopath, with the requisite inability to feel empathy, and in that department he was ideal. He'd grow into it. Eventually Watson would have to see to it he learned the fine points. The basic truths of interrogation: that the shortcut to a man's secrets was the destruction of his sense of self-worth. Psychologically undermine him with humiliation, force him to identify with his interrogators. Physical torture did that, of course, for a time. But psychological torture was more effective in the long term. Watson had learned both techniques from CIA interrogators. The CIA had always been the Professors of Torture. In the twentieth century they'd taught the Guatemalans, the Argentine military, the Chileans, the Salvadorans; they'd taught their trade in Africa, too, where Watson had learned it.

But it was hopeless to try to pass it on to Chilroy now, though Watson had the fatherly impulse to try, despite his dislike of the boy. One takes a pleasure in teaching the young the skills of adulthood. Later, later. Just now, some-thing simpler. . . .

Watson said, "You know, Chilroy, the technique you're using is time-consuming." Watson looked at the welts and blisters on the Jew's skin. "And a man can steel himself against it with some success. Much faster to sit them up, let them watch as you take a hacksaw to their genitals. Or better yet, bring in their family, play with the children a bit; these Jews have strong family instincts." He glanced at his watch. "I wish to see the American."

"Certainly, sir. This way."

They went down the hall to a padlocked double door. Chilroy opened the lock, removed the chains, and drew his side-arm. "The man is dangerous. He's under sedation, and he's handcuffed to a pipe, but . . ."

Watson nodded. Inside, they found Hayes as Chilroy had left him, sitting on the floor, cuffed to an iron pipe that ran floor-to-ceiling, staring at the barred window of the old storeroom. His left hand was bandaged; he'd lost several fingers. His eyes were red-rimmed, his hair thatchy.

"His name is Hayes, sir."

"And the Army doesn't know where he is?"

"Not so far as we know. They *are* looking for him."

Watson said sharply, "Hayes!"

Hayes looked at him. Then at his cuffs, then back at Watson.

Watson could guess what Hayes was thinking. Hayes was thinking he'd like to kill both these strangers and would, except for the cuffs. "I see why you drew your gun," Watson muttered.

"Yes, sir. He's a killer. He's quieter now that we took him off the amphetamines and hormones they had him on. But . . ."

Hayes murmured something—not to Watson or Chilroy or to himself, but, it seemed, to the shaft of light angling down from the window.

"He talks to a bird, Colonel. An imaginary bird. A parakeet. One of our patrols found him wandering the streets, talking to this imaginary bird, in English. We ID'd him with the DNA tag."

"I see."

He might be too far gone to use. But it would take a while for the drugs to really wear off completely. A better diet, a detoxification program, and probably something could be done with him. Looking at Hayes, Watson felt that, indeed, something could be done. They'd have to rebuild much of his personality, in any case. And, of course, he'd need a new face. Colonel Watson felt a queasy déjà vu, a sense of destiny unfolding. This man was to be his weapon.

"I think he'll do nicely," Watson said.

The Island of Malta.

A windy morning on Malta. The three men stood on a tarmac dock in a Maltese shipyard. The cliffs of metal hulls rose on both sides; loading cranes, like the skeletons of abstract dinosaurs, reared over them. They stood in the center of the dock, in a narrow patch of sunshine between shadows from the ships. They were warm from the sun and cold from the wind, by turns. On Hard Eyes's right the *Hermes' Grandson* was half concealed by derricks and tarps and other dry-dock devices Steinfeld had used to camouflage the craft from spy satellites.

A number of still mysterious crates and the prisoners had been removed from the ship, taken to storage and incarceration.

Hard Eyes was exhausted. He hadn't slept in—how long? Thirty-six hours? Forty-eight? He wasn't sure. The sunshine hurt his eyes, but it felt good on his neck. He looked down the dock, hoping Claire would show up and ask for him. Maybe she was already with Karakos.

"You look like you need some rest, Dan," Steinfeld told him.

"What was Karakos's assignment during the assault?" Hard Eyes asked, massaging the bridge of his nose.

"Radio room," Steinfeld said wearily. "Why?"

"Did he ask for it?"

"Yes, he said he thought he knew where it was."

"Did he go alone?"

"No, of course not." But Steinfeld looked uncomfortable.

"Who was it?"

After a moment's hesitation Steinfeld said, "Pierce and Griem."

Hard Eyes said, "And both men were killed."

"Killed by the SA."

"How do you know?"

Danco snorted. "Hard Eyes, Karakos is a freedom fighter, the real thing, a man fighting from patriotism—something you would not understand."

Hard Eyes glared at Danco. Danco only grinned back at him.

He wanted to hit Danco. In his grinning mouth. But Hard Eyes held back. He had become increasingly alienated from the other NR lately. *Don't make it worse*.

Hard Eyes turned to Steinfeld. "This morning I was working on the deck, near the hatch where Karakos was. He was down in the hold—"

"I wondered why you insisted on working there. So you could keep an eye on him, eh?" Steinfeld shook his head in exasperation, his beard whipping in the wind.

"Anyway, this time I heard him talking to Bonham."

"What was Bonham doing there?" Danco broke in with maddening irrelevance.

"Steinfeld sent him over to help unload," Hard Eyes said impatiently. "I couldn't hear most of what they said. But Bonham was offering some kind of deal to Karakos. And Karakos said he'd consider it. What I want to know is, what has Bonham got that Karakos would be interested in? What has Karakos got that Bonham could use?"

Steinfeld took a deep breath, expelled it in a long, sighing expression of irritation. "And you said yourself you couldn't hear them clearly. You could've heard what you wanted to hear."

"Steinfeld, Karakos is your old friend. You don't want to believe something's not right with him—"

Steinfeld said, "Hard Eyes, your judgment on the matter is even less objective than mine."

Hard Eyes remembered that candlelit room, Karakos holding Claire naked in his arms.

Hard Eyes said, "Maybe. But maybe not too."

He turned and walked away from them. Wondering tiredly: *Are they right? Am I seeing things out of jealousy?*

He made up his mind to forget his suspicions. If he could.

Karakos walked moodily into the barn, past the men rolling the small, bullet-scarred copter back into place. He climbed the rickety wooden stairs to the radio room, hoping to find Claire.

But it was this man Bonham who was on his mind.

"I talked to Pierce before he died," Bonham had said that morning in the hold. "I was helping out in the infirmary and . . . I was the last one to talk to him. You look surprised. You thought he was dead, right? You were in a hurry to get to that radio, seems like, so you were sloppy. He told me: You shot him. There could only be one reason for that." He lowered his voice. "You're SA, my friend."

"I ought to kill you for that insult."

"Don't play the game with me, Karakos. Pierce wasn't delirious. He was sure. So am I. But it's okay. You think I like this cornball operation of Steinfeld's? I don't care about politics, man. I'm sick of this scene."

Karakos waited, listening. Wondering if he could kill this

man here, make it look like an accident. No one would mourn him much. Bonham was a skinny, flabby, rat-faced man—what he had become had made him more so than he would have to be—and he was easy to dislike.

"I'm sick of being held prisoner," Bonham said. "I want to go back to the States. I figure you can help me. Get me a pass from the SA, a guarantee of safe passage from them. In exchange I can give you some information they'd love to have: I know who the top NR people are on the Colony. Only Steinfeld and Witcher and Smoke know that, besides me. You help me and I'll help you, tit for tat, and I'll keep my mouth—"

"Shut it now," Karakos had whispered, looking up at the square entrance to the hold in the metal ceiling. Hard Eyes had appeared up there.

There was still time to decide about Bonham. The man was dangerous, untrustworthy. But the information about the Colony could be very useful indeed.

And SA headquarters, speaking to Karakos aboard the *Hermes' Grandson*, had said, in essence: "Take your time, observe, learn what you can about this upcoming assault of theirs; learn about the NR's infrastructure, especially about their undercover operations in Europe, the States, anywhere. Gather more information about the Maltese base. We will destroy it when the time is right—you'll have plenty of warning."

And perhaps now Claire could be induced to give him something about the assault Steinfeld was planning.

She was there, in the radio room. With Lila, damn her.

The two women looked up from the decoder as Karakos came in. Lila put the decoder on hold and blanked the screen. *Does she suspect me?*

"Hello," Karakos said. He looked at Claire. There were rings under her eyes, and she was pale. She hadn't slept yet, either.

"Hi," she said, and pretended to look over something in a notebook.

There was a moment of silence; the only voice heard was the wind's, singing mournfully in the eaves.

Then Karakos asked, "Can I speak to you, Claire?"

She hesitated, then shook her head. "No, I—I've got some new stuff in. I've got to get it ready for Steinfeld."

Just an excuse. She didn't want to talk to him alone. So that was the way of it. She was having an attack of guilt. Or perhaps this Lila, who was looking holes through him, had turned her against him.

He could wait. Claire was useful to him; she misdirected the others so that they couldn't take this Hard Eyes seriously.

He would have her again in time. She was the hard type who wanted very much to let go and be soft, and that sort of woman was easy for him. She put herself in his hands like a gun, and it was a gun he would use.

TEN

THE SPACE COLONY, SECURITY.

Russ Parker was staring at the blank videoscreens, wanting to call the security checkpoints but afraid to use the vidfone. Afraid of what he'd see.

They've got it out, he told himself. They said it was some kind of sabotage program one of the radics had worked into the system somehow. Despite all the safeguards. The door that had tried to crush him, the breakdowns . . . yesterday the lights going off and coming on and going off . . . fire sprinkler systems shooting off at random around the Colony . . . laughter coming from the intercoms but traceable to nothing. The images of old Rimpler, cackling dementedly.

All part of the hypothetical sabotage program.

And they promised to reprogram the system by one. It was two in the afternoon. It should be done. So go ahead. Turn on the screens. . . .

He took a deep breath, reached out, flipped the switch. The screens lit up. "Type in access number," said the luminous green words. Parker let out a long, relieved breath and tapped the number for Security Checkpoint One.

A thing with gills appeared on the screen.

It was a sort of head, made of shiny black stuff, like glossy rubber; there were gills or vents on its jowls, corrugated tubes running from its nose and curving into its cheeks; pus running from the bright red, piggish eyes; bald head studded with black knobs. Mouth made of flaps within flaps, each one leaking a separate bright color of viscous fluid.

It was hideous, alien. But it was, viewed as a whole ensemble, weirdly recognizable. Just squint a little and the parts resolved into a distortion of . . . Professor Rimpler.

The screen's speaker gave out a sound that was pure mockery, a squawking like the noise made by one of those novelty-shop laughing boxes. Torn laughter.

Revolted, Russ switched off the screen. The image faded.

Then, impossibly, the screen switched itself back on.

The rubber face, the squawking.

He reached behind and jerked out the power cord. The screen blanked. He sat back in his chair, trying not to hyperventilate. He stood up and went to the door. He didn't want to be alone in there.

He went to get the repairmen, and then to the commissary.

While Russ was gone, Kitty Torrence came.

"He's not in," the secretary told her.

"I'll wait."

"I'm sorry, but you'll need an appointment, and he's just not seeing anyone right now."

"I'm not leaving."

The secretary pushed the call button. Two guards came into the office almost immediately.

That's when Russ returned, pausing in the outer offices to ask if the repairman had come for the viddycom.

He stopped when he saw Kitty Torrence. The guards were turning her away.

She was crying, shouting she wanted to see Russ Parker.

"Wait a minute," Parker said. "I don't recall having been asked if I'd see this woman. I told you I was coming back."

His secretary reddened. "Well . . . we thought, you know, you being so busy . . ."

It's Praeger, he thought. *He's told them to insulate me from the technicki.*

"Send her in," he said firmly, glaring at the receptionist. He was glad of something to take his mind off the black rubber thing on the screen. And he was scared to be alone in there.

He went into his office. Kitty came in and sat down in the only other chair. The door closed.

Her cheeks were streaked, her eyes puffy, but she'd stopped crying. She hadn't brushed her hair in a couple of days.

No preliminaries. "They beat him over the head just now," she said, "for nothing."

He knew who she meant, of course. "I'll look into it."

The words came out of her in a rush. "That's not enough. Let him go. You have the power to let him go. All we want is to go home to Earth. We can't cause trouble for you if we're not here. Let us go."

His mouth was dry. "I . . . it's not in my power to let him out or to let you go back to Earth. The space on the few ships the Soviets will let through is for emergency purposes only—administrative purposes." He realized he'd put that wrong.

"Administrative! Yeah, for Admin! You guys can leave whenever you want!"

"That isn't true." Oh, God, no, it wasn't true. "And as for letting him out of detention—it's not in my hands. It's in Chairman Praeger's hands alone, and I don't think you'd find him a sympathetic listener. At any rate, there's strong evidence your husband was directly involved in sedition. It's only at my insistence, frankly, that you're not in jail too."

Kitty Torrence closed her eyes. Her fists balled. "All we want is to go. To leave you all alone to your little war."

"Look, I doubt you'd get flight clearance for Earth even if I could arrange for you to go—you might lose the baby during G-stress on reentry. And, anyway, it's a big risk for anyone. There's a world war going on out there—not just on Earth but in orbit too. If the military situation changes, the shuttle could be shot down. I'll tell you something more:

There's a good chance the whole thing will blow up into nuclear war. In which case the safest place to be is right here."

"I can accept anything, even staying here, if Chester's with me."

He shook his head. "I haven't got the authority—"

She leaned forward and said, "You think we don't know about RM17?"

He couldn't speak for a moment. He saw a flicker of triumph in her face. It made him angry. But he thought, She's only doing what anyone would do, in her place.

He glanced at the door. Floundering with, "I don't know what rumors you've heard, but it's all—"

"Murder is murder."

"Now look, Mrs.—"

"Murder is murder. Murder is—"

"All *right*. That's *enough*."

He sagged back in his seat. "Look, the damn Colony is falling apart. Colony maintenance is at an all-time low. Especially since . . . the explosion. Maintenance supplies are trickling through the Soviet blockade so slow . . . we got just enough to keep going. We've got sabotage like you wouldn't believe. We've got vandalism. We've got random violence —people are getting stir-crazy. I just don't have time to take your problems on—"

"Murder is murder. You people are going to have to murder me, too, if you want me to shut up about it. Unless you let him go."

He opened his mouth to tell her not to threaten him, that there hadn't been a murder. But he couldn't say it. It was as if his voice box just wouldn't work. Not for that particular lie.

Finally he said, "I don't think I can help you." But he was writing something on a pad, keeping his body between it and the office's wall camera. "Here's a special pass to see him whenever you want."

When he handed it to her, he could tell by her suddenly guarded expression that she'd caught it; that he'd given her two things. A pass and, under it, a note. She looked at him; he looked at her. She nodded and left the office. Probably wondering how she could trust the chief of security. And realizing she had no choice.

The note read, *My office is bugged. I'll contact you and we'll meet in the Open, at the Monument. I'll let you know in twenty-four hours when the meeting will be. I'll try to help you. Destroy this, after you go out.*

He watched her go, thinking, Now I'm in it deep.

But, hell, he'd made a choice. He'd chosen sides.

Faid was a wiry, nut-brown man with a droopy mustache and large, excited eyes. He wore a rather battered Japanese action suit today, tiger-striped, and he added a large smile when he saw Russ. "This is one funny place to meet," Faid said in a rather thick accent. "It's all broken here, rather." He'd learned his English in London, and he mixed Briticisms with his bad Standard.

Russ said, "Hell, it ought to be useful for somethin'." They were in one of the closed-off cafés on the Strip, the small section of the Colony that had been designed as the recreational center for its technicki population. The shops and cafés and spas were closed now; there were no supplies to keep them open. Russ, as Security Chief, had a key to all the silly little units on the arcade.

The place was dusty—more proof that the air filters were working badly in the Colony. Normally dust was precluded wherever possible, since it increased wear on the LSS equipment. Dust was a life risk. The windows were blocked-off paperboard; the only light was from the electric lantern Russ had set on the table.

"Shall we be sitting down, then?" Faid asked, gesturing toward a table. "I think the service will be slow, what?"

Russ smiled. He shook his head. "Can't stay long." He took two passes from his pocket, handed them to Faid. "You're security, you know how to use 'em."

"I *was* security, bloody longer I'm not anymore . . ."

"I know. I'm sorry. That's Praeger's doing. But take these. It's up to you if you want to actually use them—the situation is like this: I'm going to be taking some risks. I'm going up against Praeger. Chances are I'll be arrested. If you help me, there's a big risk in it for you, and maybe not much else. But I thought you might want to, anyway."

Faid nodded. "You bloody well are knowing me too good, Russ!"

Russ pointed to each of the passes. "This one gets you into any place in Security Section; this one can be used to transfer prisoners. When the time comes, I'll want you to get this man out of detention and hide him." He gave him a piece of paper with the name and prisoner number of Kitty's husband. "I promised someone about him. And if he's loose, he just might do Praeger a dirty, which'll please the bejeezus out of me. Only, not yet. I don't want to do it that way except as a last resort."

Faid said, "You are knowing me too good." And then he grinned and stowed the passes in his pocket.

A shopping mall in Washington, D.C.

"We each get a copy, Stoner," Brummel said. "That was the deal," he added as Lopez accepted the manila envelope from Stoner.

Stoner said, "They're both there." He was looking out the window of the cafetamine shop at the glassy maze of the mall. It was almost ten at night, and the shops lining the corridors of the vast underground mall were mostly closed. Some of the cases were dark, some were lit up but forlornly motionless; they displayed clothing and toys and designer medinject units and ninja gear and sporting goods and vidinserters; the glass of the cases reflected one another, so the goods were layered in reflection, collaged with skewed squares of shine; one case mixed by reflection with another, a jumble of enticements; like a premonition, Stoner thought, of the coming time when the stuff ends in the city dumps, jumbled together again.

He felt empty and hopeless tonight; he felt bought and sold. Passing information to the enemy.

Think of the wife. The little girl.

Lopez slurped at his Styrofoam cup of speed-spiked ersatz coffee as Brummel looked at the little disks in the envelope. Which was stupid; it wasn't as if you could tell anything by looking at some loose floppy disks. Stoner shifted in the hard booth, rested his elbows on the synthetic white table-top, his chin on his meshed fingers. A waxy crueller, made of God knows what, sat untouched on a paper napkin in front of him. He asked, "When do you get me out?"

"After it is looked at good," Lopez said.

"Work on your grammar," Stoner said. "How about we find a booth, I pay for the computer time, you read through it quick right there?"

Brummel looked at him. Perspiration glazed his dark skin. "You got a reason to worry?" He glanced at the corridor, then over his shoulder at the shop. It was empty, except for the Japanese kid behind the counter.

Stoner hesitated.

The three men sat bolt upright in their seats as the room shook with a sudden roar, the windows and tabletops vibrating; the Korean boy had switched on a tape deck, blasting the heavy-metal squeal of a neopunk band. The lead singer was jeering:

Let's bring the war home
We deserve to suffer like the rest of the world
Yeah, bring the war home.

Stoner winced. "Yeah," he told Brummel, "I always got reason to worry. I don't think anyone's on me tonight. I don't see how they could have us under voice surveillance here when they didn't know—and *we* didn't know till ten minutes ago—where we'd have our meeting. But you're stupid if you don't worry."

"Come on, please, let's get out of here," Lopez said.

They left the shop, walked down the echoing corridor together, past a crowd in front of a cinema octoplex, Stoner asking, "What about the booth?"

"If we can find one with a disk drive," Brummel said, nodding.

A bald man in a saffron robe was ranting at the octoplex lines. "Those of us who know these are the last days of man," he shouted, "demand that the suffering of innocents cease! Today I make another sacrifice, my flesh for their flesh, one ounce of flesh a week until the war is over!" He held up an arm and used a hunting knife to pare off a chunk of the heel of his hand; blood ran down the blade, twined his wrist; some of the crowd groaned in revulsion; others laughed. Someone yelled, "You're not really serious unless you cut off your dick!" The man in saffron opened his robe, took his penis in hand. An SA cop on a jitney rolled around the corner, pulled up next to him. Someone screamed.

Stoner, Brummel, and Lopez turned a corner, hurrying away from the scene.

They found a number of phone/computer "grid-in" booths at an alcove in the next corridor. There were twelve; seven were vandalized, scored with graffiti, their wires hanging out. Only two of the booths had the old disk-drive slots— people didn't use them much.

One of the booths worked. Stoner tapped its keyboard for "isolated reading" and then entered the disk files. He stepped aside, let Brummel and Lopez go through it, knowing he was taking a chance. They could always take the stuff and ditch him, leaving him twisting in the wind.

"I have something else, of course," he murmured, "something I'm keeping back till I'm safe and out of the country. Something very useful to the NR."

"It looks all right," Brummel said, stepping out of the booth, not concealing his excitement very well. "It—" He broke off, staring past Stoner at the bend in the corridor.

Stoner turned to look. An SA bull, this one without a helmet, was staring at them. He raised his arm, spoke into his wrist. Then turned away, was gone around the corner.

Just a routine check, Stoner told himself. He said, "When do we go?"

"We'll be in touch. I'll contact my sister," Brummel said.

Stoner held Brummel's eyes. "Soon."

"Soon as we can make it."

"How soon is that, dammit?"

"A few days."

"*Sooner*," Stoner barked. He moved off toward the escalator leading to the parking lot.

In the parking lot he started his Guatemalan Rapido and drove out into the weirdly abstract, arrow-marked lanes between cars. Seeing a light in his mirror. Another car starting up, following. Just someone going home from the mall. Everyone goes out the same way, after all.

But when he was out on the street, he turned at the next

corner, and the car behind him turned too. A Chrysler Colony Shuttle. Hanging back, but tailing him. He took another turn, arbitrarily, watching it.

The stranger turned too.

Not bothering to hide the fact that they were tailing him. Which meant they wanted to scare him—or they were about to come down on him.

He sensed somehow that that's what it was. They were going to take him. Now.

He pulled up at a crowded restaurant and bar, double-parked, went inside as calmly as he could, going from deserted dark street into brassy lighting, noise, laughter.

"Yes, sir, are you here for dinner?"

"I'm meeting someone in the bar," Stoner lied.

He tried not to run, managed to keep it down to a trot, as he hurried into the bar, past it to the phone booths. He punched his credit card into the phone slot, and the screen lit up. Punched his home number, waited breathlessly, glancing over his shoulder. No one following him in yet. Saw his wife's worried face appear on the screen. "You okay?"

"Yeah. But . . . anything going on at home?"

She shook her head.

"Okay. Your sister there?"

She nodded.

"Okay. You make that little trip to see your mom."

Her eyes widened. "Okay."

He cut the line. She knew what to do. She'd arranged it with her sister. Her sister would put on her clothes, get in the car, drive out of the garage as fast as she dared, drive off to Falls Church, where her mother lived. They'd think she was going to her mother's. The sister wasn't a twin, but she looked enough like her from a distance that it might work. The surveillance crew, with luck, would follow the sister.

His wife and daughter would go out the back, through the neighbor's yard to a friend's house, call a cab. They'd meet at a certain motel in Baltimore.

If it worked. If the Company was fooled. There was a chance: God knows CIA Domestic could be fooled.

Stoner went to the men's room. The window was nailed shut. Risk it. He took off his coat, balled it around his fist, smashed the window glass, hoping the noise from the bar would cover it. He broke out the jags from the window frame, climbed on a sink, wormed through the frame onto slimy asphalt, expecting someone outside to grab him as he came out. No one there. A wet, trash-gunked alley. He got to his feet—saw headlights swinging into the alley to his right. He turned down a narrow walk between the restaurant and the next building, feeling his way along in pitch darkness; moving back toward the restaurant's front. Smelling urine, garbage. He emerged onto the sidewalk. The Chrysler was gone; it was around back. And there was a cab just letting a young couple out in front of the restaurant. He ran to it, got in before they closed the door, slid a fifty-Newbux note through the slot to the driver. "Go anywhere, fast!" he yelled. The driver saw the bill, changed gears, and the car squealed away from the curb.

Stoner watched through the rear window, didn't see the Chrysler. The dumb shits were still looking through the alley. The cab turned a corner and he felt a ripple of relief. Ditched them for now. Unless they had a surveillance bird on him too. He glanced up at the sky. No telltale silvery fluttering. But the birds were small; you never knew.

He'd have to contact Brummel directly, somehow. Tomorrow, if he got through the night alive.

The New York County Jail.

There were forty beds in the county jail's hospital room. Charlie was lying in the bed nearest the door.

He gave up trying to get comfortable on his back, moved to his right side. That hurt too. He shifted to his left side. After some more experimentation he found that if he remained on his left side and tucked his knees up near his chest, bunched the sheets up under his sore kidney, he could minimize the discomfort. Now and then he reached under his sour-smelling, grimy pillow and let his fingers play over the plastic cigarette lighter he'd found in a trash barrel. Some guard had thought it empty. But chances were there was a light or two left in it.

The prison hospital was bigger than he thought it would be; danker, darker, more foul-smelling. It was shaped like an enormous Quonset hut, walls curved into ceiling. The only windows, shaped like quarter-moons lying on their straight sides, were near the ceiling; they were metal-meshed, fly-specked, never opened—probably never could. The light from the windows and the ceiling fluorescents was a sort of milky glare. There was no TV, nothing to read except the heap of printout magazines over by the door. The old metal beds creaked at one another constantly, as if groaning for the patients, and the patients—or call them prisoners, or victims, or stray animals—complained and cursed. Half of them were tied to the beds with plastiflex restraints; the orderlies came rarely, so the prisoners were forced to foul themselves and to lie in it.

The place was bedlam, and the shouting, the groans, the idiotic hoots and the weeping—everyone here in pain, most everyone condemned to more pain and death—the noise of the place scared Charlie. He found himself reverting to a kind of infantile state of terror, the fright only an infant can feel, a fear primordial in its depth, all-consuming. He was caught in the State's garbage disposal, and the noise of this place was constantly grinding away, and the sound of it was the sound of the gnashing steel teeth of the State, its teeth gnashing bones and flesh.

Charlie was trying to screen it all out. Think of it some other way, he told himself. Think of it as the noise of a storm. The noise of a storm scared you when you were a kid, till you learned not to hear it.

He lay on his side with his eyes screwed shut, trying not to hear it.

His mind was busy. It cut his situation into segments, and cut the segments into smaller segments, and parsed the little segments into sorted heaps.

He could blame the Hollow Head, really. The place that was a drug. That's why he was here. Because of what the Place had done to Angelo and to him.

No. It was his own weakness. His psychological original sin. His own tendency to—what had the school psychiatrist called it when Charlie was in seventh grade? Disassociative neuroses? The need to disassociate his mental focus from himself and things around him. Drugs worked best. It was trite, it was cliché; he'd done drugs because they freed him, they just blew away his problems and anxieties.

And the Hollow Head, of course, was more than a drug. It was living drug paraphernalia; instead of you swallowing the drug, the drug swallowed you. All-encompassing. *Real* disassociation, internal and external at once.

When you left the Hollow Head, you were exhausted, sick, maybe greasy with self-disgust. Vowing never to go back. Same old story, same old hard reality.

Because you always went back, if you *liked* it—not everyone did. You always found your way there, found excuses, your feet turning toward the place without your thinking about it.

When you realized you were going to cop a buzz, you argued with yourself. Maybe only so you could say to yourself, "I tried, I fought it." But with never any real conviction in the fight.

Sure, it scared you. You'd seen the burnouts. You'd heard the stories of things happening like what had happened to Angelo. You were scared of the place, of the addiction.

The trap, the cycle, had a thousand manifestations. There were the little fantasy-induced pleasure jolts that came from watching prime-time TV—pleasure of catharsis, pleasure of fantasy release. There were bigger, more direct manifestations, even besides drugs and the Place; Charlie knew guys who wore dick tinglers. Little chem-bathed metal harness with a battery, wear it on your dick, right? Runs a current onto the erogenous nerve ends, not so much that it hurts or burns, but enough so it stimulates you sexually. Some wore another in the ass, a little pumping mechanism gently massages your prostate and gives you the nerve-sweetening current too. You didn't have the thing turned on all the time. Do that and after a while you felt nothing. No, it was hooked into a needle that ran through the skin, into the bloodstream, and built into the needle was a device that detected certain hormones. When adrenocorticotrophin and other biochemical agents were released—things released when you got *mad*—you got the jolt, maybe starting slow, building for ten, fifteen minutes. So what you did, you walked around looking for trouble and you got into fights just to give you the dick tingling and the hot rush of pleasure, and it got so you identified fighting with sexual pleasure. Which increased the odds you'd die young. But the pleasure cycle, the behavioral programming trap, kept them doing it, even though it got them beat up and busted and even though they saw their friends getting killed. If you wore a dick tingler, you got into illegal prizefights—only, if you're fighting hard, you get tingle after tingle and rush after rush, and finally you start to *come.* You *ejaculate during the fight,* punch some guy's nose back into his sinuses, *crunch,* and orgasm at the same time. It kind of threw you off, opened you up for his retaliation. And when he hits you, you get mad, which means you get another jolt of sex reward, which means you orgasm harder, so you keep coming and coming because the guy is hitting you, and you're too whacked out to retaliate and too stimulated to lose consciousness and . . . maybe he beats you to death while you quiver with sexual pleasure. Charlie had heard that it happened. Had heard, too, that the Army was experimenting with something like the dick tinglers with some of their troops.

Charlie had no desire to strap electric-shock gear on his genitals. Charlie had found another well-worn path to self-destruction. Drugs, and the Hollow Head. The cycle had been eating him alive. So he'd gotten into the Resistance. He'd joined them, he knew now, more to escape from drugs than for ideological reasons. He believed in the resistance passionately. But deep down he was there because he'd thought it would save him.

It hadn't saved him. The drug thing was like one of those movie monsters you thought was killed—and it rises up again and again. Out of water and out of flames, neither drowned nor incinerated.

And he'd shot Angelo into himself; he'd gone mad for a while; he'd killed a cop. He was judged and convicted. The sickening thing was, he understood the conviction very well. He didn't even have the consolation of feeling that he was an innocent wronged. He'd walked a tightrope over a vat of shit, and he'd fallen into it.

There was no appeal. He was here only till he healed up just enough to participate in the circus they'd make of his execution. Every day the doctors would examine him; treacherously, his body would repair itself, and with every improvement he was a little closer to his execution show. There were cameras in the ceiling, and the men in restraints were mostly the ones the cameras had caught mutilating themselves to put off their executions. He had a few days, as much as a week, and then they'd execute him.

The NR didn't know where he was. It probably couldn't help him, anyway.

He had an absurd image of his mother coming in, shouting at everyone, straightening it out, taking him away from here. *I'll be good, Mom. Just get me out.*

Shit. He didn't even *like* his mother.

The only way out of here alive was escape.

His hand closed over the lighter again. It was sweat-glossed with his touching.

Sometimes the guards came in and searched the beds for improvised knives, drugs, anything. Fouling your bed wasn't enough to keep them from searching it. They just made you clean it up first.

Next time they searched, they might find the lighter. Stiff as he was, now was the time.

He turned onto his stomach, pulled the rancid sheet over his head and over the pillow, as if trying to blot out the light so he could sleep. He lay still for a while, smelling himself, sour but reassuring, in the gray semidarkness, hoping anyone watching on the ceiling cameras would think he'd fallen asleep.

Twenty minutes, till he was sweaty from being under the sheet, and then he reached under his pillow, found the lighter. He put it between the palms of his hands and began to rub it, warming it up with friction and body heat. So the small amount of gas that was in it would expand, rise to the nozzle . . .

He pushed his head under the pillow, making a little hump under it so there was enough air for the lighter.

He decided he'd rubbed it long enough. He flicked it, watched the sparks breathlessly.

There: a translucent, blue-white flame, as faint as a burnt-out freebaser's rush, but there all the same. Enough to set the pillow on fire. The pillowcase caught.

He jammed the lighter into the waistband of his prison-blue pajamas and jumped up onto the bed, shouting, "*Shit!*

Which one of you idiots tossed that fucking burning butt onto my fucking pillow? Shit, you caught it on fire!" And he convulsively tossed the burning pillow one way, the burning pillowcase the other, onto the heap of magazine printouts. The torn pillow's ticking floated in a burning cloud, fire moths, over the three beds nearest him; prisoners yelled and cringed away, others laughed, flames rose from the burning printouts, smoke darkened the room.

A Hispanic kid was spreading the fire around, laughing and setting fire to sheets, blankets.

Coughing from the flames, Charlie backed to the door, stood to one side of it, thinking, *Maybe it won't happen the way I thought it will; could be they'll all burn to death because of me.*

It didn't matter.

And there was a certain exultation seeing the flame reaching with thin yellow spires toward the ceiling; it was as if all the bound-up anger of the patients was manifested in the fire, was dancing, restoring animation to this groaning repository of the good-as-dead.

The door burst open; guards with fire extinguishers came rushing in. No ceiling extinguishers here.

They did what he hoped: In their haste they left the door open behind them. Not thinking anyone was back there, not seeing him.

He went through the door, trying not to cough till he got far enough down the hall. He went down the blank hall, looking for a way out or a place to hide. Now what? The fire hadn't been out of hand; they'd have it out in a few minutes.

He turned a corner, came to a door. It was open. He stepped through and found he was outdoors—on the top landing of a metal stairway zigzagging down the outside of the building, four stories down into the unused concrete exercise yard below and to his left. It was gray and chilly out. Beyond the exercise yard was a high wall crested with concertina wire, cameras, and a guard tower. Charlie turned right, along the metal catwalk. Two men came out of another door, just in front of him. He saw his own face.

"That's him," the man behind Charlie's face said.

His face was reflected in an SA mirror visor. (The SA was

a private outfit. What was SA doing in the public police station? Were they that far infiltrated into the System?)

The other guy was a wide-shouldered, swag-bellied black guard—ironic that he should be working with the SA. He had a shotgun in his hands, its blue metal mouth open to Charlie's middle. "You going for a walk?" the black guard said, grinning.

Charlie said, "Trying to get away from the smoke, is all."

The SA shook his head. He had a plastic breast tag on his armored suit: SECSPEC. He was a security specialist. High-ranking SA hired by the city—or by classified defense contractors, or airlines plagued by terrorists—to bring a special expertise to making security airtight. He'd seen Charlie on the cameras, known what he was doing.

"I've got a feeling about this young man," the SECSPEC said, approaching, slapping his RR stick in his gloved palm, his voice all crackle-edged from the helmet amper. "He thought it out very well. We checked your DNA imprint, Charlie. Just now. You were taken in two demonstrations. Leftist demonstrations. You're an organized rebel with a political bent."

"Got us a terrorist, huh?" the guard said.

Charlie backed away—and came to a jarring stop against the rainwater-beaded metal railing around the landing.

"I think we're going to have to apply to the judge for an extractor order for this young gentleman," the SECSPEC said dryly. "Unless you'd like to confess your political affiliations now, Charlie?"

Shouts and smoke from the corridor to Charlie's right. To his left, a wall. Behind him, a four-story drop.

And ahead of him: the extractor.

Oh, no. Cold metal on his back. Concrete building. Metal catwalk. Concrete exercise yard below. Hard metal things in the hands of the men approaching him, the guard taking out a chromium pair of cuffs.

All the hard things, concrete and metal and barbed wire and guns: part of the trap. The hard-edged, hard-walled, unyielding concrete-hard trap. All the planes of metal and concrete contracting in on him, rushing toward him, bearing with them an inflexible conclusion: He had to die.

Right now.

If he let them take him, they'd use the extractor, dip into his brain, pluck his knowledge of the NR. Down to the approximate location of the island, Merino. Smoke. Witcher.

He had a half second to make up his mind. *It's your fault, you did the Hollow Head, risked the NR doing it, face the responsibility for once, you asshole. Do it!*

"Stop him!"

He felt the gloved hand on his arm, but he wrenched away, turned, flung himself over the railing head first, angling his body vertically, throwing his legs back, hands gripping his hips; angling to fall head down, to make sure he landed on his—

The two men on the landing looked down at the body in the exercise yard. Red splash at one end of the body. Where the head was. "Mushed his brains out," the guard said. "Hell, you ain't gonna extract nothing from *that* mess."

The Island of Malta.

Claire wasn't at all sure why she'd done it. Why she'd slept with Karakos. Why *really*.

Except that perhaps it had been a way out of the pressure.

She was sitting with Lila on a little window seat, looking out to the north. It was dusk. The tangerine light reached from the west to tinge the twig tips of the trees; the trees did slow shimmies in the wind. The sky to the north was violet. The house creaked in the sighing wind.

Lila was cleaning her gun, an H&K autopistol, but doing it with placid absentmindedness, the way a woman from the early twentieth century would do needlepoint.

Lila stole glances at Claire now and then; Claire, wearing only a robe, a little cold but not wanting to move and break the quiet spell of the moment, pretended not to notice Lila's glances. But she enjoyed them.

Enjoyed them as she thought about someone else entirely. Hard Eyes. He pressured her without even trying. She wanted him, wanted his lean, hard, angular body pressed against hers. But sometimes when she looked at him, she saw one of the man-animals of her nightmare.

Karakos had finessed her with just the right amount of fatherly teasing, joking, and protectiveness. Never assuming too much, but accepting the relationship as the most natural thing in the world. And he'd wept. Wept at the horror he'd seen in the SA prisons. She'd put her arms around him, to comfort him . . . and the pieces fell into place, the chemistry took them from there. She wondered, for a moment, if she'd fallen for what her father would have called "the oldest trick in the book." But Karakos had seemed, like her, honestly sick of the killing. Psychically wounded.

Hard Eyes, on the other hand, despite admitting to having been afraid that once, never *showed* it—and if he was hurt by what he'd seen, he kept the hurt hidden. Called "Hard Eyes," maybe, because it was hard to picture him crying. It was as if he'd locked away some part of himself.

His reluctance to *genuinely* open up, to show her his hurt . . . it frustrated her, made her feel excluded from real intimacy with him.

Made her angry. Hard Eyes's protectiveness, too, had made her angry. Had she slept with Karakos partly out of anger?

The thought made her cringe. How had she gotten into this silly emotional maze? She looked at Lila, wishing she could be more like her. Always busy with something. Totally committed. Unruffled. Never tangled with men.

Before coming back to Earth, Claire had been celibate for two years. It was as if being on Earth (mental image of the earth goddess) had opened a hillside spring of sexuality in her. Her only significant Colony affair, more than two years earlier, with Mouli, a Persian life-support-systems stress analyst, had discouraged her hugely. Mouli had been relentlessly cerebral, except in bed—when he became mechanical. She'd had a ferocious crush on him, though, till she realized that despite all his earnest pretense at listening to her, and despite his serious conversation about Colony politics and futurological projection, Mouli didn't give a damn about *her*, the real Claire Rimpler. The mental relationship was a sham; she was just pussy to him.

She knew she meant something to Hard Eyes. And she seemed to have answered some deep need in Karakos (wondering with a vague unease, *Was* Karakos manipulating her, as Hard Eyes implied? His emotional openness was almost too good to be true). But when you got involved with men, you became absurd. Unimportant things seemed significant; you became stupidly *girlish*. It was embarrassing. It was beneath her. Sexism was unfashionable with men like Dan Torrence and Karakos. But somehow it was alive and well in them. As soon as you became involved with men, regardless of the best intentions of both sides, you became subsumed to them. Co-opted.

Still . . . the tension in her, the sense that she should be doing something to make up for abandoning her father, was maddening. And sex was a very effective release from it.

She looked at Lila, the twilight's gloom making her dark skin look, in profile, like a black velvet cutout. She was laying her reassembled gun aside, wiping oil off her hands. Carefully not looking at Claire.

"You never seem to get rattled, Lila," Claire said on impulse. "You never seem to need to . . . to get drunk like the others sometimes do, or . . . I mean, even Steinfeld needs to get drunk about once a month. You never get drunk, never get involved with men. You don't . . ." She shrugged. "How do you do it?"

"There's something I do," Lila said, looking uncomfortable.

Claire was embarrassed. Afraid the woman was about to confess that she was in love with someone, like Steinfeld, that she masturbated wildly and fantasized about him.

"This is what I do," Lila said. She took a little brass pipe from a pocket on her fatigues, and a piece of tinfoil. "But only once a month—that's all I allow myself. To, um, *let go,* no? I find it does not impair my efficiency the next day so much as, um, getting drunk."

"What is it?" Claire asked.

Lila was opening the foil. Inside was a little brown lump of hardened mud. Or something that looked like it. Lila glanced at the door, as if to be sure that it was closed, and said softly, "It is hashish."

"Oh!" she'd read about it. "It's carcinogenic, isn't it? Lung cancer."

Lila smiled. "Perhaps this is so if you smoke it every day. Once a month it's much less risky than breathing the air in a city. And I only allow it to myself once a month." She broke a piece of the hash off, rolled it into a tarry lump, and pressed it onto the screen in the little brass pipe. She put the pipe in her mouth, gripped between her straight white teeth. She took a steel-gray Soviet cigarette lighter from her pocket and ran the flame over the hash, sucked on the pipe, making the tarry lump bubble and glow. The coal lit her face with a fan of soft red light. The blue-white smoke drifting up from the pipe was aromatic.

Claire was only a little short of amazed. Lila, a drug user!

Lila inhaled, held the smoke for a moment, then let it gush out and said, her eyes faintly sleepy now, "It's a very mild hashish." And she offered the pipe to Claire.

"Oh, um, no thanks."

"A guerrilla has to know the world from every—how would you say it?—from every window. From every direction. This will show you a new..."

"A new angle on things?" Claire smiled.

"You have been so tense. I've seen that. This will help."

Claire found herself accepting the pipe. The guerrillas sometimes smiled at things Claire said, as if they thought her just a little ridiculous. As if she were a naïf because she'd lived most of her life in the Colony. She didn't want Lila to think of her that way.

But her stomach contracted with fear as she put the pipe in her mouth. Would she hallucinate? Would she think she'd turned into a sea gull and try to fly from the window and fall to her death?

She inhaled. "I don't think it's affecting me."

Lila giggled. "You inhaled before it was lit. I have to light again. Put it in your mouth... yes, hold it still... good... now suck on it to inhale... good, inhale..."

Claire felt a hot sandpaper hand jab sharp fingers into her lungs, and she gagged, coughed, almost dropping the pipe. Lila was making a strange sound. Something like *tee hee*. Astonishing!

"Well, I am guessing you got some that time, Claire. Beautiful Claire. Now I will have some more..."

Lila took another puff. A long one. She didn't cough.

Claire felt pleasantly distant from things. Mentally. But physically she could feel the window seat's cushions under her, the fabric of her robe under her hand. The air currents sliding cool past her throat.

Her lungs still burned from the first hit of the hashish, but she found herself wanting another.

They traded the pipe back and forth twice more, Claire coughing both times but caring less with each lungful of the hot, dark fragrance.

"It smells like incense," she said dreamily. "But a little more . . . a little edge to it . . ."

"It makes me sleepy," Lila said, "but not like I want to really sleep. Just to lay down and dream but with my eyes open."

"You mean . . . you hallucinate?"

"No, not that kind of dreaming. My mind goes wherever it wants."

She walked to the bed with an odd combination of floaty grace and stoned dislocation. With a soft cry she sank onto it, began to undress.

Claire stared at her, thinking she should leave. Lila was going to sleep, or wanted privacy to lie there and dream. But it was so fascinating to watch her peel her clothes off. She'd never realized before what odd things clothes are, what peculiar, soft encrustations they were. And Lila was so slender, smooth; watching her limbs move was like watching the flow of a dark river at night; just enough moonlight on the river to make out the contours of currents and ripples.

"You're so beautiful," she blurted.

A flash of white teeth in the near darkness. "Come and talk to me, Claire."

"I should . . . let you sleep, or . . ."

"I'm sad, Claire. I get sad when I smoke hash sometimes. Please don't leave. Come and talk to me." She was a woman-shaped pool of soft-edged shadow on the silvery silk bed. The bed didn't look like a bed; it seemed like a sort of great soft cake, as if you could reach out and push your hand into it and scoop moist chunks of bedcake.

Claire stood, swayed with a momentary dizziness, then walked toward the bed. It took so long to get there.

But in a moment she was lying on the great rectangular cake beside Lila, lying on her back, her robe fallen open, feeling the cool air whisper over her skin, one of the currents warm as it cupped her left breast and drew on her nipple, stiffening it.

Oh: It was Lila's mouth.

Claire stared at Lila's dark head moving on her chest, her large, lustrous eyes looking up at her . . . felt a connection, a bolt of wet lightning between her breast and her vagina. The electric wetness emerging there so she could feel the lubricants cooling in the slit where they met the air.

There was a glass pane of resistance in her, telling her: *This is perverse, this is a bad idea, shouldn't get involved like this because Lila will get attached and I'm not gay (am I?), and anyway, Dan will freak out. . . .*

But the tide of sheer sexual yearning rose up in her and pushed mightily at the glass pane, which turned out to be ice because it didn't break but melted in warm, salty sensation. As Lila slithered onto her, pressed succulently large lips over hers, ground her pubis onto Claire's—not too hard, the way a man will when he's clumsily trying to turn a woman on, but with firm tenderness and a suggestion of suction so that labia sucked on labia. They rocked together, and Claire basked in the ecstatic surprise of heightened sensory input as she drank Lila's skin with her own, letting her hands skate the impossibly perfect engineering of the feminine curvaceousness of Lila's back, the supple fullness of Lila's ass. With her eyes shut, she seemed to see what she felt, a synesthesia of tactile sensations translated into the visual, Lila's elegant arcs abstracted into swirls of ruby mist and exquisite ellipses of mouse-fur gray. Their tongues, entwined, were translucent, comma-shaped bubbles that became one another and then writhed happily apart and came together again with impudent stickiness. . . .

A fulsome ache came into her stomach. Lowering itself into her groin.

As if sensing the ache's arrival, Lila moved off her—sense of fleeting tragedy; wash of sweet, cool air—and knelt beside her, exploring with her fingers, chasing hot fish of sensation up from their dark caves. And then dipping to meet them with her mouth.

Oh, Claire thought, *no. I couldn't do that.*

Lila didn't insist. But after a while Claire found herself turning onto her side, pressing her head between Lila's smooth thighs, probing for the wet, warm place between the petal-shapes of wool.

Lila's tongue on her clitoris, Claire's on Lila's, and the sensation was all mixed up; she couldn't tell her tongue from Lila's, thought she felt Lila's clit sensation in her own, they'd synthesized into one person and a gong shivered, shivered, shivered. . . .

It seemed like no time, or possibly years later—but it had been only an hour when the door opened and someone stood there, backlit in the yellow hall light.

Lila and Claire had rested. They had just begun again. Somewhere, sometime, they'd had another pipeful. And they'd begun kissing again, exploring each other's breasts with the satisfying slowness of the utterly relaxed.

And then someone had opened the door. Claire looked over. It was Dan. Hard Eyes. Staring.

Staring like he couldn't believe it had happened to him twice. And maybe because he couldn't believe it was Lila this time.

"How many times," Claire murmured vaguely, "is he going to walk in on me with people? This is ridiculous. Doesn't anyone *knock* in this place?" She sank back on the bed, giggling.

After a moment Hard Eyes closed the door and they heard his footsteps recede.

"Poor Hard Eyes," Claire said. Suddenly feeling cosmically sad for him.

Lila comforted her.

ELEVEN

MERINO, SOMEWHERE IN THE CARIBBEAN.

"The files Stoner turned over are essentially the stuff of allegations," Witcher said. "It's useful stuff. It'll help. Of course, the CIA can claim we fabricated the files. But *this*" —he tapped the screen—"this they can't deny."

"They can claim it was video-animated," Smoke said. "But we can provide the tapes to independent analysts. They'll analyze it and see it wasn't computer-formulated, prove it's authentic. Along with the general impact of Kessler's propaganda spotters and the stuff Stoner gave us, it should wake up the press."

"Like a beehive in their beds," Witcher agreed.

Smoke and Witcher were in the briefing room, standing together at the blackboard-size video-instruction monitor. It was a cool night on Merino, almost eleven P.M., but the island was quite awake: They could hear the clank of rifles on strap buckles as sentries walked by to relieve those at the rear fence. Mosquitoes whined in bloodthirsty frustration at the window screen. From the distance came the dulled thud and blurred chant of a beat-box as someone got in their R and R. Smoke wondered what it was like to relax at a party and, well, to *dance*. To laugh and slap friends on the back and dance and feel at one with a party without trying. He'd never been able to do that sort of thing, and he envied it. He thought about Alouette, sleeping now, and he missed her.

His mind swerved hastily back to priorities. He turned to look again at the screen; the crow, on his shoulder, made a raspy caw and fluttered his wings at the motion. Smoke and the crow gazed thoughtfully at the stilled image on the big, inch-thin videomonitor.

It was an image of the President of the United States. President Anna Bester, America's own Maggie Thatcher, out in a snowy field, in tan overcoat, brown pantsuit, and high gold rubber boots, walking with a fat man in a tentlike white mackintosh; she was talking earnestly to him. The President had none of her usual charismatic composure, was missing her look of it's-all-under-control-and-I'm-sanguine-about-the-future-despite-the-gravity-of-the-situation. She was scowling. The scowl showing the lines of her late middle age in spite of her face-lift.

The fat man was Sackville-West, Head of Security for the Second Alliance International Security Corporation. The SA's Head Inquisitor, Witcher called him.

Witcher hit the play button on the VCR, and the videotape began to play again; as if responding to a choreographer, the President and Sackville-West began to move, walking in matched stride. The image was a little unstable; it drew back for a wider angle and took in two Secret Service men, expressionless and wearing shades as they had for generations —old-fashioned dark glasses had become their totem of office, like the archaic costume of a British Beefeater.

"It's amazing they didn't spot the bird's eye," Smoke said. The crow made a creaking sound in its throat, as if in agreement.

Witcher spread his hands and put on a comical expression of false modesty. "My outfit makes the best surveillance equipment on the planet. And on the Colony. Anyway, the sky was with us, the cloudy backdrop, the diminished light, not much reflection. The surveillance bird is treated with something we call chameleon spackle, blends in with the backdrop. Also, the snowfield dazzled them some. And we were simply lucky. For example, the two Secret Servicemen were watching the woods almost exclusively. They were thinking assassins, because she was so out in the open, not surveillance. They really have become embarrassingly incompetent lately. It's a national scandal."

Witcher rewound the tape a little and turned up the volume. They heard bits and pieces of the conversation, perhaps forty percent of it.

"Shame about the sound," Witcher said. "They spoke softly. There was noise from the wind and boots in the snow."

"There's enough," Smoke said.

As they heard Sackville-West say, "Madame, the Fourth Estate, to put it bluntly, is the enemy of this enterprise. The press must be kept under strict rein. We ..." Garble. "If the Emergency Powers are ..." Garble. "... intolerable situation unless we take strict ..." Garble. "... bottom line is this, Madame: To paraphrase Pastor Crandall, 'In order to take control, one must first take control.'"

The President's scowl vanished; she actually laughed out loud.

Then she became grave once more. "If I'm granted the powers to control the press, I'll use them, and once I have them, I see no reason to have to relinquish them. But in order to establish police control, we'll need coordination with your ..." Garble. "... not sure of the timetable. In the meantime we'll eliminate ..." Garble.

Smoke froze the image again. "It'll shake things, and nicely."

"Your people deserve the credit, really," Witcher said. "The NR trailed Sackville-West—and very well. He must have people trying to protect him from it—and they got the bird in close enough for us to use it once they—"

"How many meetings with Bester?" Smoke asked suddenly.

"Four over two months. We've got proof of them all. This is the only one with dialogue, the others were indoors and were very top secret."

"'Why is the President meeting this man in secret'?"

"Yes, that'll work, I think."

An undercurrent in something Witcher had said began to tug at Smoke. He looked at the older man. "'Your people,' you said. 'The NR,' you said. You don't think of yourself as NR. Is that snobbism because so many NR are technicki?" Smiling to defuse the implied criticism. "Or because you think of them as a ... as a tool?"

Witcher shrugged. His lips pursed. The faint narrowing of

his eyes, the way his hands tucked into his pockets as if to force concealment and control on them, one of his little bursts of paranoia coming on. "I just can't see any reason to keep up this prying into my motives, Smoke. Don't look a goddamn gift horse in its dentures."

He turned and walked out, banging the screen door behind him.

The crow squawked softly, as if to reproach Smoke. "You're right," Smoke muttered. "I've been unsubtle." But he thought he began to see, almost intuitively. To see why Witcher funded the NR: The SA's political plans were in Witcher's way.

And Witcher had his own plans for the country.

The Space Colony, Security.

They'd apologized for waking Russ, but he hadn't been asleep.

When the SA bulls came to his quarters, it was officially three in the morning, and Russ was lying in bed arguing with himself about sedatives. *You start using them, you could get dependent on them,* he told himself. To which he replied, *That's your tight-assed Southern Baptist upbringing. Hell, give yourself a break.*

And then the chime, and he'd answered the door, found the SA bulls there.

So they've come for me, he thought wearily. *It's my turn.*

But one of them said, "Sorry to wake you, sir. Chairman Praeger would like you to come to an emergency meeting of the council."

Still murky from being half asleep, he started to ask why they hadn't simply used the screens, and then he remembered that the screens were down because the Face was still thrusting itself onto them.

"Okay," he said. Not as relieved as he should have been that he wasn't being arrested.

He printed out a preset suit, put it on still warm, and followed them to the council room.

They were sitting at the conference table, which was shaped like a backward *S*; the room was lit thoroughly but softly, from nowhere apparent. Praeger in the center, Judith Van Kips beside him as always; beside her, Dr. Tate, the Colony's chief psychiatrist. Even Tate looked tired, despite his rebuilt, unnaturally regular features, his surgical affectation of youth, some of his sixty-five years showing through the mask of a thirty-five-year-old.

Ganzio, the Brazilian, sat across from Van Kips. He was a slim, black-eyed man with a pencil-thin mustache and a penchant for gaudy suits, and now (yes, even at three in the morning!), he was resplendent in a double-breasted suit of sky blue, with blue-trimmed ruffles. He tugged on his lapels to straighten the lines of his suit, glancing at the camera, near the ceiling, that was supposed to be recording all the council meetings for the Colony's appraisal. He was unaware that Praeger had long ago had the camera disconnected.

Messer-Krellman, the technicki's union rep—nontechnicki himself and generally regarded as the Boss's lickspittle—sat to Ganzio's right. He was a ferret-faced man with an air of boredom.

There was much talk around the table as Russ opened the door. When he came in, the talk died out. They all looked at him, smiling in polite welcome.

Russ remembered the meetings with Professor Rimpler and his daughter, Claire, and how subtly at first, and then more and more clearly, the Rimplers had been excluded from the diffuse cronyism that characterized Admin's inner circle. Russ, then, had been one of the charmed circle. Now he felt the chill. He was officially, to an extent functionally, still part of the council. But in fact, he was on his way to becoming an outsider.

Feeling a queasy combination of fatigue and wired anxiety, Russ took his seat on Ganzio's left, asking, "Anyone going to clue me in on why this graveyard shift was necessary?" There was a pot of ersatz coffee on the table, and Styrofoam cups. Russ poured himself some, sipped it, regretted it.

"We have had the results of the comm system and LSS analysis," Praeger said, sighing the words, "and we've been forced to conclude that . . ." He hesitated, folded his hands on the table, stared at them for a moment. Van Kips looked at him questioningly. He went on, "That the majority of the recent sabotage and the comm system imagery interference has not been caused by radic involvement. Has, in fact, somehow been induced by Rimpler himself."

Russ felt sweat start out on his palms.

So now it was said. What everyone had been trying not to think.

"Evidently," Praeger went on with a weary dryness, "there's some sort of . . ." He glanced questioningly at Dr. Tate.

Tate shifted uncomfortably in his seat and said, "It's a sort of psyche-gestalt presence maintaining the dynamics of Rimpler's personality despite the fact that we, uh, technically cut his personality away when we removed a large part of the brain tissue. We can only speculate, at this point, about what psychic mechanism has been engaged. But I'm fairly sure some rather base, almost infantile portion of Rimpler's personality has survived as a kind of subtle electromagnetic field, which, by a sort of, ah, cyber-telekinesis, seems to be exerting its influence over the contiguous LSS computer control systems. The, ah, ghost in the machine, as it were . . ."

"Holy shit," Russ breathed.

"Yes," Praeger said. "We've accrued enough parts to replace the life-support computer system without using cerebrointerfacing. We can . . . dispose of Rimpler's brain. But we're not sure we can get to it. We sent some people in to try to shut him down—he overrode the door sensors, locked our people out. Rimpler seems to have accessed computer security systems. He's been opening and closing the detention cells at random, for example. The guards have kept the prisoners in place but . . ." He shrugged. "Obviously, if he can do that, and if he's truly aware of us—as he seems to be—he can block our access to the LSS using its security backup systems. Electrification, paralysis gas—even drawing the air from the access corridors."

"And you want me to find a safe way through."

"You're the Security specialist, and you know the Sec systems like no one else."

Russ looked from face to face, repressing an urge to shout at them. He stared at their emptied coffee cups. "You were having the meeting long before I got here. You didn't bring me into it until you had to."

"This is no time to harp on esoteric rules of procedure," Van Kips said sharply. "This is an emergency. Can you help us with it or not?"

Russ thought, *I'm more on the outside than I thought. Looks like Praeger has decided I'm a radic sympathizer. In that case, with all the usual irony that attends politics, I'll have to be a radic sympathizer to survive. No more putting it off. I'll have to make my move. Soon.*

He rubbed his damp palms on his soft paper trousers. Then, annoyed at himself, he looked down and saw that the sweat had blackened his palm with print-dye. "I'm not sure. Seems to me, if we try to blowtorch into the place, he may retaliate by opening air locks here and there."

Everyone reacted. Sharp intakes of breath, faces going pale, eyes staring as they imagined it. The Colony's nightmare. The void, the cold vacuum, always waiting outside. . . .

"The only way to be sure of it," Russ said slowly, "would be to shut down power around the Colony except for battery-survival minimum for each section. While the main power lines are shut down, Rimpler can't control the doors, air locks, anything. We can waltz in and shut him down easily."

"Battery-survival minimum doesn't provide for Security or for comm systems," Van Kips said in her most brittle tone.

Praeger nodded his agreement. "Judith is quite right. We would be unable to seal off Admin with any effectiveness, unable to communicate with the Security Forces, and unable to maintain surveillance in the technicki dorms. It would be the ideal time to mount another rebellion. We'd be all but helpless."

Russ snorted. "We'd still have most of the weapons, the armor, the trained guards!"

"It's not enough," Praeger insisted. "We're too badly outnumbered. No. Absolutely not. We can't risk dropping Security envelope. We'll have to find another way in."

Russ took a long, slow breath. He exhaled it even more

slowly. Then he said, "Okay. I'll try. I'll play it by ear, see what we've got, try to break in. But if he . . ."

Tate put in, "In my opinion, he thinks of the Colony as part of himself. He *has* gone mad—he seems to be willing to be, in a way, deliberately incontinent, to mutilate himself. But he won't kill himself."

"You'd better be right, Tate," Russ said.

Kitty sat uncomfortably on the stone bench under the Monument, in the Open, looking up through the branches of the eucalyptus trees, smelling their menthol fragrance, wondering if she was being set up in some way.

She looked up at the statue. The Monument—a man in a pressure suit, sans helmet—was carved from some dense reddish asteroid ore, memorializing the EVA workers killed —how long ago now? A year? Two? They were almost forgotten now. And the hypocrites would have to put up another for RM17.

The statue's arm was raised, hand outreaching, his face cornily expressive of awestruck yearning for the stars. Bogus, Chester would say.

It was "noon," so the mirrors and filters at the Open's enormous circular windows, at both ends, diffused the park with a homogenous golden sunlight. The air here would have made a visitor from Earth gag, but to Kitty it smelled clean, after the dorms and the corridors. The Colony was choking itself; it was an organism whose liver and kidneys were failing, whose lungs were too clogged to filter out poisons. The foul air seemed fouler in the background of social tension: the persistent rumors about RM17; the latest cuts in food rations; the arrests. And the vandalism—the insane old man's face that came and went on the comm system. The power failures and burst pipes.

She saw him coming a hundred yards away, cutting across the soccer field that no one was allowed to use at the moment—public gatherings of more than three were forbidden until Admin saw fit to lift the state of emergency—and she felt like running.

How could she trust the Chief of Security?

But Chu had surprised her. "Go see him," she'd said. "There are strong indications he's on the outs with Admin's

Council. He's had several conflicts with them. The danger is, maybe he wants to flush us out through you, to regain their favor. But I have studied the man, and I don't believe this is the case. He may be our best hope."

She got to her feet, but it was too late to run. "Hello, Kitty," Russ said, smiling wearily. He stepped onto the path and stood there awkwardly, hands in pockets, looking at his shoes, so she almost laughed at his "aw-shucks" posture. But then she realized he was staring at the grass stuck to his shoes. It was dried, yellowed. "Grass is dying out there," he said. "They watered it this morning, looks like, but it maybe came too late. Maybe not pure enough water." He looked up at her. "How you getting on?"

"Okay." Then she shook her head. "Not okay."

He nodded and moved toward the bench. "Let's sit down, talk."

"Not there." (Chu had advised her.) "While we're walking."

He smiled sadly. "You think the bench is bugged? I could be wearing a wire, for that matter. But hell, let's walk."

They strolled down the path toward the Admin housing project. "Here's the story," he said in just above a whisper. "The Colony can't go on this way. If we leave things the way they are, it'll get worse before it gets better. Now I'll tell you something about RM17. You're right about it. Now, look—I trust you, Kitty. I don't even know why. I do, though. I don't trust the other radics. Maybe I trust you because the way I read you—I could be wrong—you aren't politically motivated, not really. You just want decent treatment, a fair chance. So you're not a radic, per se—I know your husband is, but . . . the way I see it, you're a person willing to fight, but you don't have any axes to grind ideologically."

She wasn't following him. "What about getting Chester out?"

"Sure, well, I'm comin' to it." He glanced around. "I fooled with the surveillance cameras, reassigned the guards out here, but all this open ground still makes me nervous. Damn, it looks empty. Seems a shame."

"Hard to get permission to come out here lately. Kids are getting stir-crazy."

"I know. That'll change, too, if...okay, listen. What we're going to have to do is to organize a counterforce, our own security outfit, and disarm the one that exists. I have a scheme for that. We might be able to disarm the whole bunch of 'em without a shot fired. But I'm going to need commitment from the technicki underground that they'll co-ordinate with me. Move where I say, when I say. If they'll do it, we'll pull the rug out from under Admin. You'll be my liaison with the underground. That way I don't know who they are, so they aren't threatened. The thing will happen in stages. First stage, we disarm as many of the bulls as we can—I'll give you the details on that one later. Second we release the political prisoners, merge them with our new se-curity force, use it to incarcerate the old one and take control of the various sections. You look like all this's thrown you a bit."

"I...God." She shook her head in amazement. She hadn't come prepared for this. Having a full-scale rebellion dropped in her lap. A complete takeover! "But how will you keep control of it after Earth finds out?"

"We'll worry about that when we come to it. I think I can establish that Praeger's Admin was guilty of murder, for one thing."

"I—this is too much. I thought you were going to smug-gle me and Chester out or something."

"I can't get Chester out until the SA is disarmed. Those people are *not* under my command anymore, except for the simple day-to-day assignments. If I told them to disarm, they'd turn me into Praeger. They're not the Colony's secu-rity anymore—if they ever were. They're SA."

She stated it flatly. "They're Nazis."

He sighed. "I'm beginning to think so too."

They didn't say anything for a while. Finally she had to say, "I'm scared."

He nodded. "Yeah."

Cloudy Peak Farm, Upstate New York.

Hayes was inside out, scraped clean.
Sometimes he almost felt like he was shining.

Hayes was standing in the Media Center. It was at the southern edge of Cloudy Peak Farm, an annex on Crandall's private wing of the overgrown log cabin. On three sides were screens, and gear for bringing the screens alive. The fourth side was a filtered glass wall, which Crandall usually kept dialed to opaque. But it was a sunny morning near the end of March, and Crandall's doctors had insisted—so far as they'd dared—that the sunlight would be good for his health. He'd let them dial the wall to transparency.

Hayes was the door guard, standing against the room's only bare patch of nonglass wall, the door to his left, the screens directly to his right, and diagonally from him, and the glass wall directly across from him. And Crandall, with Rolff and Ben, directly between.

Hayes liked to know where everything and everyone was in the room. It was more than that he *liked* to; he'd been made that way. Made recently. (If he tried to think about how he'd been made that way, he came to an impenetrable membrane, and he had to turn back.)

He was supposed to keep track of things spatially, like a chess player visualizing the board. Because . . .

He didn't know why. He knew it was for something.

But anyway, it felt good to do it.

Crandall was sitting in an electric wheelchair, still wearing pajamas and a robe. Looking frail. Hard to believe a man that sunken, that frail, had so much power. Behind him, on either side, Rolff Getzerech and Ben stood bodyguard.

"Guards right outside the building," Hayes had told Rolff. "Guards patrolling the grounds, in guard towers, on the fences, patrolling the area in helicopters and jeeps. Guards in the hall, at the door. Radar to watch for missiles. And with all that,' he needs two more guys standing behind him all the time?"

"The NR shot him. Killed his sister. Right here in the house. For a long time," Rolff had said in his soft accent, "he would not come out from behind the bulletproof glass in his bedroom. Saw people with cameras. Even now he carries a gun on him. Even with the two guards."

Rolff stood there with unflinching patience, wearing a short-sleeved Special Guardsman's uniform, his big, meaty hands clasped like an altar boy's over the brass SASG buckle with its chrome "iron cross" inset. Rolff was Klaus's brother. Klaus Getzerech, the bodyguard and factotum for Colonel Watson. He had Klaus's delicate red lips, incongruous with the craggily chiseled face, the massive chest. His hair was so blond it was almost white; his eyes a blue so pale, they were almost silver. On his hips were a Browning machine pistol and a walkie-talkie.

Ben wore glasses, but he was as big as Rolff, his brown hair clipped into the classic Mid-American choirboy's haircut. He had a dimple in his chin and small, empty brown eyes. He was dressed like Rolff. And like Hayes too. But Hayes hadn't yet earned the privilege of attending church services in dress whites, like Rolff and Ben. They were an impressive sight coming into the little chapel under the oaks with Crandall, in their dress uniforms—modeled on Marine Corp dress uniforms but red and white. Mostly white.

Outside the glass wall, a guard in an armored uniform and mirrored helmet walked by, his visor making semaphores of glints of sun with his movements.

Hayes felt a strange unrest. *Flashing lights.*

His hand went to his gun.

But the guard walked by; the flashing went with him.

Hayes felt as if something had been taken from him just now. Like a section of his stomach had been pulled out like a drawer. He tried to think about what it was, but he felt the membrane again. So he simply took his hand off the gun, and the unrest went away.

Crandall was using a complicated remote-control box he held in his lap to switch on the screens. The big one across from him first—most of the smaller screens to Crandall's right were conference screens, for talking to the regional commanders and other high-ranking personnel. And for watching SA christenings, initiations, rites of all kinds. At ten he was to watch a graduation presentation by the boy, Jebediah. The boy Crandall called "the living destiny of my church." Just a precocious kid, as far as Hayes could tell. He'd seen him onscreen a few times. Smart, articulate, schooled in the Three Fundamental Ideas and all the ideological underpinnings. Even better schooled in it than Hayes, who knew Crandall's Revised Bible by heart. The kid, Jebediah, seemed to *understand* it better. Give him that.

On the big screen there was yet another report about the war. The anchorman claimed the Soviets were retreating. "Unilaterally in retreat," he said. Their offensive "splintered," the guy said. New Soviet mobilization in orbit. Some analysts wondering if the orbital mobilization could be in preparation for a first strike. Knock out our antimissile satellite weapons. *Maybe it's finally coming*.

People should be more optimistic, Hayes thought. Look how marvelous the world was, really. Those TV screens, themselves. We take 'em for granted, but, hey, they're amazing. Screens dancing with light. Sunlight outside the glass. Look through the glass out into the world. Look into the screens into other avenues of the world; the televisions were windows into the world. Nice thought. Made him feel shining. Positive, optimistic. Accent the positive in things. TV screens were windows into—

"Smoke," Crandall said, interrupting Hayes's rumination. "That's Jack Brendan Smoke."

Casting about for a morning news program, Crandall had stumbled on someone he knew. Crandall's jaws were clamped, muscles bunched in them.

"The source of the New Racism has deep, complicated roots," Smoke was saying on the big screen. He was sitting in a pastel talk-show setting of some kind, with a talk-show interviewer nodding patiently to his right. One of the more public television types, judging from the fact that he didn't interrupt with a lot of stupid, sensationalistic questions. "Some of its growth is the accident of circumstances, and some of it has, I think, been cultivated by coalitions of highly organized racists."

Crandall grunted at that and shifted in his chair.

Smoke went on. "There was a certain amount of backlash to civil rights legislation and racial quota hiring practices in the 1960s, '70s and '80s. But something even more important to the New Racism emerged in the 1980s, and continuously thereafter. The influx of non-European immigrants, especially Arabs, Persians, Pakistanis, people from India, from the Caribbean; Israelis, Japanese, Koreans, and Vietnamese—all these people began to seem sort of overwhelming to the average American and the average Caucasian in Western Europe. The immigrants tended to create their own well-defined cultural environments in the urban settings, changing the looks of neighborhoods, threatening the standard American religions, altering the type of service available, and so forth. But the turning point came when they began to organize for political power. They began to learn the basic political skills, grass-roots organizing, voter registration, precinct walking, the importance of ward captains, home-computer bulletin-board lobbying, school-board elections, city-council races, and perhaps most important to the Arabs especially, political patronage. Each one of these various new ethnic communities became a political force to be reckoned with."

"You're saying," the commentator asked, "that the fact that they were of non-European derivation increased the bias against them?"

"Yes, clearly. Most of these people were not Christians. Not Catholics or Protestants. Protestants and Catholics are prejudiced against one another to a degree, but not nearly as much as they are prejudiced against Moslems, Buddhists, Sikhs, and Hindus. And equally important, most European immigrants were Caucasian. The U.S. was founded by European immigrants—and their black slaves, though, of course, most Americans don't choose to recognize blacks as cofounders of the country. Most Americans could accept Caucasian European immigrants, even Hispanic immigrants —they were at least Christian—but not this other massive influx of unusually alien aliens. White Americans felt that their cultural traditions, their very identity as Americans, were threatened."

"If I understood your latest printout..." The interviewer held up a copy of the computer printout's cover page and read off the title: *"Wave of Darkness: The New Racism* by Jack Brendan Smoke, published by Penguin Printouts... uh, if I understood it correctly, you link the reaction against immigrants to an increase in racial prejudice against blacks and native American Jews."

"I do. I think that for various reasons of conditioning, psychological dynamics, and perhaps, even to a degree, instinct, a large sector of our society is basically racist by nature. I think, though, that this racism becomes active only when there are certain social and environmental factors at work. I think this xenophobic reaction, this inflammation of the territorial instinct, if that's what it is, grows and feeds on itself once it's set free. Racism against one group leads to racism against another."

"What are the social and environmental factors that bring this reaction about in people?"

"There's some evidence that sociobiological factors may be at work. For example, population density. Up to a certain level, high population density promotes a kind of adaptive acceptance of many kinds of people—but there's a breaking point. After the breaking point of population density is reached, people feel constantly threatened by other people. They tend to group with their own ethnic and cultural types increasingly in an instinctive search for protection. All this is aggravated by poverty, lack of opportunities, depression, a general sense of frustration. People look for someone to blame for all this, and they naturally blame groups of people who're obviously different. Other ethnic groups. They tend to be perpetually scanning for differences in other people that might represent a threat. After a while any difference represents a threat. And some of the ethnic political groups developed extremist splinters who implemented an epidemic of terrorist bombings, snipings, hijackings, all taking place on American soil. That fed the racism, of course.

"Another factor is the breakdown of useful family structures, the ephemeral quality of families, a trend that developed at the end of the last century. This combined with pervasively ephemeral cultural trends to produce 'wandering self-image.' People became vulnerable to identification with mass-marketed imagery. They began to feel reduced to pixels on a TV screen themselves. In the immensity of society—an immensity shown them every day in the Grid—they felt insignificant. So they turned—and were led—to excessive identification with their own race to give them a handle on identity."

"You've intrigued me by saying that people are 'vulnerable to mass-marketed imagery,' that they're being 'led.' What exactly . . . ?"

"There are organizations at work who recognize these trends as useful to them. They use them to build political power, or more accurately, to *seize* political power. In part two of *Wave of Darkness* I demonstrate—with plenty of evidence—that the Second Alliance and Rick Crandall's Second Circle church organization—these days they call it 'His Church'—are conspiring to promote racism in the United States, in order to facilitate their own political ends here, and that they are instrumental in a new Fascist power grab in Western Europe. I have new information that has not been incorporated into the current *Wave of Darkness* printout. Proof that *this racist organization has the ear of the President of the United States.* That they are—to put it bluntly— *working very closely with her* to scrap the Constitution, and *take power* here."

"Take power." The interviewer looked almost disappointed. As if he'd decided Smoke was just another crank.

Crandall snorted with pleasure. "Go ahead, tell 'im another one," Crandall muttered.

"I have brought proof," Smoke said. "I propose to show that proof here, on this program, for the first time anywhere." He opened a briefcase, took out a tiny videodisk, and handed it to the interviewer, who gave it to a technician.

Crandall sat up straight in his chair. He swiveled to his right, punched a button on his remote-control unit. A face appeared on one of the screens in the stack to Hayes's right.

"Yes, Reverend?" the face asked. A woman, that's all Hayes could tell from where he stood.

"Get me Chancelrik at Chicago Worldtalk."

Smoke was saying, "... hard to say where the SA's insinuation into federal government began, although it seems to have been in partnership with the CIA for many years. Last year they exchanged their own new techniques for submarine-silencing to the Department of Defense in exchange for participation in Defense planning committees and other projects," when Chancelrik came onto the screen.

Hayes heard him say, "What can I do for you, Rick?"

"You monitoring channel fourteen?"

"No. I was—"

"Never mind. Monitor it *now*."

"Gotcha. Okay, I've got it. That's what's-his-name, Smoke, isn't it?"

On the screen Smoke was saying, "... were photographed covertly by operatives of the New Resistance."

The screen showed the President of the United States walking through a snowy field with a fat man Hayes didn't recognize. "Sackville-West," Smoke called him.

After the film ran, the interviewer and Smoke came back on. The interviewer looked shaken. "Of course it has been analyzed for video falsification?"

"It has. And it's available to anyone for that same analysis."

"Holy fucking shit." Chancelrik's voice.

"There's more," Smoke said.

"God in heaven," Chancelrik said.

Another film came on the screen. Swarthy-looking men opening crates in what was probably the hold of a ship. Harsh lights brought in for the filming. Smoke's voice-over: "Here we have videotapes provided by the Israeli Mossad of the inspection of cargo of a ship called the *Hermes' Grandson*. The Resistance intercepted the ship and turned its contents over to the Mossad. This is a Second Alliance ship—here you see SA prisoners—and it's packed stem to stern with artillery, illegal devices for interrogation, antiaircraft missiles." One by one the items were shown as Smoke ticked them off. "And *this* carton contains nerve gas. We found two tons of nerve gas on the boat. The SA's legal presence in Europe is as a peacekeeping and police force. It would have no legitimate use for nerve gas, missiles—"

"We can claim the New Resistance stocked the ship, made up some of its own people to look like SA troops," Chancelrik said.

"Shit," Crandall said. (Making Ben look at Crandall with surprise.) "If it was by itself, we could make it look like it was bullshit. But along with the film of Bester talking to that incompetent tub of lard and the damn book . . . well, do what you can."

He cut Chancelrik's connection and cut into another line. "Johnston?" Head of SA International Security for the United States.

"Yes, Reverend?"

On the screen, Smoke was talking about CIA files that had come to his attention recently. He was talking about a man named Kupperbind. He was talking about a campaign to purge the ranks of CIA Domestic of blacks and Jews. He was talking about files—he admitted they'd been stolen from the CIA—that discussed the CIA's part in the initiation of a European apartheid.

Crandall was saying, "Johnston, Jack Brendan Smoke. *Tagged*. Quietly as possible. And tell Sackville-West I want him here by tonight. Here, in person!" His voice breaking, almost weepy with anger.

Tagged: Kill him. Make it look like an accident or like someone else did it.

"Smoke entered the country under heavy guard two days ago, recorded some interviews yesterday, and left this morning, Reverend. By private jet. The jet was bound for Mexico City. We followed by satellite recon to Mexico City, but after that . . . Witcher's people are in control of the airport there. Smoke changes planes in Mexico City and we lose track of him. Mexican immigration so far has either been recalcitrant or too inefficient to—"

"No excuses. Find him. Tag him."

The Island of Malta.

"Recon post Seven is about sixty-five miles southeast of Iraklion," Steinfeld was saying, tapping the coast of Crete on the map. "The post is the SA's key Mediterranean reconnaissance center. It coordinates satellite surveillance, it monitors transmissions of all kinds, it collates information from the various SA outposts in Europe. SA troops there number—if the Mossad is right—less than a hundred. Artillery and missile defense is minimal. So it's underdefended, it's vulnerable. The Greek government—or the SA occupation government, to be more accurate—has about three hundred men stationed within an hour of Post Seven. But by the time they're mobilized to give Seven assistance, we'll be well away."

Karakos, Hard Eyes, Danco, Lila, Levassier, and the other officers were sitting in a semicircle around Steinfeld. The briefing room was lit only by the map lamp. The back part was in darkness. Sometimes Karakos imagined he saw —or felt—things moving out of the corner of his eye back there. But when he looked, it was always gone. Sometimes he still felt the strange pressure, and the impenetrable places in his mind, the membranes beyond which he could not pass. He tried not to think about it. He tried to think about Greece. Its Nationalist salvation.

He noticed that Bonham was not there. He was never permitted at the planning sessions. They didn't trust Bonham. *Maybe,* Karakos thought, *I shouldn't trust him, either.*

Bonham had given Karakos the names of the NR operatives on the Colony. Time would prove whether the names were real or not. To test that, he must once more get to a radio. And, of course, there was the matter of reporting the assault on Post Seven.

Steinfeld went on to describe his strategy for their assault on Post Seven; some part of Karakos's mind was absorbing Steinfeld's briefing, but thoughts of this Hard Eyes were like dogs locked in some mental outbuilding, fighting and snarling in there, distracting him. The bastard was doing nothing, saying nothing about Karakos. But Karakos could feel him watching him, even when he didn't seem to be. Working against him somehow. Otherwise, why was it that Karakos still had not been told when the *real* assault against the SA would commence? Why was he still in the dark about its target? It had to be Hard Eyes. He had planted the seeds of doubt in the others, and despite all their denials, they were cautious around Karakos, and Steinfeld told him nothing. This business of the attack on Post Seven was minor, just a warm-up for the April Assault.

But he didn't dare press anyone for information. That would make them suspicious. He would find a way.

"The destruction of Seven will set the stage for the April Assault," Steinfeld was saying.

And then he looked at Karakos. Expressionlessly. But looked right at him.

Hard Eyes resented the night. It was balmy and the air was sweet as he left the house to take his turn at the sentry shack by the road. He could smell the sea, and the mosquitoes seemed to be on vacation. His mood demanded a stormy night, or at least a driving rain, and as much discomfort as possible.

Hard Eyes was stepping off the porch when someone in

the darkness came toward him from his right. He swung his assault rifle around.

"It's me." Claire.

He slung the rifle on his shoulder. It seemed heavier than it should have.

"You want to talk about it?" she asked softly.

His eyes began to adjust to the dark. Her face materialized like a ghost. He tried to not say it, but he couldn't stop: "You going to sleep with everyone else? Who's next?"

"That's not talking about it."

"I didn't say I wanted to talk about it. God, I don't know. I'm just . . . I'm human. Shit, Claire . . ."

She touched his arm. He trembled at her touch and felt stupid about it, so he stepped back from her, and she misinterpreted him.

"You decided you want no contact with homosexuals?"

"You're not a homosexual. You might be bisexual. But you were feeling things, real things, with me." His tone challenged her to pretend it wasn't true.

"Of course I did. I don't think I'm gay. But she . . . she's very tender and . . . in some way it's what I need right now. I don't know for how long."

"God. Should I take a number?"

"Fuck you, Torrence."

"I'm sorry. I shouldn't have. I'm sorry."

"I know."

"Yeah, you always say that. You know. I don't know you. You accused me of not opening up more than once, but I *don't know you*. Maybe that's my fault."

Her silence acknowledged that maybe it was.

Baltimore, Maryland.

Stoner was running even when he was motionless.

They'd changed motels twice in two days, Stoner making light of it, pretending for Cindy that he wanted one with a Gridfeed screen so she could see her cartoons. And then wanted one with a Gridfeed screen *and* a pool. Trying to hide from his little girl that he was moving them out of simple fear.

But he couldn't hide it from Janet. Stoner and his wife sat in a window seat overlooking the skating rink of the underground mall the motel was in, sipping weak cocktails in squeaky plastic cups sent up by the automated room service. Janet was sitting there rigidly, staring out at the gliding figures on the skating rink, her eyes tracing the blades that etched off-white lines into the chalky ice; Cindy was watching TV, the Japanese reactive cartoon, *Roboboy*. Cindy had the interaction box in her hand; the screen was set to receive the various *Roboboy* interactive programs, and Janet had booted Cindy's name into the flexible sound track. "Uh-oh!" Roboboy was saying. "Stoned Dr. Drugmaster has shot a hypnotic into Designer Dan! What should I do, Cindy? Should I try to find an antidote, or should I go to the Garbage Marsh to rescue my pal Lowtech without Designer Dan's help?"

"Find an antidote!" Cindy said, pushing the button for Option A.

"Me," Stoner muttered, "I wish he'd rescue us from the

Garbage Marsh." He watched Janet's face, hoping she'd smile.

But her lips compressed, whitening; trying to keep from crying.

He glanced at his watch. Eight. It would be dark up above. But here, of course, with its perpetually modulated lighting, never too bright, never too dim, it might be any time of day. The walk between the motel and the rink was still busy with shoppers and browsers moving like bees gathering pollen at the shops on the other four sides of the rink. On the far side a Silent Radio strip formed marching letters for newsblurbs and ads: DEPARTMENT OF DEFENSE REPORTS SOVIETS CONTINUE WITHDRAWAL IN EUROPE BUT INCREASE ORBITAL PRESENCE ...PRESIDENT BESTER DENIES SECOND ALLIANCE PLOT ALLEGATIONS CALLS FOR INVESTIGATION INTO 'ANTIPATRIOTIC PROPAGANDA SOURCES'... SECRETARY OF INTERIOR SWILL REAFFIRMS NEED FOR EMERGENCY PRESIDENTIAL POWERS, WILL NOT RULE OUT MEDIA CENSORSHIP, CITES WAR EMERGENCY...ACID RAIN CONCENTRATED IN TORNADOS BLAMED FOR TOXICITY DEATHS IN MISSOURI...COURT FINDS COMPLETE VINDICA- TION FOR LATE SENATOR SPECTOR. SPECTOR WAS KILLED DURING ANTIVIOLENCE LAWS PROGRAM- MING; GRAND JURY NAMED FOR VIDEOFRAMING INVESTIGATION...IN SPORTS, THE HOUSTON OR- BITERS SHOT DOWN THE...

Stoner looked away, shrugging. And saw Lopez, standing by the railing of the rink, looking up at him.

"There he is," Stoner murmured.

"Where?" Janet asked breathlessly.

"He's coming into the motel now." Where was Brummel? Stoner wondered.

Lopez came to the door. Stoner let him in, glancing at Cindy. She hardly looked up. She told Roboboy, "Apply for new memories, Roboboy!" and pressed a button.

Lopez went directly to Janet, still sitting in the window. He was wearing a brown overcoat, speckled from rain.

"It's raining up there?" Stoner said.

Lopez took off his soft plastic fedora, held it in his hands in front of him, and said softly, "Mrs. Stoner, I'm sorry to tell you, your brother is dead, or will be soon. He was stopped at a checkpoint and lost his temper with a policeman, pulled a gun. They hit him and took the gun away, took him to be questioned and . . . they put him under extractor. They know what he does. Under the antiterrorist section of the AVL laws, he will be killed, probably before AVL is suspended. I am sorry. We cannot help him."

He said all this quickly, and with a sympathetic gentleness that surprised Stoner.

Janet covered her mouth, squeezed her eyes shut, rocked in silent pain. Stoner went to stand beside her, put his arm over her shoulder. And then the implications hit him like a chilled spike: Brummel, extracted. Which meant that Lopez would soon be under surveillance.

Lopez, looking at him, saw it on his face and nodded. "We have to hurry. And I'll be coming with you. They know about me now."

Twenty minutes and they were all down in the lobby, bags sloppily packed, on the carrier beside Stoner, who was waiting at the desk for the Pakistani clerk to bring his credit card back. Wondering if maybe there was an APB out for him with a credit freeze tagged to it, which would mean the clerk's credit reader would refuse Stoner access to his funds. And would alert the police.

Cindy was crying because she'd seen her Mommy cry; she clung to Janet's legs, and Janet was trying not to cry, and dammit, the clerk was taking too long to come back with that card. Why had he taken it into the next room, anyway? He'd slotted it into the desk reader, said it wasn't working, he'd have to take it to the back room.

Oh, Lord. Stoner looked at Lopez. "I think there's—"

"Yes," Lopez said, "we'll have to leave the bags."

Stoner bent, took the small blue Tourister off the stack, handed Janet her night bag, said in a low voice, "That's it, I'm sorry, honey, but that's it. Come on."

She followed her husband and Lopez across the lobby to the glass doors, looked over her shoulder at the bags they'd left. Just once. "Mommy, we have to take our bags," Cindy said.

"Someone's going to send it for us," Janet told her, lying

with an admirable cheeriness as they went out the doors onto the walk. Wash of skating rink schmaltz music, the generic mockery of crowd sounds.

A neopunk boy in a fatigue jacket, an orange flight suit, and spiked boots approached Lopez. He had a pallid, long-nosed face and needled eyes, and he wore a headset communicator made to look like a sort of Walkman. He said, "Armando called down, says a fed copter landed on the roof and a bunch of guys who look too much alike got out of cars and ran into the mall upstairs—about a minute ago."

Lopez swore in Spanish and then said, "You find the way?"

The boy nodded and jerked his head: *Come on.* They followed him through the crowds to the door of an office with a dull black plastic sign, MALL SECURITY. Lopez glancing at Stoner with that look of inquiry. *Betrayal?* But they went past the door, around the corner into an alley littered with waxpaper cups, graffitied: JEROME-X WINS WHEN HE LOSES. A small three-wheeled truck was parked there, the words MALL SECURITY PATROL on it in the mall's colors, gold on dun. Another kid was in the driver's seat, his zigzagged haircut looking odd under the Security guard's cap. He wore a brown uniform. Lopez, Stoner, Janet, and Cindy were ushered into the little truck—a van, really—and Janet gasped. Stoner looked, saw a man in yellowed briefs tied up in the back of the van, turned to the back door. Hands cuffed behind his back; ankles cuffed together. Breathing but gagged.

"Mommy . . . ?"

"It's okay, honey, it's a joke, they'll let him go soon."

"Lay down in the back," the driver said, a teenager's voice.

God, we're in the hands of children, Stoner thought.

They lay down side by side, Lopez at the rear beside the subdued guard, Stoner turned away from him, toward his wife, the two of them holding Cindy between them. "It's a game, Cindy," Janet said, inevitably making Stoner wince. Because he knew that Cindy wouldn't fall for it.

She pretended to fall for it. She nodded and closed her eyes as the truck started moving. She was a good girl.

Stoner thought, *This is stupid, ridiculous, I'm an idiot.*

Hearing the electric motors droning, vibration coming through the floor; thinking that it was his fault they were here, undergoing these absurd contortions, he should have stayed out of it for his family's sake, or left them, the Company probably wouldn't have . . . yes, they would have. They'd have picked up Janet in case she knew where he was. Maybe to use her and Cindy as hostages to get him back. To shut him up.

But somehow this was his fault. Dragging his family through this, making them feel like wetbacks lying on the floor of a truck. Maybe in the trunk of a car next, for God's sake.

And this absurdity was made worse by its probable futility. They'd probably be busted; any second cops or CIA Domestic would stop the car, dourly smug faces would look through the front windows at the white wetbacks clinging to one another in the back.

He felt the van descending a ramp of some kind, turning; he and Lopez nudged by inertia against one another, Cindy whimpering, Janet clutching her tighter, trying to smile at Stoner.

Maybe they'll simply execute the lot of us. Cindy too.

The van was leveling out, probably in the underground parking lot.

The van stopped. Men's voices. Stoner wondered if it would have helped if he'd brought a gun.

"If I knew where, I wouldn't be out looking for them," the kid driver said to someone.

Don't come close enough to look in the back.

The van was moving again. Stoner realized that Cindy was squeaking with pain because he was holding her so tight. He loosened his grip, whispered, "Sorry sweetie."

Lopez hissed, *"Silencio!"*

The van hummed along for ten minutes, and Stoner realized, *We must be out!* and as he thought it, the light shifted its quality, became streetlight, harsh blue-white. They were on the streets.

Ten minutes more and then the kid driver said, "Checkpoint. Lay still no matter what."

The van grumbled and stopped.

Clipped voice of a young by-the-booker who sounded like

he'd just finished his stretch in the service. "You got a pass to—what the hell is that? In the back. Get out of the—"

Then a rattling hiss. A bubbling *uh-uhnk* from the guy who'd stopped them. The van was moving again before Stoner realized . . .

"Oh, God, no," Janet said. "He killed someone."

"You must be quiet!" Lopez said.

"Oh, shut up, Lopez," Stoner snapped. "Doesn't matter now."

There'd be a patrol car after them in minutes. The van wasn't fast, maybe wasn't even street-legal, was designed for trundling around the walkways of the mall. It stopped.

"Change vehicles fucking *fast!*" the kid driver yelled, banging the side door open.

They were up and moving. Glimpses of an industrial park, Cyclopean red light atop a tower, and then they were in a bigger van, thirty years old, its sides painted with surfer myth imagery, a bulging window blurrily shaped like an arrow on the side above a god-sized curl that never breaks. In the back, they sat on the metal floor.

Sirens.

"Oh, shit," the kid driver said, putting the van in gear. A lurch and a growl, the van burning rubber. "Oh—he's not on our road . . . I don't think . . . just a mile to our airstrip."

Stoner was certain that any second they'd come up against the roadblock or a Police Assault Van forcing them over, maybe taking out the rear tires with a neatly placed 20-mm shell.

But then a long, long curve as they turned off the industrial park road, down a utility road. Gravel crunched under the tires till they reached the tarmac of the airstrip. Stoner saw the Lear and thought, *No, really?*

Really. Thirteen minutes and they were aboard, the little jet taxiing down the runway, Janet, laughing with relief like a stewardess—no kidding, *a stewardess*—saw to it they were strapped in, and they were in the air. Stoner and his family were the only passengers except for Lopez and the kid driver (what happens to the guy they left in the van? The cops would find him), the kid throwing the oversize guard's cap in the corner, then beginning work on his acne, squeezing pimples methodically as they talked to Lopez.

"You heard they got Charlie Chesterton? Not sure how. But he snuffed hisself, probably so they couldn't braindrain him."

Stoner said, to change the subject, "Where we going?"

"South," Lopez said. "The Caribbean."

The kid adding, "Little island you got to call home for a while. It's comfortable, almost like a resort. It'll be okay."

Will it be prison? Stoner wondered. He still had a bargaining chip. He knew about the mole in the European NR. They might subject him to the extractor, of course. But he had a feeling that wasn't their style. So he had something to bargain with. Maybe he'd have to bargain with them for his family's freedom. Maybe he'd have to give them the SA agent who'd penetrated Steinfeld's base on Malta.

Cloudy Peak Farm, Upstate New York.

"Satelex from Colonel Watson," Johnston said, coming into the room. "He's on his way here." He showed the printout to Crandall, who was in his office, sitting at a WorkCenter; he'd been scowling over some statistics on the computer monitor. The scowl deepened as he scanned the satelex printout. Hayes was at the door as usual, watching and listening but not seeming to. Not watching and listening for any reason; it wasn't like he was *spying*. But it kept him amused, kept him from mentally roving up to those disconcerting membranes that cut him off from certain channels of free association. He listened because he wanted to feel like a part of the place. He believed in Crandall, admired him.

"What the hell?" Crandall said. "I didn't order him to come here."

It was Sunday afternoon. They'd just come from chapel, where Crandall had preached on the SA security channel, for Initiates only. Fresh from church, Ben and Rolff were in their dress uniforms, standing beside Crandall's chair.

Johnston was in a real-cloth Sunday-go-to-meetin' suit, blue serge and subtly cut. He had the sturdy, brown-haired, blue-eyed, enlightened-young-cowpoke looks that Crandall liked to surround himself with. Early twenties, very serious. Johnston stood by in case Crandall wanted to send a reply.

Crandall seemed to consider it, then shook his head. "Wouldn't get to him, anyway. Well, he'd better have a hell of a good excuse. He's supposed to be gettin' squared away to clean the chimney, sweep those little greasers out of their nest." Meaning the NR, Hayes guessed.

Hayes found himself watching Rolff. He looked a little pale. He was staring at the satelex print. Rolff looked up and looked directly at Hayes, almost like he wanted to say something to him. Then he dropped his eyes and cleared his throat. "Sir . . ."

Crandall muttered, without looking up from the computer screen, "Yes?" He'd gone back to picking through statistics.

"Permission to use the bathroom."

"Sure, Johnston's here, he can stay till you're back."

"There's something else, sir," Johnston said with a little hesitation. "I don't know if I should report on it till I'm sure . . . but I've got a good feeling about it."

"What's that?" Crandall asked, glancing up at Johnston.

Rolff was moving toward the door, but slowly, as if he wanted to hear what Johnston was going to say.

Johnston said, "The Secursearch data base has put a red star next to an island in the Caribbean. Place called Merino. Dinky place, sir. Military installation there we thought belonged to Costa Rica. Set up to look like it's part of Costa Rica. Camouflaged that way, I think. But there are a number of irregularities. Civilian jets from Mexico City landing there with unusual frequency, and we've identified the owner of one of the jets, sir. Witcher." Edge of excitement in his voice. "We think we might have a major NR stronghold. Maybe Western HQ."

"Lordy. Who all knows about this?"

"Just me and you, sir. In accordance with your directive."

"Good. I'm feelin' funny about security again. If it leaks that we know where they are, they'll run and hide again."

Rolff wasn't listening to them, Hayes realized. He was standing in the doorway, staring. At Hayes. Just looking at him, a little to his right. One hand resting on his gun butt. The other, his left, in his pocket. The hand in his pocket made a movement. Hayes saw it through the cloth, and then lights flashed. The ceiling lights. Flashing on and off, over and over, in a pattern and—oh, no—Hayes had a rollercoaster feeling inside. The room got all tunnel-dark, except for a corona of light around Crandall and Johnston, and they were moving in slow motion, looking up at Hayes, Johnston reaching into his coat, Crandall throwing his arms in front of his face. Why were they reacting that way?

And then Hayes saw that there was a gun pointed at Crandall (the lights flashed—oh, no) and the gun was in Hayes's hand, his own gun. *I'm pointing a gun at Rick. What am I doing?* Slow motion went to fast motion as he squeezed the trigger again and again, not even having to sight in, his hand doing it for him. He heard shouting, thought he heard Parakeet's voice laughing (who was Parakeet?), and then Crandall's head exploded, and the gun was tracking up to Johnston. Johnston had his gun out now, and Ben had his leveled. Something kicked into Hayes, right through the middle of him. He saw Johnston falling, knew that he'd shot him, felt another kick in the side of the head where Rolff had shot him.

His grandmother had had a record player. He heard the squeal of a record-player needle across a record. And then silence.

"The lights flashed," Ben said, "like a signal. And the guy shot Rick." Ben was crying, big guy like that blubbering. Klaus, standing behind Watson, snorted and shook his head.

Watson turned to Rolff. "What was Johnston there about?"

"About your satelex," Rolff said. "And about something he'd found. I didn't catch what. I was ... Hayes seemed to be acting funny so I ..." Rolff glanced at Ben.

You're a bad actor, Rolff, Watson thought. But fortunately Ben's too upset to notice.

Rolff went on, "I didn't catch it. You get it, Ben? What it was Johnston wanted?"

"Something about a satellite picture," Ben said, his voice breaking, nose running. They were in the dark wood living room, sitting on the black leather couch, Ben with his head in his hands.

Crandall was only three hours dead. Watson felt ... what? Mostly a kind of dreamy detachment. *Crandall was dead!* Unreal. And Watson was tired, jet-lagged, but the adrenaline of the trip—never quite sure if the Soviets were going to let you through—still had him jacked up. "I don't know," Ben said after a moment. "I didn't pay attention because I was noticing how Rolff was looking at Hayes and..." He shrugged. Then he looked at Rolff. It made Watson uncomfortable to look at Ben; such a big man, a muscle rippler, with his face tear-streaked like a five-year-old who'd scraped his knee. "You shouldn't have shot him in the head, Rolff," Ben said. "That was stupid. We can't extract now."

Not that extraction would show anything, Watson thought. But then, perhaps Rolff had done well: an experienced extracting tech might realize that Hayes had had his brain rearranged by an extractor before. Yes, Rolff had good instincts.

"And you," Ben was saying, looking at Watson. "Hayes was sent over by your people."

A shame Johnston had been there. That had confused Hayes's cerebral reprogramming. He'd been programmed to shoot Crandall and the man standing with Crandall, which should have been Ben. But Johnston had been there with Ben... so Ben was alive and might be suspicious.

To kill him, though, pretend he'd been killed at the same time as the others. That would alert Sackville-West. "This came in just ten minutes ago," Watson said. And in saying it committed himself to letting Ben live. He handed Ben a satelex. It read:

> Arrest Special BG Hayes instantly. Repeat: Arrest and hold now for extraction team. The following is text of Hayes's letter to newspaper *International Herald Tribune* dated_____. "I have decided to terminate the life of Rick Crandall, a pious hypocrite whose distortions of God's Teachings are an embarrassment to all real Christians. St. Peter has come to me in a dream and asked me to do this, and I want the world to know why I'm doing it. By the time you get this, I will be a part of history. I will have killed the Antichrist."

"He was crazy," Ben said. A little relieved, for some reason.

Watson nodded. The ground had been prepared; false

background on Hayes, which Sackville-West would be allowed to unearth, made it look as if Hayes had converted to "Christ's Army"—fanatics, the Christian equivalent of Muslim militant fundamentalists. Dead set against Crandall. "He'd decided that Crandall was the Antichrist."

Ben put his face in his hands. Rolff and Klaus looked at each other; Klaus rolled his eyes. Rolff smiled. "Rick was important to you, wasn't he, Ben," Watson said.

Ben nodded into his hands.

"He was important to all of us," Watson said. "He was the heart and soul of the Second Alliance—and its Church. We can't let him die. Our people, our movement . . . all of us, we need him too badly."

Ben, red-eyed, looked up at him. "You can't revive him. His head . . ."

"We can revive . . . what he symbolized. And we can revive Crandall as a symbol. Not as a martyr. Not yet. In time. But for now, we need Crandall himself. Or . . . an image of him. We'll computer-animate him. A generated image of him will go out on the channels, will continue giving orders, lectures, insights. Just as he would. We'll be . . . arranging it."

Ben shook his head in disbelief. "That's . . . it's not respectful."

Watson went to sit on the coffee table directly in front of Ben, so close that their knees were touching. He looked into Ben's eyes and said with all his earnestness, "It's what Rick would have wanted. He would want whatever's best for the Church. He was the glue that held it together. We have a world to make, Ben. A sacred war to fight. We need him for the morale of that war's soldiers. Do you understand?"

After a moment Ben swallowed and nodded.

FirStep, the Space Colony, Life Support Central.

The Colony's survival mechanism was operated from here. This was the Colony's autonomic breathing apparatus, its bodily thermostat, its immune system. And at the top of the spine that made the system work was a brain. It had been an electronic brain; it was now an uneasy collaboration between electronic and biological brains. Rimpler. His brain, his pared-back mind, crouching in the center of that webwork of wiring like a spider of gray matter.

Since the system was of priority importance to the survival of the Colony, it was multiply protected. It was equipped with an air lock to give it a buffer should meteor damage—or a missile—evacuate the air in the surrounding sections and out into space. It had its own temperature-control units, special layers of insulation. And there were protections against sabotage. . . .

Russ could feel Rimpler watching him.

The security cam near the ceiling was whirring. Refocusing on Russ and Rechstedder as they entered the air lock between the access corridor and the Life Support Systems Primary Computer housing. Then the camera tracked down to look at the plastiseal box Russ carried. Did Rimpler know what was in the box? Did he guess that it was his electronic replacement?

Rechstedder wore an electrician's yellow-paper jumpsuit, freshly printed out so that it rustled as he moved, and carried a stainless-steel briefcase of tools and testers; he was a dark-eyed, compact, muscular, deeply tanned West German mechanic and electech who was also the Colony's low-grav wrestling champion. Most of his free time he spent training or soaking up solar radiation in the sun rooms. He was said to be gay. He had an air of perpetual boredom whenever he was at work, as if he were only putting up with this sort of thing until his shot at the Olympics came around.

He went into the air lock first, Russ right behind him. It was a rectangular room with a door on each end; the room was about the size of a walk-in closet; military green on the metal walls, ceiling, floor. Near the ceiling, to one side of the camera, was a ventilation grate. It made Russ think uncomfortably of the gas chamber he'd seen once when he'd done consultancy work at the state pen in Austin.

The first door closed behind them with a hiss, and its locking wheel spun. *Clack:* locked shut.

Some of Rechstedder's air of boredom vanished as he turned to look at the door.

"It does that automatically," Russ told him. And there

were two SA bulls on the other side who could open it from there for them, if necessary.

"Oh, yes. Yes, of course," Rechstedder said. "I was just startled by the noise." He turned to face the door into the Primary Computer housing, frowned, studying it. "You couldn't get in?"

"We tried the lock about twenty times. It just won't accept the combination. Rimpler's overridden the—" He broke off as Rechstedder turned him a look of lofted eyebrows. Rechstedder didn't know about Rimpler's brain.

"It's too hard to explain," Russ said. "The main thing is—can you get us in?"

"I don't know till I try." Rechstedder examined the seals on the double-thick air-lock door. He pointed to a panel in the base of the door. It was bolted shut, the bolts the smooth kind that could only be removed from this side by force. "I could drill out those bolts, open the panel, try to trigger the door from inside."

Russ nodded, and Rechstedder opened his case, squatted down to work.

Russ glanced down at the blue plastic box under his arm, then up at the camera. Wondering if Rimpler knew. Rimpler could monitor the whole Colony from here. Rimpler might know that the Soviets had let them bring in another subsistence shipment that "morning." He might have listened in on the shipping clerk's report on the contents of the cargo.

Rechstedder's drills whined; tiny, spiral worms of metal sifted into small heaps on the floor beneath, and Russ thought, *I'm thinking of that thing in there as Rimpler. But is it Rimpler? It's a portion of his brain, conceivably a portion of his consciousness.* It seemed they'd cut out everything but cunning, hatred, and a sense of humor so reduced, it was imbecilic. It seemed to have some memories. It had motivation, initiative. Is that enough to make it someone? Is it *Rimpler?*

But what am I anymore? he thought. *Used to be sure of myself, of what I was, what I believed in, who I believed in. Not now.*

"There it is," Rechstedder muttered, withdrawing the drill.

He took a flat tool from his case, began to pry on the edge of the metal panel in the door.

"If we get in," Parker said, "you're going to have to help me remove something and put something in. You might be a little . . . well, you might not like what you see. When you see it, don't ask me why it's there. It was a stupid idea. It's incredible to me that Admin put it into effect."

Rechstedder snorted, and, frowning with concentration as he worked on the creaking panel, surprised Parker by saying, "*Ja*, but you know, intelligent, worldly people have stupid ideas and carry them out all the time. There are very bright, educated people who think that a real nuclear war is something a person can win. That building up arms as far as possible was something to keep away the war. That the atmosphere, the ecology, that these things would absorb any amount of poison and everything would be fine." With a sulky rasp, the panel came free and fell on the metal floor with a rattling clank. He glanced up at Parker and again surprised him by grinning. "You have a look on your face that says you did not think I would speak that way, like a man who thinks, eh? You're very much one of the Admin to think that, Russ Parker." He took another tool from his case, looked into the panel, murmuring, "So we're going to find one of those kind of stupidities in here? The intelligent person's stupidities. That's what I came to the Colony to get away from." He bent to look deeper into the panel, put a hand on the door to steady himself. "Things like—"

He screamed and went rigid, his neck cording, lips drawing back to show his teeth in a skull's grimace, his whole body shaking. The smell of burning flesh, a wisp of smoke.

Russ kicked at Rechstedder's hand, hard, with his rubber-soled boot. It clung, smoking, to the wall, seemed as immovable as the root of an old tree. But he kicked it again, as hard as he could, and Rechstedder's hand came free of the panel.

Rechstedder stopped shaking. But he was lying on his back, face contorted, eyes staring. And the death's-head grin was permanent.

Russ tried artificial respiration, tried to pound Rechstedder's heart into restarting. But it was like trying to revive a mannequin.

He stood up, shaking, and looked at the door to the computer housing. It was sealed with some nonconductive synthetic. The floor wasn't electrified. But the door was wired for electricity. There shouldn't have been enough voltage to kill a man. But Rimpler had seen to it that there was.

Russ bent, looked into the open panel. A cryptic tangle of wires. Some of them metal-cased—they could be electrified. Russ didn't know anything about electronics. No way he could open the door on his own.

He looked up at the camera near the ceiling. Saw its lens irising as it focused on his face. Maybe there was enough Rimpler left to reason with. "You . . . you built this colony, Rimpler. It is a legacy to you, man. Little by little you're destroying it. Stop it. Give it up. Let me in. Let me help you."

This is crazy, Russ thought. It's not as if he could reply.

But Rimpler did reply, in a way.

With a hissing sound from up near the ceiling. The sound of air being sucked out of the air lock.

Russ stared at the ceiling grate, dumbfounded.

"Stop it!" he shouted. "This is . . . you're . . ." Hopeless to try to talk to him. It.

He turned to the door behind him. Tugged on the wheel.

"Oh, no." Unbudgeable.

Already he felt pain in his ears, an ache in his lungs. Headache as air pressure dropped. He took a deep breath, filling his lungs, and held it, afraid his lungs would collapse. He heard a pounding in his temples, felt the tautness in his chest become a strangling sensation as he turned, snatched up a wrench from the tool case, used it to bang on the door, frantically. Explosives. Had Rechstedder brought explosives? No, dammit, the council had vetoed that idea: blowing the door could damage the Life Support equipment behind it, send the whole Colony haywire.

The damn entry door was thick; the guards on the other side might not hear him. Hell, they might be gone.

Because maybe . . . maybe it wasn't Rimpler who was pumping the air out. Maybe it was Praeger. Using this chance to get rid of him, lay the blame on Rimpler.

In which case he was a dead man.

Bang on the door. Can't hear the sound of my own banging anymore. But keep banging.

My breath. Got to take a breath. Don't. You'll lose pressure in your lungs, they'll collapse. Hold it.

The hissing had almost stopped. In its place was a high-pitched hum. Some effect of losing air pressure on his— God, the pain in his eardrums was unbearable. Something was going to burst.

Metal squealing and a cloud of darkness closing around him.

Rush of cool air on his face. Feeling cold. Then hot, a hot flash. A series of hot flashes rippling through him. He opened his eyes.

"Chief Parker?" the man in the helmet asked him. Directly overhead, looking down.

Russ took another deep breath. "I'm okay. You guys heard me bangin', huh? Jesus Christ, you took your time."

Russ said, "We have no choice."

Praeger said, "A team of technicians, working at it for a while. Insulated equipment, pressure suits—"

"Not enough. I've been looking at the security setup for the LSS. There's more he can do. But what worries me is what else he'd do when they were trying to break in—to the rest of the Colony."

They were in Praeger's office. Russ, Praeger, and Van Kips. The two of them on the other side of the desk from Russ. A desk built for two, it seemed. The room well lit this time . . .

Russ remembered her touching Praeger, arousing him while the RM17 exploded on the screen, and a surge of nausea swept him. He shook himself and took a printout from his pocket, unfolded it, passed it across the desk to Praeger. "It happened about the time Rechstedder was drilling through the door. A pipe exploded over the day-care center. Two kids nearly drowned in sludge. He meant that as a warning to us. He won't let us tinker with him. He won't give us time to break in the way you want to. He's got the capability of killing—a section at a time or the whole Colony. I think he's probably self-destructive."

"Dr. Tate disagrees with you," Van Kips pointed out, her voice silkily contemptuous. "He's the psychiatrist, not you."

"That thing—or Rimpler, if you want to call it that, he . . . it . . . it's too unpredictable to take chances like that. We have to cut the power down to local battery units. Emergency minimum. He can't operate on that. Life Support will hold out long enough for us to break in, and he won't be able to stop us."

"And the radics will use the blackout as an opportunity to run rampant." Praeger put the tips of his fingers together. "You'd like that, wouldn't you?"

Russ stared at him. "What?"

"We have a report of a rumor you're collaborating with the radics."

"That's bullshit." Russ's hands were suddenly clammy with cold sweat. "There's always a hundred stupid rumors."

"What you've proposed suggests to me that this particular rumor isn't 'bullshit.'" He pronounced the word in mocking imitation of Russ's Southern accent.

Van Kips was smiling, looking at the door.

Oh, shit, Russ thought.

"I'm under arrest," he said.

The door hushing open behind him. He felt the guards standing there.

"What are you going to do about Rimpler?" Russ asked.

"Work with a team. Protect them."

"There is no protecting them, because they're part of the Colony, and the Colony's at Rimpler's mercy."

"Rimpler won't endanger the Colony. His survival instinct will prevent that."

"He's too fucking crazy to have a survival instinct. Shit, for all you know, you cut out that part of his brain."

"I doubt it," Praeger said. "Anyway, we're going to prepare carefully to make sure the operation goes as swiftly as possible. He won't have time to do much damage."

Russ snorted. "Not much. Just the acceptable casualties, right? A few hundred people, maybe. But what's that, after sacrificing everyone aboard RM17? What's a few hundred more?"

Praeger rocked back in his chair, smiling faintly, unaffected. "Take Russ here, to detention," he told the guards. "He's no longer Chief of Security. He's unemployed now."

"Yes, sir."

There were two of them. Big, confident, quiet. Russ went between them down the hall, passive. But at the core he buzzed and shook, like Rechstedder.

They walked past his office. Russ stopped. "Any objection if I stop in, just send a note out on my line to let 'em know I'm out of commission? I had some meetings set up, and I don't want to hang anyone up."

The guards were mirror-helmeted, as they always were when they were busting someone. But their body language spoke hesitation. They turned to one another and spoke on their helmet radios, without external volume. Then one of them nodded. "If it's quick."

If he'd been anyone else but their former boss . . .

He nodded, palmed his office door; the door slid aside and he went in. The guards waited politely outside. The light came on, and Russ sat at the console, typed out a quick message to Faid. A message he was instructed to take to Kitty Torrence.

He sent the message, then he went outside, and they took him away and locked him up.

The Island of Crete.

There was no one around, but Hard Eyes felt closed in. It was dark out, but Hard Eyes felt as if bright lights were shining on him.

He and Danco were the point of Steinfeld's assault, moving up the cracked, one-lane road, a quarter of a mile inland from their beachhead on the rocky shore of Crete. The assault teams were in four units of nine each, moving toward the SA's Post Seven on foot. They were moving in a fairly tight column now; when they reached the outer defenses of the post, they were to split into four squads, each with its own fire mission, for the attack on SA Surveillance Post Seven. Hard Eyes and Danco were at the head of the column, each carrying an auto assault rifle.

The darkness was thick on the ground, and in the olive

orchard to the right and left; the olive trees were shadows in shadows, their tops faintly glazed by starlight.

It was a mild, moonless night, windless, cool but not cold. "It's so damn quiet, Danco." Hard Eyes whispered. "Not even crickets."

He looked over his shoulder and could just barely make out the man coming behind them in the column. Not a man: it was Lila. There was supposed to be someone beside her. He wasn't there. Hard Eyes dropped back beside Lila. "Where's Karakos?" Hard Eyes asked softly.

"He said he was going to the rear to speak to Steinfeld."

Something out to the right caught his eye. Hard Eyes stared into the darkness of the olive orchard. There: a small red star, just a wink of minute light, and then it was gone. As if hastily extinguished. A match. Someone lighting a cigarette in the orchard in the middle of the dark night. Someone stupid.

Hard Eyes hissed, "Danco! Lila—freeze where you are!" The word went down the line; everyone stopped moving. He took his rifle in his right hand; with his left he put on his headset. "Squad One to Four, do you copy?"

A crackle. Steinfeld's voice: "Hard Eyes? What's the delay, everyone's stopped—"

The air split open, humming. Bullets ripping it open. Muzzle flashes in the orchard, the thud and rattle of gunfire. Lila screamed. Someone else behind them yelled in pain. Hard Eyes felt something smack his left hand and he spun, lost his headset, staggered; and suddenly his hand was slick with wet warmth. A wave of dizziness and nausea whipped through him. He went down to his knees and shouted unnecessarily, "Ambush—we've been ambushed. Pull back!" He tried to take his rifle in both hands, but his left hand was numb, was like there was a lump of frozen meat between his wrist and the gun; he couldn't hold it up that way. So he planted his left knee on the ground (the air whining, humming as rounds whipped past him), propped the gun barrel on his right knee, fired from the hip into the orchard, spraying at the muzzle flashes, probably not hitting anything, wanting to suppress them so the others could get back (wanting to run himself, his bowels vised with fear). He emptied the magazine, saw a shape loom up in front of him.

He dropped the rifle, fumbled for his pistol—but it was Danco.

"Hard Eyes, what you doing, come *on*—" Then the two of them were up. Hard Eyes stumbling along behind Danco, feeling a stab of guilt even through the throbbing ache traveling up his arm and the nausea and fear: *Left my gun behind. We don't have enough guns.* But the air was still flying apart, humming with invisible bees; bees whose stings killed and maimed. Hard Eyes almost fell across Lila. Lying sideways across the road (it was funny, he could *see* better now, maybe it was some adrenaline reaction). Hard Eyes said, "Danco, it's Lila—" He said more, which was lost in the rattle of gunfire and someone's scream. He bent and found her arm, felt it move under his fingers. She was alive. He gripped her upper arm with his intact right hand, tried to lift her. Weak from blood loss already.

"Danco!" Danco cursed but took her other arm. Between them they half dragged, half carried her to the ditch that paralleled the road. They stumbled down into the ditch, four feet deep, used it for partial cover as they dragged her through the darkness, back toward the sea. Stopping so Danco could put a belt tourniquet on Hard Eyes's left arm— the tourniquet, after a few moments, hurt more than the wound. And they stopped again so Hard Eyes could vomit. They went on, carrying Lila, coming across three more bodies, each completely inert. Slipped in puddles of blood more than once. Steinfeld had set up protective-fire units here and there down the road to try to cover their retreat; they'd fire a few bursts, retreat a few steps, go into position, fire a few more bursts . . .

Hard Eyes felt a wave of weakness kick the pins from under him; he stumbled and fell to his knees. Lila drooping to the ground between him and Danco. "I can't carry anyone," he muttered, disgusted with himself.

In broken bits filtered through the gunfire, Hard Eyes heard Willow shouting at Carmen to get back to the beach. Danco yelled, "Willow! Are you hit?"

Willow scuttled up to them, Carmen beside him, ignoring him when he told her to go back. "It's Lila, she's alive," Hard Eyes said. Surprised at how hard it was to talk. Such a small wound, a shot to the hand, funny how it could make you feel.

Carmen and Danco took Lila, and feeling weightless now, Hard Eyes trotted on ahead, back toward the beach. Behind, the gunfire continued but more sporadically now.

Once he paused and held his injured hand up to silhouette it against the sky. Two of the fingers were gone. The little finger and the fourth finger. Stumps a quarter of an inch above the palm. His stomach lurched. He went on.

Somehow his pistol was in his right hand. Someone was running at him, and he raised the pistol, then lowered it, recognizing the bearish silhouette. They crouched down to talk. "Steinfeld . . . where's Karakos?"

"I don't know. Maybe hit. He was at the point with you."

"No. Just before the ambush, he went to the rear."

Hard Eyes knew by Steinfeld's silence that he understood. Hard Eyes said, "How bad is it, do you know?"

"Not so bad. You stopped us right before we walked into the worst of it. The bastards are on the beach, too, of course, but I've shifted to the alternate beachhead. Radioed the boats to pick us up there—head for the alternate and try to make sure everyone else does too. And listen: No wounded stay behind. If they look like they're not going to make it, then it's a matter for triage. Because of extractors."

Which meant: Kill anyone who wasn't likely to make it alive.

Thank God Claire was out to sea, on the ship's comm station.

Hard Eyes said, "Yeah." And moved out, dizzy, but feeling more together now.

After a while he was trudging down a beach road with three other NR; the sea hissing to one side, a rocky field to their left; the SA ambush was well behind them. The road was blue-black against gray, stony sand. Someone was lying by the side of the road up ahead. Facedown. Hard Eyes knelt beside him, found a penlight in his belt. It was Ali Mubarak, one of the Egyptian immigrants to France they'd rescued from the camps. A quiet little man, always eager to please everyone; someone who would've liked to've had more friends than he had. Hard Eyes had always meant to get to know him better.

Now he had to shoot him.

Ali was murmuring, and sometimes he'd try to weep a little, but that hurt, so he'd stop weeping and gasp. Hard Eyes turned him enough too see that he was gut-shot; the movement made Ali cry out in Arabic. Hard Eyes could see that the guy's belly was ripped open, sternum to groin; it was a boiling mass of blood and ragged entrails. Hard Eyes pictured Ali stumbling to this spot, holding his gut closed with his hands, trying to make it to the alternate rendezvous. Collapsing here. He wouldn't survive the trip back. But if the enemy found him, they might put him in an oxygenator, keep his brain marginally alive. A dead man's brain could be subjected to an extractor if you kept it oxygenated. The SA had been waiting for them here; they might have an extractor waiting too. Hard Eyes had the .45 pistol in his hand. He pressed the pistol to the back of Ali's head.

"Don't," Ali said in English.

Hard Eyes looked up at the stars. He tried to pretend that someone else was pulling the trigger.

_____Thirteen

FirStep, the Space Colony, Brig.

Russ Parker sat in a clean white room on the bed bench that folded down from the wall, staring at the clear, unbreakable plastic panel that blocked the doorway.

He sat there, rocking slightly, wondering if Rimpler would kill them quickly—the walls would sunder, the Colony would be sucked into the void and death—or if he might simply shut down the systems bit by bit, destroy the water supply, turn off the heat. Let the cold of interplanetary space soak in and make thousands of crystalline corpses floating in the dead shell of the Colony.

Remembering the insanity-twisted face on the monitors, Russ was certain that Rimpler would eventually kill them all. He was only waiting for the provocation.

The provocation that Praeger was going to give him.

And Russ had to sit there and let it happen. The detention cell was a mockery; the walls were solidified laughter. He boiled inside with the need to *do something,* and what he could do here was pace, piss, and pout. That was just exactly all of it.

He blinked. Something interrupted the line of his unseeing stare. There was someone standing in the doorway. An SA bull in a mirror helmet.

The doorway hissed into the wall, and the bull gestured.

Russ thought, *Maybe I'm going to an air lock. To join the crew of RM17.*

He stood up and walked like an automaton to the door. The guard stepped aside and gestured again; Russ put his hands behind his back; the guard put the plastiflex cuffs on him. Then Russ preceded him down the hall. They passed other cells, these with at least four people apiece in them. Kitty's husband Chester watched them go, shaking his head slowly. In the next cell down was a woman alone, an Oriental.

They passed through two electronic checkpoints, a door opening for them at each one, before they got to the admitting office. The young, helmetless SA sitting at the desk said, "Let me see that transfer pass again." He had a reedy voice that didn't go with his affectation of great authority.

The bull took a pass from a Velcroed pocket and handed it over.

Russ looked at the guard who'd escorted him from his cell. He was smaller than most of them. And his uniform didn't fit very well.

The desk guard asked, "You don't want another escort?"

"No." The bull's voice came filtered through the helmet PA.

"Okay." The kid shrugged. "Take him to Praeger directly."

But they didn't go to Rimpler's office. They went to Russ's. The guard unlocked the door with a card-key and said, "Inside."

Russ went in, expecting to find Praeger there. But the office was empty. Except for an empty SA armored uniform draped over his chair—and a helmet sitting on the chair's seat. Russ turned in confusion to the guard—and froze.

The guard had come in and closed the door behind him; had taken off his helmet. It was Faid. Grinning. "I'm sorry. You wanted the passes to get that other man out, right, mate, but I couldn't leave you there. And anyway, this is what we decided to do."

"Who's 'we'?"

"You sent a message to Kitty Torrence, what? She is contacting the NR. All the NR but one have been arrested, two hours ago. They are take our leader, Chu, bloody damn, because there is a message from some ruddy bastard on Earth. Everyone arrested NR but me."

"You!"

"You would not have giving me the cards if you knew I was in the Resistance, what?"

"I'm glad you didn't tell me. So you went to the SA dorms, got a couple of spare suits . . . this one for me?"

"Yes, mate. There are two hundred technicki rebels waiting for you to tell them to move. This is through Kitty Torrence. She is talking to everyone about the RM17, don't you know. Everyone, they are angry. And yes, the suit is for you. A good idea or not one?"

"A good one."

Praeger, Judith Van Kips, and Dr. Tate were staring into a console screen. Tate was seated, the other two stood behind him; they were looking at diagrams. Probably of the LSS Computer housing. Praeger looked up in irritation as the two guards came into his office.

"Well, what do you want?" Praeger demanded. "Why didn't you announce yourself on the—" He broke off as the taller of the two guards pointed a gun at him. A .357 autopistol. "If you call anyone in here," the taller guard said, "I'll shoot you. I guarantee it." He removed his helmet with his free hand. "Have you begun on Rimpler already, Praeger?" Russ asked. He tossed the helmet onto the table.

Praeger said, "This is very stupid, Russ."

"Answer the question."

"No. We have not."

"Mighty pleased to hear it. Faid, take Praeger into that room there. Don't let him say a word. If I give you the signal, or if it sounds like there's trouble in here, you shoot him in the head. You understand?"

Faid nodded. He drew his gun and gestured with it.

Praeger's face was flushed; his lips trembled with fury. But he walked stiffly into the next room. Faid followed and closed the door behind them. Russ smiled easily at Judith Van Kips. She looked at him like an angry mannequin. Russ said, "You're the new Security Chief, Van Kips. That's what I hear."

"What of it?"

"You're giving the orders now, and the men know it. This is what you're going to do: Tell *all* SA units they're to meet at the ordnance center. Tell them it's for disbursal of new equipment. They'll be getting new armored uniforms and new weapons which just came in on the shuttle. They're to line up and wait. They'll be called in one by one. Once inside, they'll undress, hand over the old gear and . . ." He smiled crookedly. "And then we'll give them something new."

"You'll kill them?"

"Don't be absurd. This is going to be a bloodless coup. Or it will be if you let it be. We'll cuff them, gag them, take them out into the maintenance corridor and into storage. One of our people will put on the armor. And one by one we'll have them all. They'll be put in Detention."

"You'll never take Ordnance. It's well guarded."

"We already have. They trustingly let Faid and me in, and we threatened them with high explosives. They gave us their guns and we've let our friends in. Two hundred of them."

"But I won't play along, you know that. I'd rather you killed me."

"Would you rather I killed Praeger?"

She became a thing of wax, still and pale. Then she laughed, almost explosively. "I know you. You have an overblown ego that supports an overblown sense of ethics.

You'd never shoot a man down like that. Just execute him."

Russ went to the door into Praeger's chambers. "Faid! You're going to hear a gunshot! Don't do anything to Praeger even when you hear the shot, unless I tell you to!"

"I understand," Faid called.

Russ turned to Tate. "This thing with Rimpler is as much your fault as anyone's." He pointed the gun at Tate's chest. Van Kips backed away from Tate.

Much of the missing age returned to Tate's unnaturally young features. He stood up and took a step backward. "I don't think you'll do that," he said after a moment. "You're not a natural killer. And after all the hours I spent trying to help you."

"And reporting on me to Praeger. Yeah, I know about that. But you're right. I'm not a natural killer. I don't know how to do this without getting sick."

Russ squeezed the trigger; the gun leapt in his hand. Tate's chest burst open, sprayed red onto the console. Tate spun and fell. Blood dripped down the computer's monitor screen.

Sure enough, Russ was sick to his stomach. He took deep breaths and turned to Van Kips. Managed, just barely, to keep from vomiting.

"Judith!" Praeger called. Then, to Faid, "That redneck has shot her!"

"She's all right, Praeger. I shot Tate."

Van Kips moved to the seat and sat down. "You'll be convicted of murder."

"Maybe. We'll see. Anyway, you can tell I'm committed now, I guess. Wipe the blood off the screen and call your people. Tell them what I told you to. And no one else will have to get hurt."

She looked at the door to Praeger's chambers. "I believe you'd do it."

Russ nodded.

She took some tissues from a drawer and thoughtfully cleaned the blood off the screen.

And then she did as she was told.

The Island of Merino, the Caribbean.

On a hot afternoon, and on the island of Merino, in a small, air-conditioned bungalow with cool blue walls and wicker furniture, James Kessler, Julie Kessler, Stoner, and his wife, Janet, were sitting on a wide sofa and in wicker chairs, watching satellite television. Cindy and Alouette were on a field trip with the NR's day-care unit, collecting seashells.

Attached to the television was a Media Analysis microprocessor, booting up Kessler's Media Alarm System. On the smaller monitor next to the big wall-screen, arrows, exclamation points, and capsule analyses flashed as the system interpreted Worldtalk's propaganda.

"How many of these did you send out?" Stoner asked.

Kessler said, "Witcher sent out more than three million media-alarm software disks. Spent three or four fortunes doing it. But it's having its impact. Congress has been inundated with letters." Kessler said it with a quiet satisfaction. Julie reached over and squeezed his hand. Her other hand lay on her pregnancy-swollen belly.

On the big screen, the Worldtalk-produced drama *Ghetto Cop* paced itself through a series of archetypal confrontations. The blond, blue-eyed hero was confronted with a dull-witted higher-up who tried to mitigate the cop's macho dynamism—in short, a liberal—and the hero plowed right through his boss's misgivings and went out to kick some ass; the hero was confronted with drug addicts and whores who were reluctant to give up information on the doings of a Zionist terrorist ring hiding in the ghetto, and the hero beat the truth out of his informants, plowed right through them to the next obstacle where the hero was confronted with the miscreants, who were reluctant to give up their sniping positions, and the hero kicked down their doors and . . .

The media-alarm system went *ping*, and the propaganda analysis appeared on the little monitor screen:

THE FOLLOWING IDEAS ARE PROPAGATED BY THE STORY IN THIS EPISODE OF *GHETTO COP*.

Liberals are dupes.

Terrorists, no matter what their color, typically hide in ghettos, implying collusion with ghetto residents.

Ghetto residents are mostly whores and junkies.

Ghetto residents know where terrorists are hiding and what they are up to, implying that the non-terrorist residents are somehow part of the conspiracy.

Terrorists plan to blow up grade school, therefore terrorists hate white children and wish them harm.

Terrorist sees news report of new Soviet invasion, remarks, "Time we did our part," implying that all terrorists are in league with the Soviet Union.

Terrorists are Jews (or Arabs or blacks).

Violence with no holds barred efficiently eliminates terrorism.

THE FOLLOWING BACKGROUND DETAILS FOUND IN THIS EPISODE OF *GHETTO COP* COMPRISE SUBLIMINAL SUGGESTIONS APPEARING WITH A FREQUENCY THAT ADDS UP TO NINETY-SIX PERCENT PROBABILITY OF DELIBERATE INSERTION BY THE PRODUCERS.

During scene in which terrorists make plans to blow up white middle-class grade school, there are seven objects arranged in the background of their hideout to form subliminal shape of the Star of David.

During the scene in which the hero confronts the liberal demagogue the titles of books on his office shelf all have one word which is larger than the others; the large words taken from each title and reading left to right are: "DEATH" "FOR" "YOUR FAMILY" "BLACK" "SUPREMACY" AND "JEW" "SUPREMACY." "LEADS" "TO" "YOUR POVERTY." The titles are too small to be picked up by the conscious mind.

In the scene in which the hero breaks into a whorehouse, a TV screen in the back of the whorehouse's living room, behind the main action,

shows the following images, almost too small to see:
A BLACK MAN RAPING A WHITE WOMAN. AN ARAB
KIDNAPPING WHITE CHILDREN. A HASSIDIC JEW—

"You get the idea," Witcher said as he came into the
room. He turned off the air-conditioning and stood in the
back of the room, rocking nervously on the balls of his
feet. "What you say we switch channels. Smoke should be
coming out of the hearings about now. Yeah, there it is."
Kessler'd switched to a news channel. Smoke was standing on the steps of the Senate building at a portapodium
with several congressmen. Stoner recognized Senator Har-
old Chung and Senator Judy Sanchez, who were there
with Smoke for a quick news conference after the Senate
hearings. Smoke had given testimony on the SA.

Senator Sanchez was reading from her notes. "We feel
there is strong evidence that the Second Alliance has been
involved in an active conspiracy essentially to do away with
the Bill of Rights; to eliminate SAISC enemies through the
courts and the AVL laws by means of an illegal video evidence tampering which fabricates false evidence for use in
court; there is, further, substantial evidence that Worldtalk
Public Relations Inc., which is owned by the Second Alliance International Security Corporation, deliberately and
willfully inserted illegal subliminal ideation into television
programs of their production; that the SAISC repeatedly violated conflict-of-interest laws by using their influence to
place their operatives and cronies within the ranks of the
CIA, CIA Domestic, the FBI, and the police departments of
every major city in the United States. We further feel there is
indeed strong evidence that the Second Alliance conspired
with Anna Bester, the President of the United States, to de-
vise a plan eliminating congressional decision-making power
and freedom of the press, under the cloak of declaring a
State of Emergency..."

Cameras flashing, as if the flashes were the light given off
by the awe and amazement of the reporters; gasps from Mr.
and Mrs. Kessler and Stoner, who were astonished the investigation had gone that far.

"It's Smoke," Witcher said. "People took him seriously
because he won the United Nations Literary Committee

prize, used to be a major figure in the academic world. He's been pushing things in the Undergrid, sending films and interviews and programs to the underground stations till he could get it on the networks. I guess it just built up in a sort of ground swell . . ."

Smoke stepped to the microphones to make a statement. "There can be no mistake. If we don't act quickly, we're going to lose the United States of America—and not to the Soviets. The Soviets are a danger, but there's a more immediate internal danger—"

A confusion of sudden movement on the steps behind the people at the podium, a bang, a rush of men in uniforms . . .

Smoke was not at the podium.

The image wobbled as the camera trucked around as the commentator yammered confusedly. A crowd of people bending over someone on the steps. The crowd parted just enough to give Stoner a glimpse, as someone ran to call an ambulance—

Smoke was lying there, his chest bloody.

"Oh, Jesus," Julie said. "God, I'm glad Alouette isn't here."

"Oh, no," Kessler said.

Witcher said, "Stupid." He snorted with contempt. There was no grief in his voice, but it creaked with anger. "Stupid bastards. They shot him, and that makes it worse for them."

Stoner said, "You see the guy who shot him? I couldn't see him. Oh, fuck. I need a drink. You see him? Was he black? I figure they'd set up a black guy or an Arab, maybe, to do it."

Kessler said, "The public won't fall for that. The SA's stupid to do it now, in public."

Hands shaking, Stoner went to the bar to pour himself a drink. "Chances are the order went out to kill him before the investigation went public. They failed to contact their man to pull him back in time. Stupid is the word, all—"

"Shush!" Julie said. "They're going to say something."

A flushed, wide-eyed woman reporter came onto the screen. "Uh, I can definitely confirm that Jack Brendan Smoke has been shot while speaking at a news conference

—we are told that he is alive but 'probably critically wounded,' but we have no definite word on that yet—"

The Island of Malta.

Hard Eyes shook his head in disbelief. "Satellite reconnaissance. You must be kidding."

Steinfeld said, "I don't see what's so unlikely about it. They could have spotted us coming, set up the ambush—"

"Steinfeld, they knew precisely what route we were taking—"

"They could have been collating their information with ongoing reports from their surveillance—"

"Oh, what *shit*! You're suffering a massive case of denial, man!" Hard Eyes was surprised he'd shouted at Steinfeld. It didn't seem possible. They didn't speak for a moment.

They were in the little back bedroom that Steinfeld slept in. The room was monkish, dusty, almost bare. The morning light was diffused to a blush by the window shade. Steinfeld sat on his cot. His face sagged; his eyes were ringed with sleeplessness. Hard Eyes was pacing around the room. He paused to look sullenly at his maimed hand. With only three fingers, it looked like the paw of an animal.

Staring at the stumps of his fingers, Hard Eyes said, "They knew we were coming. We lost a fourth of our people and we achieved nothing." He turned to Steinfeld. "For the sake of the people that we lost—the people who are dying now . . . for Lila . . . Lila's dying. Steinfeld, we've . . . we've got to . . . to *assume* that—" A strangling fury rose up in him and clenched his throat so that he couldn't say anything else for a moment.

Steinfeld said, "But to start a witch-hunt now when morale is so low . . ."

A soft knock on the door.

Levassier came in, carrying something in his remaining hand. He handed it to Steinfeld, all the time looking at Hard Eyes's own disfigured hand. Then he smiled at Hard Eyes and shrugged as if to say, "Not so bad, really."

Steinfeld read the printout twice, and then looked at Hard

Eyes. "I don't want you to take this as a confirmation of what you've been saying—it isn't necessarily Karakos. But apparently we've had a defector from the CIA. A man named Stoner. He says we definitely have an SA mole. Right here on Malta . . ."

Hard Eyes slumped against a wall in relief. "We'll move out of here?"

"Yes." Steinfeld turned to Levassier and made it an order. "Now. Contact the Mossad, ask them about Haifa. Just get us off the island . . ."

"I have to bring more news," Levassier said, looking at the shaded window. "Our Lila is dead. She died . . ." He shrugged. ". . . a few minutes ago, in the Valetta hospital."

Hard Eyes felt the rage turn in him; it turned inward. He was angry at himself for feeling just the faintest streak of relief that Lila was dead.

Steinfeld put his head in his hands. "She was, perhaps, our best."

Hard Eyes nodded. Then he said, "What about the mole —what about Karakos? You do understand that it must be Karakos . . ."

Steinfeld looked up, hesitated. Then, slowly, he said, "I don't know. I don't know who to believe. Anybody could be a traitor, Hard Eyes. With the extractor. Even you."

FirStep, the Space Colony.

The Colony was blacked out. Dark. It looked like a dead thing hanging in space. Even the Soviet blockade ship, orbiting a spare twenty miles away where it could keep an eye on all approaches to the Colony, called in to Colony Comm Center to ask if the Colony was in danger.

But the Colonists were there, alive, sitting in the darkness and semidarkness. The only illumination came dull red from the emergency panels glowing over the doors.

Russ had switched off the Colony's power. Nearly all: only the emergency battery power remained, the bare minimum to sustain Life Support. And only for two hours.

* * *

Russ moved down the ladder in the eerie silence of the maintenance access shaft, his rubber-soled boots making almost no sound on the rungs. He wore a hard hat with a light on it, and where he looked, a blob of colorless light pooled on the wires, tubes, and microprocessor boxes lining the curved walls.

Russ saw LSSCH LEVEL stenciled on an oval hatch. He stepped onto a metal grid under the door and swayed, almost losing his balance on the narrow ledge. The black throat of the shaft yawned behind him. He clutched at the door, his fingers found the wheel, and he hung on; felt the shaft suck at his back, felt sweat maliciously tickle his neck. He took a deep breath and got his footing. Then he turned the wheel and opened the door, climbed through. He was in front of the air lock that led to the LSS Computer housing. The door was open. It was dark in there, except for the faint, malevolent shine of a small, round red light like a demonic eye.

He couldn't go in.

If he went in, the door would slam and the air would suck away, and this time no one would come.

Rimpler can't slam the door, can't draw out the air, Russ told himself. *He hasn't got the power to do it anymore. You're safe. Go on in.*

Russ took a step toward the door. And stopped when his lungs seized up, an ice giant's fingers closed around his chest, tightening. He wheezed and shook with a surge of fear that was like an electric current. He struggled to keep his bowels from convulsively opening in his terror. Ashamed to be found dead that way.

Psychosomatic. There's air here. He forced himself to take a step, and another, and he was inside, committed. The icy hand went away, and the electric feeling, replaced with a dull ache of fear. *He can't do anything now! He's shut down!*

Russ saw the open panel on the door across the chamber and, in his mind's eye, saw the tanned, confident West German crouching there, reaching into the door and shaking with electrocution.

Russ blinked, and the dying man was gone. Only his toolbox and the LSS Computer replacement unit remained, on the floor where they'd left them.

Russ said, "Come on, now." He took the printout diagram from his pocket and bent, diagram in hand, beside the door. He looked at the diagram and matched it up with what he saw in the panel. He reached in. *Don't touch it. Electrocution.* But he found the lever for the emergency manual override, something that wouldn't have worked while Rimpler was still powered, and pulled it down. The door clicked and moved out a quarter of an inch from the jamb. *If I put my fingers in it, he'll slam the door shut, smash them.*

Using up his reserves of willpower, he pushed his fingers into the margin and pulled the door back. It slid easily into the wall.

The little room beyond was all convoluted arrangements of component shelves, consoles, dials, numbers. He was dazzled by its cryptic intricacy.

Should have brought a tech with me, he thought. *I'm lost.*

But he'd elected to come alone because of what had happened the last time he was here. The man who had died... this way he risked only himself. Stupid. An act of guilt. He had felt that, being Admin Security, he had some culpability in the death of all those aboard RM17. Guilt blinds you.

After twenty minutes of looking and staring at the second page on the diagram, he found the unpretentious metal box containing the LSS Computer guidance unit, and what was left of Rimpler's brain. He unscrewed the panels, opened it. Inside was a black metal box that was sloppily soldered where it interfaced with other units. It looked jury-rigged.

That was it. A man's brain was in there, in that box. And all that remained of the man. An ambition, a dream, and an irrational rage. All in something little bigger than a cigar box.

He clipped the wires, removed the box, his hands shaking. "I'm sorry, man," he said. *Had* to say it. "Rest in peace."

Russ put in the purely electronic unit, following directions on the diagrams.

Then, carrying the cybercerebral interface box, he found his way out and back up to the power station. An hour later the Colony lit up like a Christmas tree.

Russ took the box containing Rimpler's brain to a jettison air lock. He thought he could feel impotent fury tingling in his hands as he carried the thing into the air lock, but of course he was imagining that. . . .

He left it there, in the air lock, and went back to the control chamber. He told the jettison tech, "Seal it." The air lock sealed off. Then Russ closed his eyes. And feeling the tech gawking at him, the guy trying not to laugh, Russ said a prayer, ending in, "Ashes to ashes, dust to stardust. Be part of it forever." And then he nodded at the tech, who pressed a button, opening the air lock so that the atmosphere in it, and the little metal box, were sucked out into space and gone.

The Island of Malta.

Karakos could feel Hard Eyes glaring at him as he came into the room. He saw Hard Eyes from the corner of his eye, standing by the window. Steinfeld was lying on his cot, staring at the ceiling. Levassier was sitting on the edge of the cot beside him. Staring at the floor. They looked comical that way, one looking up, the other looking down.

Karakos felt the tension in the room like a bubble, pressing him back, so he stayed in the doorway. "They told me you wanted me, Steinfeld."

"Lila died."

"Oh, Lord. God no."

"Yes."

"The ambush was a terrible thing. I was almost shot myself, many times," Karakos said. "I was lucky."

"Yes."

"Well . . . I am sorry to hear—"

Steinfeld interrupted. "I am telling you this because I

want you to take Claire's radio duty. She was very close to Lila. I don't want someone distracted by . . . well, I prefer she rest now. So report to the—"

Hard Eyes had crossed the room, was standing by the cot, staring at Steinfeld, pointedly not looking at Karakos. "This is . . ." He shook his head as if he couldn't believe it. "It's stupid. You're going to let *him* on radio call? He knows we're pulling out."

Karakos looked at Hard Eyes. "What?"

Steinfeld snorted. "He *didn't* know. But I was going to inform him, true. Yes, Karakos, we're moving out. In just under two days. The entire HQ staff. We'll establish a new base in Italy. We'll be leaving here in forty-eight hours."

Karakos struggled to maintain his mask. He wanted to shout, "*Damn you, no! That'll be a day too soon.*" But he said, "Italy? Where?"

"Steinfeld . . ." Hard Eyes said warningly. "There's no reason to tell him, especially when he's going on radio—"

"Shut up!" Steinfeld snapped, glaring at Hard Eyes. Steinfeld had the look of a man who's angry from weariness. "This man has worked with me for years. I know more about him than I know about you. I want no more of this idiotic divisiveness in our ranks."

Hard Eyes turned angrily toward Karakos, who stepped aside, and Hard Eyes shoved roughly past him, stalked away down the hall.

Steinfeld said, "We're moving to somewhere near the town of Bari on the coast of the Adriatic."

"Bari!" Karakos was surprised. Bari and the entire coast around it was supposed to be an SA stronghold. The man they called The Cutthroat was in power there, an SA major who was said to disdain gas and the other mass-killing methods as being economically wasteful. "You bring them to the sea, you cut their throats, you push them off the cliffs, one-two-three, no messy mass burials, no expensive gas chambers, simple, effective, and fast." Tellini The Cutthroat tolerated no rebellion within striking distance of Bari.

Karakos smiled wanly and said, "You look surprised. You've heard the stories about Tellini. I'll surprise you some more: Tellini is *our* man. The SA are not the only ones with extractors; we have one, just one, in Rome.

Tellini was extracted by Witcher's best man, put under extractor post-directive. Now and then he does things we want him to and doesn't remember doing it. He will protect our base without knowing he's doing it. The SA could put him under an extractor and find nothing. But the post-directive is in there." He stood and put a meaty hand on Karakos's shoulder. "I'm telling you this because...I want you to know I trust you. Because you have been with me so long. You are like part of me. I..." He turned away. Karakos was surprised by the warmth of the gesture and the tears in Steinfeld's eyes.

Karakos clapped Steinfeld on the back. "Thank you, my friend. You will not regret it." And then he went to do his radio duty.

FOURTEEN

FirStep, the Space Colony.

Russ sat on the desk in the admissions area of Detentions and felt a foolish shiver of vicarious happiness as he watched Chester coming through the door, running to embrace Kitty Torrence.

Praeger was right, Russ thought. I'm too soft for this job.

Other prisoners were emerging. A group of women now: Judy Assavickian, Angie Siggert, an Oriental woman—Chu, or something—and the black twins, Belle and Kris Mitchell, hugging one another, crying with relief. Belle and Kris looking as if they'd been routinely beaten about the face.

A group of men came out, and then Faid, walking up to Russ in a tentative way, almost on tiptoe, and Russ knew he was carrying bad news.

"Chief—" Faid's voice broke. "There are being only half as many prisoners as there should be . . ."

Russ went cold inside. "Did you talk to the guards who were here?"

"Not yet, but the prisoners say the bloody bastards took people away every day for the last week and they never came back and, chief, I don't thinking they are letting them go."

"No. No, I don't think they did either."

"I wonder," Praeger said, "if you have even the slightest inkling as to what's going to happen to you, Russ, eh?"

Russ leaned against the wall of Praeger's cell with his hands in his pockets. Praeger looked small and pink sitting in the corner of his white-walled cell. A guard in full uniform—except, they didn't wear the helmets now—stood at the door. He was one of Russ's people. Russ said, "I can't believe you did it."

Praeger acted as if he hadn't heard. "UNIC won't stand for it. NASA won't stand for it. The European Space Agency won't stand for it. The American government."

"We've been getting transmissions again. The American government has big problems of its own right now. The President of the United States is going to be impeached."

Praeger laughed softly. "A silly rumor. Nothing will come of it."

"They seemed pretty certain about it, friend. How did you do it, exactly? Did you put them alive and kicking out into space, Praeger? Did you at least kill them with sedation first? Twenty-seven men and women taken from the cells and vanished."

Praeger shrugged and said offhandedly, "I told them to do it the way they thought best. I know the bodies were jettisoned."

"I feel like hitting you. Just holding you down and hitting you." The desire to do it was a buzz going through him. "But what I'm going to do is, I'm going to try you for the murder of the people on the RM17, and for the murder of the prisoners in your charge, and, if the jury agrees, I'll execute you. And Judith. A *technicki* jury. I think they'll go for it."

Praeger stared at the floor. He swallowed so you could see it, and said, "You're getting yourself in deeper and deeper."

"I was in deep a long time ago."

"Not Judith, Russ."

"Oh, yes. If anything she's worse than you are. But the SA bulls, all of them, will be considered on a case by case basis. The SA's going to be prosecuted in the U.S., it seems. If that happens, I'll ship them down."

"Chances are none of this will happen," Praeger said rather distantly. "The Soviets . . ."

"They're withdrawing. Most people think they aren't going to fall back on nukes. We have too many missile-carrying submarines. They lost too many in the war. And anyway they're scared of nuclear war as much as we are."

Praeger said nothing.

"We're overcrowded with prisoners, so I'm going to have some put in here."

Praeger shot him a look of pure venom.

Russ chuckled. "The idea of being in with the hoi-polloi repel you? Yeah, you'll have to crap in front of them too."

"This making you feel better, Russ? You think you can take this thing over and the people on Earth will shrug? Russ—it belongs to Earth. It belongs to those nations. They won't take this."

"Sure they will. We were about to go into the black, before the shit started coming down. We're a moneymaking proposition. If we're unanimous, if we're united here, we'll be making them an offer they can't refuse. They need us, more and more they need us economically. And we'll tell them what the Admin did. We'll tell them about RM17 and about the other murders. And I think they'll understand."

"'If we're united here.' You're a Communist."

"You say that like you mean I fuck my mother. No, I'm not a Communist. But I'm making Kitty Torrence and her husband the technicki reps. He for electrician ratings, comm ratings and mechanics, and she for the other labor levels. And *they're* Communists. Me, I ain't a Red but I guess I've gone a ways to the left. And that's *your* fault, Praeger, you did it to me, you pushed me to the left. I don't like it over in the left: it's cold over here."

When the NATO spacecraft came onto the screen, Russ was almost disappointed. It was gliding into position so sedately. It looked sluggish and about as impressive and threatening as a tugboat. It was a cylindrical thing with a lot of spokes at one end. The Soviet ship was moving, too, jets firing here and there as it jockeyed about.

Russ was in the Colony Comm center, surrounded by banks of screens showing the Colony inside and out and, like the one before him, views from the tethered satellites extending miles from FirStep's hull. All the small views of various other environments in and around the Colony added up, on the banks of screens, to one collective video environment, a chamber of video swatches, checkerboard pattern of shifting grays and electric-whites and misty greens and the Bible black of space; the room lit with a light made of other lights; and it was a place made of other places.

Faid and Chester sat beside Russ in bucket-seated swivel chairs. They were all a little drunk. The occasion seemed to call for it, so Russ had broken out his treasured fifth of Kentucky bourbon and they were sipping it from plastic cups.

"They really going to do it?" Chester asked, his voice slurring. "They going to fight it out?"

"Hell yeah," Russ said. "And with this fight we're either fucked or we got it made."

They watched as the ships approached within two miles of one another. They saw the ships on separate screens, monitored their positions with instruments, Faid muttering, "If that ships are blow up, bloody 'ell, some debris could come here and be smashing us, mate."

Russ nodded. "Or a stray missile . . ."

With comical but inadvertent simultaneity, they took another sip of bourbon. Thinking: *Good chance we'll be dead in five minutes*.

The conflict took less than five minutes. Less than *one*. The ships seemed to be just looking at one another. Chester raised their frequencies, and they heard a babble of Russian and fragments in a Missouri accent ("... we've got alignment but no... [crackle] reads five-seven-oh [crackle] ... good thing you can't smell anything through ... you're going to owe me that shortcake—") and then there was a flash, just a little flare on the NATO ship on screen 6, a matching flare on the Soviet ship on screen 7, and a pencil of light on screen 6 as the eight-megawatt Fluorine-based laser, near infrared and showing red tinged, lanced out and caught the Soviet missile. They couldn't see the missile, but they saw the wink of light as it exploded. And then a crackle and a confused shout on the Soviet frequency and a big smear of white filling screen 7. And, on the Soviet frequency, a nerve-wracking squeal. Four seconds of noise that expressed the murder of the Soviet ship's electronics; implying the murder of more. Then static-edged silence.

Chester said, "Jesus. All those men are dead now. Just like that. Poof. *Shit*."

"Blockade's over," Russ said. "Just like that, poof. Too."

Chester was looking at the instruments and the screens. "We're okay. No debris coming our way."

Russ drained his cup and sloshed some more in. In a drunken mock of a high moral tone, Faid said, "We should not drink more, mate, now that we know we are not going to die, what?"

"We don't need that excuse," Russ said. "Hell no. We got plenty more reasons to drink. We'll drink to the Soviets who died on that ship. Who called and asked if we were okay when our lights went out."

"I'll drink to that," Chester said.

It was almost midnight on Merino, and they were still watching the television. Stoner was bleary eyed and blurry brained, from TV and from drinking, but they were afraid to silence the big flat screen. Too much was happening. The Stoners and the Kesslers—Cindy asleep on the couch with her head on Janet's lap—were slumped here and there about the dark room, looking ghostly in the blue light of the TV screen. Wanting to go to bed. But things kept happening. The war news: the sense that it was either going to end, or detonate. The announcements of the arrests and indictments; the demolition of the American SAISC. The calls for the President's resignation. NATO's promised investigation into the European SA. The announcements of a new administration in the Colony and the arrest of Colony SA. The assassination attempt on Smoke. The announcement that he was not badly hurt, that he was off the critical list. (They'd sent a messenger to tell Alouette.) The editorials, the interviews, rehashing all of it. The Soviet defeat in orbit, the Soviet withdrawal from blockade positions under renewed air attacks from NATO.

There couldn't be anything more, Stoner thought. Time to try and sleep. *Try.*

On the screen a political analyst was droning about the likelihood of the opposition candidate's winning the next presidential election. Comparisons with Watergate, the Iran/Contra affair. "But of course this is something far worse: what we have here, at least in the minds of many, is treason on the part of the President herself—"

Stoner was just getting up and stretching, ready to go, when the political analyst was preempted, and an excited young announcer came on and told them that "the Soviet Union has expressed its desire to call a cease fire to the war in order to negotiate a peaceful end. Secretary of State Carnegie has said, and I quote, 'We feel that the end of the war is at hand. The Soviets are indicating they are ready to surrender.' I—" The newscaster cleared his throat. "Ladies and gentlemen . . ." His voice choked with emotion. For once the cookie-cutter newscaster was gone, the man behind the glossy image emerging, moved by the emotional electricity of the moment. "Ladies and gentlemen—ladies and gentlemen, *the Third World War is over.*"

Cloudy Peak Farm, Upstate New York.

"The crisis is very real," Watson said, "and it's going to mean drastic retrenching. But it's only a setback on one front."

Sackville-West shook his round head so that his jowls

waggled. "It's not a *setback* on this front. It's a *complete defeat*. The President will be forced to resign. Our American bank accounts are already frozen. CIA Domestic is under investigation by the Justice Department—and our people who were in the Justice Department are under arrest. American public opinion is ninety percent against us. Even the Fundamentalists. They're pretending they're horrified, had nothing to do with us. Worldtalk's assets frozen. Worldtalk Grid projects seized. Indictments and more indictments. The Colony fallen, Praeger taken. Most of it happened through the press, the underGrid, the networks."

"You sound bitter," Watson said coldly, "and that's ironic."

There were four men in Cloudy Peak Farm's comm center, in person, including Carlton Smith, the SA's Special Education Coordinator, tall and bushy browed, with short, receding brown-blond hair and always the pipe and the faint smile as if the biggest problems were just a matter of father and son talking it out. He was the father of Jebediah Smith.

Watson and Sackville-West were there, and Klaus, whom the others assumed was there simply because, as Watson's bodyguard, he went everywhere with him.

There were others on the video conference lines, four other SA chiefs in various parts of the country, and in various states of panic and disgust.

Watson, Smith, Klaus, and Sackville-West were seated around a small, round conference table Watson had brought in. Smith and Old Sacks had glanced at Klaus when he'd sat down just as if he were an equal, but they'd said nothing about it.

Watson went on. "I mean, Sacks, you really sound as if you're angry about all that's happened. As if you're angry with other people. But you, Sacks, *you* were in charge of security, you were the one who allowed yourself to be recorded in conversation with the President, recorded and photographed discussing a very sensitive matter. You were the one who let Stoner get away. So you won't be surprised when I tell you that you are being replaced."

Sackville-West's head jerked up. Jowls jumping again.

His eyes went piggish, his skin vermilion. "Replaced by who?"

"Klaus, here. I have looked at the matter from every angle. He has been extractor approved. He has an extensive background in Security." He added a lie: "He was in charge of my station Security in France."

Sackville-West turned to the screen. "Gentlemen—I—the buck is being passed here, I am a . . . a scapegoat for . . . for . . ." But after that, all that came out was inarticulate fragments and sputters. Perhaps because of the way the men on the screen were looking at him. Watson went to the door and called, "Ben."

Ben came in and stood behind Sackville-West's chair. He spoke gently to Sackville-West. Ben was mildly embarrassed. "Sir. Come with me, please."

"And—where might that be?" Sackville-West demanded.

"Debriefing," Watson said smoothly, sitting down. "And retirement. Ben . . . ?"

Ben nodded. He put one hand on his gun and the other on Sackville-West's shoulder.

The old man shuddered and sat there a moment, breathing through his mouth, sweat glossing his forehead. Then he stood up, upsetting his chair, and walked with a kind of roly-poly dreaminess out of the room, Ben close behind him.

Ben shut the door behind as they went out.

Watson sighed, rubbed his hands together, and said, "Now. The Soviets have removed their blockade from the Atlantic ports. They're talking cease fire and negotiation, and all this is generally being taken as a sign they are close to surrender. Thanks to the crisis here it behooves us to remove ourselves and our projects from the U.S., to take them overseas . . ." He smiled at Smith. "Yes, even the people of Colton City. And all the kids in your charge. We'll transplant the town to Britain. We're strong there now, and, after all, the roots of the Caucasian Prime are in Europe. In a way we'll all be going home. In a month, we'll be ready to announce the formation of the Self-Policing Organization of European States."

He paused dramatically, looking at Smith and Klaus, and looking into the camera that conveyed his image to the men on the screens. He wasn't as good at this sort of thing as Crandall had been, but until the new Crandall was video-fabricated, he'd have to deploy all the leadership faculties at his command. "Rick is in seclusion, as you know, but he has asked me to be his spokesman—I believe you all got his signed statement to that effect—and I have the joy to inform you that we have some very good news indeed to offset all the bad news that's plagued us lately. The good news is: Europe is essentially ours, though NATO is withdrawing its support. We will get no more help or credibility from them. But it doesn't matter a bit. We are being incorporated into the military infrastructure of our adopted European nations. The government of every European nation where we maintain a presence is a government we have established. And in a month they will announce SPOES, essentially a 'united states' of Europe, united for reasons of defense, and by philosophical alignment. Anticommunist, antiimmigrant, nationalist-central and of course a strong advocacy of racial purity. And yes, it's that simple."

Tamping his pipe, Smith nodded, like a TV father hearing Abraham Lincoln quoted. But he said, "If we could hear it from Rick, I mean, in person . . ." He lit the pipe; its aroma slithered through the room.

"You will, shortly. He'll be taping an announcement. He'll be announcing the retirement of Sackville-West, Klaus's stepping into the job, our move to Europe, and the formation of SPOES."

"'Formation of SPOES,'" Jaeger said. "You make it sound very easy." Jaeger spoke from his screen. He was a stocky, pug-nosed, thin-lipped man, an ex-football player who'd failed in three bids for the U.S. Senate. His munitions company had designed the Jaegernauts.

"Resistance on the legitimate political level is almost nil," Watson said. Not a lie but surely an exaggeration. "And as for the fringe groups, like the NR—well, they're being taken care of. Klaus?"

Klaus cleared his throat and threaded his fingers together. He wasn't used to having to deal with people this way. "Yes—it is all coming together very nicely." Klaus rumbled. "Our man in the NR, on Malta, has warned us that they are about to relocate, so we have moved up the date of our

surgical strike against them." He glanced at his watch.
"Twelve hours from now, the majority of our Sicilian air unit
will carpet bomb the area. Our troops will move in by helicopter to do the mopping up, I think you call it. We expect
the strike to destroy Steinfeld himself and the core of the NR
leadership."

Smith nodded. The smile was still there, but he was pale,
and the hand bringing the pipe to his mouth was leaving a
crooked trail of smoke. "I see. And as for the relocation—
you feel we will be, um, allowed to leave?"

"We've got a lot of friends still. They're lying low, of
course," Watson said, "but they'll help us. Friends in immigration, customs especially. We'll get everyone, ah, significant out. And most of Colton City. You can be sure we're
going to take good care of Jebediah." He smiled at Smith.
"You should be very proud of that young man. He's our
future. I can tell you that Rick is thinking of Jebediah in
terms of his successor. One day, ten years from now, after he
has been properly prepared . . ."

Smith's smile became genuine. He fairly glowed.

Watson congratulated himself on winning Smith over. The
others seemed ready to go along. They were desperate, after
all . . .

Things were going badly, in one sense. But in another
way, everything was falling into place.

Watson and Klaus were alone. The screens were blanked.
Smith had gone to call his family in the privacy of the guest
room.

Watson leaned back in his chair in the silence, and
wondered how long he could keep the rest of them from
knowing that Crandall was dead. And wondering who he
should tell.

Klaus lit a cigarette and said, "This SPOES State . . .
Praeger is right. It's not going to be so easy. There is probably going to be a reaction, a resentment against the new
governments by the regional nationalists. They will know
that the figureheads are being manipulated by foreigners.
And there are still opposition parties, still political resistance, especially in Germany and Italy . . ."

"Italy is always fighting itself. Its internal chaos will

make it easy for us. Within our organization, there is no chaos. But I suppose you should know there's another method . . . a bigger picture . . ."

Klaus looked at him expectantly. Watson wondered how much he should tell him. Well, Klaus was really and truly *in* now. Still, he mustn't tell him everything.

Watson went on, "I've been in conference with the Worldtalk people. We are going to create our own national leaders, much the way we're re-creating Rick Crandall. We'll use video animation and computer-designed psychiatric models to create for each country a kind of . . . well, a false idol, the ideal demagogue for that country. He'll look and sound like that country's ideal leader, incorporating in his speech and mannerisms all the cultural characteristics of the quintessential Frenchman, Brit, Dutchman, German, Greek, Belgian, Italian. Of course, people have been doing this for years but not so literally. In America the political P.R. specialists do something equivalent, packaging their candidates, so their candidates seem to have all the right qualities for the great average American's taste. In public our man will only be seen in the distance. For security reasons all interviews will be done via screen. We'll have to invent a private life for him. In one case we'll be co-opting the public life of a certain national favorite—we'll alter the man's image to suit our needs. And the man himself will be entirely under our control. Extractors are marvelous things . . . we're just beginning to explore their potential."

Klaus shook his head in amazed disbelief. "It'll never work."

"Klaus, you underestimate the power of the Grid. The media is powerful—it's what wrecked our work here in America, and in a remarkably short time. People will believe in our creations. They *believe* the men they see on TV—and most of them never see them in person, really know very little about them."

Klaus sat in silence for a moment. Then he said, "Yes. Perhaps you're right. Still, we're going to be observed: we want to eliminate the mongrel gene pools, the lesser races. But Europe is sensitive to Genocide after Hitler."

"Much of it will be done . . ." He hesitated. This was too

sensitive to tell Klaus about yet. The virus was a very serious matter indeed. When you are contemplating the extermination of millions, you must be more careful than anyone has ever been before. "We will talk about that later. When the time comes . . ."

The Island of Malta.

At three A.M., Karakos stepped out the back door of the villa, closing it carefully behind him. The sentry was on the other side of the house for the moment. Carrying his satchel, he turned, stepped into the darkness, took only one step toward freedom and safety. And then the darkness grew the shapes of men.

They moved in all around him, and he froze as one of them shined a light on him. It was Steinfeld. "When are they coming, Jean?" Steinfeld's voice came out of the darkness above the glare of the light. The hurt in that voice was unmistakable.

"Who? What is— I was going to Valetta, to . . . well I have private matters . . ."

"And you needed the bag you're carrying? We'll have to have a look in that bag. Please, Jean. Tell us when they're going to come." The light angled up to shine in his eyes. He looked away—but the other men switched flashlights on, to shine in his face, so many he could feel the heat of the beams.

"This is insane—"

"The SA has arrested Tellini." Hard Eyes's voice. "We told you he was NR to see if he would be arrested. He was. They didn't try to salvage him with extractors. I guess they bought the bullshit about our extractor techniques being too subtle to detect. They took him away and shot him, in front of his men. He was loyal SA. That means you told them our story about him."

"I see," Karakos said. "Disinformation." His own voice sounded very far away to him. "And you acted your part very believably, Hard Eyes." There was a strange kind of relief in him, and it came as a surprise. He closed his eyes against the light, but opened them when Steinfeld said:

"I must insist you keep your eyes open, Jean. So you used the radio to tell them about Tellini," Steinfeld said, "and our people in Bari saw them take Tellini the Cutthroat away. And that is some good to come from this, anyway. And you've told them we're going to Italy—so they'll be here sooner. How soon?"

"It doesn't matter if you know—you'll leave in time, I'm sure, anyway. They are coming in two hours from now. Just before dawn. Now please. My eyes hurt."

Steinfeld lowered his light, so the others lowered theirs too.

"Put the bag down, Jean."

Karakos thought of running. Useless. He dropped the bag. "I won't make any more transmissions for you. They have made me so I will not knowingly do anything against them."

"Yes. The extractor." Steinfeld was silent for a few moments. They could hear the sawing of cicadas, the muted rumble of the sea. "I had hoped to take you back to the States, perhaps restore you to yourself with our own extractors. But we could never be sure of you—we couldn't know for sure we'd taken out everything they put in. So . . ."

"I understand." Karakos felt airy, distant from things. No fear at all. Steinfeld came toward him and took his arm, and they walked off into the night together.

"Where will you go?" Karakos asked.

Steinfeld told him, because in a few moments it wouldn't matter what Karakos knew. "Now, we go on the assault. Sicily. While most of their forces are here, attacking the empty base. Afterwards, Haifa. Israel. The Mossad have set a base for us up there." Steinfeld sounded as if he might cry. But his grip on Karakos's arm was like a beartrap. "You know, I hate these extractors, Jean. Look what they force us to do. And what do they leave us—what are we to believe in? We can't even believe in our enemies. There is no trust at all now. And can I even trust myself? Who knows, maybe someone put me under an extractor once and told me I believe what I believe. If beliefs are so malleable, then we are nothing but computers in flesh, and that is a very ugly thought, Jean."

"I think . . . I think there *is* something more. Even when I do the SA's work—and I admit I could never have done anything else, once they changed me—but even then, there was a . . . a kind of shadow of something. Maybe cast by my soul. A taste of regret, of longing for . . . I don't know."

"It is a great relief to hear you say that, my friend." Steinfeld stopped walking. They stood together in the middle of a field, and Karakos looked up at the stars. He heard Steinfeld cocking his pistol. Steinfeld said, "Thank you for restoring my faith in the soul, Jean. Thank you, and I'm sorry . . ."

Then came the father of all thunders, and the starry night up above them poured icy cold down into the hole Steinfeld's gun made in his friend's head, and filled his mind with forever.

Hard Eyes found Claire sitting in the kitchen, sipping from a little porcelain bowl of tea she held in both hands. She was wearing her fatigues and boots, her rifle leaning up on the table beside her, ready to go. They were short-handed; no one would be staying behind this time. She didn't look at him when he came in. He stood awkwardly in the doorway. He looked at the night-blanked windows, and then at the bulb over the wooden table, and then back at Claire. She still wasn't acknowledging him.

"Claire . . . I'm sorry about Lila."

She sat the bowl down hard enough to make it slosh onto the table. "Is Karakos dead too? Was that the shot I heard?"

Too. "Yes. Ask Steinfeld. He was—"

"I know!" She glared at him. "And you told me so."

"Look that's not what I'm—"

"Bullshit. You're glad she's dead. And he's dead."

"You really rate yourself highly. Glad Lila's dead? She was one of the best. We'd be better off losing *you*."

The words had come out of him on a wave of anger, and he regretted them.

She went red. But her shoulders slumped and her face crumpled. He went to stand beside her and she turned and she was in his arms like a stone falling into a well. "I'm sorry, Hard Eyes. She was hard to lose."

The shouting of the NR and the drumming of helicopters brought Bonham awake. He sat up in fear—sounds at night did that to you when you lived with these bastards. He went to the window; there was an iron grating over it. Bonham had been arrested earlier that night, and brought here and given a sedative. They had insisted he take it. And they locked him away. He was still muzzy from the sedative but it had nearly worn off and all that noise... and now he saw what made it. A number of big helicopters and two cargo trucks. They were just slamming the doors on the trucks, which went grindingly away almost immediately. The NR were getting into the copters... and Claire was with them.

Bonham pulled on his clothes, then went to the door and tried to open it. Still locked. There was a piece of paper on the floor, a corner of it still under the door. He picked it up, turned on the light and read the message penned in big block letters on the ruled paper. It was from Claire.

> WE ARE LEAVING YOU HERE. THE SA IS COMING. TRY TO
> BREAK OUT AND YOU MIGHT SURVIVE. SOME OF US
> WANTED TO EXECUTE YOU, SO THIS ISN'T SO BAD. THE
> PEOPLE YOU BETRAYED ON THE COLONY ARE FREE
> NOW, AND YOU WERE NEVER ONE OF US, AND YOU
> DON'T KNOW ANYTHING ELSE THAT COULD HURT US SO
> STEINFELD SAID YOU COULD LIVE. GOOD LUCK.
>
> CLAIRE

"Good luck," he muttered. "Thanks, bitch."

He looked around the room. The bedframe was all there was to use. He pulled the mattress and boxframe off, disassembled the metal frame, and took one side of it in his hands. He began to batter at the door.

The Island of Sicily.

The Israelis were committed. "Everything short of declaring war," they told Steinfeld. "And yes—your request for back-up in a preemptive strike has been granted. We can give you eight Z-90 fighter-bombers and two escort air-to-air fighters."

The Mossad's surveillance satellite had given them the details of the SA's European HQ. It was shaped like a skewed four-leaf clover ("or an iron cross," someone said), with four broad approaches, between the ancillary buildings, to the main operations building. The axis of the cross ran north-south. The northeastern road was Entry One; northwestern was Entry Two, southeastern and southwestern were Three and Four. It was a quarter mile in from the coast, eight miles east of Palermo on the Tyrrhenian Sea. It was protected with radar, and with satellite surveillance, and with missile emplacements. With cannon and a no man's land of mines and concertina wire.

The SA's aviation unit sent its squadron out at four A.M. The Israeli radio listening posts picked up the departure codes identifying the copters accompanying the jets. And the radiomen of the six NR transport copters accompanying the Mossad's complement of fighter planes knew those codes. The six transport copters had been repainted to resemble SA copters. As they approached the base, the SA radar techs demanded they identify themselves. They gave the SA code.

"You're back early," one of the SA radiomen said. "Over."

"Yeah, we're ahead of schedule."

The helicopters moved in at five hundred feet; the fighter bombers were behind them but rapidly catching up. Two minutes more. And then there were more questions from SA control. A visual check confirmed the copters were the right type, but the planes seemed to have the wrong configuration. And they couldn't be *that* much ahead of schedule. Still, they'd had the right code . . .

"No," said the XO, hearing all this a little too late, "that was the departure code. The return code was—"

But by then the bombing had already begun.

MALTA.

Another island, other bombings. The SA hitting four places on Malta where the NR had been an hour before; buildings that were lit up as if they were occupied. Inviting themselves to be targets...

Empty buildings.

At one of those places, the old villa, Bonham ran from the building, his hands bleeding, seeing the VTOL jets coming in to strafe, the bigger jets diving and letting missiles go that sank neatly into the barn—the barn throwing itself into the air in a fountain of fire. Bonham screaming, waving his arms, "You idiots, don't! Don't! I'll work with you, I'm not one of them—you morons, you cretins, you jerks, there's *no one here!* This is a *decoy!*" A chopper was coming in, swinging its minigun toward Bonham. Bonham ran toward it, waving his arms, shouting hysterically, "There's no one—"

The minigun round that caught Bonham in the center of the chest was big as his thumb, and coming hard at a range of only forty-eight feet. So his chest quite literally exploded under the impact, and he was dead before he could mouth another syllable.

Sicily.

They were descending into flame. They came down into a sea of molten air, churning with cinders, swirling with the orange and red and yellow fires.

Hard Eyes jumped from the chopper, fell six feet to an ankle-jarring impact on the asphalt of Entry Three, and turned to shout at the others, getting them off and running, leading them onto the road and into the tunnel of roaring light.

Between sheets of flame that sucked the oxygen away, flame bannering and billowing from the windows of the big square barracks and wooden office buildings and pressboard mess halls and computer bunkers; flame reaching above them in sheets four stories high, rearing like some mythical entity, a god of the elements. At intervals parts of the buildings were smashed, flattened outward into the Entry in rings of embers and burning timbers where the bombs had struck. Concussion bombs and incendiary bombs.

Hard Eyes looked over his shoulder, saw Claire and Danco, Willow and Carmen and four others running behind him, gasping, firelight tiger-striping their faces. He turned and, running, carrying his assault rifle with his maimed hand—the finger stumps aching—fumbled in his shirt for his dark glasses, unfolded them and put them on. It didn't help much. Entry Three was a forty-foot strip of asphalt, melting on the edges, running straight to the heart of the SA's European HQ. They ran down the middle but the heat sucked the perspiration off them, made their skin ache and rasp in their clothing; successive walls of smoke burned their eyes, left them choking, gagging as they ran, inhaling cinders, feeling their nostrils coating with ash, beginning to cough up blood, lungs searing with every white hot breath. Dizzy, wobbly on their feet from oxygen deficiency, Hard Eyes yelling into his headset, "Steinfeld —not enough air, we can't—there's no one alive here anyway. Do you copy?"

He pressed the little instrument to his ears; it was hard to hear over the blustering of flames and the rolling booms of explosions, but he made out, "Keep going . . . clear up soon, we couldn't reach the—" Static.

They came to a place where the Entry road was nearly blocked by flaming timbers and burning sections of ragged wall. There was a narrow path between the fallen building on the right and the burning structure on the left. Hard Eyes turned, mimed *Hold your breath!* and led them onto the path—eight feet wide, flame on either side sucking the air away, roaring . . . Hard Eyes glanced back, saw Claire staggering, her knees buckling, her head down, hands over her mouth. She was a red silhouette against a backdrop of yellow flame. He ran back to her, took her by the arm, and they stumbled on, lungs bursting. He thought they'd fall but they emerged into the open road, ran through a wall of smoke, into a wash of cool air.

And gunfire. Gratefully drawing lungfuls of cleaner, cooler air, they threw themselves flat, slapping rifles into firing position. Bullets sang overhead.

They were forty yards from the central building. It was a rectangular five-story concrete building, utilitarian-brutish, unpainted, its windows shuttered with metal slitted for gun muzzles. Muzzle flashes from those windows. Other NR teams were emerging from the other Entries, coming at the building from the four points of the compass. The frayed ends of smoke and the distortion of heat waves refracting massive firelight gave them partial cover. Up ahead, parked at an angle, was a small armored car, its front doors showing the SA cross, a Christian cross with the iron cross at its center; it was abandoned but it looked intact. Hard Eyes squeezed Claire's arm, yelled over the roar of flames and the crack of gunfire, "You okay?" She was still coughing but she nodded. He shouted hoarsely, "Get behind me when I start moving, stay low!" He signaled to the others to stay directly behind Claire. He laid his rifle down beside her. "Hold on to that for me."

And he ran in a crouch—keeping the armored car between him and the HQ Central—up to the side of the car, looked in. Empty. He opened the driver's side door, got in, keeping below the dashboard. Someone had seen him: machine gun rounds struck sparks from the hood of the car, gouged the asphalt beside him. Squatting behind the car, the others in his team returned fire. Hard Eyes found a tool kit under the seat, and set to work on the car's ignition. His hands shook, but the car started. He put it in gear, got it moving forward, laid a wrench on the accelerator at an angle that would keep it moving about ten MPH. He peered over the dashboard, angled the car for the machine gun emplacement, behind sandbags, where the front door had been . . . Hard Eyes shouting into his headset, asking for suppressive fire from the Mossad chopper moving in overhead . . . the chopper opening up at the windows with its miniguns . . .

Hard Eyes opened the door, slid out—feeling a giant's hail of machine gun rounds hammering the door. Thirty feet to the doorway. Twenty-five. Hard Eyes let the car slide on ahead, took a grenade from his bandolier. He pulled the pin with his teeth while opening the gas tank's cap with his free hand—working clumsily with the three remaining fingers—MG rounds whistled around him as he dropped the grenade into the tank and ran behind the car shouting, his team flattened, everyone throwing themselves face down. Hard Eyes flattening with his face buried in his arms, as the car plowed into the the the sandbags—

The explosion slapped the sky and vomited a wave of heat; the hair on the back of Hard Eyes's neck incinerated and he winced with the pain of the shock wave. But less than a second later he was up, catching the rifle Claire threw him, turning to fire past the yellow flames, the burning hulk of the car, into the building—

"Shit!" Carmen's voice. Hard Eyes saw her dragging Willow into the cover of the building, under the windows. The side of Willow's head was missing and it was useless, he was dead.

A rocket from the chopper blew in one of the ground-floor windows, near the corner, forty feet down from where Carmen was hugging Willow's body. Hard Eyes ran past her, shouting, "Come *on*!" and she followed, they all followed, they climbed into the smoking socket of the window, burning their hands on the edges, coughing, firing bursts at anything that moved. Two men went down. Carmen shot a woman in a dress who was probably only a secretary. Then a man in armor stood in the doorway, firing. Hard Eyes and Carmen and Claire ducked behind a desk. Rounds from the gunman in the door chewed the fiberglass desk apart, Danco whooping as he came through the window only to be knocked back out as he was hit. Hard Eyes jumped up, firing at the figure seen dimly in the smoke. The guy staggered but his armor held against the assault rifle's rounds. Carmen shrieking, "FUCK YOU FUCK YOU *FUCK YOU!*", running at the door while the armored SA paused to reload; Carmen with a hand grenade in her teeth, jerking the ring, tackling him, the grenade between her and the SA bull (Hard Eyes thinking: OH FUCK NO), the grenade booming, shaking the floor, ripping them both apart and killing another SA around the edge of the doorway...

Hard Eyes and Claire stood up, slapping fresh clips into

their rifles, ran to the smoky doorway, coughing, firing, coughing, trying not to look at what remained of Carmen, coughing, firing at men who came around the corner in the hall, coughing, rifles jumping in their hands, Gutman behind them with a grenade launcher taking out another guy in armor at the end of the hall, Hard Eyes and Claire reeling back from the shock wave, coughing, getting their footing, firing again and again toward the muzzle flashes, the blurred shapes of running men; trying not to see Carmen's bloody grin, her severed head; Hard Eyes holding back hysterical laughter, coughing, sprinting down the hall, jumping over bodies, firing, firing . . .

After a while, no one fired back.

FirStep, the Space Colony, the Open.

"You don't want to go back," Kitty said. "Be honest."

"I promised we would," Chester said. "We will. But you're just not in shape to take a shuttle trip till after the baby's born."

They sat in the grass, basking in reflected sunlight beside the Open's playing field; they were watching a touch football game, listening to the music from the Colony's folk quartet over the P.A. that Chester and Russ Parker had set up. Russ himself was quarterback on the Admin team, which was definitely taking the worst of it, losing 44 to 12. The Open was thronged, the crowd around the playing field dancing, drinking wine from Admin's formerly private stock, laughing. Admin with Technicki; a multicolored crowd shifting with restless energy, making Kitty think of a World's Fair she'd been to as a girl. With her brother Danny. Where was Danny now?

Chester laughed. "What's so funny?" she asked.

"The looks on the face of the storage officers when we came in and Russ told them he was turning Admin stores over to the technicki—for a party! 'A party, sir?'"

They both laughed. And she felt better than she had in months. "Oh, hell, Chester. The blockade's down. Russ's offering you an important job. A job like that on Earth . . ." She shook her head. "Chester, let's stay."

He slipped an arm around her. "I knew you'd come around if I kept my mouth shut."

Haifa, Israel.

The brassy light of Israel. Gold domes, great swathes of white walls, a maze of narrow streets, ambience of the ancient . . . beyond the domes and tile rooftops, the heartbreaking blue of the Mediterranean. A furious sun was baking it all, trying to cook it back into the sand.

Hard Eyes turned away from the window, disoriented by the shadowy, air-conditioned room, the row of consoles and print-out gear and screens against the right-hand wall. There were three men and a woman sitting in the dark wooden chairs on the thick rug, watched over by the portraits of generations of Israeli politicians on the walls, a gallery of bitter smiles and dour optimism. And there was an old-fashioned pendulum clock, the sort with springs and hands pointing to the hour, that said *tick tick tick tick . . .*

Bensimon, the Mossad's military attaché, sat behind the brown metal desk. He was a bearded man with deepset black eyes. He wore an Israeli military uniform and gold and red embroidered yamulkah. There were pipes in a rack on the desk but he made no move to smoke. He seemed a little in awe of Steinfeld.

Steinfeld and Witcher sat across from him, Claire sat between them.

"Will Captain Danco not be coming?" Bensimon asked.

"No," Steinfeld said, shifting in his chair. "He was wounded. Rather badly. But he's expected to live. With luck he'll be at the next meeting."

"Good." Bensimon looked at Hard Eyes, gestured toward a chair that stood empty to Steinfeld's left. "You do not wish to sit, Captain Torrence?"

Captain Torrence? "No thanks," Hard Eyes said. Amenities. Weird. "I was sitting for hours on the helicopter and the ship. Let's get started."

Bensimon shrugged. He put his hands together, cracked his knuckles, and said, "We did quite well in Sicily. It is a great victory for you, Steinfeld. Their records, perhaps half of their European leadership—all wiped out. Colonel Watson, however, apparently survives. He is believed to have recently arrived in Rome. Now as to the next step: I have been in touch with a friend at the American embassy. The new President makes great noises about the SA in Europe, but will not consider moving against them militarily, for a variety of political reasons which come down to this: the American public is sick of war, and it is hard to disentangle the targets from the people they are hiding behind. To attack the SA the US would have to attack Italy, France, Britain, all the countries where . . ." He made a dismissive gesture. "You see the problem. But our intelligence tells us that the pogroms are ongoing. The European apartheid proceeds. Israel also cannot yet declare war. But we have committed everything short of war to helping you. Especially intelligence, logistics and recruitment. Some air support. But we are already weathering accusations from Italy about the attack on Sicily . . ."

There was more talk, much talk of specifics and talk of money. And then Bensimon invited them all to lunch at a "very nice place not far from here." How strange, Hard Eyes thought, to be invited to lunch. At a "nice place."

Witcher said, "I'm sure we'd all be delighted—I wonder if we could have just five minutes alone here. And we'll join you downstairs. There's something we need to discuss . . ."

Bensimon nodded, and stood, smiling. "Of course. I have something to do anyway. Downstairs in five minutes." He smiled and went to the door, paused, and turned to them, a little embarrassed. "Ah, please permit me to . . . to express my admiration." Steinfeld nodded. Bensimon left the room.

Witcher turned to Claire, and said, "I have some news for you, young lady."

God. How weird to hear her called "young lady." Everything seemed strange today.

"The Colony?" Claire's voice was small, tentative. Which was also weird.

Witcher nodded. "I understand there was some doubt about your father's . . . about what happened to him. There isn't now. I'm sorry to tell you he's dead."

Claire swallowed, and after a moment said, "Go on."

"The Colony has been taken—you've heard that. The technicki control it and a few rebel Administration personnel, specifically a man named Russ Parker."

"He's with Praeger."

"Not anymore. In fact, he's arrested Praeger. It's very probable that, by now, Praeger has been executed for murder. Evidently he had a number of people killed . . ."

"Do you know who?"

"I don't have a list. You can find out for yourself."

"What?"

"Our people are now on the, uh, ruling council, whatever you call it, of the Colony. The Colony is effectively an NR enclave. In fact, we believe the SA may know about our retreat in the Caribbean. Everyone in our Caribbean headquarters—everyone who wants to—will be removed to the Colony. Once things are stable there."

"But if the SA find out—"

"We're not going to advertise it. And if you do your part, the new board of UNIC, NASA, and the U.S. Orbital Army will be working to protect the Colony. It'll be one of the safest places in existence."

"What do you mean—my part?"

"They want you to take over as Chairperson. As the new Colony Chief. You're the daughter of the man who designed the place. You have experience in Admin Council. You're someone UNIC and the NASA people can relate to. They'll accept the new order there with you in charge."

"God. Me in charge."

"Yes. And we want you there—" He smiled. "Because you're NR." After a moment he said. "Well? What do you say?"

She turned and looked at Hard Eyes. Then she looked at Witcher. Then she looked at the floor and frowned. No one said anything. Except the clock on the wall that said *tick tick tick tick* . . .

"I feel different about a lot of things," Hard Eyes said.

He was sitting up, holding Claire in his arms, in the hotel room's double bed. The bedclothes had been thrashed onto the floor; the sheets were rumpled like a great carnation around them. Moonlight from the double glass doors onto the balcony silvered them.

"I was childish about Lila and Karakos," Hard Eyes said. "I wasn't thinking of what you went through. I wasn't really *seeing* you, then . . . Claire, don't go back."

"I decided."

"Claire—"

"I have a responsibility to it. To my dad, too. Steinfeld and Witcher both said it's the best work I can do for the NR. I'm going."

She reached up and touched his face and her fingers were shocked by the tears on his cheek. But she didn't change her mind.

Washington, D.C.

Across an ocean, Smoke lay partly propped up in a hospital bed, feeding crusts to his crow. The crow sat on a perch in a square brass cage, the door of the cage wide open, on a table to Smoke's left. Beside the table was a cot, on which Alouette slept, curled up. She had insisted on sleeping in the same room with him, to keep him company. The TV was on, but Alouette could sleep through anything. It was because of her—because the nurses could deny her nothing—that the hospital had grudgingly allowed Smoke to keep the crow here with his cage open.

To the right of his narrow bed was a machine that fed him through a tube in his right arm. There was a bandaged hole in his chest, just under his sternum. A TV on the wall across from him chattered happily about peace negotiations. The Soviets. The new President. The disappearance of key American SA personnel. Not a word about the European SA. It was like the Iran/Contra hearings in the last century; then, too, the investigators had looked just so far and no farther. The Iran/Contra investigators ignored the evidence linking the President; they ignored evidence of Contra and NSC involvement in murder, and in smuggling tons of cocaine to finance the rebels. It was now as it was then—as if they didn't want to see certain things. Didn't even want to think about them.

On Smoke's lap was a clipboard and a letter he'd scrawled to Steinfeld. He wondered who he could trust to take it . . . so that Witcher wouldn't intercept it. Witcher wouldn't like the last paragraph.

> *I'm worried about Witcher. Did he ever give you his lecture on World Government and why it's the next step? He has it all worked out, or so he thinks. He doesn't like the SA's notion of a world government. He prefers his own ideas. His personal vision of One World. He doesn't even hint about his part in it. But I think we should both be worried about him.*

Smoke tore the sheet off the clipboard and stared at it. Then he tore it into many small pieces and let them drift to the floor.

He sighed. He no longer ached all the time, no longer felt feverish. But he was tired. Needed to rest. After he got out of the hospital, there would be work. There would be no rest for the handful who felt the chill; who acknowledged the shadow of the Eclipse.

The Puerto Rican nurse came in and said, "You want me to turn off the TV? You look tired."

"Yes please. I've lost the remote." He closed his eyes and lay back. "Turn it off."

THE END OF VOLUME TWO

QUESTAR®

... MEANS THE BEST SCIENCE FICTION AND THE MOST ENTHRALLING FANTASY.

Like all readers, science fiction and fantasy readers are looking for a good story. Questar® has them—entertaining, enlightening stories that will take readers beyond the farthest reaches of the galaxy, and into the deepest heart of fantasy. Whether it's awesome tales of intergalactic adventure and alien contact, or wondrous and beguiling stories of magic and epic quests, Questar® will delight readers of all ages and tastes.